Soul Reaper

Ubiquity Book 1

Allyson Lindt

For my eternal dragon

Chapter One

Home again. Michael almost laughed at the thought. His colleagues called heaven or hell home. His was Franklin, Tennessee.

He stepped through the glass door labeled *First Angelic Non-Denominational Church of Faith.* There were few times in history was something more appropriately titled. A deep sense of serenity settled over him. A place like this held its own power, granted by occupants' belief and faith, rather than just recited words from a page.

Another day, he would have taken a seat in the chapel and reveled in the peace. More important things waited. Critical, if he understood correctly. He took the stairs to the right and headed up. On the second floor, he knocked on the apartment door.

The man who answered emanated a faint glow. It wasn't as bright as one hundred years ago, but an aura dimmed and eventually vanished when an agent of heaven or hell fell. Fortunately for Izrafel, his descent was by choice, and his glow had a secondary source.

"I'm glad you could make it." Izrafel opened the door wider.

"I'm sorry I took so long. I was in Tibet when I got your email."

"Clearing your mind of decades' worth of thoughts?"

Michael should do that sooner, rather than later. "More like helping a monk find inner peace." Izrafel would know he meant literally. Michael had coached him through the same thing many years back, and it was why he was here now.

"This is Toby." Izrafel nodded to a young man pacing near the window. Even in streaming daylight, the guy shimmered like a string of multi-colored Christmas tree lights refracted through crystal.

This was bad. Michael hid a frown. That level of fracture… Early hints of regret twinged in Michael's chest for what was probably about to happen. *Let me be wrong.*

Toby whirled fast and teetered before holding onto a stack of books. His eyes grew wide when he saw Michael. "Whoa, you glow too." He stumbled forward, hand outstretched. "Pretty."

Izrafel stepped between them, wrapped an arm around Toby's waist, and then tugged him to sit on the couch. "We met in a bar. Had more in common than our preference in men."

Toby's aura sparked and hummed in an impressive light show. Then there was his childlike fascination with everything in reach. Michael had no doubt. Like Izrafel, a cherub shared the man's body. Toby's confusion made it seem as though his hitchhiker wasn't intentional.

"Oh, wait." Toby trailed his fingers over the fabric on the lumpy sofa, stroking, as if every pass was a new experience. "You're the guy who can tell me what's going on, right?"

Michael kneeled in front of him. "That's me. What do you know so far?"

Toby met his gaze for the first time, and terror replaced awe. The emotion spilled from him in waves that nauseated Michael. The downside to an angel feeling human emotions was when those emotions were tangibly potent.

Toby's aura spiked, jagged shards of color, and he scrambled back on the cushion, pulling his knees up close to his chest. The ethereal scent of cotton candy filled the air. "Don't send me back. Please. I like it here. It's nice. Don't make me go." He used his hands and heels to scoot away from Michael in tiny, slow movements.

That was the cherub talking. He shot his hand out and grabbed Toby's wrist to stop him from crawling too far. At the same time, he let just enough power flow through him to calm the man. Boy? This guy was barely twenty-five. Izrafel was picking them up young. But it wasn't Michael's place to judge.

"Toby." Michael forced strength into his words. "I need you here."

The flare around the man died a little, and Toby's pupils shrank to a normal size. "Yeah. That's me. Izzy said I was possessed. I don't believe in that God shit. Are you a priest?"

"Not quite." Michael kept a tight grip, trying to strike a balance between holding the man captive and not hurting him. This wasn't the part of the job he hated, but that bit was coming soon.

Michael could give him the honest, straightforward answer. The cherub sharing Toby's body should have popped into existence in heaven or hell and begun its life serving demons or angels.

If that happened, it would have fulfilled its purpose until it earned the right to a name and became a full-fledged agent. Instead, it had appeared on Earth, a place where nothing could survive without a physical form for long, and sought the closest available vessel, in order to survive.

The concept was hard to grasp for someone in full control of their senses. He wouldn't make Toby struggle through an explanation, given the man's state of mind. "You have an angel living in you." Michael might as well go with the possession approach. They'd established Toby was familiar with the concept.

"Angels don't exist. And only demons possess people."

Heat pulsed through Michael's hand where he held Toby's wrist, and Michael pushed another calming wave into Toby. "You know something's in you, is that true?"

Toby nodded.

"What do *you* think it is?" This was always the difficult part of an evaluation. Michael needed to determine if the host and cherub were happy together or should be separated. The former created someone like Izrafel. At peace with themselves and somewhere on the power scale between a human and an angel.

The latter was more likely and far more painful to the host.

"I don't know. But I want it gone. Am I stoned? Did someone slip me something?" Toby's pupils dilated. "Don't send me back. Please. The bar was fun. The people were friendly. I got laid. Have you ever gotten laid? *Wow*." That would be the cherub again.

"*Toby*." Michael hated to use heavy levels of power on a mortal. Their bodies weren't built for it. "Do you want it gone?"

"Yes. Please. Make it stop."

"It's going to hurt." Michael used to tell them it would be fine and they wouldn't feel a thing. After sitting through a couple of hosts screaming in agony, he decided honesty was a better route.

This was the part of the job he hated.

"I don't care. Get it out of me."

Michael nodded at Izrafel, who took Toby's other hand and stroked his thumb over the man's knuckles.

"Look at me." Izrafel's voice was calm. "Don't pay any attention to him. I'm here, all right?"

Toby nodded.

Michael drew in a deep breath and mentally tugged on the ethereal threads running through Toby's body. Best to do it fast, like ripping off a bandage. He yanked.

Toby's scream filled the room and shook the windows. The rainbow around him danced and splintered. He jerked to get away, but Izrafel and Michael held him tight.

Michael struggled to ignore the pain and terror spilling from Toby, and keep his focus on the task at hand.

The reaping seemed to stretch on and on but in reality, only took a second or two. Silence crashed over the room as Michael sent the cherub to heaven, so it could start life properly. In a few months, or years, it would earn the right to shift to a physical form, and then it could come back here as its assignments allowed and enjoy getting laid on its own time.

Toby collapsed back against the couch, unconscious.

Michael sank back onto the carpet. "He'll be out for a little while, but he's going to have a hell of a headache when he wakes up." Speaking too effort. He'd poured too much of himself into protecting Toby from the pain.

But he'd recover in a few minutes. Far faster than Toby would have without Michael shielding him.

Izrafel raked his fingers through his hair. "So that's what it's like when it doesn't work out. That sucks."

"At least he found you before someone from Ubiquity got to him."

"About that." As Izrafel spoke, he moved to the kitchen to grab a glass of water and a bottle of pills, and then brought them back to sit on the end table.

"Nope." Michael would rather take a few minutes to collect his wits before moving on, but that was his cue to leave. "I don't want to hear it." When it came to anything to do with the mockery of a joint initiative heaven and hell called Ubiquity, Michael's favorite spot to be was anywhere else.

If he left now, Michael could catch the next flight out of here. Another agent might phase across the ocean in a blink. He preferred his physical form, and enjoyed human modes of transportation, when possible. There were rumors of a witch doctor in Peru who performed actual magic.

"You want to hear this." Something in Izrafel's tone made him hesitate.

Michael was going to regret asking. "What is it?"

"They've got one there."

"One…what?" The place was teaming with demons and angels. All had been cherubs once. But they'd earned their names. Their right to come to Earth.

Izrafel nodded at Toby. "One of those. Fractured aura, the whole deal. Except she's different."

"How?"

"You want the list? She came from hell, and she knows it. As in wasn't human, she's a demon, present tense—name's Uriel. Lucifer pulled strings to get her a reaper job. She doesn't remember who she is or anything before she got to Earth. Oh, and she doesn't have any idea she's carrying a passenger."

Fuck. That sounded bad. "You know her personally?"

"Yup. Lucifer introduced us. Said she might need a little extra help. Not that I mind keeping an eye on her. She's an absolute blast to talk to."

Lucifer said… No. Lucifer named the cherubs that came out of hell, just like Michael and Gabriel named those from heaven, but he wasn't a hands-on guy. Lucifer passed them off to someone in middle management and moved on.

"Why haven't you told her?" Michael asked.

Izrafel fiddled with the fringe on the edge of a couch cushion. "I want to, but I wasn't sure if I should. Right now, she's not hurting anyone, you know, the way it should be, and if she's a project of Lucifer's…"

"I understand."

Izrafel needed to keep a low profile. Hanging onto a cherub wasn't exactly sanctioned, and Michael helped anyone he reformed lay low. Going toe-to-toe with an original like Lucifer was the opposite of keeping one's head down.

No one liked to mess with the three remaining originals. Fortunately, Michael was one of them, and company politics were the kind of bullshit he liked to step over.

"I'll look into it," Michael said.

"Be careful with her? She doesn't have the same lust for power and deception that a lot of them over there suffer from. She deserves better."

Michael couldn't make any promises, so he swallowed the ache that came at the start of any new pursuit, kept his mouth shut, and gave Izrafel a thin smile.

He couldn't ignore one thing though—the same question that always haunted him. Would this be the job that made him regret what he did? Would this be the cherub that convinced him to fall, and leave all of heaven and hell behind?

Chapter Two

Other demons fight for these jobs? Ronnie blinked to restore the moisture to her eyes and keep them from glazing over. The computer's flat-screen monitor mocked her: Flowers, porn, perfume, candy. *No. No. No. No.*

She clicked each as a *Pass* and moved on to the next person's *suspicious activities* in the queue. Some holier-than-thou agent of heaven, a representative for *the other side*, would have their chance at the same list she vetoed, and if they decided it was important, they could chase down the lead.

They wouldn't find a cherub there, even if they decided to pursue. As a reaper—sorry, *retrieval analyst*—for Ubiquity—*the* internet search engine for Earth—part of her job was to manually assess results of what mortals searched for online when the automated system flagged a *possible cherub.*

When it came right down to it, this meant she spent a whole lot of time looking at normal individuals with some kind of fetish or addiction.

Or, since it was a freaking online search engine, regular everyday people just shopping for the perfect gift for their loved ones.

Did she have loved ones? The unwelcome thought gnawed at her, and she shoved it aside. She was working, not bemoaning her lost memories. Not that work took a lot of focus.

The next individual's search results flashed onto her screen—online games, social media, twenty-two email addresses.

Yawn, fucking yawn. The odds were something like one in five gazillion a potential would exhibit anything close to cherub-like behavior.

She flopped against her chair with a grunt, the mesh seat yielding before it snapped back into place. She rolled her eyes as far back as they went to distract her from the monotony. Someone needed to adjust the algorithms. This person wasn't a cherub, just bored at work. Imagine that.

There were ways to spice up an afternoon. If her boss wasn't breathing down her neck, she'd sneak away and visit Irdu. Could she come up with an excuse to stop by the developer's office anyway? *He wanted me to bring him some data.*

She'd probably used that story a few times too many. If she kept taking advantage of her friends-with-benefits relationship with Irdu while they were at work, someone was going to notice.

Still, being bent over his desk, while he pulled her hair and slid inside her, sounded even better than normal right now.

She squeezed her thighs together, and turned back to her computer. She should be grateful for this job. The whole missing memory thing meant she probably wasn't any good at whatever she actually trained for, and if she wanted to stay on Earth—and who wouldn't really, so many chances to *feel*—she needed money for things like rent and food.

But damn if it wasn't so freaking tedious some days. She'd rather be out there—wherever *there* was—trying to figure out why her past vanished from her mind.

"Back to work, demon." Raphael's barked order reached her with a jolt of electricity that zinged through her chair and crawled like tiny ants over her entire body before it seeped out her soles. *Great.* Static crackled through her hair as if she'd made out with a balloon.

"Holy fuck. Was that necessary?" Ronnie didn't know why he took issue with her. He wasn't zapping any other demons on staff.

"I don't care whose pet you are. Watch your language."

She wasn't anyone's pet. And language? Really? Fucking totalitarian, angelic fuck took this dogma shit way too seriously. It wouldn't do her any good to remind him she preferred to be called Ronnie instead of demon or pet. He'd find a way to twist the request and use it against her.

The moment he was gone, she set her queue to *Away*, grabbed her water bottle, and rolled back from her desk. Outside the building's wall of windows, green and blue, dotted with the occasional cloud, taunted her. At least her cube came with a view.

She'd take a stroll past her *mentor's* desk, and then detour past Irdu's office on her way back.

She wove her way through rows of cubicles toward heaven's side of the room. Ariel, Ari for short, had the enviable corner desk. Her window looked out on twice as much rolling landscape. She stood a couple of inches taller than Ronnie, even more so in the high-heeled boots Ari adored. Her flame-colored curls bounced around her tan, freckled face in a never-ending waterfall of corkscrews.

A perk to being an agent—pesky things like genetics didn't apply. Their appearances reflected the way they saw themselves, and since most of Ronnie's colleagues thought highly of themselves, there weren't a lot of ugly angels or demons.

Ari was one of heaven's top performers. At the head of the cherub capture list every month. And somehow Ronnie managed to land her as a trainer. Heaven's stats must be suffering, but Ronnie wasn't going to point that out. She leaned her weight against the back of Ari's chair and peered over her shoulder.

"Can you take a break?" Ronnie hoped the answer was *no*. She liked Ari's company, but naughty office desk sex… that was a hard thing to forget now that the idea was in her head.

Gaze straight forward, she held up an index finger and pointed at the lead on her screen. "Yes!" Enthusiasm filled Ari's triumphant whisper.

"Yay. Another dead end."

The words rushed inside Ronnie's head like a shock. Did she think that? It certainly sounded like something she'd think.

"No. It really doesn't." The taunt echoed in her skull, sounding like her, though it wasn't her thought.

Now she was arguing with herself? If that was the case, why could she almost swear she *heard* the voice? Like a dream or a memory…

She waited a few seconds, but silence greeted her.

Ari spun to face her. "You up for taking this one without any outside interference?" Ari nodded at her screen. She must have found a potential cherub.

The offer cleared away the odd sensation of another voice in Ronnie's head. Maybe she shouldn't have called it *voice*. But when she extracted cherubs, they passed through her as she sent them to hell, so she was familiar with sensation of a second party talking in her head.

Ronnie read over Ari's shoulder, processing the list of searches and purchases. A little unusual but nothing off the charts. Until she saw the jewelry. Lists and lists. All of it cheap trinkets. Silver, quartz, costume shinies. Watches, chains, a lot of it masculine.

"Gotcha." There was that weird mental voice again.

She shook her head to jar the voice loose. She didn't remember ever talking to herself like that. Wherever it came from, Ronnie or somewhere else, it made a good point. A sharp tingle raced inside. Her instinct was never wrong about these.

"You're welcome," said the mental voice.

"You drive; I'll just observe." Ari grabbed her purse.

Of course Ari wanted Ronnie to do the phasing. Not that Ronnie was complaining. Most of her colleagues couldn't easily travel long distances the way she did. It required a shift out of the mortal body to melt into the ether, and then she had to transverse space. Unlike her, most agents couldn't travel in an effortless blink. It was supposed to be a painful, draining process, so a capture mission in another state permitted a lot of time to get there and back.

Despite Raphael's efforts, Ronnie didn't have separate rules regarding how long a job should take, so no one expected her and Ari back today.

Omaha was new territory to Ronnie, at least as far as she remembered. It sounded like fun. They'd take in the sights while they were there.

She intertwined her fingers with Ari's. A rush of power roared through Ronnie as she focused on erasing their physical forms and becoming ethereal. Their world blinked out of sight, and a suburban street replaced the Ubiquity offices.

Cherub, cherub, where was the cherub? Ronnie scanned up and down the street. A trickle of disappointment flowed through her. The place looked like every other town: houses lining the sidewalk, the occasional tree, and cars dotted along the curb.

Ari pulled her phone from her purse and showed Ronnie the GPS coordinates from the Ubiquity search engine logs. The location was precise, but her phasing wasn't if she'd never been to a place. She didn't have built-in satellite navigation.

"Go left."

Creepy voice.

"Because your limited experience makes you an authority on creepy."

Whatever. Ronnie thrust the odd thoughts away and turned left. A warm breeze kissed her bare arms with hints of humidity. At least it was a gorgeous day.

"Shopping after this?" Ari asked as they made their way down the street.

"No money."

Ari shrugged. "Window shopping, then. And ice cream."

"I'm in." Ronnie couldn't fight her grin. It wasn't desk sex, but good ice cream, the right kind of sweet and rich, was its own kind of tantalizing.

Within a few moments, the residential neighborhood thinned, giving way to a strip mall with a diner on the corner. The afternoon sun illuminated random splashes of metal in the parking lot as cars raced by on the main road. The roar of traffic was light, despite the looming rush hour.

It seemed as likely the cherub would be here as anywhere, especially given the *Free Wi-Fi* sign in the window, but no one stood out as a target. A cherub tended to be naive, overly enthusiastic, and very friendly. Like a new puppy. Ronnie scrunched her face in disappointment. Did they miss it? No. The tingle in her veins was still there, and it never let her down.

"What can I say? I'm good."

Yeah, that was definitely odd. Maybe she was rediscovering her ego.

"Afternoon, beautiful." A harsh edge underlined the seductive greeting, mingling with the growl of engines several yards away.

Ronnie whirled toward the sound and the pull of her instinct. He stood between the dumpster well and the chain-link fence behind the restaurant, shielded from the view of passersby. Loose gravel crunched under her sneakers as she crossed the short distance between them. He leaned against the stucco building. Even farther out of sight. *Perfect.*

"Your show," Ari whispered and took two steps back.

His open designer track jacket showed off gold chains gleaming against his tan. She had to raise her head to look him in the eye, but she had to do that with most people.

His dark eyes narrowed as his gaze traveled up her body and lingered on her chest. His lust crawled over her skin and sent a shiver down her spine. Something wasn't right. If there was a cherub in the man, he should be living every sensation to the fullest. He shouldn't be so composed. So…intimidating.

"Hi." She caught her bottom lip between her teeth, studying the gleam of his watch. How long had it been since the cherub moved into this body? It didn't matter. It wouldn't be for much longer.

Ari's instructions replayed in Ronnie's head. *Get close enough to touch him, keep the contact minimal, and draw the cherub out.* The familiar mantra helped her slide into the extraction. From there it would pass through her, and the right words would send it back to hell.

"Lucky bastard."

Huh? Ronnie didn't miss home that much.

"Are you sure it's safe for you out here, little demon?" Intense creepiness destroyed any innuendo in his flirting.

How did he know what she was? A cherub shouldn't possess that kind of knowledge or recognition.

"Maybe he's more than just a cherub."

"He certainly isn't one of us." Great. Now Ronnie was talking to herself. The moment the thought materialized, doubt followed it. She didn't have time to linger on it.

He sneered and lunged, moving so quickly his hand blurred in the afternoon light before he backhanded her. A ring connected with her cheekbone, knocking her off balance. Concrete bit through the denim of her jeans when her butt slammed into the ground. She muttered a string of curses and fingered her tender cheek.

She shouldn't still feel the sting. Because her physical form was a reflection of her self-image, any wound should heal the instant it happened. Still watching him, Ronnie scooted back as his foot came down where her ankle had been. Fear spiked inside, and her heart hammered against her ribs. What the fuck was going on?

"A little help, here," Ronnie called over her shoulder.

"You're doing fine," Ari replied. "But you're going to have to fight back soon."

Fight? What the hell? This was supposed to be easy. It had always been easy before. Ronnie rolled away when he lunged. Gravel embedded itself in her bare shoulder. She should have worm something with more coverage than a tank top. She winced and brushed away the larger rocks. Why was he making this so difficult?

Ronnie forced her tone to stay even as she tried to negotiate. "It doesn't hurt if you don't struggle."

"Like you know that."

Stupid mental voice.

"I'm all for playing, pretty demon." A threatening growl obliterated the man's smooth baritone. His intentions—violent and hate-filled, clawed their way along her nerve endings. "But why don't you join me in my body instead of pulling me into yours?"

She scrambled to find her footing. Her ankle twisted when she hit a crack in the asphalt at the wrong angle, and she landed on her ass again. The shock raced through her spine and reverberated in her skull. He couldn't kill her though. Could he? Terror lingered on her tongue, tasting like copper and bile.

"What are you doing?" Ari's bored tone floated through the air behind Ronnie. "Sparring practice? Bag it, and let's go get ice cream."

She made it sound so simple. Why hadn't anyone taught Ronnie how to fight? Was that something she knew before, in the pocket of memories she didn't have access to? "I don't know how."

"Quit screwing around. We all know how to fight."

"Except maybe for those of us who lost our memories," Ronnie reminded her, irritation heavy in her voice.

The cherub's gold chains flashed in the sunlight as he closed in on Ronnie. His gravelly voice rolled over her skin. "Are you sure you want to do this? If you're struggling, maybe you want to let me have your power instead. There's room in here for more. It would be easier that way."

A response, not hers, echoed in Ronnie's skull. *"No it wouldn't."*

Something unfamiliar rushed through her as if oil were sliding under her skin. It electrified her senses. The sensation was foreign, but it was also less threatening than the cherub.

She drew on the new well of power. It sped through her, replacing confusion with confidence. Without conscious thought, she looked inside herself with her second sight, as if dealing with a cherub, and saw dark ribbons of power racing unhindered along her veins and muscles.

The feeling continued to flow into her limbs, moving them in fluid motions she didn't know she was capable of. The cherub lunged, and she dodged, the foreign ribbons of ink driving her actions. Was this what it was like to be a marionette? She'd care about that later. Right now, she was winning.

The cherub stumbled, and Ronnie shot her hand out and locked onto his wrist.

"See? That wasn't so hard."

With the taunt, the new feeling in her limbs faded. What *was* that? She filed the experience away for later. Taking a deep breath, she set aside part of her consciousness to fog the thoughts of anyone passing by. Since most people preferred to pretend Ubiquity's odd actions didn't exist, inspiring mortals to ignore them came as easily to Ronnie as phasing from place to place. It was time to finish the hunt.

Vibrant streaks of violet and silver wove through the host's aura. She visualized the wisps of the cherub intertwined with the man. It wasn't something she saw with her eyes, but when she connected with the cherub's vessel, an image—a knotted chain of tangled ribbons—filled her mind. She followed the strands of cherub and unraveled them one-by-one.

Her eardrums recoiled at the loud howl reverberating off brick and concrete. Why the fuck was he screaming? That was as new as his fighting back.

Ari's hand rested on Ronnie's arm, voice low but encouraging. "You're almost done."

The physical contact gave Ronnie something solid to focus on besides the howls of agony. She closed her eyes and drew the strands out of the host and into her. The roars grew louder, losing the cherub's gravelly tone, as she absorbed more and more.

Ronnie imagined winding the vibrant threads into a little ball. The screaming threatened her hearing. The uproar was horrible. It made her feel as if she was torturing a puppy. She wrapped the wisps inside her head and shoved them to the back of her mind.

Silence crashed around her, and she opened her eyes. *Thank God.* The job was done. Her surroundings swam around her. She blinked. Blinked a few more times. The fence and dumpster became distinct again.

Exhaustion weighed her bones, and despair bubbled in her mind. She swallowed a sob.

"Let me out. I'm not one of them. You don't understand." The cherub whispered inside her thoughts.

Ronnie muttered the incantation to exorcise it from her body, and seconds later, the cords rushed away from her to hell.

Examining herself for physical damage helped pull her from her fractured thoughts. Her tank top was torn in at least three different places, and something slimy and sticky covered her jeans. *Gross.* She needed to change. And crash.

Her legs wobbled, threatening to give out. None of this was right. The cherub was too aware. Too coherent. And too violent. Nausea churned inside and it took a severe force of will to make herself move.

"Took you long enough." Ari's tease helped ground Ronnie further. "You never told me you forgot how to fight."

Ronnie stuck her tongue out at Ari. "I didn't remember I was supposed to know how. Thanks for your help, by the way."

"You did great."

"Whatever. Speaking of, I don't think I'm up for ice cream." Wow, she really must be sick.

Ari's smile was sympathetic. "I completely understand. My first fighter caught me off guard too. But you did fantastic."

"First...?" Ronnie struggled to process the words through the haze of exhaustion. "I didn't think they ever fought back."

She raised her eyebrows. "Who told you that?"

"I..." Ronnie stared at her shoes as heat flooded her cheeks. No one told her. It was part of the knowledge Lucifer stuffed into her head, to help her cope without memories. "I don't know. Someone, I guess."

Ari tugged Ronnie's fingers, drawing her attention back up. Ari's voice was kind. "Whoever it was lied, or just didn't know. Think about it. Would you want someone taking your body from you?"

"No. I'd like it back now, please."

The voice in Ronnie's head wanted its body back? An involuntary chill rolled down her spine. *Beyond creepy.*

"That makes sense, I guess." Ronnie gave the cherub's former shell one last glance. The host should wake up in a few minutes, dazed, a little confused, and no worse for the wear, minus an extra voice in his head. *Lucky bastard.* "Do you want a lift back?"

Ari glanced around, fiddling with her fingers, attention drifting up and down the street. "I'd better. There's not much to see here anyway."

After dropping off Ari, Ronnie headed to her apartment and collapsed. If she was lucky, this exhaustion would knock her into a deep sleep for a few hours, so she could erase the more potent bits of what she'd just experienced.

Chapter Three

Ronnie wasn't lucky.

Her thoughts buzzed like an alarm clock with a broken snooze button, until she wanted to scream and yank her hair out. She needed a distraction.

Her physical form provided a lot of options—so many things felt and looked and tasted and sounded incredible.

It was too early to go dancing. But that might be a good thing. Normally she could lose herself in the emotions of the people around her, but after what she'd just been through, that might make her worse.

She didn't have enough money to buy good ice cream. She and Ari would have split something, but on her own, she was too broke. Cheap wouldn't sate the craving.

Ronnie could go anyplace in the world and watch. Listen. Take in the vast array of scents. But traveling reminded her of work. She needed to think about something else right now.

Sex.

Not with a random stranger. That too effort, and if they didn't know what they were doing…

She had her phone out in a blink, to text Irdu. He was one hell of a sexy incubus, and he was oh so good at helping her discover where her buttons were.

He was one of the best things she'd discovered since she arrived on Earth. According to the clock, he was still working, but he'd be done soon.

What are you doing after work? She texted him.

His answer was there seconds later. *Depends. What did you have in mind?*

Me.

That line should be so old by now, he typed.

She smiled, the playful teasing already blanketing the chaos in her mind. *I guess it's a good thing I'm cute.*

Among other things. Be there at 5:01.

He was being literal. He was one of those more powerful demons who could blink… well, in the blink of an eye.

She needed to occupy herself until then. A change of clothes was a good start. Why was she still wearing these sticky jeans? She shed everything. Could she afford to throw it all out? It would be nice to just erase the entire afternoon.

Ronnie took a quick shower. Water hot enough to sting flowed over her shoulders and down her back. It would be nice if it seared away the cherub's touch… Its fury and lust… Everything.

She tugged on a loose pair of shorts and a T-shirt. It was all coming off again soon anyway.

She stepped into her living room, and her heart skipped when she saw Irdu waiting on the couch. No one else could get into her apartment with the wards up. The protections weren't a lock, so much as they distracted an individual to the point where they focused on the wards instead of their reason for arriving.

Irdu had told her the first time he was here, they didn't work on him, because he was too focused on her. Talk about a swoonworthy line.

He was thin and tall—of course, everyone was tall to her—with Kool-Aid red hair, and the most captivating amber eyes. And big, thick, strong hands.

And then he was gone from sight. He pressed into her back. "What happened to your face?" He brushed his fingers over a tender spot where the cherub had smacked her.

Why hadn't that faded? "Bad day at work?"

"Then I'm double glad you called." He glided his hands under her shirt "And got all dressed up, just for me." His breath was hot on the back of her neck.

The physical contact, the lack of hesitation, and his deep voice settled in and made her pulse race for new, delicious reasons. "I did. You're early."

"My asshole boss doesn't notice if I sneak out fifteen minutes before five. I wasn't getting anything done anyway, after I got your message."

He lay a row of kisses down to her shoulder, then scraped his teeth along the tender flesh.

She sighed in appreciation. "I'm not complaining."

"If you were, it would mean I was doing something wrong." He bit harder, and glided his hands up to cup her breasts.

She arched her back, pressing her front into his touch, and her ass into his front. His erection dug into her, teasing and promising more. This was exactly what she needed. "You're definitely doing everything right."

"Everything?" He rolled her nipples between his fingers.

The sting. The pleasure. The need. It all wove together and wrapped her in sensation. She whimpered in response.

He teased her breasts and bit into her shoulder, holding her captive. She could break away, but she didn't want to.

He increased the intensity of his touch, of the pressure, until Ronnie was squirming. When she looked, she saw the pale flow of green and gold flare bright around his fingers. He was slipping the slightest hint of his power into this, enough to keep her on that edge of almost too much. To push her toward wet and needy, but not let her slide over into orgasm.

Her head was light and floaty. The combination of pleasure and pain almost made her climax.

Irdu pulled away. She didn't have time to register disappointment before he tore her shorts down her legs. Fabric ripped and burned against her skin. He hadn't destroyed the shorts, but she doubted they'd ever be the same again.

"You're not wearing panties." His voice was gravel.

"Because you keep tearing them off and I only have so many pairs left."

He slapped her ass.

The sting reverberated through her, humming in her thoughts. Fuck, she liked that.

"I have to decide if I'm okay with that, or if I need to buy you more." He slapped the other cheek.

She gasped. The pain should be gone before it manifest, but he knew how to make it linger. Yet another benefit to having an incubus as a fuck buddy. "It gives you easier access if I go without."

"True." He slipped his hand lower, between her legs. "It gives you easier access too." He glided between her folds to tease her opening, then slipped toward her clit. He didn't linger in either place long enough to do more than tease.

"What would you do if I started wearing more skirts to work, with nothing underneath?"

"Hmm…" His lips vibrated against her skin. "I'd hope you were fingering yourself under your desk, and that bastard Raphael was jerking off in his office at the thought."

"You wicked man." She slipped her own fingers between her legs.

Irdu grabbed her wrist. "No."

Her other hand was free, but she preferred his touch anyway. "I'd rather you were the one jerking off in your office." She pressed her bare ass back into him, grinding into his erection.

"I'd rather I was under your desk, licking that delicious pussy, and trying to make you scream." He finally moved his touch back to her clit.

She swore tiny jolts of power danced through the sensitive nub. The idea of him going down on her in the office, along with his skilled fingerwork, pushed her over the edge. She came hard, grinding into him, letting herself live in both fantasy and reality.

She was just sliding away from climax when he forced her to her knees. The rough texture of the carpet dug into her knees.

So fucking good.

Irdu pushed her head down, and lifted her hips, so her ass was angled in the air.

He thrust inside her without further fanfare, filling her almost to the point of uncomfortable, but not quite.

He found her clit again. He was keeping her sensitive, and the feeling was too much, in the best possible way.

Ronnie tried not to squirm away, but her body had other ideas. She couldn't go far, though. He slammed inside her, hitting the right angle every time.

Her orgasm was more drawn out this time, slowing drawing her toward that peak and then lingering there, before letting her tumble over.

She fell into the delicious onslaught on her senses.

His familiar grunts, the stutter to his thrusts, said he was coming too.

She felt it when he spilled inside her, the flow of energy between them, mingling and merging.

They both knelt there for a moment, letting silence settle in, and reveling in the lingering feelings.

Irdu slid out of her, gathered her into his arms, and carried her to the couch. He lay down with her half on top of him.

His touch was gentle again. He was still clothed, and the various blends of fabric bit into her bare back.

Everything with him was sensory overload. It was amazing.

He kissed lightly along her back, and up to her neck. No teeth this time, just tender lips and fingers.

"You're tense. What's up?" he asked.

She'd almost forgotten about the whole voice-in-her-head, fighting-cherub thing. His question dragged everything back with fresh potency. She wasn't mentioning she'd heard voices, though.

Hell, she probably imagined that part. "Did you know sometimes cherubs fight back?"

His laugh wasn't comforting. He cut it short. "You're serious."

"Don't make fun of me." The request slipped out with a whine attached to it.

"I'm not." He kissed the edge of her ear. "You really didn't know?"

"No one ever told me."

"Not even Lucifer?"

She sat up with a scowl. "What was unclear about *no one*?" She couldn't keep the irritation from her voice. Why did everyone think she was making this up?

Irdu sat, too. He tugged the crocheted throw off the back of the couch, and wrapped it around her. "I'm sorry. I believe you. I would have told you if I'd realized no one else had. Cherubs fighting back is part of the curriculum. It's probably one of the biggest reasons Lucifer has me writing code instead of reaping—he doesn't want me to know how to fight."

Ronnie didn't know what Irdu had done to piss Lucifer off, but it meant the incubus got the shit jobs.

"Why is this coming up now?" Irdu's question was sympathetic.

She pursed her lips and raised her brows. "Why do you think? I reaped someone today who fought back."

"Are you all right? Is that where the bruise came from?" He cupped her face and traced a thumb along her cheek. Concern filled his gaze.

Why was she still marked? "I—" If she wasn't mentioning the voice, she couldn't very well say it was the only reason she could fight back. "Ari was with me. I figured things out pretty quickly, but apparently Lucifer doesn't want me to know how to fight either."

"I'm glad you're safe." He brushed his lips over hers. "I'm glad you texted me."

She wanted to slide back into the playful teasing. "You're always glad I text." It felt forced. He had to hear that.

"You don't have any complaints either."

"None." She managed a laugh. "Thank you for coming." The unintentional innuendo helped her mood a little.

So did his constant touch. "Classy. Try this one instead. *Thank you for making me come so many times.*"

Her chuckle came more easily this time. "That's not what I meant. Though yes, thank you for that, too."

He wrapped her in a loose hug, and trailed his fingers along the back of her hand. "Do you want to order takeout? Or I can go grab something. There's this place in Vietnam I've been dying to try."

She wanted to. He'd buy, it would be delicious, and they'd stay up all night talking, leaving them too tired for work tomorrow.

But there were too many unanswered questions, and she couldn't ignore them much longer. "Next time?"

"I'm just your booty call, I get it," he teased.

She leaned her head on his shoulder. "Not *just*, and it's not like you mind."

"Not even for a second. Give Lucifer my love?"

"Right. That'll make the conversation go well." She didn't ask how he knew where she was heading. Most of her colleagues were aware she had an unusual direct line to Lucifer. He was about the only one who didn't give her grief for it.

Irdu kissed her one more time, crushing his mouth to hers, sending need and comfort pulsing between them. "Good luck," he whispered when he pulled away.

She was going to need it.

Chapter Four

Michael leaned back in the chair, plastic and metal creaking beneath him, and propped his feet on the desktop. Dirt flaked from the dried, caked-on mess on the bottom of his boots and littered the polished oak. The sight of the hardwood surface—free of any scrapes or scuffs—made him smirk. At least some things were predictable about Lucifer.

A key rattled in the lock, metal scraping metal, and the office door swung open.

Michael raked his fingers through his hair. Maybe he should have changed before popping into hell. Chasing a sociopathic cherub through the muddy fields of Kansas wasn't exactly his shining moment this week. He could have at least showered. He scratched the scrub brush of dark beard covering half his face. Or shaved. But he was anxious to make his move. Living for centuries didn't grant the kind of patience most people assumed it did.

"Morning," Lucifer said with disdain. "You have something against my desk, Taxiarch?"

Michael hated that nickname. An archaic title from a time best left in the past. A point in history with *her*. He glanced at Lucifer and crossed his feet at the ankles. The desk wouldn't take any damage. Lucifer liked his antique furniture and polished-to-the-point-it-reflected wood surfaces too much to let that happen. Besides, Lucifer knew Michael hated being referred to in military terms—regardless of the language—so the aggravation flowed both ways.

Michael glanced at the non-existent watch on his wrist and let impatience leak into his voice. "Are you keeping bankers' hours now?"

Lucifer dropped into the chair on the other side of the desk and leaned forward, steepling his fingers. "I didn't realize anyone was waiting."

The office was as much Lucifer's home as any place, so he knew the moment Michael walked through the locked door.

"I should have called ahead. My apologies."

Lucifer didn't look impressed. "I heard you had a run-in with a rogue and a fallen angel. I'm surprised you didn't get here sooner."

"What makes you think Izrafel told me anything that would bring me here?"

Lucifer raised an eyebrow.

If Lucifer already had an idea of what Izrafel told him, the concerns probably had merit. A sliver of self-satisfaction tickled his thoughts. Every once in a while, it was nice to have the upper hand. "I want in at Ubiquity." He didn't really. But he had to see this demon for himself.

"What happened to *this is the stupidest idea any of you have ever come up with, and I won't be a part of it*?"

"I need a new approach." It was a safe answer. Whether or not Michael agreed with Ubiquity, or with heaven and hell's goals there, no other place housed more information about potential cherubs. "I'm not asking. I'm letting you know as a courtesy." Like Lucifer and the third original, Gabriel, Michael only answered to Him. Neither of Michael's counterparts would stop him from walking into the job.

Besides, he couldn't ask flat out about the girl Izrafel mentioned. Lucifer never answered direct questions. The best way for Michael to get his information would be to hang around the office and get to know this Uriel for himself.

Lucifer stood. "You're right. Do what you want. I don't even care if you tell anyone who you are. Whatever your reasons are for being here, they're your own."

Michael kicked back from the desk, more dirt falling around him and settling on the nauseating, busy carpet, and stood. The mess wasn't enough to obscure the cheap Vegas remnant. He paused on his way halfway to the door, and turned back to Lucifer. Asking probably wouldn't do him any good, but his curiosity won out. What kind of answer *would* it get him? "Is there a reason you jumped the queue and shoehorned the new demon into a spot at Ubiquity?" Michael asked.

Lucifer's expression stayed flat. "I'm sorry, which one?"

That was what Michael thought.

A strange tingle raced over his skin as the air grew thick around them. The sensation of the atmosphere pressing in on him from all sides vanished almost before he registered it. He knew the feeling but wasn't used to it happening in a flash. Someone just phased in. He spun toward the new arrival, and every inch of him froze.

She barely came up to his chin. Black hair trailed down her back, and her tank top showed off smooth, pale skin. Brown pupils laced with red stared back at him, unblinking.

Izrafel was right about the aura. Fractured and broken like a million shards of golden glass mixed with red and black. Michael couldn't pull his gaze away. She was cute in a sexy, almost deceptively beautiful kind of way, but agents tended to be attractive. There was something else about her.

Who was she?

And why did seeing her hum along his skin, leaving a tantalizing layer of curiosity behind?

"Weren't you leaving?" Lucifer's irritation cut through the staring match.

Michael would save the questions, at least until after his shower. "Yeah, I'm going."

There was something about the way she held herself. He shook his head to clear away the confusion. There would be time for details later. There was always time later.

*

Ronnie materialized from the ether, already anticipating the comfort of Lucifer's office—the closest thing she recognized as feeling like home. His door was halfway open when she arrived. He sat at his desk, so she pushed in with a brief announcing knock.

Ronnie exhaled in relief when his familiar aura seeped into her. As one of the three remaining originals, he held his own little corner of hell. Instead of being generic day-to-day blahness, it radiated a lived-in vibe that came from millennia of occupation. As she got far enough inside to see the rest of the room, she froze, all coherent thought evaporating. Lucifer wasn't alone.

"It's not... Maybe? Mikkel?"

Lucifer stood. He crossed the room, coming to a stop in front of Ronnie, still looking at the stranger. "Weren't you leaving?"

"I'm going." The guest glanced at her before moving to the exit.

It wasn't always easy to tell the difference between an angel and a demon. But a real angel, one who served order instead of looking for the loopholes which allowed chaos, carried a different aura—a smooth glow instead of a kaleidoscope of fractured light.

And the arrogant man walking out of the room was more distinctly angel than anyone Ronnie ever met. The situation, on top of the last twenty-four hours of her bizarre life, perplexed her. Who was he? Angels in hell weren't unheard of, but they disliked hell's methods, so visits were rare.

She watched him leave. With his dark hair, light eyes, and an obvious disdain for the most powerful demon in existence, he made her pulse and heart race. What kind of things could he teach her about her senses? He—

"If you'll stop swooning, I can kill that fucker. Right here and now. Draw your sword."

The vicious words in Ronnie's head, filled with hatred and venom, almost made her stumble.

She stared at the door long after he walked through it. What was that about? A painful rhythm beat against her skull—a jackhammer against bone.

"Ronnie?" Lucifer's kind tone drew her out of her fog. He nudged her to follow him on his way back toward his desk. The large chair hissed a little with forced airflow when he lowered his large frame into it.

Ronnie shouldn't drool over her boss, but Lucifer's presence always delighted her as much as his aura comforted. He was gorgeous in that *I'll devour your sense of reason* kind of way. Maybe part of the attraction was the taboo—no one was more off limits. That never stopped her from reveling in his presence.

"Fuck, you're pathetic. Do you want to hump every celestial you meet? We'll kill Mikkel later. It's fine. Vengeance has waited this long."

Nice. *Not.* But the voice was a forceful reminder of why she was there. She dropped into the chair across from Lucifer's desk. The entire room shared the auburn sparks of his aura. Like aloe on a fresh burn, the residual power soothed the ethereal and emotional sensations lingering on her skin and chased away the tension of her encounter with the cherub.

He studied her with orange eyes—his one inhuman feature. "You're a mess."

"Thanks. You don't look so hot either."

Stupid voice. It didn't help any that Lucifer's words stung—and not in that *spank me harder* kind of way. Ronnie closed her eyes and breathed deeply, using the ambiance of hell to find her center. It didn't help as much as she wanted.

"What happened?"

Ronnie still wasn't sure. "I was in a fight. With a cherub. And I thought I was going to die. Or something. Can one of those things kill me? And I didn't know what I was going to do. Except then I fought back. I don't know how. There was this voice. I mean, I guess it was there before I got to the cherub, but not much before. It wasn't me, but it was in my head. Maybe. I heard her whisper. And then I knew what to do. Like I was fighting, but it wasn't me, and—" The words tumbled out in fragments as she tried to make sense of them.

"Stop." He unfolded himself from his chair, springs squeaking as he stood. He moved to her side of the desk and leaned against it. "How did you manage to get a black eye?" His thumb slid over her cheek.

The memory of the smack rushed back. "He hit me."

"Wow, you're a bit of a whiner, aren't you? Move over, let me drive."

Disorientation blurred the edges of her thoughts. It was similar to the sensation during the fight yesterday. The impression she wasn't quite in control.

She pushed back, and her world swam into focus again. "Did I mention this voice in my head? It's loud. I'm pretty sure it's not me, but maybe it is.

41

I'm having a hard time ignoring it. I don't think it's normal to have a voice living in my head. I mean, that makes people crazy. I'd rather not be crazy. I already don't remember my past. What if this means I'm mental? Does insanity come after amnesia?" Why was she rambling?

"Because you're terrified and woefully underequipped for this life. I know a solution to that."

"Uriel."

Her full name. Lucifer only used it when things were serious. She clung to the force of that single word and used it as a focal point to ignore the background noise in her skull.

"Slow down and start from the beginning," he said.

It took strength to talk and suppress the strange voice at the same time. "Ari got a ping on a cherub, and she let me have it so I could practice. There was this guy all decked out in gold and expensive clothes. And he attacked me. Full-on punch throwing, kicking, and some seriously scary kung fu shit. I don't think I want another assignment like that."

"You did great. No. Wait. That was me."

It was hard enough not vomiting as she relived the fight. She wasn't giving any attention to the voice, to let it make things worse.

"It sounds like you did fantastic." Lucifer ran his finger over her bruised cheek.

His touch alone was soothing. The throbbing ebbed as he pulled the pain away from her. Lingering traces of his aura mingled with hers and made it easier to think. It was more though—a tenderness she craved from him. That hit of softness that always lingered under her skin when he made contact with her.

She concentrated on the sensation, letting it fill some of the cracks in her psyche. "Except, you know…the voice, the fighting back, everything about it that wasn't status quo."

"He wanted me. You don't want me. You don't even know what I am."

Great, the voice in her head, that sounded like her, was keeping secrets from her. That was sane. Not. They were having a serious conversation when Ronnie got home.

"Because that's so much saner than just listening to me."

Lucifer tilted his head to the side, watching but not interrupting.

Ronnie's story spilled out again. "Ari said it happens, though. Why didn't you warn me they fight back sometimes? And then it was like I knew things I'd never been taught. How to fight…" Something she couldn't quite grasp flitted at the edge her mind.

"It's okay." Lucifer rested his hand on the back of her neck, holding her head in place as he looked her in the eye. "You're all right now?"

"Well, you know, except the whispering. This voice in my head won't shut up. And it's ranting about vengeance and death—it's possible mine is at the top of its list. That angel guy who just walked out of here certainly was. And how did the cherub know I was a demon?"

"You're all right. That's what matters."

The brush off rocketed deep inside her, filling her with ill-ease and making her muscles tense like a coiled spring. "Maybe, but I would have preferred it go smoothly, like it's supposed to. And Ari texted me last night. She said I was in trouble for leaving and not coming back yesterday, even though it was an out-of-town capture."

"Raphael?"

Ronnie nodded.

He reached for his phone receiver. "I'll take care of Raphael. How's it going otherwise?"

At least Lucifer cared about that. Not enough to move her under a different manager, but he'd already pulled strings to keep her from working with Irdu. She didn't want to see what her next option was.

"Well…" It ate at her to nag about the problem, but updates were non-existent since she arrived at Ubiquity. While she knew three months was nothing in the grand scheme of eternity, she was starting to worry she'd never figure out who she was…before. "Have you made any progress on figuring out how to get my memories back?"

Lips drawn into a thin line, he studied her for a moment before replying. "I actually think I have an idea, but it's too early to tell. I'll need to talk to some friends. For now, take a day off. You bagged a cherub more than a thousand miles away. You're not expected back in the office yet, regardless of what Raphael says. Who, I'm dealing with now."

She hesitated with an unspoken question. She didn't want to come off as a complainer—especially with him already brushing her off—but she had to know.

He paused with the phone halfway to his ear. "Yes?"

She traced the toes of her shoes over the random cluttered patterns on the carpet. "Why are we hunting cherubs? Like really why, not the reasons preprogrammed in my head."

The sympathy in his eyes evaporated. "It's the natural order of things." A cold edge lined his retort. "They should exist in heaven or hell, not roam the earth with no direction. Heaven wants to prove it's doing a better job than hell, and hell fights back. It's always a numbers game. Go home. Rest. Then get back to life as usual."

She flinched. The answer didn't surprise her, but his delivery and shift in mood left a dull ache in her chest. "Okay."

"Company rhetoric. That's not like him."

"Good point, voice." The doubt that bled through her was disconcerting. Lucifer was her guide and mentor. She should be able to trust him.

She concentrated on erasing her physical form. The world faded as she became ethereal, and milliseconds of sweet silence flooded her thoughts as she phased back to Earth. It didn't last long enough. In a single second, Lucifer's office was gone, and she was surrounded by the small box she called her apartment. Tangible again, reality rushed back.

This sucked.

Chapter Five

Being allowed to take a physical form gave agents a choice—stay in heaven or hell, or live on Earth. Even though their physical forms came with limitations that their ethereal bodies didn't, most of agents chose to live here. *Feeling* meant a lot more than existing in the ether.

Like so many of Ronnie's Ubiquity colleagues, her studio apartment was in the middle of a little Tennessee suburb. Not the fanciest place on Earth, but it *was* on Earth, and that was what mattered.

With a sigh, she flopped onto the mattress on the floor. Worn cotton sheets caressed the portions of her back her tank top left exposed, sapping some of the heat from her skin. She closed her eyes, not wanting to see the small stack of breakfast dishes in the nearby sink or the armful of clean laundry draped over the orange chair next to her.

She hopped to her feet. *Screw this.* She didn't have to be at work. It was too bad Irdu and Ari both did.

Still, there was no way she was wasting a day off by lying in bed and drowning her sorrows in music.

"At least you're not always boring."

She almost smacked the side of her skull to shake the noise away, but inspiration struck before the self-induced headache. It was an insane idea, but she was already hearing a voice, so this couldn't be much worse. She strode into the bathroom and looked in the mirror. Dark eyes, almost red, stared back. Yup, that was still her.

"What do you want?" She didn't know why she was talking out loud. It could obviously hear her thoughts. She guessed the action made her feel less crazy.

"Out of your head."

That made two of them. "Is that an option?" Could she evict voices from her skull? Maybe that was some kind of therapy she didn't know about. That would really be all kinds since mental health knowledge wasn't necessary to her job.

"As if I know. I haven't been up here any longer than you have."

If the voice was Ronnie, she was kind of bitchy and very not helpful.

"I'm not you, and I'm not the voice. *I'm Metatron. I'm* His voice."

The words clenched in her gut, and bile rose in her throat. Great. Ronnie wasn't just losing it, she thought she was possessed by an original angel. One of the first four created. She wouldn't let it— *her*—know the impact it had on her. "Like the bad

guy from those stupid transforming robot movies?"
Ari loved those things.

"That's Megatron. I'm Metatron. Which you're already aware of. I can read your thoughts. You've figured that out, haven't you? And you're not insane. Well, maybe you are, but I'm not a symptom of that."

"All right, not-me. Then how do I get rid of you?"

"Just like I know what you do, I don't know any more than that, beyond my past life and knowledge. All I remember is someone—"

The voice choked off, and a sharp stabbing pain rocketed through her gut, as if Ronnie had been stabbed. She doubled over and clenched her stomach, but nothing was there. The pain ebbed and then vanished.

"Was that you?" It was harder to speak than she expected.

"I died. Then I woke up in your head. That's all that matters. It's a bit fuzzy for me, but the more time you've spent here, tangible, the more I've seen of your life."

Was this a product of Ronnie's magic-fed education, then? Something evoked by lessons of the originals?

"No. I'm Metatron. Pay attention."

At least if Ronnie was going to lose it and fall into some kind of past-life reincarnation fantasy, she picked someone powerful to model herself after.

The voice made a noise that was somewhere between a growl and a sigh. *"Don't believe me, then. I may not have answers now, but you're a little dim about the world around you, so I assume I'll extract them before you do."*

"That doesn't sound so bad. Then we're separate and both happy?"

"My form, everything except this core of me, was destroyed. The odds are good only one of us comes out of this intact."

"Fuck."

"Exactly. Any other questions? Want to talk about the weather next?"

Ronnie wanted to stop indulging a voice that may or may not be her, who was all but threatening to destroy her once it found a way.

Sitting around here talking to herself wouldn't change that.

She was mostly broke until payday, but she had a couple extra dollars for coffee, and then maybe she'd go visit her one friend outside of work.

"You've got friends? Poor bastards."

She'd ignore that. Only partly because admitting she heard a voice was crazy. She was pretty sure letting it ruin her free day was another step toward insanity.

Half an hour later, iced coffee with extra chocolate and whipped cream in hand, she stood in front of a building a few blocks from her apartment. On the outside, it wasn't much to look at—a single glass door amid of an entire block of them.

The only thing to make this one stand out was the church's name: *First Angelic Non-Denominational Church of Faith.* She'd told Izzy a dozen times the name was clunky, but he swore it was appropriate. And apparently it had been that way for over a century, so it must be working for him.

The main chapel was to the left of the entrance. Izzy's apartment was up the stairs on the right, which was where she headed.

Izrafel was one of the fallen. *Falling* meant an angel or demon surrendered their ethereal power and became mortal. Some fell because they no longer believed in what they did. Others reached the point in their personal evolution where they wanted to do and be more. They experienced so much as ethereal beings, they opted for mortality and a chance to learn and grow as humans.

His chapel was the most comforting place she'd ever been. On Earth anyway.

His door flew open seconds after she knocked, and Izzy grinned. With his messy brown hair and the ability to successfully rock a muscle shirt and pair of skinny jeans, he looked like one of those guys who graced covers in the romance section of bookstores. This, oddly enough, wasn't the reason single mothers flocked to his sermons. He was also a genius with kids.

"Izrafel?"

A waver of recognition rushed through Ronnie but vanished again just as quickly.

He grabbed her coffee and took a long drink before setting it on a table against the wall just inside the doorway. Hands free, he wrapped her in a giant hug.

Ronnie squeezed back with a smile and a muffled greeting. "Morning."

"Hey, angel." He let her go and stepped back. "Shouldn't you be working?"

She loved the nickname. No one but Izzy considered them all to be the same, just calling different places home. She faked a cough. "I called in sick."

He laughed and nodded to the couch. "I didn't even think you got sick days over there. I hate to rush you, but I'm almost on my way out the door. Talk while I finish packing?"

She chuckled. Of course he was still cramming things into a suitcase when he was supposed to be leaving.

"Where are you going this time?" She dropped onto his couch and immediately sank several inches into the soft, worn upholstery. She loved Izzy's apartment. Bookshelves stuffed to overflowing lined the walls, and more books decorated the floor. And coffee table. And kitchen counters.

Like most agents, when he was an angel, he was gifted only with the knowledge he needed to do his job. As one of the fallen, he craved as much information as he could hold in his skull.

His voice carried from the bedroom. "Fiji. Researching coconuts."

She relaxed further at the hint of a joke in his tone. He was a religion scholar. When he wasn't discussing faith with his congregation, he traveled around the world, searching for the foundations of beliefs. *What do coconuts have to do with that?* He'd tell her when he was ready and probably less pressed for time.

"Speaking of your research..." She needed to ask now before she lost her nerve. It shouldn't be a big deal, but she was about to imply she was going insane. She forced the question out. "Have you ever come across any mention of sane people—or not-sane people—hearing voices? Who claimed they were dead angels?"

The rustling in the other room stopped, and he stuck his head out of the door, eyes narrowed as he locked his gaze on her. "What? Who's hearing voices? You?"

She winced. *Crap*. He did think she was crazy. "A friend?"

"Shit." He dragged a duffel bag and suitcase out of the room, set them by the front door, and then kneeled in front of her. Her peered into her eyes as if he hoped to uncover something hidden in their depths. "How long have you—"

The blare of a horn drifted up the stairwell and through the window.

He hopped to his feet and offered her a hand up. "I'm sorry, angel. Cab's here." He furrowed his brow and studied her for a moment longer. "If the plane tickets were refundable, my trip would wait. I don't think I'll have internet or cell service where I'm going, but I'll only be gone a week or so. We'll talk as soon as I'm back, I promise."

At least he took her seriously. The thought wasn't as comforting as she wanted it to be. That just meant they might both be insane.

Chapter Six

Ronnie poured herself a cup of coffee from the breakroom pot. Normally, she tried to avoid the free stuff. Whichever demon inspired free work coffee did it wrong. And it was a demon; angels didn't take risks, especially with something so important.

Though she'd only been at work for a couple hours, Raphael's glares were devouring her composure.

The angel from Lucifer's office was here too. She wasn't sure what he was doing, besides inhabiting a normally empty corner office. Ronnie caught glimpses of him several times, and the distraction, even if he was a sexy bit of angel, was still a distraction.

One made worse when the voice in her head screamed bloody murder—literally—every time he was around.

"Let me kill him and both problems are solved."

Nice. Not.

"Hey, you're back." Ari's perky enthusiasm dragged Ronnie out of her thoughts.

Ronnie dumped a liberal amount of sugar in her cup and faced Ari. "I'm sorry Raphael gave you crap for coming back without me."

"He's a big grumbly teddy bear when you're not around. I handled him." Ari turned toward the vending machines at the far end of the room and nudged Ronnie with her shoulder in the process. "Do you have any plans this weekend?"

Trying to get her memory back—which, besides hounding Lucifer, involved a lot of mass-media consumption in the hopes something, anything, would be familiar. Wondering why she didn't have plans beyond that. Same old stuff. "Probably not."

"Want to go dancing?" The clatter of coins clinked in rhythm with Ari's words, followed seconds later by the thunk of her candy bar rolling from its spot and dropping to the bottom of the machine. "I know the most perfect, epic place ever. I swear you'll love it."

"Oh, yay. You can be one of the in *crowd. A lifelong goal achieved."*

The voice's sarcasm made Ronnie's smile even bigger. Being alone with her thoughts recently moved to the top of her list of least favorite things, and she loved music. "I'm in."

They snagged a table near the back of the breakroom, and Ari leaned in, voice low. "Have you seen the new bossman?"

Of course Ari had answers. She knew everyone. A flicker of giddiness tickled Ronnie. "Who is he?"

Ari laughed. "Sorry. You're serious?"

Ronnie was getting real sick of being asked that question.

"He's a lying, vindictive, cruel asshole who deserves to die slowly and painfully."

The voice's words sliced through Ronnie with the same impression of inky ribbons that filled her when fighting the cherub but this time with trails of blackness. It left a path of euphoria and vengefulness in its wake.

She pushed the strange sensation aside. Had she forgotten this angel or never been told? No, there was no way she wouldn't remember him.

"He's Michael." Ari looked at her with heavy expectation.

"Told you so."

"Want to tell me more than that? Like how the fuck to get you out of my head?"

"If I had that answer, I'd be gone already. Or, more likely, you would."

Why wasn't Ronnie surprised?

"So, he's important?" Ronnie knew she shouldn't have to ask. Everything about the conversation told her she should already know this, but since she didn't, this was the easy way to find out.

"Like *the* Michael. The Creator's right hand. The original angel."

"Oh." Of course. Another of the four originals—Lucifer, Gabriel, Michael, and Metatron. According to Lucifer, most demons and angels went their entire existence only meeting the one who named them. Lucifer took Ronnie under his wing.

Another now occupied their office, and a third may or may not live in her head.

"Why is he here?" Ronnie's sparse knowledge said Michael's response to Ubiquity was: *That's the stupidest idea I've ever heard, and I won't be a part of it.*

Which meant he was smart, in addition to being attractive, and pissing off a voice she hated. No agent from the higher ranks worked for Ubiquity. They'd actually earned the chance to help people directly. And the originals... Gabriel and Lucifer's schedules held more than she could fathom, so as long as things ran smoothly here, they stayed out of the picture. This Michael must be the same, right?

Ari leaned closer, forearms resting on the table, and her voice dropped in volume. "I've only heard rumors. But supposedly, something very specific brought him back. Supposedly, something hell is doing."

"Like what?" Hell wasn't doing anything. Except making Ronnie, and others like her, watch computer monitors all day.

Ari clamped her jaw shut and scooted back from the table. "Nothing specific. Stuff. I don't know." The words tumbled out on top of each other. "I need to get back to work."

"Wait." God damn it. Ronnie was on her feet in an instant and spinning to follow Ari out of the room. "What kind of stuff...?"

Ronnie's forward momentum stopped, and her question trailed off when she saw what—or rather, who—sent Ari scurrying away. Michael stood near the breakroom doorway, gaze locked on Ronnie.

He cleaned up nicely. The short growth of beard was gone, he'd swapped out the tattered shorts for jeans, and the sleeves of his beige button down were rolled up halfway up his forearms. Strong, muscled, tan forearms…

And she was staring. She pulled her eyes away, cheeks heating. What was it about him? The aura of power he radiated? She wasn't used to seeing it on anyone, even the higher-ups. Lucifer hid his, and she'd never met Gabriel. Maybe heaven was just flashier.

"You." His reply dragged Ronnie from her rambling thoughts. "I'm here because of you."

He was here for her? A loud hiss echoed through her skull, followed by a rush of electric inky streams filling her body.

"I'll destroy him now. Move aside, child."

The unexpected venom, combined with a surge of power inside her but not hers, stole Ronnie's balance and ability to puzzle over whether or not Michael was being facetious. Though motionless, she stumbled, but caught herself before she fell.

He furrowed his brow and reached for her. "Are you all right?"

"Don't touch me."

Her body jerked away without her permission. With the snarled words, more black seared through her. Each new burst left her oddly disconnected from her thoughts, and with a euphoria that convinced her she could do anything. Was *the voice* trying to control her? She didn't know what the sensation was, but she wanted it fucking gone. Now.

If she turned her focus inward, she could almost see the dark strands weaving through her the same way a cherub intertwined with a human host. Why did she have something like that inside her? Was that Metatron? It didn't matter. The feeling was foreign, threatening, and if she had to be honest, terrifying.

Michael continued to study her, his frown deepening with each passing moment. As she poured half her concentration inward, tugging at the foreign threads of what she could only call power, the rest of her focus went into forcing what she hoped was a natural smile onto her face. "I'm fine. You're not really here for me, right?"

"Don't you dare do this. Let me kill him, and then you'll know what fine is."

The sharp tone steeled the voice's words. A wave of weakness blanketed Ronnie, and she lost strength in her limbs, making her stumble again.

"You don't look fine." Michael's voice was heavy with concern.

She'd be great as soon as she tucked the voice—or whatever, *whoever*, it was—far, far away.

"Stop calling me the voice. *Use my fucking name. Let me destroy that foul creature, and we can sit and talk about reaching a solution that benefits us both."*

That was the stupidest thing Ronnie'd ever heard. She might have rolled her eyes if she weren't pouring so much energy into not looking crazy while talking to Michael.

A wash of inky black ribbons raced through her, more intense than before, and the edges of her vision swam, the walls dancing around her. Her world went black.

* * * *

Every few seconds, Michael glanced at the demon curled up on his office couch. On the surface there was nothing wrong with her except… Right before she'd passed out, her aura surged dark and then almost vanished.

It was still pale, but no more so than some of the other agents in the office. In contrast, before she noticed him in the breakroom, it was the same bright, shattered gold mixed with red and black he saw in Lucifer's office. The fractured aura wasn't the only that clue she hosted another entity. A lot of agents sparkled with that kind of chaos. The way it flared and ebbed was a strong indicator. Why didn't anyone around here pick up on that?

Michael tried to tell himself he couldn't keep his eyes off her because he was concerned. There was more to it than that. Was he really so shallow he just liked looking at the petite, stunning brunette?

Lucifer had taken a special interest in her. Why? He didn't play favorites. The last time he took this kind of interest in someone was…

A phantom pain echoed in Michael's chest at the thought of Metatron, and he shoved it aside.

Lingering on her memory didn't do anyone any good. Metatron's destruction hit Lucifer as hard as anyone. He could deny it all he wanted, but Michael recognized his own grief on his counterpart's face that day so long ago.

If Lucifer singled had Uriel out for a specific reason… She visited him in his office, but most denizens of hell did that eventually. If she was unique, did she know it? Would asking her directly do Michael any good? And why, every time he looked at her, did the desire to protect her from anything and everything wash over him?

The leather of the sofa creaked when she stirred, and her eyes fluttered open, her red-eyed gaze taking a minute to focus before locking on him.

"Are you doing better?" he asked.

With Lucifer, the direct route to anything was a waste of time, but Michael couldn't operate that way with everyone else. It was why he told her she was the reason he here. Life was complicated enough without games and second-guessing motives.

Her aura flared—a rich velvety red like a twilight sky with no stars. Her eyes rolled back for a moment, and then her entire glow dimmed to a faint smudge of brown. She took a deep breath and sat up. "Where am I?"

Not quite what he asked, but her talking was a start. At least she wasn't wobbling anymore.

"My office. You passed out, and we don't really have a protocol for agents getting sick." Since they didn't. "This was the only alternative I could come up with." He couldn't exactly take her to a hospital. Their physiology might be human, but because they healed in an instant from most wounds, things like needles didn't agree with them.

That and a lot of agents never got the heartbeat or body temperature thing down. Too hot, too cold, too fast, too slow—there was almost always something about them that wasn't quite right.

She rubbed her eyes and stood. "I guess that makes sense. I'm sorry. I'm probably keeping you from your job. I have work of my own to do." Her aura flared again, muddying before flickering and fading, and she pressed her palm to her forehead.

"It's all right." He was next to her in an instant, guiding her to sit. "Nothing we do can't wait another few minutes, or even hours or days."

She gave a bitter laugh and leaned forward, resting her elbows on her knees. "Right. Tell that to Raphael."

Desire rushed through him. To wrap her up in his arms. To trail his fingers through her hair and kiss her until the world stopped spinning around them. He pushed the impulse away. It wasn't the images that disturbed him—he knew how to banish thoughts of lust. It was the other emotions. The urge to treat her differently. To abandon fairness and—

He obliterated the impulses before they rambled further. "I'll tell him personally. But not until we're done here."

"You could have taken me home or something." The corners of her mouth twitched up.

"I wanted to have your friend do that. Ariel, right? But she said you kept wards on your doors only you could get past." Another odd thing on his growing list. What the angel described was something only Lucifer did. Why would this demon know tricks like those?

"Ari," she corrected him. She stood again, this time without any incident, and raked her fingers through her hair.

"Angels and demons don't shorten their names." A name was a job. It made a cherub into more. It was a thing of pride. Cherished by those who held one.

Color was returning to her cheeks. "Of course they do. I don't go by Uriel. Talk about awkward rolling off the tongue in about half the languages on the planet." Her laughter was light and natural, like water over crystal.

"What would you prefer I call you?"

"Ronnie."

A heavy stone dropped into his solar plexus. That was what he'd called Metatron. A pet name, the only one Michael ever used. He couldn't hide his grimace. "How do you get Ronnie from Uriel?"

"I don't know, I just do. How you do you get Bill from William?"

"I don't." He had to know.

Uriel was emblazoned on her back, the large red tattoo-like sigil looking the way so many from hell wore their names. And her tank top showed enough of the symbol for him to recognize it. But too much of everything she'd said, the way her aura acted, what Izrafel… Something was going on.

It was too bad he couldn't tell if she would answer any of his future questions with lies. Like any angel, except for reading auras, his gift of seeing a being's truths only extended to mortals. He didn't need to be *His will* when it came to other heavenly beings. "It sounds more like it's short for Metatron."

Her aura flared again, the yellow almost vanishing in a sea of black and red. She collapsed onto the couch, sinking into the cushions as the glow around her all but vanished.

Would she faint again?

No, she stayed upright. She intertwined her fingers so tight her knuckles turned white. "It sounds like a lot of things. Why would you use that word?"

He had no idea what to make of her response. "It's not a word, it's a name."

"Whose?" There was no way she was faking this. She looked terrified.

"She was one of the four originals. Yes, I said four." It felt odd to add the qualifier. Metatron was all but obliterated from their history. Her betrayal was considered worse than Lucifer's. Most were only created with knowledge of the three. Their curriculum was preprogrammed, so the moment they became an agent, they held all the knowledge deemed necessary to their jobs.

Once upon a time, everyone knew the originals. Lucifer was His advocate, which was why Lucifer chose to walk away and rule in hell instead of staying in heaven. He was always looking for the other side of the story. Michael was His will; Metatron, His voice; and Gabriel, His vengeance.

At the mention of a fourth, she didn't even flinch. "I assume because there were four of you."

That was interesting. "Most of you don't know that." He dragged his gaze from her when she squirmed.

"Why not?"

Not only did she know Metatron's name, she was surprised no one else did? She just got more and more intriguing. "They stripped her from the standard lesson plans after she was destroyed."

The sludgy gold aura leaked from her again, this time swirling and dancing around her instead of flashing and overwhelming. For a moment it looked as if she might cry. She rubbed her face and dragged in a few shaky breaths.

He wanted to reach for her. Something. He'd never seen this before. Even when a cherub and host clashed, their auras didn't muddy and fade.

Someone knocked, and the door opened a crack, enough for Ariel to peer through. "I'm sorry to interrupt."

All of a sudden, the light around Uriel—Ronnie...*that would take some getting used to*—returned to the same red she displayed around the office, almost as bright.

Michael didn't know what to make of any of it. He returned to the chair behind his desk. "You're fine. What can we do for you?"

"Raphael said to come check on things." Ariel stepped farther into the room, leaving the door open the crack she needed to fit inside. She shared a smile with Ronnie, but stared at her feet instead of looking at Michael.

"Is that all he said?" Dripping sarcasm flavored Ronnie's question. "You're sure it wasn't something like *I don't care who she's talking to, tell that demon to get her spoiled butt back in her chair right now?*"

Ari lifted her head long enough to glance at Uriel before turning her attention back to her shoes. "Maybe."

Office politics. *Fantastic.* He wanted to know more about what Uriel was thinking, but he didn't think he'd get answers from her. Whatever was going on with her energy, she may not hold up to more questions. He had confirmation enough—she was different. Even if Lucifer wasn't favoring her, he'd done something unusual during her creation. It was another piece in a bizarre puzzle.

He looked between the two women. "Uri—Ronnie's not going back to work today, she'll be back tomorrow."

"But—" Ariel and Uriel spoke in unison.

He held up his hand. "I'll talk to Raphael." He looked at Ariel, and pinked flared across her cheeks when she finally made eye contact. "Make sure she gets home all right."

Chapter Seven

If Ronnie hadn't been walking a fine line between insanity and wondering what Metatron would assault her with next, she might be amused by the almost tangible hero worship in the room. She was pretty sure Ari would have dropped to her knees and spit-shined Michael's shoes with her favorite sweater if he asked. And she'd enjoy every second of it.

It was disturbing and funny, and that wasn't the tiniest bit of jealousy growing inside.

"Don't get attached. We'll destroy him soon enough."

Between the threats to flay Michael where he stood, and the whimpering *the voice* did in Ronnie's head at mention of Metatron being stricken from common knowledge, Ronnie was learning to love this new element of her thoughts.

"Sarcasm doesn't suit you. How do you know I'm not His voice, driving your directions?"

Because He didn't dictate that way. He was more hands-off, a trust-His-employees kind of guy rather than a micromanager.

"Just because you think you know everything doesn't mean it's true."

Whatever. She was done listening to the vindictive, petty bullshit. Ari waited for her in the doorway. With the afternoon off, as soon as Ronnie got home, she was researching *how to remove dead angel brain stains*. On a search engine other than Ubiquity's.

Ari fumbled through a polite goodbye to Michael, and Ronnie bit back a smirk. When he stepped closer to shut the door behind them, the impulse to lean in and kiss him raced through her. *Where the hell did that come from?*

She put it all behind her when Ari and she made it outside moments later. The sun warmed her skin, and she turned her face into the heat, enjoying the crisp scent of fresh flowers and trees. At times like this, when she could enjoy all the pleasures that came with having a physical body, she knew exactly why angels and demons vied for Ubiquity jobs.

"You're sure you're all right?" Ari's question drew her back to the now.

Ronnie nodded. "You don't really have to make sure I get home. I don't want to take you away from work." She added a teasing lilt to the second part of her statement.

"Whatever. No one is going to knock me out of the number one spot in half a day. Also, we're not going home. Today's the kind of day made for blowing off responsibility."

"I like the way you think. What did you have in mind?" That was why Ronnie adored Ari.

Research could wait a couple hours. It wasn't as if Ronnie would get more crazy in that time. Besides, if it was someone else's voice, that meant she was sane, didn't it?

"Tell yourself whatever you need in order to sleep."

The Ubiquity offices occupied their own building in the middle of an office park a few miles from Nashville, isolated enough to not worry about mortals seeing agents phasing in and out. On perfect days like today, she missed the people. So whatever Ari had in mind, Ronnie hoped it involved downtown. No reason to travel to another state when conditions were perfect locally.

"There's someone I want you to meet." Ari grabbed Ronnie's hand.

Ronnie wasn't sure what to think of the statement.

"He might be able to help with your memory."

"I can help with your memory. You just have to stop fighting."

"Does help involve you obliterating me, like the last time we had this conversation?"

"Maybe," Metatron said. *"Details don't matter if you're gone, right?"*

That wasn't a solution that interested Ronnie. While she knew better than to hope Ari might be right, she couldn't suppress welling optimism. "I'm in."

The Ubiquity front lawn vanished, and Ronnie smothered the urge to count the seconds until they rematerialized. She wished Ari didn't take so long to relocate them from place to place, but since she knew their destination and Ronnie didn't, Ari drove.

After several agonizing seconds, they arrived on a sidewalk with a smattering of people. No one seemed in a hurry. Small groups of two and three strolled by, heads ducked together, or pointed at shop windows, laughing and chatting. The atmosphere was intoxicating.

Did Ronnie's job for hell, pre-Ubiquity, involve people? She never got tired of having them around.

Lucifer had told her she'd never been among humans until now, though.

"Did it ever occur to you they call him the Prince of Lies for a reason?"

Stupid voice. She was pretty sure Lucifer was sick of her always asking about her memory. If he knew any information that would make her leave him alone, why would he hold onto it?

"I'd say ask him, if you really want to know, but..."

"Maybe you were only there for the most recent conversation," Ronnie said. *"But I guarantee, it wasn't the first time I've asked him for help."*

She wasn't letting this non-conversation with Metatron ruin a perfectly wonderful afternoon. She stowed the nagging questions and followed Ari into one of the windowless shops on the street.

Ronnie paused just inside the door, letting it swing shut behind her, and inhaled deeply. The rich aroma of fresh coffee filled her lungs while she studied the room. With no windows, the only light came from a sparse arrangement of sconces along the wall. The floor melted into the shadows and then reemerged with tables and chairs sprinkled throughout the room.

She didn't think there was anyone else there, but a flutter in the energy around her pinged her with recognition and drew her attention to a girl behind the counter. Ronnie studied her for a moment. What made her different from the average person? The tingle inside Ronnie reminded her of tracking a cherub, but that couldn't be right, could it?

"Look closer."

On second thought, if the voice cared, Ronnie didn't.

As they approached the register, Ronnie read her name tag. Apparently the girl was Claire.

"Hey." Claire gave Ari a warm smile. "Your usual?"

"Two of them." Ari half-turned to Ronnie. "You'll never taste a more awesome caramel latte the rest of your existence."

"That's an impressive recommendation," Ronnie said to Ari. Ronnie couldn't take her gaze off Claire for more than a few seconds, despite her desire to ignore anything a voice in her head was interested in. Every move the barista made was deliberate—gliding her fingertips over the handle of the espresso machine and pausing with each ingredient as if enjoying the scent for the first time.

When her gaze met Ronnie's, she ducked her head and went back to work. Ronnie really needed to stop staring. She followed Ari to a table at the far end of the room.

"It's too bad you were passed out." Ari took the tiniest sip from her drink before setting it down. "I mean, I guess it wouldn't have happened then but still. You completely missed it. Michael was so worried about you. Doting, hovering, making sure you were taken care of. Can you teach me how to do that?"

"How to pass out? I don't think that's the kind of skill you can just learn."

"Aww. Do you have any idea how lucky you are? He's *the original* original. Does that even mean anything to you? The *first* angel."

"I guess." Ronnie would correct her if she thought it mattered. Lucifer was the first; Michael even confirmed it. But nothing changed—the world didn't stop spinning, their jobs would still be the same—if Ari thought Michael was older, and it would let her revel in her hero worship a bit longer.

"You guess? Really? I don't care where you're from. He exudes everything positive ever."

"He is sexy." Ronnie bit the inside of her cheek the moment the words slipped out. It wasn't that fraternizing with colleagues was against the rules. Angels hooked up with each other plenty. And demons with other demons. That whole appreciation for a physical form made some seriously horny agents of heaven and hell.

When Irdu wasn't available, her vibrator was her favorite appliance, even though she'd never tell the coffee maker. Angels didn't touch demons though. As if demons were beneath them.

Ari shrugged. "Of course he's sexy. I mean, you don't hold a position like that and think poorly of yourself, right?"

Ronnie couldn't argue with that. Something flashed out of the corner of her eye, and she whirled toward it. What was that? Everything was the same as it before. A counter, a cash register, pastries under the counter, and Claire.

Ronnie blinked and looked again. Claire glowed. It was faint. If the coffee shop was any brighter, it wouldn't be visible. Even the few extra lights over the counter obscured it enough to make her doubt the aura was there. That explained the tingle in Ronnie's veins. She turned back to Ari, who drummed the fingers of one hand on the table, expression unreadable.

Ronnie nodded toward the register. "Is she…?"

"A cherub? What do you think?"

"I told you to look closer."

Even if she was having a hard time ignoring the voice, there was no way she was listening to her cryptic, frequently sadistic advice.

"We talked about this. My name is Metatron."

And she definitely wasn't calling it by the name of some long-dead angel no one even talked about anymore.

"Fuck you."

"How long have you known?" Ronnie asked Ari.

"A while. I don't know. She's been working here longer than I've been coming here."

"But…" None of this made sense. "You're a top performer. You're a master of following the rules. How come you never took it?"

"Her. Not it, her. The thing about rules is there tends to be room for interpretation. For instance, we're in a coffee shop even though I promised to get you home safely. I'll get you there eventually, just not yet. If she ever needs to be sent back, she will be."

"It's not the same." Even as Ronnie ran an argument through her head, her own logic balked, agreeing with Ari. "We have to send them home. It's the entire reason we have these jobs and the right to live on Earth." Ronnie pushed her chair back, wishing she could find the confidence to match the words falling over her lips. "If you won't do it, I will."

"All right. If you feel like you have to."

That was odd. Why wouldn't she want to send a cherub back to heaven? Ronnie stepped toward the counter, and a wash of images slammed into her thoughts. Memories of the last cherub she took, the screams overlapping with the fight, mingling into an agonizing mess with the voice asking how she knew it didn't hurt.

She tried to force her feet forward. This was her job. If Lucifer was right, gaining this form was what cost her memory, she'd surrendered—temporarily or not—any ties to her past to do this.

Claire looked up, blue eyes wide, half a piece of chocolate caught between her teeth. "Can I get you anything?" Her question was muffled.

Doubt smothered Ronnie's decision. There must be a reason Ari refused to take her. What was she missing?

"You mean besides everything? Let's see. She's not hurting anyone, she just wants the same chance at a body and life as any of us... Do you want me to go on?"

It didn't matter that those were some really good reasons. The Ubiquity guidelines implied no exceptions.

"Because they're telling you everything. Uh-huh."

Fuck. Ronnie couldn't do this. Not because of the voice, but because she trusted Ari's reasons. Ronnie shook her head. "No. I'm good." She turned back to her seat and dropped down with a scowl. What was she doing?

"Why should you enjoy life but be allowed to take hers?"

Ronnie wasn't taking her life, just sending her back home. Besides, she earned her chance on Earth. Claire hadn't even done her time in the proverbial mail room yet.

"Are you sure you've earned it? That's a confident statement for someone who doesn't even remember what she was doing before she got here. What's one cherub, give or take, in the grand scheme of things?"

Ronnie gritted her teeth. Stupid, reasonable, obnoxious voice.

"You're welcome."

Chapter Eight

Ari's smile flickered before she hid it behind her coffee cup. "See?"

"Yeah, I get it." Ronnie didn't completely. She still couldn't articulate what made her not capture the cherub, but her conflicting thoughts kept her from acting.

Without warning, the chair next to them was occupied. Even seated, the new arrival, who phased into the chair as quickly as any shift Ronnie ever completed, was at least six inches taller than her. Standing, the height difference would probably be closer to a foot. His blond hair was pulled into a ponytail at the base of his neck, but his goatee was jet black. Odd combination, but it worked on him.

"Hello, handsome. Long time no see."

The greeting made her grit her teeth, and lit her caution censors on fire. How did Metatron know someone Ronnie didn't?

"Same way I know Michael. Except this gorgeous angel didn't murder me."

He gave Ronnie a wide-eyed glance before he turned to Ari. "I thought you were busy this week."

She leaned back in her chair, posture casual and relaxed. "Someone earned me the afternoon off." She nodded at Ronnie. "This is who I was telling you about. Ronnie, this is Gabriel. It's his coffee shop."

An original. Of course. One took her on as a student—which apparently no one did, one acquired a job at Ubiquity just to see her, number three lived in her head, and now the fourth studied her as if she was under a microscope. What made her so special?

"Me."

They didn't know a crazy dead angel lived in her head.

"Just Gabe."

"I thought originals didn't shorten their names."

"You've been talking to Michael." Was Gabe disappointed?

"Yes."

"I have the utmost respect for him, but he tends to be a bit old fashioned."

Oh. She didn't like the hint of condescension in his voice, and she really didn't appreciate the embarrassment it sent flitting through her. She shifted her attention to Ari. Who, in sharp contrast to the submissive, almost worshipful posture in Michael's office, looked relaxed and at home here.

Gabe offered his hand in greeting. The instant Ronnie's fingers brushed his, warmth pulsed through her. It tossed away traces of exhaustion, leaving her feeling as if she'd just woken from the best sleep of her life.

"Whoa." Even the voice was faint.

God, that was amazing.

He raised his eyebrows. A tiny smile tugged at the corners of his mouth before he pulled away. "So you're what hell's turning out these days."

Was that an insult or a compliment?

"Who cares? Did you notice he's kind of sexy?"

Of course she had. She wasn't stupid.

"Are you sure?"

Ronnie focused on the new—she could only describe it as energy—flowing through her, and returned the smile. "Apparently."

He traced his gaze over her face. "Is it true you don't remember anything before Ubiquity?"

At least he got to the point.

Her pulse increased, heat flooding her skin under his scrutiny. But something about him tickled her memory. "That's not much of a secret."

"I'd like to help. I'm glad you let Ari bring you to see me."

"That was easy."

The word *help* triggered hope inside. Lucifer told Ronnie he'd look into it, and her memory should come back on its own, but never suggested more than waiting it out. Would she finally get answers? "So you've seen this before?"

"It's rare, but it happens. Every once in a while, when an agent takes on a physical form, the shift from quasi-mortal clashes with their heads. It's like their spiritual body doesn't know how to meld into a new shape."

He better have more than that. More substantial than the same crap she'd already been fed. Especially since, unlike everyone else, she didn't have any problems shifting between her two forms.

"So I won the amnesia lottery. Go me."

"Something like that. I'm surprised Lucifer hasn't done more." There was no trace of mocking in his voice.

Even though his words echoed her thoughts, defensiveness surged through her. "He's tried."

"I'm sure. But having someone else on your side can't hurt. Is there anything else you can tell me?"

"She has a voice living in her head, and she's too big a pussy to either obliterate me or step aside and let me have control."

Wait. Ronnie could obliterate her? How would she do that?

"I'm not giving you that answer."

Because Metatron didn't know. If she did, she would have done it already. "I don't remember or know enough to say if anything else about me is unusual. Is there a list of symptoms or something I can look for?"

"Have yo—" A single glance from Gabe, and Ari clamped her lips shut, jaw clenched.

That wasn't odd at all.

"At least you're paying attention. I like you sarcastic."

He turned back to Ronnie. "Not really. That's why I need to know anything and everything in order to help. Even if you don't think it's significant, I might."

"I really like ice cream. Is that unusual?" This wasn't getting her anywhere. It was too early in the conversation to be giving up, but she was spinning her wheels again. "Why would you help me? I'm not one of yours."

"In the beginning we were all His creations, and in the end, we're all His creations. Just because you call a different place home doesn't mean you deserve any less respect."

"He's an idealistic sap, but it's kind of charming."

She wasn't going to agree. There was no way she was giving a voice in her head that satisfaction.

"You can't lie to me any more than you can lie to yourself. Actually, it's probably harder for you to lie to me."

Whatever. Ronnie rested an arm on the table and leaned in. For a brief moment she considered telling him about the voice. However, unlike Lucifer and Izzy, she barely knew Gabe, and she didn't want his first impression of her to be she was crazy. "I can't think of anything specific, but I promise I want to try."

The three of them spent the next few hours talking about work, life, hot vacation spots, and pretty much everything random. Gabe occasionally prodded Ronnie with a question he might as well have summoned from nowhere-ville. Had she ever visited the Middle East? How did she feel about cherries? Did she prefer silk or wool?

The conversation was nice, but she didn't feel any closer to answers.

Her phone chimed, and she reached for her purse without thought.

Gabe raised an eyebrow.

She resisted the urge to purse her lips. "Sorry. I didn't know we'd be doing something important or I would have turned it off." Did that sound sincere?

The message was from Irdu. *Who does a demon have to fuck to get a permanent get out of work free card like yours?*

She couldn't hide her smile at the teasing. *I'm available, but I don't know about that card.*

Lunchtime quickie, and we can figure it out? Irdu typed.

"Am I keeping you from something?" Gabe's condescension was back.

She was supposed to be cowered by that, wasn't she?

"Don't piss off the sexy angel man."

Another reason to do mostly that. "Actually, I had plans for lunch. I didn't realize we were going to be here so long."

"Sorry to tie you up." Was Gabe surprised by her approach?

Good.

"I'm going to stick around here, if that's okay," Ari said.

Ronnie was great with that. She loved Ari's company, but the angel didn't get along with Irdu. "Sure. Catch up with you later?"

Ronnie replied to Irdu as she strolled from the coffee shop. *If you're on the menu, lunch sounds good. Meet me here, we'll get up to something wicked.* She sent him the address.

He appeared in front of her a second later. His scowl caught her off-guard. He looked between her and the coffee shop. "Gabriel? Really?"

His tone didn't thrill her either. She'd just been talked down to by an original angel, she didn't need the same from a friend. "And?"

"So, first you pass out—which demons don't do—and wind up in Michael's office—"

"You know about that?" And if one more person reminded her the passing out was abnormal, she was going to scream.

"Do you know where we work? *Everyone* knows about it. Raphael made sure of that."

Because apparently gossip was one of those things that was awesome with a physical body. Go figure Raphael headed up the rumor mill.

"And now you're hanging out with Gabriel," Irdu said.

She didn't like the accusation in his voice. "I didn't know this was where we were going." She had stuck around for a while, but did it really matter. "And, so what?"

"One, they're angels, and two they're originals." Irdu crossed his arms, and his jaw was tight. "If you're tired of being called Lucifer's pet, how much worse do you think it's going to be when the office thinks you're just an original whore?"

"Excuse me?" Ronnie almost choked on the words, but that didn't stop her from shouting. Disbelief and hurt rocketed inside. This was worse than being slapped.

*

Fuck. Irdu couldn't take that back. Why did he even say it? He didn't care who Ronnie slept with. They'd both been with other people.

Other demons.

"That came out wrong." He'd also waited about two beats too long to say so.

She raised her brows. Fury crackled through her aura like a fireworks show. That was new. "I'm having trouble figure out how it could have sounded right. Maybe I haven't fucked Lucifer enough to have that answer?"

Great. Now she was mad. He was irritated. And he should backpedal. He should apologize.

But she also couldn't be doing this. For all the reasons he just gave her.

And because he'd sworn to Lucifer that he'd do whatever he could to keep her away from Gabriel. Not that he could tell her that.

"I'm sorry." He poured sincerity in the apology. "So, yes, people will talk, but fuck what they think."

"Which is that I'm an *original whore*." She ground the words out through her teeth.

He scrubbed his face. Would groveling help? Was it worth it?

For Ronnie, maybe.

Though, he wasn't sure why. "You're never going to let me live that down, are you?" He tried to shift his tone toward something lighter and more playful.

"Would you if I said something similar?"

He heard shit like that all the time. Well, not exactly like that. Fucking around was in his nature, and used to be part of his job description. "I'm sorry."

She stepped away from him. "You know what? I'm busy after all. I can get judged anywhere. I could go back and plant myself in front of Raphael if I wanted a scathing assessment of all I'm doing wrong with my life. I don't need it to hear it from the one person I thought got me."

If she wasn't going to hear him out, he wasn't going to stand here and shout at her. "Fine. Enjoy your day off."

He phased out before she could reply. Childish? Probably?

Did he care?

Yes.

No. He'd go find something else to distract him. He appeared outside the city library. One of the best places to meet hook-ups. Smart girls and guys were fucking kinky.

Except he couldn't put one foot in front of the other, and make himself walk inside.

Was he actually not in the mood to get laid?

He needed to get the fight with Ronnie out of his head first. Anger and frustration surged through him. She didn't deserve this kind of space in his thoughts. No one did.

Except, he'd given up a management job for her, and pissed off Lucifer in the process. She already had a pretty permanent residence in his thoughts.

That was scary. No. Wrong. Intimacy didn't terrify him. It was just frustrating. Maybe this was a good time to start keeping his distance from Ronnie.

As he stood in the middle of the library steps, debating the pros and cons, people brushed past him. Their emotion bled through him, and it should have been intoxicating.

He was too distracted. The concept of *give up Ronnie* ached to even consider. Out of this entire fucked-up mess that was his life as a demon, he hadn't met many people he liked. Tia—his sister, Izzy, and now Ronnie.

Was he jealous of her time with Michael and Gabriel?

Jealous of a couple of angels? Fuck that. With their holier-than-though bullshit, they weren't worth his time, and they weren't worth Ronnie's.

He shouldn't have phrased things the way he did, but she needed to keep her distance, and he wasn't sorry for telling her so.

Chapter Nine

Ronnie picked another green pepper off her pizza and added it to the growing stack on the side of her plate. Ubiquity bought lunch for the monthly staff meetings, a nice gesture. It made perfect sense too, since a bunch of borderline sensory junkies worked for them. What better way to willingly bring together a group of beings who found joy in the simple task of eating?

She was glad Irdu wasn't here. Developers didn't have to mingle with reapers. And fuck him. His cruel words still bounced in her head, the next day. He'd texted once, and she ignored him.

That was the end of that.

If she thought about it too much, it welled in her chest and pricked her eyelids with tears. It wasn't easy to find friends here—not with everyone knowing Lucifer pulled strings to get her the job.

She didn't ask for that. Not that she'd complained, but she hadn't done anything special to get his favor.

At least Ari was still talking to her.

One by one, management called the names of the people with the top capture counts for the month. Five angels, including Ari, all ranked high enough to be recognized.

Ronnie had two problems with these assemblies—or rather, what they represented. Since this was only her third staff meeting, and she already recognized these flaws, she was curious how they escaped everyone else's notice. First, if someone was last to the meeting room—as she was today—that person got the pizza no one else wanted. She eliminated another vegetable, and stabbed it with a plastic fork. The action made her feel better than it should have.

Her second issue tied back to the cherub in Gabe's coffee shop yesterday. How many more were still out there courtesy of Ari passing them over? And if she was ignoring cherubs, how was she consistently getting top recognition? Ronnie already knew why no one was asking. Prying into *was the system rigged* meant deconstructing the one thing so many of them looked forward to. This job.

Not only that, but how was Ari getting so many legitimate pings? She averaged one every other day. Ronnie was lucky to identify one a week, and she was never wrong when she picked one to go after. Was Ronnie that bad at identifying them in the queue, or was Ari that lucky?

Not that Ronnie begrudged her the success. When Ari dropped back into the empty chair next to her, the *congratulations* were genuine.

"Thanks." Ari's smile was flat. She tossed her reward certificate in the middle of the table and turned her attention back to her pizza.

A sliver of self-satisfaction trickled inside Ronnie. Maybe she wasn't the only one who saw the ridiculousness in this ceremony after all. "At least you get free sugar out of it."

The corners of Ari's eyes tugged up, and she held up the gift card to a local ice cream parlor—the only real bonus to these events. "Good point. Want to go with me after work to spend this?"

So she still had one friend. That was nice.

"Of course." Ronnie pushed aside the rest of her food. She wasn't going to suffer through cold remnants of wilted veggies and weak sauce with the promise of desert nirvana waiting.

"Did you think any more about what Gabe said?" Ari asked.

Thought about it, was frustrated by it, and rolled the entire conversation over and over in her head until she was dizzy—it was better than dwelling on the fight with Irdu. "I guess."

"Is there anything else you can tell him?"

Ari had never expressed this much interest in Ronnie's missing memory. She was sympathetic, but that was it.

Not that Ronnie minded the concern, but the out-of-nowhere bit of it caught her off guard. Maybe she was reading too much into it since no one really tried to help before. "Nothing." It was hard enough to tell Lucifer she was hearing a voice. As kind as Gabe appeared yesterday, he was still mostly a stranger, and he still wore that mask of arrogance. She wasn't willing to share that much information with him.

"You care what he thinks? Or are you just worried he might be more interested in talking to me than you?"

Ronnie cared about not being labeled insane.

Ari drew her lips into a thin line as she studied Ronnie. "You're sure? What about what happened with that fighter?"

"What about it?" The question set off more miniature alarms in Ronnie's head. Ari told her the fighter stuff was status quo, and Ronnie didn't tell her how she won the fight in the end. Or rather, that it hadn't been Ronnie who fought back.

"Nothing." Ari shook her head. "We should probably get back to work."

Something was off about the conversation, but Ronnie couldn't place it.

"Because you're not trying hard enough."

"Or nothing's there, and a stupid voice is making me paranoid."

Around them, everyone stood, tossed away their plates, and broke into small clusters to chatter and try to waste another five or ten minutes before they logged back into the queue. Regret mixed with sadness twinged through Ronnie. Ari was just trying to help, same as Gabe. Telling them everything would increase the odds of that happening. So why couldn't she bring herself to do it?

"I'm starting to wonder if you even need me here. You'd probably talk to yourself even without me around."

She certainly wasn't stopping Metatron from leaving.

"Ha ha. If only it were that easy."

"So you do know more than you're telling me."

"I didn't say that," she replied. *"Just that I know it's not easy. Believe it or not, I don't want you here anymore than you want me in your skull."*

Ronnie ignored the bitter taunt and the part of her that agreed, and made her way back to her desk. At least she had ice cream to look forward to after work.

Pings rolled into her queue one after another as soon as she logged in. Dud after false lead after not-even-close scrolled by. As she rejected each one, she wondered again how Ari and the other top performers landed so many captures.

Another ping. She hovered over the *Pass* button as she scanned the details. She jerked the mouse cursor to a neutral part of the screen as she continued to read and process. There wasn't anything specific, but the undeniable tingle racing through her told her this was a hit. *Score.* She clicked the *Capture* button and grabbed her purse off her desk. Time to see the world.

She was far enough into her training that taking Ari with her was optional. A request she could make if the situation concerned her. The tingle humming under Ronnie's skin demanded she do this alone.

Right before she phased, she sent Ari a quick text:

Off to Israel, back in time for ice cream.

Nervous apprehension flitted through Ronnie as her surroundings melted into narrow streets, towering buildings, and more stars than she'd seen in a single place. She stared up at the sea of black sprinkled with a gazillion sparkling white dots. So gorgeous.

It took her a moment to pull her focus back to the task at hand. Why was she here in the middle of the night? Or whatever time it was? She checked her phone: 2:00 a.m. Perfect. Not. Where was she supposed to find her target if most people were sleeping?

In the distance, a large shadow of a wall loomed over it all. A sob echoed inside her skull. Great, what now?

"It's all... It used to be so... No. What happened?"

Her vision danced and swam. She still saw the cars and bikes lining the streets and the stone structures climbing toward the sky. But she also saw what was there before. The rolling hills, a smattering of adobe huts—

She shook her head to clear away the images, but they didn't vanish. How did she know what was here before? It almost felt like a memory. Instead of drawing her out of the vision, it spiraled her further into the sensations and emotions. Her heart fluttered, and she turned down a side street without questioning where she was going.

"This past isn't yours."

Something irritating buzzed in her skull, but she needed to be somewhere. Of course it was hers.

She grabbed more strands of the memory and tugged.

"No."

There was no power, no resistance, behind the protest.

Ronnie wove through an alley, turning without knowing why or where she was going. She strode past a large brick structure, blocked off by a gate, and kept wandering. Fences and walls circled large portions of the area, but it was a simple task for her to shift to an ethereal form long enough to pass through.

Even in the middle of the night, warmth radiated from the sand, and caressed her skin. A hint of cool ran through it all but only enough to tease.

A tiny portion of her mind asked if being here, seeing this *other* past, was the key to unlocking her memories, but she couldn't grasp the thought long enough to consider the truth of it. The flutter in her chest grew as she strolled farther from the structure, and her surroundings looked more like crumbled stone buildings. Still, fragments of *what used to be* superimposed, and amid the ruins, she saw houses and vendor stalls.

She turned another corner, and in her mind, saw the temple that once stood there. An abrupt stop, feet frozen, a sob rose in her throat. It wasn't a sacred house of worship anymore. The decrepit walls barely reached her waist in some areas. Time eroded so much. The landscape was desolate. Empty. Abandoned.

"Leave. I don't want to see this."

Ronnie sank onto a nearby step—or what had once been one. Loss dug a hollow in her chest. Confusion churned in her thoughts, and doubt clenched in her gut. Nostalgia, joy, and agony rose inside. She dropped her face into her hands. What did she think she'd find here? And why did this place and its state of ruin grab at a jumble of emotions she didn't understand?

Something vibrated against her leg, jarring her from the dreamlike state. She shook away the haze and grabbed her phone from her purse.

A text from Ari. *Ice cream?*

Ronnie rattled her head to clear away whatever was going on, and the present seeped back in. Right, she was there to find a cherub. Did she really wander that long? The stars faded from the sky as dawn crept in. She needed to get back home. There was nobody here. She'd wandered far enough off track that whatever registered in the queue was somewhere else, and she wasn't knocking door to door or looking in windows for it. Apparently, she was about to have her first failed capture. She sent back a quick, *Be there soon.*

"It's beautifully tragic, isn't it?"

She jumped to her feet and whirled at the intrusion. The unexpected newcomer stood just inside the crumbling walls. He wore a black jacket and matching slacks with a white button down shirt, and topped with a *kippah* and *tallit*—skullcap and prayer shawl. In the predawn light, without the disruption of city lights, the faint glow surrounding him was distinct. Apparently she didn't have to knock on every door near her GPS coordinates after all. She'd found her cherub. What she couldn't find was the motivation to do her job.

"I didn't mean to startle you, demon." He tipped his head in a bow. His Yiddish was flawless. Wait, she understood Yiddish?

She stepped back, too much surprise cluttering her thoughts to decide what shocked her most. The cherub she took a few days ago knew what she was as well. That didn't make sense. Supposedly, a cherub who popped into existence outside heaven or hell didn't know anything except the basest survival instincts and a desire to experience everything.

"How do you…?" She trailed off, feeling silly asking her question aloud.

"Know what you are?" The corner of his mouth tugged up. "Your aura glows brighter than any one of the stars. I walk out here during the early hours when no one is around to stop me or care. You're easy to spot in a ruin like this. I don't suppose…" He turned his gaze to the sky. "No. That's not appropriate to ask."

She wasn't surprised he saw her aura, but she didn't expect him to be articulate about it. This wasn't some random cherub who just hopped into the nearest body a couple of hours ago. He knew too much about living life in general. Like Claire in Gabe's coffee shop, he was acclimated to his surroundings instead of rampantly licking everything that looked interesting.

Ronnie's Ubiquity training tried to butt in and whisper she needed to take him, send him to hell, and move on. She was too captivated by the unexpected conversation. "I'm not easily offended. Ask away."

His smile returned. "I don't suppose you're old enough to remember this place in its original glory."

"I am. She's not."

More memories tickled her thoughts. Of waiting for someone. Of her heart hammering against her ribs and her stomach fluttering. It all vanished with a growl and a flash of nothing, and she blinked at the rapid shift in her mind. "No, probably not."

"What a shame. It was gorgeous, I promise you."

He was talking as if he'd been there. That made no sense. Cherubs didn't start popping into existence on Earth until the last century or so. This wasn't right. Except he knew things. He knew why she was here. And he was talking to her.

"Nice. You'll spare him if he'll give you answers? If not, then what? You'll pout in a corner?" Venom filled Metatron's words, but hurt and anguish lay underneath.

Ronnie shouldn't know what Metatron felt, but emotions rocked under her skin, as if they were her own.

Ronnie's fingers twitched at her side, and indecision pummeled her thoughts. She left Claire alone, but the queue didn't send Ronnie to her. Then again, this stranger… What could he tell her? Was one failure really a big deal?

He nodded at Ronnie's hand. "Please don't."

More ambivalence taunted her. His request didn't make it any easier to take him.

He took a step back. "I know you're supposed to eliminate us, but I'd rather stay here. You don't have to tell anyone you found me."

None of what he said made any sense. She knew on an intellectual level what the words meant, but couldn't piece together why he said them. She could only think of one response. "It's my job."

"It is. But I've already chosen my path." He gestured to his clothing. "Do you think taking that from me will change who I am?"

She swore she was missing key information in this conversation. At the same time, he was right. The traditional clothing, the way he wore his hair. He already sought enlightenment and helped others find it. From his outfit, his preferred method of education was religion. Sending him to hell wouldn't change that. "How do you know why I'm here?" she asked.

He closed the distance between them, stopping less than a foot away and locked his gaze on hers. "You should probably ask the person who sent you. I stopped doing training centuries ago." He grasped her fingers between his and kissed the back of her hand. "Just promise me you won't tell them asking was my idea."

"I—" What was she doing? She had hold of him. A couple of seconds, and she could extract the stray cherub. Except the desire wasn't there. Whether he spread the word with his followers or was a really horrible priest, he was doing more to help people delve into themselves than any angel or demon could. Was taking that from him worth getting a certificate of recognition at the end of the month? "I won't."

"Thank you." He turned on his toe and strolled back into the ruins of the temple, across the dirt-strewn floor. He disappeared from sight past a wall on the far end.

What was that?

Her phone vibrated in her purse again, and she fumbled for the device.

You on your way or not? Ari asked.

Be right there. As Ronnie phased back to Ubiquity, she tried to stash the onslaught of questions but couldn't. What was going on?

Chapter Ten

"I'm wounded you didn't remember me." Gabe's low voice rumbled against Ronnie's neck as his chest pressed into her back. He rested his hand at her hip, holding her close.

With every new touch, desire pulsed through her veins. How did she forget something like this? She leaned into him, memorizing the texture of his shirt against her bare shoulder blades. Her skin burned with exquisite agony for each new touch. It thrummed through her, beating in time with her heart.

"If I had a choice, you'd be the last thing I forgot." Why did she say that? This moment, each sensation—it was all incredible, but there was a lot implied in that statement.

"Hmm..." The vibration tickled her skin. "You do have a choice."

"If that's true, why hasn't someone told me?" She didn't want to talk. She wanted him to roam her body. Glide under her clothes. Caress every inch of her.

"I'm telling you now." He slid his hand under her tank top and rested it on her stomach.

A few inches higher, and he'd brush her breasts. Her nipples hardened at the nearness. "You could have told me before."

"I didn't feel like I had your full attention." He wrapped his fingers around her wrist, rough and demanding, and spun her to face him. Dark haired, clean-shaven, Michael stared back, not Gabe.

Shock rolled through her. That hadn't been Michael's voice, though. She'd only talked to each of them once, but she knew… Didn't she? She didn't. She'd forgotten what each man sounded like. This had always been Michael. She only loved him. Only desired his touch. Need filled her. To sink back into him. To run her hands over his entire frame.

He rested a hand on the small of her back, the other cupping her cheek. "I swore I would move mountains for you if I had to." He sought her mouth with his, and the feather light kiss rushed through her, making her head swim. It was gentle, undemanding, and all-consuming.

He broke away enough to trace his thumb over her lips. Each new caress tingled under her skin.

"That I would surrender everything—eternity, glory—all of it. For you… I lied." His voice shifted to a quiet snarl.

"What…? No." The words cut deeper than she expected. Were those tears pricking her eyelids? Why did that sting so much? Sharp agony tore through her gut. A physical pain, it might as well have been rending her in two. She gasped and choked on a thick liquid. Stepping back, she looked down. His sword was buried to the hilt in her stomach, dark red pooling around it and spilling over his blade and hand.

His gaze bored into her. "There is no redemption for what you've done. Never forget that."

The edges of her vision blurred and faded, blackening as she sank to her knees. She didn't know which hurt more, his words or his blade. Though the pain in her middle faded, the one in her chest throbbed harder.

Ronnie opened her eyes wide in shock, every inch of her screaming in pain. She struggled to catch her breath, but she couldn't gasp, despite her need for air. Sit up. She had to sit up. Except she couldn't do that either. Her body wasn't responding to her instructions.

"Wow. That must suck." Her own voice drifted to her ears. But she hadn't said anything.

"You're a bit slow on the uptake, aren't you?" Ronnie's voice said.

"Metatron?"

"Suddenly I'm not *the voice* anymore? Tell me, how does it feel to be the one stuck on the inside? Oh wait, you can't talk. *Ha.*"

Ronnie needed to wake up. Knock herself out of this dream. Get back control of herself.

"Not necessary, not happening, and fuck you."

Her body was moving—rolling out of bed, tugging on a pair of shorts, wandering into the kitchen for coffee—it was all familiar. But she wasn't doing any of it. She watched as someone else drove her. She didn't know how Metatron gained control. Was it because Ronnie let her guard down to sleep? Because she was distracted by the dream?

"What should I do today?" Metatron mused aloud in Ronnie's voice. "Maybe watch a little TV, have some tea, devour your soul."

"What the hell?"

A laugh rumbled through her. It shook her chest, made her smirk, but emotionally, Ronnie wasn't amused. "I'm kidding, of course. I know you're a coffee girl."

Fuck this. Ronnie didn't care how Metatron wrested control. Apparently, whatever she'd struggled to hold back for the past few days was more serious than she realized. There was no way she was surrendering her life to a disembodied voice with some long-dead angel's name. Ronnie's determination rolled under Metatron's wicked amusement.

"You've lost your say in this matter." Ronnie's fingers flicked on the stereo. She closed her eyes as the rhythm flowed through her, and the carpet caressed the soles of her feet as she danced.

Something flickered behind her eyelids. It was a visual of the electric web filling her body. Ronnie wasn't sure how she knew, but she was certain the power wasn't hers. There was a good chance it belonged to Metatron, and while it was a long shot, Ronnie hoped it connected the two of them. Either way, it was going to go. She would've smiled if she could.

"Stop." Metatron said.

"No." Ronnie was taking her body back.

"Oh, come on. Really? Who says it's yours?"

Ronnie was done negotiating with the stowaway. She focused inward on the black strands, the way she extracted a cherub from a human. It might not be the right thing to do, but her knowledge was limited, so she went with what she knew.

The pieces Ronnie thought of as *the voice* ran far and deep in her veins. *Shit.* She'd never dealt with cherub so integrated with a human host. She grasped at loose wisps and pulled them toward the center of her being. She tugged mentally, and searing pain rippled through her. As the invading threads receded, invisible razors sliced across her back and legs.

The pain snapped Ronnie from the excruciating ritual. Metatron's presence raced back in, chasing away the oppressive pain. Metatron's threatening electricity rocked Ronnie's entire frame.

"Mine," Metatron taunted her.

Ronnie knew what cherubs did to their hosts; training said the host persona eventually ceased to exist. If Metatron was a cherub—and really, what else could she be—was Ronnie about to lose herself forever, inside her own head?

"For the billionth time, I'm not a fucking cherub."

No. Ronnie wasn't going to let that happen. Anger fueled the vow. Whatever Metatron was, Ronnie wasn't going to let her glide in here and steal what little life she remembered.

Whether it was Metatron's temper tantrum or something else, Ronnie anticipated the pain this time. She focused on the wisps threatening her.

She grasped the strands weaving through her body and mentally yanked.

Agony sliced her, and her entire body felt as if it was shredded an inch at a time. Heavy breathing reached her ears. Panting, but she didn't feel it. And then she did. Breathlessness accompanied the pain. She gritted her teeth, and her jaw responded, enamel grinding on enamel. Ronnie was winning.

"Please don't. I'll be good. I'll behave. I'll let you stay in control. Please?"

The begging made it easier to stick to her decision, and not hearing someone else use her voice pushed her past the mounting agony. She wasn't going to lose herself to a hitchhiker…or whatever Metatron was. Ronnie steadied her breathing and pictured the web as it tangled with who she was.

She grasped the last bits of Metatron, fighting back a scream as the ethereal pain threatened to consume her. She wound the foreign strands into a ball, and then boxed it into a back corner of her mind.

"Please don't. Please. I can't."

A soft sobbing echoed in her head. She reined in the voice. Metatron's crying grew into panicked hiccups, making her wince. Why did Ronnie feel so bad about fighting her back? Was the entity already that integrated with her? She didn't know how much time passed, but the eviction left her drained.

Ronnie dropped back against the nearest wall and slid to the floor. She opened her eyes, forcing herself to recognize the apartment around her—the battered kitchenette, the orange easy chair, the mattress on the floor. She held her arms stretched out in front of her. How did they look so clear when they were on fire? *Right. It's not real.*

She should do something about the pain. She should… Her mind didn't work. A portion of it was ripped away. What should she do? Go out. That made sense. If the pain was in her apartment, she'd go somewhere else.

Irdu.

Did she want to do that after the fight they had? After the horrible things he said?

He apologized. It was still a shitty thing to say, though.

But she needed to get outside of her own head. Desperation and bits of Metatron clawed inside. He was safe.

She grabbed her phone and sent him a text. *I need you.* She wasn't in the mood for playful tonight, though. *Please? I know it's late.*

Come on over.

Ronnie breathed a tiny sigh of relief at the brief and immediate response. She slipped on a pair of sandals and phased out of her apartment.

And then she was in his living room. He had a much larger apartment than she did—a benefit of making a decent salary and having been on earth for at least a couple of decades.

And right now all she cared about was that he stood in his bedroom doorway, in nothing but a pair of boxers, watching her with concern.

"Come here." He crooked his finger.

She crossed the room and fell into his arms.

He cupped her face and lay soft kisses along her lips, her jaw, her neck, and back to her mouth. "Tell me what you need."

She shook her head. She didn't know. Comfort. Safety. "Sanity."

"I don't have a lot of that, but it's yours." He slid his hand to the back of her head, holding her captive, and nipped at her lips.

The despair that gnawed her insides raw faded. She dug her fingers into his chest, needing something, anything, to hold onto. "Thank you."

He dropped his arm around her waist, and broke the kiss, but didn't pull away. With each moment that passed, her tension drifted further away, and her pulse slowed closer to normal.

Irdu guided her to the couch, sat, and pulled her to sit next to him.

It was so easy to curl into his side. Could she hide here forever?

He trailed his fingers through her hair. Such a simple gesture, it almost made her sob with relief. "I'm glad you texted me," he said softly. "I don't like fighting with you."

"Me neither." She also didn't want to get into the details of why they'd disagreed. It needed to be hashed out, but she couldn't do that right now. Was that selfish of her?

"I was an idiot. It's up to you how much more you want to delve into that."

"I don't. Not right now." She snuggled closer. "What happened?"

What was she supposed to tell him? *I've been hearing a voice and tonight it took over my body.* Would he thinks he was crazy, or just making shit up to get attention. The latter was probably preferable. "It was just a dream. It didn't sit well with me."

"So it wasn't a sexy dream." He trailed his fingers lightly up her arm.

The barely-there contact raised goosebumps in its wake, and chased away phantom pain. She wanted more of that. A touch to sink into. A passion to devour her thoughts. Something to replace the lingering ghosts from her sleep and consequent possession.

Ronnie shifted to straddle his legs, and draped her arms around his neck. "It started that way, but it ended on a very bad note."

"Do you want help writing a new ending?" Irdu glided his palms under her shirt and skated up her sides, just brushing the edge of her breasts.

"I want a total do-over."

He slid his touch to her shoulder blades, where her wings rested when they were summoned, and a pleasant shiver raced though her. That bit of her back had always been extra sensitive.

He pulled her into him, to claim her mouth. With each nip and peck, the kisses grew hungrier.

Ronnie moaned into the sensation, grinding into his lap.

"Tell me which parts of the dream were good, and we'll go from there," he murmured against her lips.

Ice slid through her veins on a whispered memory of *original whore*. "Nothing that compares to what you're doing."

"No? I bet it was that cute girl in advertising."

She could follow that line of questioning. It led down a playful path. "Pretty sure that's your dream."

"But you're always there, making out with her." He dragged his mouth along the curve of her neck.

Ronnie sighed and leaned into the kisses. "And you're just watching?"

"Only at first. Are you going to give me a little hint about what made things start off sexy? I'd love to know what kind of dreams make you wet." His coaxing growl rolled over her skin, blending with his touch. His heat. "It's not like you were dreaming about Gabriel."

She froze. She recovered quickly, but not quickly enough.

Irdu's hands stilled. "Are you serious?"

No. She wanted the comfort back. The light teasing. The promise of more to come. "I didn't say anything."

"You didn't have to."

"He ran me through with a fucking sword."

"Is that a euphemism?"

Ronnie sighed and stood. "No. It's very literal. He tried to seduce me and then he killed me and it fucking hurt. And I woke up screaming."

"What kind of a kisser is he?"

She clenched her fists and jaw. "Are you kidding me? I had a dream that some arrogant, condescending original angel lied to me, used sex to get me to let my defenses down, and then *killed me*. How do you think any of that is arousing or sensual?"

"I don't—"

"Neither do I. It was a mistake coming here." Ronnie blinked from the room before he could say anything else stupid.

Fury raged inside as she appeared on the sidewalk near her house.

"Did someone get her feewings huwt?"

And now Metatron was back. *"FUUUUUUCK!"* Ronnie screamed into the night.

*

Irdu didn't know what was wrong with him. He was acting like a jealous, possessive boyfriend.

He wasn't any of those things. What he had with Ronnie was supposed to be fun, no strings, and no pressure.

Just thinking that made him clench his jaw.

He'd justified taking a demotion for her, and now he was getting his panties in a bunch because she was fantasizing about other people.

That was so, so bad.

He sank back into the sofa and scrubbed his face. Maybe it was time to move on from Ronnie. He'd let her be a distraction for the last several months. A way to forget that he was spinning his wheels when it came to his own life.

He needed to get back to what mattered.

Ronnie matters.

He ignored the part of himself making the argument. Tia mattered. Finding a way to get out from under Lucifer's thumb, without risking his sister's life, mattered.

Sex as a whole was fantastic.

Sex with Ronnie was better.

Eternal servitude to the lord of Hell put a damper on it all.

Besides, unlike all the sensory junkies who worked at Ubiquity—including Ronnie—he'd been human before this life. He didn't walk into demonhood with the same uncontainable awe for all things physical.

Nobody else besides Lucifer and Tia know it. Her survival depended on Irdu keeping the secret. He was one of the first, decades ago, to pick up a cherub hitchhiker.

Except unlike the way things were handled now, he'd adapted, and Lucifer had not only made him a full-fledged demon, but granted immortality to Irdu's dying sister, in exchange for using him as an experiment.

Talk about literally selling his soul.

Irdu wouldn't do anything different, if he had the chance to do it all over again. But that wouldn't stop him from searching out ways to get Tia free of his contract.

He wasn't going back to bed anytime soon, because that meant dwelling on what happened to Ronnie. He'd hit the internet, for the infinitieth time, and see what kind of information he stumbled on this time.

Ninety-nine percent of it was bullshit, but the nuggets of reality he'd found over the years, combined with Izzy's input, would get him an answer eventually.

And now was the time to focus on that, rather than the sexy little demon who made his pulse race and his blood boil and overwhelmed him with unreasonable jealousy.

Chapter Eleven

Ronnie thought she'd locked Metatron away. She hadn't even noticed the lack of talking when she was with Irdu, and now it was back.

"Fooled you."

A low, cold rage simmered inside Ronnie over the fight she'd just had. How dare he? Shaming her? Even if she'd acted on the impulses or fantasy, fuck him. But she'd had a bad dream, and he got pissy about it?

"Nobody likes you, everybody hates you…"

And that. Ronnie could so do without that. Why was Metatron silent while Ronnie was with Irdu?

"Because I don't care what you do with your fuck boy. I'm watching and learning."

No. That wasn't right. Metatron didn't watch anything silently.

"Sure I do." The retort didn't carry much weight.

Ronnie liked the silence. It was almost enough to tempt her to go back to Irdu. Try to make things right.

"Poor little demon. Willing to give up her pride for a friend."

Almost. Ronnie wasn't willing to swallow her pride for that asshole, just to get a little more mental silence.

And she wasn't stupid enough to believe Metatron's reasons for staying quiet.

"Are you sure?"

Ronnie rolled her eyes. She focused inwardly the same way she had earlier. She expected the pain this time, and managed to keep from screaming in agony.

The light-headed inability to think wasn't so easy to ignore. She felt like she'd locked away half her brainpower. What was she doing? What should she be doing?

Donuts. She liked those. She'd go get donuts.

Milliseconds later she landed in front of the convenience store.

The doors slid open, and artificial air rushed over her skin. She nodded at the clerk but didn't make eye contact. It took concentration to remember who she was and what she was doing while maintaining some picture of sanity. The donut case was empty. Despair pricked her eyelids, and she blinked back the abrupt and irrational desire to cry. They were just pastries, not worth getting worked up over.

"Prepackaged works in a pinch."

She nudged the taunt aside, wishing she could eliminate the pain with a simple thought as well. She refused to hear Metatron mocking her failure, or experience her glee at her minor victory. She grabbed a plastic-wrapped package of something frosted and cream-filled. Her throat ached, and her eyes burned with unshed tears she couldn't explain as she made her way back to the counter. She swallowed and forced a smile while she paid.

"Miss, are you all right?" The cashier's question was distant compared to the chaos assaulting her mind.

"Let me out."

Violent sparks pulsed in time with the demand. Shaking her head, Ronnie phased out of the store. She barely found the presence of mind to cloud the cashier's thoughts and make her disappearance seem inconsequential as she vanished. She didn't know where she was going, but she couldn't stay there. *Fuck. Where was I going?*

The nothingness of being intangible soothed her burning flesh in a way she wasn't used to, filling the invisible cuts. She needed this to stop now.

It only took a second of deliberation to settle on a destination. Hell.

"No." Metatron's command rang in Ronnie's ears and rattled her skull.

"Shut up."

Ronnie appeared in the ethereal realm and wrapped herself in the soothing energy. Too bad she wouldn't be there long. Lucifer would drag her somewhere they wouldn't be overheard, to drown her in a lecture disguised as sympathy, and things would go back to normal.

"At least you're realistic."

"Shut up." She told herself the voice wasn't there. Metatron didn't exist.

Unlike Earth, a physical place, hell was ethereal at its core. The plane of existence didn't have any shape or form outside what its inhabitants assigned it. A lot of the older demons kept a permanent home there, even if they were allowed to spend their time on Earth, because it was easier to bend things to their will. Rumors suggested some of them shaped their corners of hell into beautiful places with forest groves, sweeping fields surrounded by mountains, and glorious castles.

Ronnie didn't know if it was true—or at least she didn't remember—but any of those spots must be better than the sterility of the main offices. Tile stretched as far as the eye could see, meeting off-white walls broken up by the occasional door.

At least that made it easy to find Lucifer's office. She had no idea where the other doors led, but unlike the rest of the flat, beige boredom, his door was textured, stained a rich maple color, and sported a gorgeous tree carved into the oak. No other like it in the endless hallway. She knocked on the worn wood and waited. She tapped her toes on the tile, and drummed her fingers against her leg. *Nothing.* She knocked louder, and irritation crept over the tentative calm settled around her.

She growled at the lack of response. She needed answers. Now in hell, the comfortable power pouring over her helped her clear her head and wrap her thoughts around what happened.

She didn't know what caused Metatron's takeover, but sleep kept Ronnie from actively trying to block Metatron from her mind. Could the odd dream be related? Whether that was the case or not, she didn't dare sleep until she figured things out. If there was a chance of it happening again—

The door in front of her swung open, and she jumped in surprise.

"Ronnie?" Lucifer studied her, brow furrowed. "It's the middle of the night in Nashville."

"I know, but I had this dream, and then the voice…" She clamped her mouth shut. He didn't know what happened over the past few days.

If she wanted to appear sane at all, especially since she was about to complain about problems with the voice in her head, she should at least try to be coherent. And she dreaded the thought of pissing someone else off. She wasn't wrong when it came to Irdu, but she couldn't mentally handle rocking another boat. "I couldn't sleep. The details could take a while to explain."

"Let's go get coffee, and you can tell me about it."

Her neck loosened at the concern in his tone, and some of her tension ebbed. "I want to, but no." Ronnie hovered in the doorway. She wanted to be in his office surrounded by the familiar. He told her once that before she became a full-fledged demon— before he gave her the name and the job that allowed her to manifest physically—she served *him* exclusively. She spent a lot of time hanging out in this small room. He said her loyalty was why he gave her special attention. Her paranoia, courtesy of Metatron, wondered if that was the whole truth. "Can we just stay here?"

He stepped aside. "Of course."

She was still on edge, distressed from the dream and waking up possessed—she didn't know what else to call it—but the pain of snatching control of her body from Metatron was fading.

The frustration of arguing with Irdu wasn't.

She must have imagined Lucifer brushing her off the last time she was here. His greeting tonight was more like what she was used to. She settled into the chair across from his desk and tucked her legs underneath her.

He stayed on her side of the desk and leaned back against it. "What's going on?"

"I had this dream." The memory rushed back, and images lit her skin on fire with lust and pain. Honesty was one thing, but there might be bits of the dream she didn't need to get explicit about. "It was nice and peaceful and serene, and then Michael ran me through with a sword."

The twitch in Lucifer's expression was so slight, she might have imagined it. The way his eyes narrowed, the purse of his lips. "Are you having trouble with the new management at work?"

It was a reasonable question from someone who didn't know the details of her life over the last few days. So why did she feel as if he should have asked something else?

"Because you're more observant than you like to admit."

And she was back. "Not really. I still hate Raphael. But I'm pretty sure that's not related."

"No, that sounds pretty status quo." The corner of his mouth tugged up.

His smile beat back any sneaking reservations she had. "But there's more. Remember last time I was here I said I'd heard a voice?"

"Yes…"

She shook away her suspicion at his measured response. He was waiting for her to explain, that was all. "When I woke up after the dream, I wasn't in control of my body. It was."

He crossed his arms. "I see."

Shit. He thought she was crazy. She never should have told him. Was it too late to say *just kidding*?

"Probably."

Stupid non-existent voice she was ignoring. "That's it? I just told you I'm hearing a voice, and it's making me do things against my will." She couldn't help the desperation that crept into her tone.

"I'm still processing. It's got to be terrifying for you. I'm sorry. Does she call herself anything?" He unfolded himself and rubbed her arm, his tone kind.

The question made her grind her teeth, and she wasn't sure why. Maybe because up to this point, she hoped the nuisance was some kind of cherub, and those didn't have names. Did this mean her problem was common after all? That wasn't reassuring. "Do most voices call themselves specific names?"

"I don't know about most. It happens."

"And do a significant percentage of them claim to be a destroyed and dishonored angel? Like, say, Metatron?"

His shoulders stiffened "And she took control of your body."

"That's what I said, yes." Ronnie couldn't read his body language enough to know what it meant, but she knew it wasn't the comforting encouragement he exuded when she arrived. Did he think she was crazy? Was he upset? Was it because of the name?

"Or maybe, it's because he misses me, and he's sad you're here instead."

"Not cool."

He shoved away from the desk, raking his fingers through his hair, no longer meeting her gaze. "But you could still think."

Did he sound disappointed or was the lack of sleep and support from Irdu making her paranoid? She wanted to believe it was the latter, but his behavior over the past few days told her he hid as much as he said. "Yes. That's how I got control back. I'm okay, right?" She didn't want to whine, but she couldn't help it.

"Do you still hear her now?"

"Notice how he doesn't call me it*?"*

Ronnie had, and that sent ants crawling over her skin. And why wasn't he answering her question? She wanted reassurance, not redirection. "Yes."

"Are you ever confused about which thoughts are the voice and which are you?"

"I'm not *insane*." Ronnie barked out the retort before she could consider how it sounded. She bit the inside of her cheek and ducked her head. "Tell me you know what's going on, please? That I'm all right."

He kneeled in front of her. "You're fine. And you will be…fine."

She wanted to be comforted. Needed it so bad, but she couldn't ignore the hitch in his voice. "What's going on?"

"I don't know."

"He's lying."

"Why are you so certain?"

"Prince of Lies. Also, experience."

Ronnie needed to believe Lucifer. He was her link to answers. To home. "You promise you'll tell me if you find out anything?" she practically begged. She didn't like this helplessness.

He rose then moved to the seat across from her. "Go home, get some sleep. And make sure you let me know if things change."

She swallowed hard as she realized he avoided her question again. *Fuck.* Metatron was right. "Sure. Okay."

"You have to be at work in a little bit. You can sleep here on the couch if you want." He sifted through a stack of paperwork in front of him, not looking at her.

Once upon a time, the offer would have tempted her. Half an hour ago, she probably would have said yes without hesitation. But she couldn't shake the feeling he was lying to her, and she was tired of people pushing her aside. "I'll be fine. Thanks for seeing me."

If Lucifer was going to keep things from her, she'd find someone else to answer her questions.

"Gabe."

If Ronnie thought Lucifer was being vague, Gabe made him look like an encyclopedia. She wanted someone who shared the answers they had.

"Good luck with that."

An image flashed through her mind, distinct and almost-tangible, of leaning into Gabe. A pleasant shiver ran through her at the thought of his warm breath on the back of her neck. Now conscious, she realized it wasn't her reaction. Physically, she wanted his hands roaming her body. Mentally? Emotionally? There was no connection.

Then again, those links hadn't been working so well for her.

She phased back to Earth, a few blocks from her apartment. It was still late. Or was it early now? The traffic, while thick, progressed at a decent clip. A blanket of velvet blocked the sun, but light peeked around the edges of the skyline.

Shops filled the older buildings—consignment clothing, coffee, art, a bakery she discovered when she first moved in.

Even if Izzy was still out of town, the chapel would be open. His janitor kept an eye on the place while he was gone, so people could congregate without him. Ronnie hoped he was back. He saw something in her when she visited the other day, and she needed to know more. Besides, in the few short months she'd known Izzy, she never found a reason to doubt him. He didn't stare at her like a curiosity or tell her everything would be fine when it wouldn't or make promises he didn't intend to keep.

And his taste in men was wicked good.

She nudged the glass door, and it swung aside and then closed behind her without a sound. Silence swooped in and wrapped her in comfort. It felt wrong to do anything but tiptoe. She climbed the stairs to knock on his door.

Nothing.

She checked her phone. Almost six. Izzy liked insanely early hours. Maybe he was in the church? He was probably still in Fiji, but desperation and the need for a friend nudged her toward the chapel anyway.

She stepped through the doors. Two sections of pews stretched in front of her, one on either side. A pulpit stood at the head of the room. Izzy normally took the bench in front of it; he was more of a conversationalist than a preacher. The benches were worn like the walls outside, but clean and polished. The energy in the air was unique. Soft, sweet, and like satin against her bare arms.

What drew her here? Why was she certain it was where she needed to be? Her eyes adjusted to the room lit only by candles. Someone sat near the center of the aisle on her left, head bowed, a soft glow radiating around him.

She took a step back and then another. She didn't want to disturb a worshiper, even if he wasn't a human. As calming as this place was, her answers weren't here.

"Good. Let's go for waffles."

An uncontrollable yawn wrenched her jaw open. She'd rather go back home and sleep for another hour or two before work.

"I second that idea. You snooze all you want."

Right. Ronnie wasn't sleeping because she liked being in control of her body. She also had no reason to stay here.

"Don't leave on my account." Michael's distinct voice didn't shatter the silence so much as roll over the edges of it.

Another snippet of her dream flashed through her thoughts—the agonizing tear of a sword cutting through her flesh.

Betrayal throbbed in her head. Her fingers itched for something she didn't understand and twitched with the desire for vengeance.

At the same time, her chest ached with a longing to be wrapped up in his arms. To brush her lips over his. To feel his mouth trail along the back of her neck.

Ronnie shoved the disjointed compulsions aside. Was the dream a memory of the past? Was that why Metatron hated Michael so much? Or were the vivid images planted by Metatron specifically to fuck with Ronnie's brain? If so, why did every emotion the dream generated feel so real?

"I didn't mean to bother you," Ronnie said.

He stood and turned without making a sound. "You're not. There's plenty of room in here for both of us. Though if you're looking for the priest, he's in Fiji."

She grabbed her left arm with her right hand to keep the conflicting thoughts and feelings from making her shake. Terror, betrayal, and trust warred for her attention. Since she was pretty sure at least two of those weren't hers, she wouldn't give them credence. Metatron could take her fucked up emotions and sulk in a corner far away from her. "I know. I was hoping I'd find something here anyway."

A tickle of a smile pulled the corner of his mouth. "Lucky me. I'm here."

A phantom pain started in her stomach and spread horizontally between her spine and navel. It took restraint not to look down. There was nothing there. It was just that fucking voice playing with her head. "I tend to wind up here when I need peace." Why was she explaining this to him without hesitation? "It's calm—the kind that only comes from a place where the occupants have such a solid grasp on themselves and their lives that their souls are at peace."

He strode to the aisle and walked toward her. "There are days I wonder if anyone besides me notices that feeling anymore. What drove you to look for peace so early in the morning?"

As he drew closer, a storm of electricity forced itself through her veins. The rush would have knocked her over if it hadn't held her upright.

Her posture shifted without her permission, feet sliding to shoulder width. As she drew her hand from her arm, twin swords shimmered into existence. It took her longer to come to grips with what happened than for it to actually happen. When she stopped moving, she held two thin, curved blades—one leveled at his neck, the other near her waist.

She leveled her narrowed gaze at Michael. "I'll tell you what you can do for me." Her voice tore from her throat, but it wasn't *her* speaking. "Today you surrender what you took from me so long ago."

Rage, not hers, coursed through her skull, making it hard to pluck out her own thoughts. Took from her? Ronnie grasped for a meaning. She knew Metatron wanted him dead, but even in the short amount of time Ronnie had known Michael, she couldn't fathom him betraying anyone.

He stopped just outside the range of her blades, jaw clenched, voice low. "Metatron."

He knew she was there. The realization sat cold and heavy in Ronnie's gut. How did Metatron escape? If she could do this even when Ronnie was actively trying to keep her locked away... How did she stand a chance against the fourth original?

Chapter Twelve

Before the swords appeared, the yellow-red portion of Ronnie's aura vanished. Rich, dark ink flowed in to replace it. Angels hadn't been taught to summon swords for centuries—projectile weapons took less power and focus to control.

Every instinct told Michael to draw his blade. To defend himself. If she lunged, the few feet between them would vanish in an instant. Even if he weren't in one of the last truly holy places left in the world, he'd fight the instinct with his dying breath.

The twin blades in her hands, each the length of her forearms with a gentle curve, shone with their own light. She held the right one high, pointed at his neck, and the left closer to waist level. He'd know those blades anywhere. They were Metatron's.

The design and color didn't set them apart, but the *tsubas*—the hand guards—bore her name in dim, flashing red marks. All the grief and regret he repressed for millennia rushed back. What had Lucifer done? "Metatron."

"You do remember me." The voice was Ronnie's but edged and sharpened. "Should I take your life quickly, or draw it out?"

This wasn't possible. He watched Metatron die. Held her until she was an empty shell. "My life is yours. I've always told you that."

"You've lied before."

Even as she held her ground, the black enveloping her flickered, and a hint of red broke through like the first ray of sun after a night of storms. "Ronnie?" he asked.

"Don't call her that." Metatron's demand rattled the pews. "That's my name, not hers."

Izrafel was right. The clashing auras belonged to two different beings. But Michael had never seen two agents—each with so much power—inhabit the same physical form. A fallen took a cherub with no will or direction of its own, or a cherub found a human host.

No one could stay sane with two distinct and strong personalities sharing a head.

Experiences like the one at Izrafel's rattled Michael, no matter how often he experienced them. Ripping out a soul out and sending it back home… He hated doing that.

This was worse. This demon—Uriel—added a new layer of complexity. It wasn't his right to evict her from a life she earned. But guilt from eons ago gnawed at him with the need to rescue Metatron where he failed before. "I'm sorry for what happened back then. You have no idea."

"I have a little bit of an idea." Metatron shifted the top sword, nicking his skin with the tip. "How long has it been since you were ethereal? I bet you've got enough of a bond with this body that I could make you suffer for a long time. And this little toy of Lucifer's is powerful. I could annihilate you in the end."

"You could, I'm sure of it." This angel he almost surrendered eternity for. Had she been conscious this entire time? The possibility horrified him. "I wanted to stop Gabriel. It doesn't change anything, but I tried."

"I—" Her stance wavered, and red flared in her aura to dance with the black. "Stop him from what?"

"From carrying out your execution." Saying the words, after all this time, sent daggers through him. None of them spoke of it after the fact. Gabriel explained, invisible lines were drawn, and no one mentioned again why Metatron died. "I begged, I pleaded, and he was so furious about what you'd done."

"You're lying. I didn't do anything. But you…" She wobbled.

"*Give me back my body.*" Ronnie's yell tore through the chapel, echoing off the walls. Red and yellow flared around her, shattering the black and obliterating it. Her swords dissolved into a pile of black glitter at her feet and then vanished.

*

The pain wasn't as intense as the last time Ronnie evicted Metatron, but it still ripped away pieces of her thoughts and strength. She dropped to one knee, gasping for breath. The cool wood of the chapel floor seeped into her palm, and she swayed.

Michael was at her side in an instant, hand on her arm. "Uriel?"

Holy fuck, that hurt. Tears pricked her eyelids as she blinked away the confusion and looked up at him. "What did she mean to you, and you to her, for so much raw hatred to fill her?"

"Everything."

A simple word, infinite meanings. Ronnie might be moved at two individuals capable of so much love for each other. If it didn't threaten her sanity.

"Thousands of years ago, I was ready to give up immortality for her. The only thing left there now is regret."

In Ronnie's skull, Metatron screamed for release. For vengeance against…she didn't know anymore. For an end to the confusion. Ronnie didn't blame her for the last one. But if Metatron was in Michael's past, Ronnie would let her stay there. At least until she posed another threat to Ronnie's future. Right now, getting answers was her priority.

Ronnie prayed he could do that for her. She might not survive another twenty-four hours kept in the dark. "You'll tell me what's going on, won't you? Please?"

He traced a thumb over her cheek. The intimacy caused a collision in her head: shock, familiarity that wasn't hers, and comfort she needed but couldn't say why it was better coming from him.

"Whatever I can, I promise." He glided his palms down her arms to grasp her fingers and then helped her stand. Hand on the small of her back, he guided her to the nearest seat.

This sucked. She pulled one knee up and hugged it to her chest, her foot flat on the pew. She chewed her bottom lip, darting her gaze around to ground herself. She finally looked at him again. "What happened just now?"

"I have a theory, but I'd like to hear your side of things first."

Why did she think he'd be more helpful than anyone else? She rested her chin on her knee. "If I had any information, maybe it wouldn't have happened twice in one night."

He settled onto the bench, facing her but leaving space between them. "Start at the beginning, and we'll figure it out together."

His reaction to her being possessed—she couldn't think of a better word for it—and his almost being decapitated was far calmer than hers. Maybe someday he'd teach her that trick. A bitter laugh slipped out, and she shook her head. "Let's start with you're not the first to say that to me, and I'm not any better off now than I was before."

"Who else have you talked to?"

"Lucifer. Gabe—sorry, Gabriel."

"Did you tell them everything?"

Why did everyone keep asking her that? Probably because she hadn't. But it was as if each of them knew there was more under her explanation. Expected a more complex answer than she provided. Her jaw worked up and down, and then she let out a slow breath. There was no threat here. No false pretenses, none of the superiority Gabe radiated. Michael was safe. She wasn't sure how she knew, but she did.

"No." Well, she told Lucifer everything, but it hadn't done her any good.

"Why not?"

"Because neither one of them is telling me everything."

"I get that from them a lot." His dry tone would have made her smile if the mood was lighter.

Instead, it added to her flailing mental state. "Really? Even Gabriel? Aren't you heavenly types supposed to stick together? Bros before hos or whatever?" She tilted her head to the side, unable to keep the sarcasm from her voice.

"Angels are capable of just as horrific things as demons are, the same way you're not inherently evil. You know all about free will and open-to-interpretation from Lucifer."

Right, Lucifer was the original loophole finder. The catalyst for demons coming into existence. For some reason, Michael's version of the rhetoric didn't bother her the way it did when Lucifer spouted it. She got the impression Michael believed it. She might as well lay it all out for him. If he hadn't already heard, he would eventually, and unlike the others, he witnessed her *change* firsthand. "I don't remember anything before about three months ago."

"Go on."

Not what she expected. He was listening instead of shrugging her off. She pushed forward.

"It happened when I took on a physical form. At least, according to Lucifer that's when it happened. I don't remember anything about myself or my existence, or anything else before that time."

"Do you remember the other day in my office? I told you there was no protocol for what had happened to you, because agents don't do things like get sick and pass out?"

Like she could forget that. She was pretty sure that was when her life started to crumble. "I remember, but Lucifer said this happens sometimes." The words sounded stupid now, regardless of how many times she'd said them in the past. "Gabriel agreed. That on very rare occasions, getting a mortal form doesn't agree with an angel. I'm being naïve, aren't I? This doesn't actually happen."

God, she was an idiot. It was too simple. Why did Gabriel lie? Why did Lucifer?

Michael's expression softened. "You're not naïve. It happens, but not the way they've spun it."

She lowered her chin until her forehead rested on her knee. Hope crept in, and despair pushed it aside. "They said all it would take is something to trigger the memories." Her voice was distant and muffled, even to her own ears. "That I'd get them back." Her voice cracked. "That it was only temporary." If they lied, would she be forever stuck without her past?

"And they're probably right. They've been doing this Ubiquity stuff for decades. They know better than I do." He scooted closer on the pew and trailed his fingers through her hair.

When Irdu did that earlier, it soothed, but expectation lay underneath. With Michael, the warmth of his touch, his fingers caressing her scalp, calmed her in a way she didn't anticipate. Did he mean the touches for her or Metatron?

Despite the soothing contact, his words were bullshit. Ronnie stared up at him and twisted her mouth in disbelief. "You're a horrible liar."

"So I've heard. Here's the truth. I don't work for Ubiquity—or didn't until a few days ago—because I don't agree with their methods. It's red tape with no room for interpretation."

The raw honesty was the most pleasant thing she'd encountered in the last few days. "I wouldn't say *no* room."

He raised his brows. "You mean like Izrafel."

"What?" Izzy didn't have... He fell. His lingering aura was because he never used the last of his power. It wasn't because he had a cherub. *Shit.* "How did I miss that?" She already knew the answer. Last time she saw Izzy, she didn't think keeping a cherub was an option.

"I hope he's not upset I outed him." Michael gave a dry laugh. "Who are you talking about?"

"There's a girl working in Gabriel's shop, and she's not exactly out in the open but not hiding either. And this rabbi I met in Israel. It's not on the books or anything, but I get the impression sometimes management looks the other way."

"That's new. Regardless. I didn't agree with Lucifer and Gabriel then, and I still don't. I look for individuals who host cherubs, whether it's angels or humans. I find them one at a time. This whole assembly-line hunt-and-destroy thing concerns me."

"Maybe he wasn't really... Is it possible he's telling the truth about me?"

Random, and a good question, but not what Ronnie wanted to focus on. Michael's interpretation of dealing with cherubs was so different from the company bullshit and made a lot more sense. "What do you do instead?" Ronnie asked.

"I talk to each of them. Figure out if they're a threat to themselves or other people, work with them to decide if they want the life merging leads to, and if things go well, I help the cherub integrate with the host."

Like what she'd seen in Israel. So she hadn't made a mistake walking away?

"I'm not integrating *with you in any way, shape, or form."*

"That makes two of us," Ronnie said. "What does that have to do with me? Do any of them think they're dead, powerful angels?"

"No. They're all cherubs. I guarantee it. What's happening to you I've never seen. I can talk you through integration. I don't know if it will work with two such distinct personalities, but—"

"No!" Ronnie exclaimed out loud, overlapping Metatron.

"Don't you dare." Metatron was vehement.

At least they agreed.

"Okay." He didn't flinch. "We'll figure out something else instead."

Sunlight spilled through the high windows at the back of the building, casting the chapel in a glittery array of colors from the stained glass above their heads. The jeweled light struck his aura and danced with it. Serenity and peace filled her thoughts, along with the memory of a temple in Jerusalem. In her mind, she sat across from Michael after a long night of talking.

"I did. Get out of my memory."

There was no power in the voice, but sadness joined the foreign emotions rolling through Ronnie.

Michael brushed a strand of hair off her forehead. "Two agents, one body? You're struggling with each other to find out who wins. My guess is the fight is holding your memories captive."

Every time he did something so familiar…so intimate, it set off a chain reaction in her skull. She loved the touch and the way it made her think he cared. She didn't know him though. Was he like this with everyone? She couldn't see the man she met in the office being touchy-feely. What made Ronnie so special, and why was she comforted by his simple actions? "What do we do about it? You don't hate me for not wanting to be her, right?"

"No." There was no hesitation in his words. He raked his gaze over her and shifted closer on the bench. "I don't want you to be her. Besides, judgment is really more Gabriel's flaw."

Did that mean he saw Ronnie when he looked at her? She liked that. "But what if me being myself destroys her?"

"We'll have to figure out a way to keep that from happening. Has she been there as long as your memory loss?"

Ronnie almost sobbed in relief that someone was having this conversation with her seriously. She didn't know which of them was crazier, but she was grateful someone supplied answers other than *wait and see*. "Maybe, but I don't think so. Since…" Had it really only been a few days? "It started a day or two before I saw you in Lucifer's office. Metatron started talking to me—arguing really. Since then, she's figured out how to take over my body, and she really wants you dead."

"I see."

Ronnie's gut sank at the lack of anything substantial in his response.

He wrapped a hand around her wrist before she could stand, and another surge of want filled her. His actions, the touches, the looks, the way he brushed his fingers over her skin, made her believe it was for her. A childish fantasy? Maybe, but he knew it was her here, and he didn't pull away or flinch.

Ronnie shouldn't stay, but for the first time since she woke up with no memories, someone was answering her questions directly and not just paying her lip service. Insecurity about whether he was here for her or Metatron kept her from holding his gaze. His palm was warm against her skin, sending longing to join her already jumbled emotions. What would it be like to kiss him? To let him press her against a wall, his mouth against hers, tasting him, and falling into the moment?

She plowed the thoughts aside. "What do you know that might help me?"

"A lot of things, probably. At the beginning of creation, while there were only angels, Metatron and Lucifer were close. It was the first time any of us had seen real love. It was scary sometimes how in sync they were."

"You'll never know what it feels like to have that kind of bond—or worse, to lose it. Lucky bitch."

Ronnie inhaled a shaky breath at the sensations, and pushed Metatron back. "But it didn't last."

"No. When he left to form hell, she stayed in Heaven. He didn't plead with her, but the hurt at her betrayal on his face... Even I recognized it. Things were never the same between them again."

"If I have one regret..."

That bastard. Lucifer had looked Ronnie in the eye when she said Metatron's name and never told her the voice tormenting her held the same nickname Ronnie did. What else was he keeping from her? Suddenly, her suspicions from earlier felt more founded in reality.

She rested her palms on the bench between them. "Was that when she was destroyed? Did Lucifer have something to do with it?" Metatron blamed Michael, but Ronnie had a hard time believing he was capable of it, unless he was the best fucking actor in the universe. Even Lucifer didn't hide his feelings that well.

"Lucifer's rage when he found out she was dead... He destroyed entire sections of hell, and it took him decades before he spoke to anyone. He wasn't responsible."

"Because *you* are." Metatron forced the words past Ronnie's lips. Ronnie kicked her back, but couldn't suppress Metatron's mottled emotions anymore.

At the outburst, Michael stiffened. He *did* know the difference between Metatron and her. His response cemented the idea his gestures *were* meant for Ronnie. "Gabriel killed her. He found out… He said she was trying to ascend. While it's true we're all supposed to become more, her plan involved destruction—of the creator, of everything around her. She wanted the world for herself. When Gabriel confronted her, he gave her a chance to atone, and she didn't take it."

Thoughts and feelings that weren't Ronnie's surged inside. Michael didn't have the story right. That wasn't true. It was so very far from reality, she might burst at the seams with fury. She wrapped her arms around herself to keep herself intact, but Metatron wasn't pushing her aside. She was shattering, and it ached deep in Ronnie's heart and gut. "That's not right. No. It can't… I— She wasn't…" She looked up at him, trying to smother Metatron's emotions and find her own.

"I didn't want to ascend. I was willing to give up eternity for you, Michael. How could you doubt that?"

Ronnie couldn't do this. Metatron was falling apart and threatening to take her along for the ride. Metatron wanted to believe Michael, but the rage had been with her for so long, forcing her love to contort and twist. Her conflict knocked about in Ronnie's skull like an avalanche, and she couldn't find her mental footing long enough to come up for air. Ronnie wasn't going to lose it here. Not again. Metatron wasn't taking control.

Every inch of Metatron struggled to leave, and Ronnie refused to let her drive them away.

"Please. We need to go now. I can't deal with this."

So Ronnie wasn't unstable, the voice in her head was. Great. She was staying. But so many questions remained unanswered; she didn't know what to ask first. She needed to sort her thoughts before putting them into words. Her stomach chose that moment to grumble, reminding her she'd been up for a while and hadn't eaten yet. "Do you want to go get breakfast?" she blurted out.

His eyebrows rose almost to his hairline.

She didn't know what to do with that response, or lack thereof. "Unless you have places to be."

"Not at all. Not for a couple of hours anyway." He relaxed, and the creases in his forehead vanished. "You'd think living as long as I have, I'd have learned to keep up with shifting social trends. But I'm still getting used to things like women asking men out."

He thought... Her cheeks flamed at the realization. "I wasn't— I didn't mean like a date." Oh geez, that sounded rude. "Not that I wouldn't. But I know angels don't... Not with demons."

"Shut up. Go home."

"I just meant—"

He covered her hand with his. "Breakfast sounds great. We don't have to define it as anything else."

She wrapped her fingers around his. "I know the perfect place."

"Let's go, then."

The implied trust wiped away more of her tension, and his touch was nice. Izzy's chapel blinked from view and became a city street just a couple of blocks from her apartment.

He shot her a glance.

Did he expect something more extravagant? Isolated? Something else? They were in a historical, restored part of town, so the buildings were all brick with wrought iron wells and aluminum awnings. "It's not super high class. I bet you're used to nicer places."

"It's perfect. There's a lot to be said for simplicity."

Chapter Thirteen

Michael let Ronnie lead. She seemed to know where she was going, and he enjoyed the heat of her fingers as they intertwined with his. He was still focused on how quickly she brought them here. A blink of an eye, with no obvious strain on her part.

It took a lot of power to do that. More than most agents had.

What happened in the chapel shook him. Metatron was alive… sort of. And haunting this beautiful demon's world. His heart ached for Ronnie. Her pain was almost tangible.

And try as he might, he couldn't ignore the question that kept bouncing in his head—if he had to destroy Metatron to give Ronnie life, could he?

He stowed the thought for later and tried to focus on what she was saying to the hostess. They seemed to know each other. Ronnie grabbed a menu and nodded at Michael. "It's for him."

The woman looked at their hands, still linked, and laughed. "Make sure you let go of him long enough to let him look."

Pink raced across Ronnie's cheeks. She was a wonderful combination of naïve, forward, and bashful. She still adored the world around her, even when a war raged in her own body.

Someone like that deserved to live.

The hostess led them to a booth at the back of the restaurant and dropped onto the bench seat across from him before sliding him the menu.

He looked between it and her. "You're not having anything?" He'd never met an agent of heaven or hell who turned down a meal. Especially from a place she seemed familiar with.

She chewed on her bottom lip, brow furrowed, before saying, "Waffles, extra strawberries, and lots of whipped cream, syrup, and butter."

He couldn't help his smile as he flipped open the menu. He should have known she'd have a favorite, and it would be sweet. "Is that what you recommend?"

She rose and leaned over the table, and pointed to things as she spoke. "If you like fresh fruit, yes. *God*, the strawberries? I swear they grow them out back. So good. But the grilled cheese is epic, and the soup is so yummy, and the scones are to die for."

He wasn't looking at the menu. She was far more captivating. The way her eyes lit up when she talked about something she enjoyed. The tiny smile that never left her lips. It was a sharp contrast to the frustrated demon in the chapel.

She's beautiful.

Her gaze met his, and she dropped back into her seat. "What?"

"Apologies." He pulled his attention away. "It's just been so long since the world was new to me, I've forgotten what it feels like to appreciate things so much. It's incredible to see."

"What was it like?"

He couldn't find a point of reference for the question. "What was what like?"

"Your first time out. Having a body. Experiencing the world."

"It's been a long time." So long, he hadn't thought about it in hundreds of years. Watching her experience the world around her gave him a new appreciation for the physical form he took for granted.

She stuck her tongue out. "I figured, you being older than humanity and all that." Her voice was all teasing, no implied insult. Not that he minded. Vanity didn't lie to him about how old he was.

Her question dredged up memories he rarely touched. He reached back for an answer to her question. He wanted to be honest. Not that he had a choice, but she was looking for beauty, and he wanted to convey that.

He shook his head and focused on her again. "It was wonderful. The sun on my skin, the scent of flowers, and cherries. Oh, the first time I had cherries. And the sand between my toes. Not a lot of shoes way back then."

She grinned. "I love the beach. I wish I lived closer. Maybe I can get a transfer. Was it weird that there weren't a lot of people?"

With each question, he tried to step back and see where she came from. It gave a new perspective to his experiences. One he liked a lot. "Not really. If there were that few people now, all of the sudden, it would be odd. But considering we watched humanity grow, it was stranger to see people than to not, at least back then."

When she was like this, her aura calmed. The fractures vanished, and the light he recognized as hers shone bright.

He ordered the same thing she was having. They talked as the food came. Swapped stories about all the places he'd visited that she insisted were exotic. They finished their meal as she shared stories of her limited travels.

He'd been to each and every place she mentioned, but saw them in a new light from her perspective. It was true, several of them had changed in the eons since he was there, but many were still the same.

The sun crested the skyline, rays of bright light peeking through the windows. She yawned and tried to stifle it. Despite the exhaustion in her eyes, she never stopped smiling. He couldn't take his attention from her for more than a couple of seconds at a time.

"I have to be at the office soon." She sounded as disappointed to say it as he was to hear it.

And she wasn't the only one. "I understand." He paid the bill and escorted her outside. As they stepped onto the sidewalk, it felt natural to take her hand. It was an intimate gesture, but it felt right. Essence sparked between them. Ice and sugar. Something he was starting to distinguish as Ronnie, rather than Metatron. "Maybe next time we'll call it a date."

"Maybe." The morning sun flashed in her eyes, adding to the shine. "I hope so."

Something shifted between them, and he was caught off guard when a blast of heat rushed between their clenched hands. She tightened her grip, and her aura flashed, muddy and fractured at the same time. She wasn't completely herself anymore.

"Uriel?" He didn't know if he could stop whatever happened by calling her name, but giving her the anchor of an external sound should help. She wrenched from his grip and backed away before he could reach for her again. "I'm sorry. I need to go." With the apology, she was gone.

His chest ached with sympathy for the chaos he just witnessed. If she lived with that every day... How was she staying sane?

* * * *

Ronnie reappeared in her apartment, her thoughts a rampant mess. More emotions than she knew existed swirled through her simultaneously. Things she couldn't identify but made her heart bleed and her soul weep and her skin hum. Even worse, she was almost certain most of the feelings weren't hers. She understood Michael's impact on Metatron—they'd shared something she couldn't begin to comprehend. But why did it hit her so hard? Tears stung her eyes, and electricity pricked her palms, searing them with the memory of the twin blades Metatron summoned, making Ronnie itch for the sensation again.

"*Stop.*" Ronnie barked the single word out loud. It echoed off the bare walls and swirled with the chaos in her head.

"I can't. I don't understand."

That made two of them. This wasn't Ronnie's memory. Whatever happened back there didn't have anything to do with her. Except it did. What Ronnie shared with Michael was him and her. The rational part of her didn't question it.

"Sleep. Please? I'm tired. I need to understand. I need... Please?"

Fuck that. Ronnie focused on thoughts and feelings she could say with certainty were hers, and turned toward the bathroom. She stripped off her clothes as she walked. The last thing she would do was surrender control over the things that belonged to her. She was going to take a cold shower, jar herself awake, and go to work. Metatron could sleep. Forever, for all she cared.

A new thought nudged the corner of her mind, and she shoved it away before it formed. She didn't know if it was hers or not. Water cranked to icy, she stepped under the stream and let the drops bite into her skin. The external discomfort gave her something to focus on. She was the one feeling it, not someone else. It wasn't a misplaced vengeance from thousands of years ago.

She stayed under the water until her teeth chattered. She focused her every thought on the world around her. The sensation of the terrycloth gnawing her frozen flesh and bringing warmth back.

The tile against the soles of her feet. The rush of morning traffic outside her window.

"What else is Lucifer lying to you about?"

The thought made her stumble. But it wasn't hers. She could ignore it.

"But it is yours. You want to know as much as I do. You heard Michael. The girl in Gabe's shop wasn't a fluke. Neither was the rabbi. Or Izzy. Izrafel for hell's sake. You think he's been flying under the radar since he fell? Not with that church. Gabriel knows what's going on with us, and so does Lucifer."

Three hours ago, Metatron wanted Michael dead. Now she was quoting him?

"I can hear your thoughts. Even the ones you hide from yourself. You want answers too."

All Ronnie wanted was her memory and life back, and to know how to evict the long dead angel from her skull.

"That makes two of us, but it was my life first."

Whatever the petty struggles of a couple of higher-ups, thousands of years ago, weren't her concern. She didn't care.

"Liar."

Maybe. But that ought to make it easier for her to fit in. She dressed on autopilot, grabbing random things from the closet and dresser. Work would provide another distraction. Besides, it didn't matter who pulled strings on her behalf. Something told her if she missed one more day of work, Raphael would find a way to fire her. Then she'd be out of a job, possibly out of a body…

Tears pricked her eyelids. She dragged the back of her hand across her cheeks hard enough to cause friction. Why was she crying? Frustration welled inside her. She couldn't lose her job. If she got sent back to hell, she might never find out what was going on.

"If you get sent back to hell, you lose your right to shift to a physical form. If Lucifer's telling the truth, don't you think you'd get your memory back at that point?"

If Lucifer was telling the truth. She swallowed the bile rising in her throat.

"My point exactly."

Ronnie took a deep breath, and when she exhaled, tried to compel the chaos out of her brain. It didn't work. She gave her bed one final, mournful glance, phased out of her apartment, and seconds later appeared in front of Ubiquity. After a short stop at the coffee shop on the main floor, she forced her feet to carry her to the elevator and then to her desk. She logged into the cherub queue with less than a minute to spare before her shift started. At least Raphael couldn't bitch at her about being late.

"Cutting things a little close, aren't you, demon?" Raphael's sharp voice sliced down her spine.

She ground her teeth until her jaw ached. She wasn't going to turn around. He wouldn't have the satisfaction of seeing her annoyance. "I didn't realize we could be penalized for *almost* breaking the rules."

The lack of sleep, combined with the jumble of Metatron's confusion sluicing through Ronnie, threatened to push more past her lips, but she bit back any further response.

"You can't be." The threat didn't vanish from his voice. "But I'm not worried about it. You'll do something by the end of the day."

"Slit his throat."

The idea was more tempting than it should be. Her fingers itched against her keyboard, not depressing any letters, but *clacking* enough to make noise. "I need to get to work."

The next few hours dragged by, minutes ticking away like centuries. She scanned one flagged set of search results after another. Nothing, nothing, nothing. She rested her chin on her hand. More nothing, a little bit of not even close, and a dash of nada.

Her eyelids drooped shut, and she pinched her cheek to snap herself awake. But she was so tired. Her eyes dragged closed again. Black ribbons swished through her, and a hiss of victory, not hers, flitted into her thoughts. Her chin slipped from her palm, and the combination jarred her awake.

She needed something to keep her conscious.

Quickie in Irdu's office?

Not likely. Not after the possessive, judgmental bullshit he'd put her through.

At least this nagging whisper of sadness was her own. Maybe she should mope about him longer. Then she'd know it was her feeling it.

Coffee was a better idea. She set her queue to *Away* and wandered into the breakroom. The numbness of exhaustion was pleasant—it kept her from living the chaos—but she couldn't give into the drowsiness.

She snarled at the empty coffee pot.

"Make more."

Ronnie might have, except defiance kept her from agreeing with anything Metatron said. Instead, she slid a bill into the soda machine and pressed a green button. She exhaled a grateful sigh when she pulled the frosty can from the machine. Its chill soothed as she trailed it along the inside of her wrists, and after a minute, over her cheek. The cold snapped more alertness into her. She popped the top and then chugged half of it. The icy sugar hit her stomach with a thunk. *Right, skipped lunch.*

"Afternoon." Michael's greeting drifted from behind her.

When she spun to face him, he was studying her with concern in his gaze. She almost choked on her next sip as the muddle of emotions surged inside again. *Not now.* She couldn't deal with this. Maybe later. She pasted on a smile and turned to leave. "Hey." She was already brushing past him as she talked. "Can't chat. Have to get back to the reaper line. Later."

"Ronnie, wait."

She couldn't. She wasn't going to listen to the command or promise of comfort in his request. And she couldn't stay there and have that conversation.

"What? You don't want to stick around and chat and swoon?"

Ronnie didn't *swoon* over Michael. And she *did* want to chat. She just wasn't sure she could handle it right now.

"*Please?*"

"*I thought you wanted him dead.*"

"*I thought he killed me.*" Metatron's response carried another wash of confusion with it. "*I need answers. We need to talk to him, if you won't let me sleep.*"

"*Definitely not.*" Ronnie settled into work without taking any more breaks, terrified another journey from her desk would mean running into more people she wasn't equipped to deal with. When she hunched over the keyboard, as long as she was scanning the queue, no one bothered her.

Her plan got her through the rest of the day. Fifteen minutes left on the clock, and she could call it a week. *God,* she loved Fridays. Not that she wanted to head home. Home meant alone with her thoughts.

"*We could go find Michael.*"

"*Not even tempted for a second. Not if that's where* you *want to be.*"

"*So you're going to stay awake for eternity, avoid anyone and everyone even though you adore people, and generally make yourself miserable just to spite me? I'm intrigued. And not at all wounded.*"

Ronnie dropped her forehead into her hand. Stupid, logical, fucking voice. If she was so smart, why didn't she just tell Ronnie what she was doing there? How to get rid of her? Obviously neither one of them wanted this.

"*I know. I'm just not saying.*"

"*Right. Because you're making yourself miserable just to spite me.*"

"*Fuck you.*" Venom filled Metatron's retort.

And things were back to predictable. That shouldn't be a relief, but it was.

"Demon." Raphael sounded far too cheerful for her sanity.

She paused her queue and whirled in the chair to face him. "What can I do for you?" She didn't care that exhaustion and sarcasm leaked into her question. He never tried to hide his animosity for her.

His smile sent ribbons under her skin, making every one of her fingers itch. She tried to be subtle about wiggling them to work out the excess energy.

"You're on your own, starting Monday," he said. "You've learned enough. Ari needs to focus on her own work."

That wasn't so bad. So why didn't the crawling inside cease? "Is that all?"

"She's not going to be there to cover your ass anymore." His tone was quiet and threatening, brimming with heavy smugness. "I give you a week before you crumble and have to beg someone else to pull some strings for you."

Ronnie couldn't rise to the taunt. There was no reason to fight back. He was a bitter, sad angel with bitter, sad dreams. The itching in her hands grew, calling to a recent memory she couldn't quite make solid. "I appreciate your input."

Her palms clenched, but not into fists. *Oh, swell.* They were curving around two grips about to appear in her hands. The sensation was identical to when Metatron pulled the swords on Michael this morning. Ronnie was seconds from letting it happen

again, and this time she didn't know if she could—
or even wanted to—stop Metatron from striking.

"Really?"

The enthusiasm attached to the single word was enough for her to grasp the last threads of her exhausted reason and mute the urge to decapitate Raphael in the middle of the Ubiquity offices.

"We both know you fucked your way into this job. That'll only take you so far." He leaned closer, voice low.

She spoke through clenched teeth. "You're probably right, but it ought to be enough to get me off work ten minutes early on a Friday. Have a good weekend."

She phased back to her apartment before she could do anything rash.

"Spoil sport."

She was too drained to argue. She sank onto her mattress, sitting on the edge, staring blankly at the floor. How much longer could she fight this battle before it destroyed her?

Chapter Fourteen

The visit to the chapel that morning was supposed to help Michael think. To clear his head and remind him of better days when churches and temples were more than just demonstrations of wealth and power.

He leaned back in his office chair, rolling the morning over in his head. Work at Ubiquity continued outside his door, but he didn't pay it any attention. Why the push for this job again? Middle management resented him for being on-site, the entire operation ran smoothly without interference, and he was getting more answers from Ronnie outside the office than he did while working.

The air shifted around him, pressing in on his thoughts. Instinct propelled him to his feet and toward the door before his mind processed why. The sensation matched what he'd experienced earlier when Metatron made her appearance. He focused on the sight a few rows of cubicles over. Ronnie stared down Raphael, a violent swirl of black, red, and yellow encasing her.

Even without hearing the conversation, her posture and aura hinted at its nature. He watched the scene with morbid fascination. He should step in, but the compulsion to rescue an innocent wasn't there. Whatever Ronnie was doing, she radiated power. She wasn't helpless. It didn't bode well for Raphael.

As abruptly as Metatron's presence surged through the office, Ronnie vanished. An instantaneous phase, as if a switch flipped.

With the disaster averted, Michael turned back to his office. The pieces were all there, but he didn't know how to put them together. Logically, there was no way Ronnie could be Metatron or even be hosting her. Gabriel destroyed her. But instinct, familiarity, and a warped sense of hope made him believe Ronnie wasn't off her rocker.

He dropped back into his chair and rubbed his face in frustration. Where did this fascinating demon come from? He glanced up when a shadow passed by his door. Maybe someone could give him a direction. "Raphael, do you have a minute?"

"Of course." Raphael turned, sneer vanishing into a smile in an instant.

Michael nodded to the chair across from his desk and waited until it was occupied to continue. "What happened out there?"

"Nothing."

Michael didn't need any sort of empathy to feel Raphael's animosity. "Listen, I'm not here to try to change the system or step on anyone's toes. My job is not to tell you how to do your job."

Raphael's shoulders relaxed, and he sank more comfortably into the chair. "Okay?"

"But I am curious about Ronnie." The name amped the tension in the room tenfold.

Raphael clenched one hand into a fist. "What about her?"

Not the reaction Michael hoped for. "Where did she come from before this? These are coveted positions. She must have done something impressive."

"You'd think that. But if she did, it's not the kind of thing angels in polite circles talk about."

Michael raised his eyebrows. "Oh?"

There was no joy in Raphael's chuckle. "She just showed up one day. No one had heard of her. Lucifer demanded the next open job. She bumped a cherub out of line that I pushed for months to get named. On top of that, the moment Gabriel heard about her, he demanded Ariel mentor her. One of hell's demons, and I have to surrender my best person to babysit."

That explained the animosity. Michael tried to keep his tone sympathetic. "Whatever my colleagues are up to, it's not Ronnie's fault. We don't hold anyone responsible for others' actions."

"I don't know why you're so sure she's innocent. She's spoiled, whiny, and doesn't deserve to be here. Angels work hard for these jobs."

"How do you know she didn't?"

"I get it." Raphael stood. "This isn't an open discussion. You've made up your mind. I heard you were better than they were. I guess that's not true."

Michael wanted to be patient, but the conversation irritated him. Regardless of how open-ended the rules were, few things irked him more than a judgmental servant of heaven. Especially when it came to trivial things such as who did or didn't have a desk to sit at. He tried to stash his aggravation. "Have you ever given her a chance?"

Raphael leaned forward, hands on the desk, face inches from Michael's. "I don't care how many guys she blew at the top to get here. I won't be pushed around by someone's slutty little pet."

The assumption. The insult. The arrogance. Rage and righteousness unlike he'd experienced in centuries spilled through Michael. He rose and summoned his glory. When his wings sprouted from his shoulder blades, it sent a shock of agony through him. Had it really been that long? He ignored the pain.

"Is this what we've been reduced to?" His voice rattled the blinds. "Petty office politics? Backstabbing? Bitching about the competition instead of excelling in our own way? You're one of His servants. A being of glory and light. And you've allowed yourself to be reduced to this fleeting moment in time that won't matter in five years, let alone halfway down the road to your eternity?"

Raphael's eyes grew wide, and he stepped back. "I… I didn't mean… I'm sorry."

"*Get. Out,*" Michael roared.

The moment Raphael was gone, Michael waved a hand. His door swung shut and all his blinds flipped to closed. As his physical form rushed back to replace his angelic one, he sank back into his chair. Why did it take so much out of him? Even worse, he didn't have any more answers now than before, just hell of a lot more questions.

*

Irdu felt the shift in the air, a massive surge of power that entire building probably noticed.

He knew that sensation. In lighter doses it hummed over his skin and danced in his veins and made him hard just picturing the demon it belonged to.

But nothing good could come of Ronnie bleeding that much power.

He was blinking down to her desk before his mind caught up and asked *what are you going to do?*

He didn't know. Whatever it took.

It didn't matter. Her seat was empty and she wasn't in the building anymore. The floor buzzed with chatter and residual energy.

Tia sat next to her, and was watching Irdu with expectation when he turned to her.

"You missed quite a show." She managed to pull off simultaneously amused and terrified as if that were a natural state for an individual.

"What happened?"

"Raphael was an ass. Ronnie got pissed. He didn't just imply, he outright stated she'd slept her way into Ubiquity. I didn't see the next bit, but that's when the air kind of crackled and burned, and then she was gone, and he was storming away trying not to look like he was running."

Wow. "Are you all right?" He needed to know that. Tia was his number one priority.

"I'm fine. She's probably not. Raph probably isn't either, but fuck that guy."

Fuck that guy indeed. Irdu puffed out a long breath. He wanted to check on Ronnie, but he might make things worse.

He'd ask Tia to go, but they didn't advertise that they were related. Since demons didn't have those kinds of connections. If she showed up, she'd have to explain to Ronnie why they were there… The two women rarely talked, so it would seem odd…

Tia quirked her mouth. "Aren't you going to make sure she's all right?"

"We're not exactly on speaking terms."

"So, apologize."

He snorted. "What makes you think it's my fault?"

"Because you're the one worried about the confrontation." She was too observant for his own good. "Go see if she's home. Bring sweets. Either she lets you in or she doesn't. The former, and you both feel better. The latter and nothing's changed, except now she has sweets. If she kicks you out, leave the sweets."

Irdu laughed dryly and kissed Tia on the forehead. "Don't ever stop being brilliant."

He make a quick detour to Switzerland, to pick up the milk chocolate with hazelnuts that Ronnie liked so much, and then phased to the landing in front of her apartment. No popping inside for him this evening.

He didn't have to wonder if she was home. The same static that lingered in the office radiated from her place.

Irdu knocked, and held his breath.

When Ronnie opened the door, she fixed a narrow-eyed glare on him. He swore the red in her eyes was dancing.

"What?" She snapped off the word.

He held out the elegant gold gift bag. "Chocolate?"

She pursed her lips.

"And a real apology. And a non-judgmental ear."

Her stony expression faltered, and she sniffled. She took the bag and stepped aside. "Come in. And please don't be an asshole."

Should be easy enough. Right?

He joined her in her apartment. "I heard what happened from the rumor mill. I thought you might need a friend."

"Are they saying I freaked out and I'm a total spaz?" She crossed the room and flopped onto the couch. The arm was on one side of her and the gift on the other.

That meant he was sitting on the floor or in the uncomfortable easy chair.

He knelt in front of her. "They're saying Raph was a total asshole, and you didn't hesitate to tell him so."

"You mean you didn't stick around and swap stories with him about what a slut I am?"

Irdu cringed. He deserved far worse than that. "No. He was in Michael's office, or I would have taken him on myself. I'm not here to make this about me, but I'm sorry for what I said the other day. For how I reacted. For all of it. I'm here because I'm worried about you."

He hadn't meant to slide into a rambling apology, but the words tasted right as they spilled out. Better than trying to pretend Ronnie was just a fling. That he didn't care when she was hurt.

Some of the rigidity evaporated from her neck and shoulders. She grabbed the gift bag and peered inside, then raised an eyebrow. "You went to Switzerland for me?"

It wasn't exactly a difficult trip. "I'd go to heaven and back." Wow, that was cheesy and stupid. Why was he being so sappy?

Because he wanted to see her smile.

The corner of her mouth twitched up.

That was a good start.

*

Irdu was way at the top of Ronnie's list of people she didn't want to deal with right now.

Metatron ranked higher, and she needed a little mental solitude.

Besides, right now he was almost sweeter than the chocolate he'd brought. Almost. She broke off a piece and popped it in her mouth, trying to find the right words.

He knelt in front of her, watching, saying all the right things.

What happened when he got pissed off again? Would it be Round 3, and then Round 4, and so on, of the insult game, until she got smart enough to stop letting him into her life?

Why did she care? Why didn't she kick him to the curb? Because he silenced Metatron?

No. Because before all of this started, he was one of the only real friends she had. It was real, wasn't it?

And sometimes—okay, a lot of time—she wondered if they could be more.

"I know you can't keep giving me chances," he said, as if reading her mind. "I'm not asking you for an endless string of forgiveness. Use me if you want. Scream at me. Fuck me. Or tell me to leave, and go find someone else to talk to. Something has been bothering you for days, and I want to see you better."

Damn it, he sounded like he meant that. What the hell. She might as well spill her guts. She was telling everyone else, and it wasn't getting her anywhere. Time to see if she could really destroy whatever this was between them.

"I'm hearing a voice," she said. "One that no one else hears. She calls me names. She torments me with violent images. And she wants me dead so she can have my body for herself."

"That sucks."

She raised her eyebrows. Not the answer she expected. "You're not going to badger me with questions or call me crazy or tell me to be patient, the answer will come to me if I just sit on my ass long enough and pretend the people I've told care about a solution?"

"I don't know what I'd ask. It sounds pretty straightforward. I don't know where I'd find a solution—I wouldn't even know where to start. I do know it has you stressed out, and that sucks."

Ronnie sighed. Damn it all to fuck it. Why did he have to walk in here and be understanding? She set the gift bag on the floor, and patted the now-empty cushion next to her. "If we go through this again, I'm not letting you back in my apartment."

"That's fair." He sat next to her, close enough to press his leg into hers. "I wouldn't let me back in either. Unless I was really horny."

Her light laugh was the best sound he'd heard all day.

"Tell me whatever you need or want to. I don't have answers, but I have two ears," he said.

Ronnie paused for a heartbeat. It should have been longer. But at this point, she'd told the story enough times, and gotten enough blasé answers, she might as well be reciting a fairy tale. She told him about how the voice said it was Metatron.

How it swooned whenever Michael was around, which was a nice change from it wanted to kill the angel.

How it wanted to kill Gabe. Which was a nice change from it swooning.

And how it was completely silent when Irdu was nearby.

He didn't interrupt. His face spanned a range of expressions from concern to surprise, lingering sometimes on anger.

Ronnie finished her word vomit and waited for the inevitable question about if this meant she was going to fuck Michael.

Irdu grasped her fingers loosely, and met her gaze. "I'm so sorry you're going through this. And to do it alone… I kno— it must be so stressful and frustrating."

"Yeah. It really is." She could call him on the incomplete thought, but she didn't have the emotional capacity for that.

"Michael said he could help?" Irdu's voice hitched. It was slight. She wouldn't have heard it if she didn't know him.

She tensed. "He said he'd look into it. They've all said they'd look into it. He also bought me waffles this morning." She didn't need to add that last bit, but she was pushing buttons.

Irdu frowned. "With strawberries? Extra syrup, butter, the works?"

"Yes."

"Did it piss off the Metatron voice?"

Not the question Ronnie expected. "Sort of? I'm still a little fuzzy on if she wanted to be there, or was upset that it was me there."

"I don't blame her for that."

Ronnie stalled, not sure how to respond. "You want Michael to buy you waffles?"

"I mean… sexy original angel, right? He seems to be the nicest of all of them."

"He is…" Was this really going all right? Ronnie didn't dare believe it. "But, I mean, he didn't bring me chocolate from Switzerland."

Irdu kissed the back of her knuckles. "I don't know how to say this, because I don't want you to take it wrong."

"Too late?" Her gut clenched. This was it. Everything was about to fall apart. She'd have to kick him out. She'd be forced to lock him out of her life...

"I'm kind of jealous of Michael. I kind of can't stand Gabe from what little I know of him…"

Ronnie's mood slipped further, and she pulled her hand away.

"I don't have a problem with you hooking up with either of them," he said. "I have a problem with what if they hurt you? What if the rumors hurt you?"

So far this wasn't as bad as she expected. "I'm a big girl. I can make those decisions myself. I know the potential consequences."

"I get that." He dragged in a deep breath. "I also… I'm not willing to give you up. Not without a fight. I don't care if you sleep with them, but I don't"—He scowled—"There's more between us than casual sex. I don't want to pretend anymore that there's not."

A sound escaped her throat that fell somewhere between a laugh and a sob. "I might be amenable to that."

"Good." He lifted her chin and brushed his lips over hers. "So let's try this again. What I should have done last night. This morning? Tell me what you need."

"I have what I need." She shifted on the couch to lean her head on his shoulder. "But if you really want me to buy your apology, I believe there was some mention of Vietnamese food."

He nudged her upright again, and kissed her on the forehead. "As you wish."

He vanished from her apartment, and was back fifteen minutes later, with two paper bags of something that smelled delicious.

Ronnie wasn't sure what they were eating, though he tried to explain it. She just knew it was the perfect combination of spicy and tasty.

They chatted and laughed for a couple of hours. It was the most normal and relaxed she'd felt in more than a week.

He held her until her eyes refused to stay open.

"Get some sleep," Irdu said. "I'm going to track down Izzy. If anyone has answers, he will."

Ronnie liked that idea. And that he gave her specifics. It was so much better than *I'll look into it.*

Irdu kissed her one more time, and then he was gone.

She sank back into the cushions, letting exhaustion wash over and through her. She could sleep all weekend and it wouldn't be enough.

"Holy fuck. I thought he'd never leave."

Chapter Fifteen

Ronnie was torn—she could call Irdu and ask him to come back.

But that meant he wouldn't be out looking for answers.

She could join him, but if she was with him, she'd be too exhausted to be useful.

One thing she knew—sleep wasn't happening anytime soon.

"How much good is this doing you?"

Staring blankly at the floor? As much good as anything. Ronnie's brain was oatmeal. The poor sleep the night before, combined with the onslaught of foreign emotions while talking to Michael, plus the murderous rage toward Raphael—which she tried to convince herself was Metatron's—was all too much. Ronnie wanted to sleep for a week.

"No one's stopping you."

And at the root of it all was Metatron.

At least when Irdu was around, the angel was silent. Another reason to lo—like his company so much.

Defiance wasn't going to take Ronnie much further, but she would hold onto it for as long as possible. However Metatron landed a home inside her head, whatever she wanted, Ronnie refused to surrender her body and sanity just because.

"Not just because. There are lots of good reasons. Me, for instance. I wouldn't be sitting here moping, I'd be getting rid of you and then enjoying life."

The words triggered something in the back of her thoughts, and she scrunched up her face, trying to force it into a solid concept. Getting rid of... Could she?

"You tried. You failed. Remember?"

No. A new surge of possibility nudged away some of her exhaustion. She'd tried to contain the voice the way she would a cherub. But with a cherub, she didn't stop at containment.

"You're too tired to think this through. Take a nap."

If Metatron didn't want Ronnie doing it, she was probably onto something. Once she drew a cherub from its host, she exorcised it. She sent it back to hell. If this thing—whether it was some remnant of an ancient angel or just a random hitchhiker—could be contained like a cherub, why couldn't Ronnie use the remainder of the ritual to send it home? Michael didn't want Metatron destroyed, but this would give her a chance at someplace less...occupied.

"Except that I'm not a cherub, and you're the hitchhiker."

Was that fear she heard in Metatron's voice? Not that it mattered, Ronnie was doing it regardless. She closed her eyes and sank into the same meditation as early that morning.

She was prepared for the excruciating pain this time. Still, when she tugged the metaphysical threads interlacing with her soul, she teetered from the intensity. With the strands of Metatron wrapped into a tight ball in the back of her mind, she muttered the words to send a cherub back home.

Daggers rocked through her skull. That was new. The edges of her consciousness blurred with the impression of her head being wedged in half and pried apart. Control slipped away. She fought back. She wouldn't surrender.

Somewhere in the background, a heavy pounding forced its way into her awareness. Her tentative grasp on excising Metatron scurried away, and the darkness rushed back through her.

She dropped her forehead into her hands, gasping around the splinters of pain. What interrupted her? Another knock echoed through the room. Door. Right.

"Nice try. Maybe next time."

Ronnie stumbled to her feet and crossed the short distance to her apartment door. Did Irdu come back? She took a few more deep breaths to compose herself, and yanked it open.

Ari's cheer melted into a frown when her gaze met mine. "Are you all right?" she asked.

Company. *Thank God.* Ronnie stepped aside to let her in. "Tired. Happy it's Friday. What's up?"

"Dancing. You still in?"

Some of Ronnie's exhaustion seeped away. Surrounded by people, with a good beat coursing through her, and so much noise she wouldn't have to hear herself think? "Absolutely. I probably need to change. I completely forgot. I'm sorry."

"Pft." Ari made a straight line for the closet. "After what you did this afternoon? You're allowed to forget."

Right. Everyone knew about that.

"You're welcome."

Ronnie forced a laugh. "It wasn't a big deal, really."

"It was awesome. Raphael's a dickhead. I can't believe he said that to you." Ari tossed her a red top that tied at the waist and neck but would leave Ronnie's back otherwise exposed.

Ronnie snagged the shirt out of the air. It was one of her favorites. She didn't get to wear her wings often, and while they weren't actually physical when summoned, she hated having her shoulder blades covered. It was a kind of stifling she couldn't quite put into words. "I guess."

"And I don't know what happened after, but Michael said something to him, and the entire freaking office knew. Michael was in his full glory. Can you imagine? An original shedding all constraints and letting everything show? I wish I could have been in the room to see that. All that power. It must have been awe-inspiring."

Ronnie saw Lucifer do it once. Summon his full power—wings, mace, the whole bit—when he bitched out a demon. She could go the rest of eternity without being on the receiving end of that kind of fury. "Sounds glorious. Really."

Ari stuck her tongue. "Don't sound so enthusiastic."

"I can show you full angelic glory. A million times better than that pussy hitchhiker Miss Angelic there has."

What was Metatron talking about? Great, the voice in Ronnie's head—the thing making her doubt her sanity—was going crazy too.

Ronnie snatched a skirt from the air when it flew toward her. Another of her favorites, it stopped halfway down her thighs, and the black leather was a stunning contrast against her skin. For the first time, she really took note of what Ari was wearing. Off white all around, from the ruffled top, to the calf length skirt with a slit almost to her hip and four-inch heels. Even the scarf tying her hair back was pale.

Ronnie wanted to talk about anything but how powerful original angels were. She changed quickly and grabbed her purse off the nightstand. "Where to?"

"Wait." Ari wrapped a loose hand around her wrist. "One more thing. Think of it as a finishing touch." A pair of auburn wings the same color as her vibrant curls shimmered into sight. When she flexed them, they spanned wider than her arms. Lying flat against her back, they almost touched the ground. "Now you."

"We can't go out like this." Who was Ronnie kidding? She totally wanted to go out like this. Even as she argued, she summoned her own. She didn't need a mirror to know the black feathers appeared almost instantly. Not as large as Ari's, but like the rest of Ronnie's appearance, how she saw herself—not power—dictated wing size. Flat against her back, they reached just to the bottom of her ass. It was incredible, as if she was whole again. Had she done that a lot before she lost her memory? Kept her wings out?

"Not if you were a cherub. No body, no wings."

"Go to hell."

"I'd rather send you."

"We can get away with it just this once." Ari intertwined her fingers with Ronnie's. "You're going to love this place."

Ronnie's apartment vanished and was replaced with a city street, and a vibration thrummed through her feet. The line at the club wrapped around the building. Some of the people wore nothing but black, and glittery fabric swathed others from head to toe. As they drew closer, she caught sight of an awkward bulge on someone. Correction. That was a naked, flaccid penis. Heat flooded her. He wasn't wearing anything but glitter and body paint.

She didn't have a problem with nudity. With appreciating the human form—hers, someone else's... But how did anyone walk with something like that just hanging out there? Wasn't he worried about it getting caught on something? She forced her gaze toward the people wearing wings. So many different kinds. She flexed hers as they approached. This place was awesome.

Music spilled from the open doors. She smiled at the sounds rocking her. As they took their place in line, whispers of light danced around some of the other patrons. Ronnie did a double take as a series of tingles tickled her skin. She and Ari weren't the only angels there. There were even cherubs in the line.

Instinct and indoctrination pulsed through her. It was her job and duty to send cherubs back home. But even as she thought it, her discoveries of the past few days raced back. These individuals wanted the same rush from life she did. Besides, Lucifer was keeping things from her, most of the management at Ubiquity was asinine, and she was off the clock.

"Way to justify your laziness."

And the best reason of all—because she didn't want another fucking voice in her head, even for a couple of seconds.

The line moved fast, and they were inside within a few minutes. Throngs of people filled the dance floor and rested at tables along the edges. Alcohol and sweat tickled her nostrils until she swore she could taste them—scents that should be revolting, but filled her with energy. The throbbing music spoke to her, calling her onto the dance floor. Flashing neon strobed, turning the room into a series of grotesque stills.

She inhaled, trying to take it all in. "This is amazing. There's so much energy here." The music swallowed her awe. Talking was going to be impossible, and that was fine with her.

Ari ducked her head close, fingers still intertwined with Ronnie's. "Right? So worth it."

They wove their way through gyrating bodies and the gorgeous rainbow of auras, which blended and competed with the dim lighting in the club. The energy was almost tangible. Somewhere along the way, they stopped trying to navigate the crowds and lost themselves to the rhythm. It was easy to dance to the frantic music.

Bodies brushed Ronnie's, crushed against her, overwhelmed her senses. A whiff of perfume. A hand on her ass, sliding between her thighs before jolting away. Hot breath on her cheek from a random stranger. It invigorated and seduced her.

Any number of these men or women, if she asked, would join her in a dark corner. Crush their mouth to hers. Melt into her as she wrapped a leg around their waist and pushed her skirt to her hips.

Ronnie drifted away from Ari as they slid from one song to the next. They'd meet up again later, or not. Exhaustion still lingered on the edge of Ronnie's senses, but the ambient energy made it easy to ignore. She could drown in the sensory overload here and be happy.

A pair of hands rested on her hips, and a familiar rush pulsed through her, erasing the weariness. She knew that sensation but from where? It was the same intoxication she experienced in the coffee shop. *Gabe.*

"I was hoping you'd be here tonight." He brushed her ear with his lips.

A tiny whisper of logic—or was it that annoying voice—tried to remind Ronnie of

Michael's story. And that she barely knew this guy. And that…

She wasn't listening. The almost erotic sensations of the room amplified his every touch. Was sleeping with a powerful angel anything like being with an Incubus? Did his power make up for any hang-ups he might have?

A tiny bit of her knew it was the room making her horny. Right now, she didn't care about the *why*.

He swayed with her, front against her back. His hard length pressed into her when she ground against him, and dampness grew between her legs.

She whirled and draped her arms around his neck. He looked good. Black T-shirt, jeans, and that same odd but alluring combination of a blond ponytail and black goatee. Every new caress sent another jolt through her. Liquid energy soothed the cracks in her fractured psyche. The heat from his body swept along her skin. She wanted to submerge herself in him.

"But…"

Metatron quieted, vanishing in the noise of the night. Ronnie liked that. He drew her closer, hands gliding to the small of her back. His breath warmed her skin when he spoke, but she couldn't make out the words.

"He's not worth hearing anyway." The taunt was barely a whisper.

"What?" Ronnie asked.

He dipped his head closer, trailing his nose along her neck until her body pleaded for more. His words were distinct this time. "I need to talk to you."

She nodded and followed him from the dance floor, letting the trancelike feeling surround her. With his fingers intertwined in hers, the pleasant hum of being near him filled her. She hoped he'd lead her to a remote slice of wall. As they gained more distance from the dancing crowd, reason seeped in. Cool air kissed the sweat from her skin and chased away some of her arousal.

She almost found the presence of mind to wonder what she was doing. They found a table, as removed from the crowds as possible, where conversation should only require a little yelling. Ronnie reluctantly tucked her wings away. Even though they were ethereal, she felt them when they did things like pass through chairs, and that made sitting awkward. But at least she'd enjoyed the freedom for a little while.

Before they could take their seats, Ari seemed to appear out of nowhere. Ronnie didn't know if she was disappointed or relieved by the interruption. The longer they stayed separate from the crowd, the more her head cleared. If that was the kind of emotional contact high she got here, she was coming back with Irdu.

Ari tossed her arms around Gabe's neck with a squeal, burying her face in his chest. His hands rested at her hips, and squeezed before nudging her back. Ronnie should be jealous, shouldn't she? For Ari or herself? She wasn't sure.

"I'm so glad you made it." Red flushed Ari's face.

He nodded at the chairs and waited for both of them to sit before dropping into his own seat.

"Wouldn't have missed it for anything. Except maybe Armageddon."

Ari giggled.

Awkwardness itched in Ronnie's palms, making her want to fiddle with something as she watched the exchange. Gabe's body language didn't match Ari's. His shoulders were drawn in and one ankle rested on the other knee. She leaned in, arms on the table, facing him, eyes wide and smile bright.

Crap. She was infatuated with him. And Ronnie just shared a more intimate dance with him than she thought was possible in public without getting arrested.

He gave Ari's fingers one last squeeze—his face showed he saw the attraction too—before turning to Ronnie. "Have you remembered anything else?" he asked.

"Who cares if she likes him? He won't live long enough for her to act on it."

Ronnie thought Metatron liked Gabriel.

"No. I wanted to use him to make Michael suffer. I didn't realize the asshole tried to kill me."

Of course. At least Gabe was still worried about her missing memories. The thought didn't comfort her. "I think I've been to Jerusalem before."

"Really?" His eyes grew wide.

Ari sank back in her chair, fiddling with her purse. "Like almost every other angel or demon ever." She glanced at Ronnie. "Sorry. I'm not being mean, but it's true."

"Then, no. Nothing significant." Why was Ronnie even chasing down this road? Michael was the only one to give her answers.

"Do you hear voices?" Ari blurted out. Gabe scowled in her direction, and she shrugged. "You were going to ask anyway."

Yeah, this was definitely awkward. And there was no way Ronnie was admitting to hearing things. "Of course not."

"Really, she doesn't. Not plural, anyway. There's just me."

Gabe gestured around the room. "You see it, right? The angels, the humans, the cherubs?"

"I do." Odd question. Were there angels who couldn't see that kind of thing? Did he think Ronnie was underdeveloped in some way?

"Just your tits."

Ronnie so didn't need that.

He reached across the table and traced a finger over the back of her knuckles. Instinct sparked in her brain, wanting to jerk away. Not liking his hands on hers or that he did it in front of Ari. However, like before, his touch sent a tingle through her that muffled Metatron, and fuzzed Ronnie's thoughts. She knew from the pitch of his voice he spoke quietly, yet she heard every word. "Can you tell for sure, all of them, which are angels and which are cherubs?"

A *yes* flew to her lips out of instinct, and she swallowed it. Her failed cherub capture raced through her mind, bringing all her unanswered questions with it. "I think so."

"She can't," Ari said.

He fixed another narrowed gaze on her before turning back to Ronnie. "Tell me honestly. I promise I won't think you're crazy or have you pulled from your job or anything like that. Are you hearing a voice?"

Ronnie swallowed, and hesitation weighed down her tongue. That addressed her serious concerns about speaking up, and her brain thought it might split from indecision. She couldn't trust him, but the heat flooding her limbs said she had to.

"Yes," she said.

Chapter Sixteen

Some of Ari's irritation vanished. Gabe's expression stayed neutral, and his voice kind. "I don't have a solution for you, but I think I can tell you what's going on. At least a little bit."

"Really." Ronnie couldn't make her tone anything other than flat. Michael already told her what was going on. Unless Gabe knew the details of how she acquired Metatron. And why didn't he surrender any of this in his coffee shop? Hearing him out was far more attractive with Metatron quiet. Ronnie couldn't even make out her snide words.

He nodded at the dance floor again. "It's why we're here tonight. I wanted you to witness firsthand. There are rumors…" He wove his fingers through hers, eyes never leaving her face. "Instead of sending cherubs home, some angels are pulling them from their hosts and internalizing them."

This ought to be interesting. How would Gabriel spin it? "Why?"

"It means more power without having to earn it," Gabe explained. "Kind of like an extended battery."

Michael neglected to mention that. Then again, Michael seemed more concerned with rehabilitation than power. Was Gabe accusing her of keeping a cherub for her own gain? She didn't like the implication. Worse, if Gabe went to Raphael with the information rather than Lucifer, would it cost her the Ubiquity job? "I've sent every cherub back home. I swear it."

"I'm not saying you kept one. At least not on purpose." With his thumb, he continued to trace tiny circles along the back of her hand. The contact acted like a muffler on the voice in her head. "I just wonder if maybe you thought you sent one home, and you didn't."

"No." She almost told him about Metatron to defend herself. But for some reason the name died on Ronnie's lips. She couldn't keep the questions from running rampant through her thoughts. His explanation was nice. It was convenient and straightforward—and too easy. But if he was offering helpful answers now, maybe he'd confirm some of her suspicions. "If it's a cherub, can I get rid of it the same way I do with the others?"

His lips drew into a thin line. "I don't know."

So much for him being helpful. Ronnie sank back in her chair with a sigh, breaking the contact between them.

"You already tried that, remember? Almost tore you apart, because you're a reckless amateur."

"Maybe I should try it again, if for no other reason than to piss you off." A reminder of the earlier pain flashed through her head. Maybe not.

The conversation tapered away from the voice in Ronnie's head and shifted to other topics. Ari drew back in, smiling, laughing, and occasionally tracing a finger along Gabe's bicep. Metatron provided a running commentary, and Ronnie found herself agreeing with the snark on more than one occasion. She still wasn't certain why they were here.

Not that she minded the club, but as she looked out at the dance floor, she'd much rather be dancing. With a sexy incubus rather than the object of her best friend's affection. Sliding into intoxicating seduction and his skilled touch. It was odd to be concerned about something trivial in the grand scheme of dead angels living in demons' heads, but a squicky feeling lingered in her gut that she might stand between Ari and Gabe.

Maybe Ronnie needed a little air to clear out the compulsion to dive into sensory overload. She shoved back from the table. "I'll be right back."

"Wait." Gabe half stood.

Ari tugged him back into his seat. "She'll be back."

Ronnie resisted the urge to roll her eyes and wandered away. She had no idea where she was going. Sitting in on the edge of the throbbing beat without moving to it drilled into her thoughts. She just wanted some silence. She rushed out the nearest door marked *Exit*.

The evening humidity blasted her cheeks, and the door muffled most of the noise when it swung shut behind her. She dragged in a few breaths of exhaust-laden air. It didn't help her clear her thoughts. *Go figure.*

She leaned back against a nearby wall, and tilted her attention to the sky. The city lights muted the darkness and obscured the stars. Longing echoed in her chest, followed by a pang of homesickness. She should go back to Israel and star watch there. Except Israel wasn't her home. What an odd impulse. Would anyone come after her, if she just vanished? Would they send someone like Ari after her? Of course not. Ronnie wasn't a cherub.

She had no idea how long she watched the sky. The music from inside blasted for a moment and then vanished again, but she didn't look.

"Are you all right?" Ari's soft question wormed its way into Ronnie's thoughts. "You've been gone a while."

Ronnie dragged her attention back to city level. "I'm good. Just thinking."

"About what Gabe said? Do you think maybe you have a cherub in you?"

"I don't know what's going on with me." It seemed as though Ronnie didn't know much at all. "But maybe that's a direction to look in."

"I had an idea about the entire thing." Ari stepped in front of her, and the toes of their shoes met. "If you want to hear it."

Not that Ronnie had much hope for a real answer at this point, but there was no reason not to listen. "Sure."

"What if I could help?"

It was so simple and straightforward. That alone was enough of a reason for Ronnie to like the idea. Plus, it made perfect sense. "I've already tried to extract it myself. Do you think you could draw it out?"

Ari nodded. "It's what we do. It can't be easy to perform on yourself. But..." She held out her hands, palms up. "...maybe with me being removed from the situation, I could pull it off. I don't know how you're so certain it's not a cherub, but even if it's something else, if it works, it'll be a load off your mind. And if that's what's keeping you from remembering, maybe it'll knock something loose."

Was Ari's logic warped, or was Ronnie being paranoid? The idea of being alone with her own thoughts again was too appealing. Ronnie rested her palms against Ari's. "I'm in."

"I've never had a willing victim before."

"With any luck, that'll make it easier. Just make sure you leave the *me* bits intact."

"Of course." Ari inhaled until her chest puffed out and then let the breath out slowly. "Here goes."

The seconds ticked away, and Ronnie waited. It should feel different, right?

"Moron. I can't believe you're trying thi—"

A sharp slice tore through Ronnie—a million razor blades forcing their way out of her skin at the same time. She bit the inside of her cheek to keep from screaming, but a gasp escaped.

"Make her stop."

"Are you okay?" Ari asked.

"Keep going." Ronnie forced the words through gritted teeth. "I think it's working."

More agony wrenched through her, tearing at every inch of her. Blackness danced at the edge of her vision, and she squeezed her eyes shut. She bit her cheek harder, trying to focus on the physical pain instead of the ethereal, and another whimper tore from her throat. *Please, please let her be almost done.*

A switch flipped, and the pain stopped. Was it over?

"Holy fuck. We're never *doing that again."*

Fuck was right. *God damn it.* Ronnie opened her eyes. An odd sprinkling of relief mingled with her disappointment at Metatron's voice. The weakness she experienced when she tried to extricate the voice herself was absent. However, haze and confusion still circled her as she struggled to make sense of her surroundings. She blinked several times to clear away the odd vision, but it was still there. Ari stood on the far side of the alley, fists clenched, eyes narrowed, staring up at Gabe.

"You were warned." His low voice rumbled the ground.

Warned about what? What was Ronnie missing?

Ari's expression wavered, but her reply was firm. "What gives you the right?"

A million tiny pinpricks rushed and danced over Ronnie skin as the atmosphere shifted. Gabe's wings appeared—flawless, taller than he was, black and white, lined with gold—and his aura flared vivid and golden. *"I do."*

The two words shook the building, vibrating more than the music inside.

Ari stepped back, and her bravado vanished behind a mask of uncertainty. She turned her attention to Ronnie. "I'm sorry." Ari disappeared.

What the fuck? Ronnie rested her weight against the wall, still trying to make sense of the scene.

The glow, the wings, and everything summoned around Gabriel vanished, and he was himself when he faced her. He closed the distance in a few long strides. "Are you all right?"

"Why did she stop?" Ronnie winced at the dry rasp in her voice.

"I stopped her." He settled a hand on the back of her neck, gliding his thumb over her cheek. "You were screaming."

His touch rooted out the lingering pain and chased it away. She wanted to jerk from his grasp, but it healed her. "I was? I didn't know."

"Are you all right now?"

Except for the fact that being so close to him fogged her thoughts. Desire pulsed over her skin, the sensation the same as the rush of being engulfed in a crowd. Despite the knowledge Ari was infatuated with him, warmth spread over Ronnie, tingling in her breasts and throbbing between her thighs. Was his presence doing that to her? Was it intentional? She forced herself to speak. "I'm fine."

"Good. I was worried."

"About me? Why?" The attention encompassed her. The physical reaction was there, but emotionally, it didn't feel right. She wanted him to shove her against the wall. To wrap her legs around his waist. At the same time, the idea repulsed her.

He leaned closer and brushed his lips over hers.

Tendrils of pleasure snaked through her, and she kissed back. *No.* She wasn't interested in this. Ari liked him. Or whatever was happening between the two of them. Despite the mental protests, Ronnie's body wanted something else. To be closer to the hum of power. She rested her hands on his chest, memorizing the texture of T-shirt stretched over muscle. She parted her lips, and his tongue accepted the invitation, sliding into her mouth and dancing.

She groaned and pressed into him, wanting to feel every inch of his body against hers. Liquid lust spilled through her, and she needed more.

Stop.

She was pretty sure that was her, not Metatron, arguing with herself. He glided his other hand down her spine, and she arched her back at the feather-light sensation, grinding against him. He sought the hem of her skirt and inched it up.

"I will not be ignored! Especially for him."

The roar echoed through her skull, and she broke away with a gasp, stumbling back. For the first time since Metatron had arrived, Ronnie felt a whisper of relief at her presence.

Gabe furrowed his brow. "Are you all right?"

"I will destroy someone for what was done to me. If you like his company so much, it can be him."

Images tore through Ronnie's mind, mimicking her dreams, but this time, Gabriel ran her through.

"Let me out!"

"No." Ronnie recognized the tickle of summoned weapons against her palms, and mentally pushed back. Gabe might set her teeth on edge, but she wouldn't destroy him for that.

"YES!"

"Uriel?" Something lingered behind the concern in Gabe's eyes. Fear? Not of her. She was nothing compared to an original.

"But I am. Let me kill him."

"I'm sorry," Ronnie mumbled. She phased back to her apartment before he could reply.

Her knees hit the mattress when she appeared in the tiny residence, her inability to act spilling in tears down her cheeks. Seven different flavors of frustration, exhaustion, and confusion poured over her, pinching until it bled. She fell to the side and pulled her knees to her chest, struggling to fight back the fear and pain. She just wanted to sleep. But she was never letting Metatron out again. This was *her* life.

"We both know he killed me."

"You said Michael killed you."

"Gabriel wove something around you back there. You recognized it, even if you couldn't name it. You believe anything he says over Michael?"

Ronnie snarled at the empty room and then spoke aloud rather than hear her own thoughts. "Michael was willing to surrender eternity for you, and you thought he ran you through. I don't trust your judgement."

"Says the demon talking to herself in an empty room. My memories lied. I see that now. Gabriel did this to me. He'll pay."

"Go. Away." Her soft command echoed. She grabbed everything she found inside she knew was hers and built a mental wall around it. *"My life."*

"You think you can really keep me out that way?"

Ronnie expected Metatron's taunt, but not her hesitation. Was that a trace of fear radiating from her?

"That's yours."

But it wasn't. Ronnie steeled her resolve. Something in Metatron was terrified she might not be able to take control again. Good. At least Ronnie was pretty sure she'd make it through the night as herself.

* * * *

Sun warmed her arms, and the wind whispered through the sand around her. Canvas-draped wooden stands where vendors hawked their wares bordered the lane. No one stood near her on the sand-packed road, but non-stop chatter filled the air.

Why was it so loud? Bright colors called to her from one of the stalls, and she wandered in for a closer look. Amazing scents greeted her—cinnamon, flowers, fresh bread. Scarves lined the table, satin brushing her fingers as she examined the clothing. The longer she lingered, the softer the chatter became.

"Does the lady see something she likes?"

She snapped her head up at the sound of Gabe's voice. Beige swathed the man staring back at her, hiding any distinguishing traits except his piercing green eyes.

Betrayal overrode her fascination. An irrational need to get away shoved her back, and she dropped the scarf. It wasn't him, and even if it was, it was okay. She trusted Gabe.

Except she didn't.

She stepped away, struggling to control her fear. The chatter returned, assaulting her and making her stumble. Why was it so loud?

Another booth sat farther down the road. It didn't call to her from a distance, the way the first did. Nothing stood out about the empty table or the two men behind it. But she was drawn to it anyway. The noise didn't die as she approached, not like before. Comfort kissed her cheeks, and she smiled. One of the men smiled back.

The other stepped forward, scowling. "We're not selling anything."

Lucifer? The voice and name stung for reasons she didn't understand, and her chest knotted. She wanted to linger. To find out why he was so upset. But the words didn't come.

"I have what you're looking for." A female voice carried over everything. It was familiar. Eerily so.

She was reluctant to leave the comfort behind but compelled to talk to the feminine stranger. She sat at the edge of the market, dressed like the other vendors in nondescript brown swaths. Ronnie studied her for a moment, bathed in recognition she didn't understand. "Do I know you?"

"Not nearly as well as you should." She pulled the veil from her face, black hair whipping around red eyes in the breeze.

Holy shit. Ronnie took a step back, disbelief hammering in her skull. It was a mirror image. The voice was hers, but outside her head. "I don't... What?"

Mirror-image-her approached and took her hand. The chatter vanished in an instant, shoved away by inky threads of power. Mirror-image-her smiled. "It's really this easy. No one else can help you but me."

Ronnie sat up with a start, heart hammering and ears ringing. She didn't mean to fall asleep. Unlike the first dream, this one felt forced. Less vivid and more metaphorical. A distraction on Metatron's part? Was Ronnie still in control of her body?

"Don't you trust me?"

"Stupidest question ever."

"I didn't feel like taking over."

Was Ronnie blocking her? Tentative relief would have flooded her, but whispers of the dream still floated through her head. It wasn't terrifying like the last one, but it didn't give her any more answers. Her thoughts were muddled. Did she really feel that way about Gabe? About Lucifer? And how was she supposed to help herself when she didn't have any solutions? Stupid subconscious, playing stupid games with her already fractured thoughts.

"Yeah, blame your subconscious."

Ronnie closed her eyes and pressed the palms of her hands against them, watching the stars dance against the lids.

Chapter Seventeen

Another night of sucky-ass sleep. If insanity didn't drive Ronnie over the edge, insomnia might. It was Saturday. That should mean sleeping in, being lazy—something. But she wasn't going back to bed. A week ago, she would have hung out with Ari, but she wasn't answering Ronnie's texts. Which, when she let herself think about it, might be a good thing. She wanted to believe what Ari did the night before was in her best interest, but doubt nagged her.

Someone knocked. *Please let it be missionaries of some sort.* At least that would be a fun conversation, and Metatron might not have a death wish for them.

"How's it feel to finally be right about something?"

Ronnie straightened her clothes the best she could. Maybe she shouldn't have fallen asleep in her clubbing outfit. Then again, she wasn't sure she cared. She wasn't exposing herself to the world. Ronnie yanked open the door, and her breath caught in her throat. Nope, definitely not missionaries. Michael looked incredible in a T-shirt and shorts.

"Sorry, what? Too busy drooling."

"Great. Your swooning isn't much better than your blood lust."

"Yeah, about that…"

Ronnie wasn't in the mood for Metatron's mood swings. She couldn't help smiling at Michael, though. "Hey."

"Am I interrupting something?" He nodded at her outfit.

"Nah.…" The false bravado slipped away. It felt cliché to say, *What, this old thing?* Besides, she liked being honest with Michael. "I forgot to change before I fell asleep."

"Did I wake you, then?"

"I also forgot to change when I woke up." Too many more nights of tossing and turning, and she'd be forgetting a lot more. Maybe that was how she lost her memory. Had she done this before? Was Metatron there before she lost her memory?

"You keep asking yourself circular questions. Let me take over for a while."

"Nope. Not interested."

Michael still stared at her, brow furrowed. She checked of herself. Skirt wasn't riding too high. Did she have mascara smeared across her face? "Is something wrong?"

"No. Just waiting to see whether you're going to try and eviscerate me or just brush me off." The corners of his mouth twitched up, and light danced behind his eyes.

Oh, that. Considering the number of ways their encounters started and ended, was he bored with something as basic as her in a mini skirt? "I wasn't planning on doing either."

"It's okay, really. Actually, I was wondering if you wanted to spar with me." He traced his gaze over her in a lazy path. Unlike with Gabe, she didn't feel a creeping desire to cover up. Her thoughts were still clear and vivid. Her own.

"Mostly."

And sparring with him sounded like a horrible idea, only partly because Ronnie didn't know how to fight. "I almost tried to decapitate you the other day."

He rubbed the back of his neck, looking at the ceiling before he turned back to her. "That's in the past. No big deal and all that."

And he was lying. *Fuck,* she was too tired for this. He was supposed to be the one person who didn't do that. "Try again."

"I was hoping it might jar something loose. After what happened yesterday morning, I know the knowledge is there. If we can chip away at your memories, it might help us figure out why Metatron is in your head."

That was closer to the truth, but not all the way there.

"He wants to see me. Sucks, doesn't it?"

It hurt to admit Metatron was probably right. But at the same time, something was tempting about spending the morning with Michael. Images of the night before flashed through Ronnie's head—the kiss with Gabe, the tension, the want. When she sank into the memory, she still felt his touch on her skin. Enticing and disconcerting at the same time.

"You should give Gabe another chance. We should go right now."

"Reverse psychology. Nice." When Metatron wasn't spewing emotion, it made it harder for Ronnie to tell which thoughts belonged to whom. Especially because yesterday morning Metatron wanted to gut Michael and string him up.

"We can do this later." Michael broke into her internal debate.

"No, it's not that. I just don't think I have that knowledge. Lucifer told me it wasn't a dangerous job. That I didn't need to know things like how to fight."

"If you've been okay without it up until now, I'm sure Lucifer's right. There's probably nothing there." Michael frowned and rubbed the back of his neck again.

Ronnie was going to have to teach him how to lie. Then again, it was kind of endearing that he couldn't. "No, I haven't been okay up until now. I nearly got my ass kicked by someone a couple days ago, and it would be nice if I knew how to defend myself. At this point, the only thing that would save me from a mugger would be my immortality, and even then he'd get away with my wallet."

His shoulders relaxed, and he finally looked her directly in the eye. "If the knowledge really isn't there, even locked away where you can't get to it, I can teach you. Since you're not from heaven, I can't impart the lessons to you the way you'd learn back home, but I can physically show you a couple of things. At least enough to fend off a mugger."

Ronnie grinned. That sounded far more appealing than logic said it should, but she liked the suggestion. "Yeah?"

"We have to keep you safe." The genuine warmth in his words sank into her and chased away her exhaustion. This wasn't like last night when a fog blanketed her. The thoughts and feelings were Ronnie's.

"Give me five minutes." She stepped aside enough to let him in. She took the fastest shower in history, scrubbed the makeup off, and then yanked on a pair of sweats and a T-shirt.

Four and a half minutes later, she joined Michael in the living room. "Let's go."

She expected him to take her hand and dash her away to some grand and exotic locale. Maybe to train with the monks in Tibet or to China to meet a kung fu master. She didn't know why, but it might be because Gabe and Lucifer enjoyed flaunting their power.

Instead, they walked. *Wait, does this mean we're on a date?* No. Not after she scurried away. He didn't ask for an explanation. But Ronnie owed him one, as much for her reassurance as his. "About how we left things after breakfast..."

"You seemed to be in a hurry. Are you doing better today?" He was so casual about the whole thing.

"Because he realizes he made a mistake. He really misses me."

At least she wasn't sulking right now. "I think so."

He rested a hand at the small of Ronnie's back to point her down the correct street and didn't break the contact after they turned the corner. Her satisfaction grew when an incoherent snarl echoed in her skull. Every few seconds, he'd glance at her, catch her gaze, and then smile and turn his attention back to the street.

The four- or five-block stroll was pleasant, and the conversation flowed easily. The buildings grew nicer the farther from her apartment they traveled. The condos they stopped in front of raced toward the sky, all concrete and glass, with balconies and no window cooling units. There was even a doorman.

Michael nodded at him and led Ronnie inside. The temperature in the lobby was perfect. Literally. It enveloped her without a sticky film of humidity or the stench of chemicals. The understated elevator ride took them to one of the middle floors. No one was in the hallway. Then again, it was early on a Saturday. If the other residents were lucky, they still slept.

It was a spiffy glimpse into Michael's life, but it didn't make sense, given their plans. If he was going to teach her to fight, they couldn't do it here. One, there was no way these condos were big enough—the doors were too close together. And two, his downstairs neighbors would hate them if she and Michael did any moving around. "Did you forget something?"

"No." He led her through the first door they came to.

It was a nice place. Sunken living room, plush navy carpet, and almost as much metal and glass as on the building's façade. Ronnie never would have pegged him for modern, but she liked the look. Still, unless his instruction was all theoretical, she didn't know how they'd practice here.

"This way." He gestured toward the doors on the far side of the room. The moment they passed through, the air sank into her skin like satin. Instead of a bedroom or office, a vast series of practice mats stretched out in front of them. Wooden blades hung on one wall, and a tremor of power mingled with the scents of chalk and sweat.

She knew the sensation. Ethereal. Unearthly. They weren't on a mortal plane anymore. Was it possible?

"Duh? You know hell isn't the only way people get into Lucifer's office, right?"

Good point. Any door could lead to a spot in heaven or hell if the angel or demon opening it was powerful enough. That meant... They were in Michael's corner of heaven. And he decorated it like a dojo. "Neat." The word slipped past her lips without thought.

"Thanks. Leave your shoes and socks at the edge of the mats."

"We do this barefoot?"

"Duh?"

"I'm new to this. Sue me."

"We do this barefoot." He set his own socks and shoes aside, bowed to the dojo, and then stepped in. "I promise, it's more comfortable. And it keeps the mats from getting torn up."

"I'm trusting you." She set her sneakers and socks aside and moved next to him. "You're the expert."

He squared his feet shoulder width apart and nodded to the spot across from him. She faced him and mimicked his posture, but wasn't sure what to do with her hands. She let them hang limply by her sides.

"Now, you just need your swords."

She twisted her mouth, crossed her arms, and glared at him. She wasn't about to reach inside Metatron for those, or however it worked. "Not funny."

"You did it the other day in the church."

"*Metatron* did that in the church. So one, I don't know how, and two, be grateful because when she does that, she's screaming for vengeance, and there's no guarantee I can stop her."

"I promise I'll behave. Just let me show you how it's done." Taunting filled her words, but pleading lay underneath. She almost sounded desperate.

Michael raised his hands, palms toward her. "I know it was her. But that means you can do it too. It's your body. Think about how it felt."

"Incredible. I missed that sensation."

"I'd rather not." This wasn't going as planned. He was taking the news about the dead angel stuck in her head a lot better than she was, and she wasn't sure she liked it.

"You're right." He grabbed a wooden practice blade from the rack at the edge of the mat, and gave it a few swings. It was about the same length as his arm, maybe an inch in diameter with the slightest curve near the end. He nodded to the collection. "Pick something, and we'll start."

"Really?" How wicked awesome was that? He was actually going to teach her to use a sword.

She crossed the floor in a few short steps and tried several of the practice weapons swinging each one, trying to mimic Michael. None of them were right. Something compelled her to grab two: one longer like Michael's, and a short, dagger-length stick. Familiarity raced through her.

When she turned back to face him, he raised an eyebrow but didn't say anything. He resumed his original stance in the middle of the mat and waited for her to do the same before he spoke. "We'll go slowly at first. I just want to see how you react naturally to things. That will show me where and what to work on."

She could do this. He believed in her. And she probably knew these things deep down inside. She had to, right? Most demons and angels did.

"When I attack, just try and block me." He stepped in with a simple swing, a motion so slow it was painful to watch. And he still tagged on the arm.

Fuck. What was wrong with her? "I wasn't ready."

"No worries. Again?"

She copied his posture this time, except her left hand dangled, useless, by her side. Why did she grab a second weapon when she didn't know how to use one? He stepped in slowly again, and this time she caught the first swing. Elation rippled inside until she tripped on the follow-through.

When he gripped her hand and helped her up, a pleasant wash of desire rushed through her. Warmth, affection, familiarity.

He sucked in a sharp breath through clenched teeth. Was he irritated already?

"I'm sorry for being slow."

"You're fine." He assured her, and the sincerity in his eyes confirmed his words. "It's not that, I promise."

"Look…" Annoyance leaked into her voice. "I told you I don't know any of this. You can't *test my skill* because I don't have any. Stop backing me into a corner and show me what to do."

"You're right. Try this instead. Close your eyes."

Ronnie snorted in irritation. She couldn't be any worse though, and at least he was patient. "Fine."

"Focus on the energy around you." His voice was low and even and sounded as if it came from behind her. He trailed his hands down her arms until both blades hung limply at her side. The subtle scent of sunshine and blossoms filled her head, along with the impulse to lean into him, and the desire to have his lips along the back of her neck.

This was different from any other man she'd been with. More sensual than sex. Was that possible? All of her sank into it, not just her body. Warmth danced along her skin and coiled with her thoughts before it wrapped her fractured nerves in salve. Irdu was need and lust and hunger. Gabe was deception and guilt. Michael was safety.

He pressed against her back. It would be so easy to fall into more than training right now. It was so tempting.

"Concentrate on what belongs to you, what's brushing your skin—the electricity in the air, not the physical." The steady rhythm of his breathing soothed her. "Do you feel what I mean?"

"Yes." She did, intensely and vividly. She was in a trance. But not an externally induced one like last night. This was all hers, evoked by Michael's attention and patience. She couldn't remember a time when her thoughts were so calm. She concentrated on his words and followed each instruction. She didn't know how she was going to fight like this, but the experience was pleasant enough that she didn't care.

It was too quiet. When did he stop talking? The air shifted around her. It was so subtle, she doubted she'd recognize it under other circumstances. Like a light breeze caressing her skin. Being in tune with her surroundings, she noticed it as easily as she would a strong gale. Even as she opened her eyes, she shifted her right arm to chest level, and raised her left to cover her gut. She reacted before she could process her own movements, deflecting Michael's blow with the larger blade, twisting under his arm, and coming to a stop with the wooden dagger resting at his stomach, dull blade nudging his skin.

I did it. Giddiness flowed through her. And then the rest of her world came into focus. One of his arms was still held captive above her head, blocked by her sword, and his free hand gripped her other wrist.

He locked his gaze on hers. The softness from earlier was gone, replaced with fire, lighting her up. "Just like that." His voice dropped an octave.

She wanted to show she understood but didn't want to move. Every inch of her begged to close the distance between them, to rest her hands on his still-heaving chest, to see what it would be like to kiss him. Was she even allowed to do that? He was one of the holiest of holy. Was he above that kind of thing?

Gabe wasn't. This was different. More subtle, but at the same time, more alive.

Something clattered behind her. Michael dropped his practice weapon. His breathing mingled with hers. Intensity smoldered in his eyes. She wanted to fall into that sharp combination of light and dark.

He glided his palms along her arms until he reached her hands. His touch drew desire down her skin. He loosened each of her fingers, and the wooden blades fell to the ground. The rest of the world faded into the background until she and Michael were the only things in existence.

"I don't know what it is about you." Gravel lined his words. "But you're temptation wrapped in wonder. I've never met anyone like you."

He dipped his head and pressed his lips to hers. This was safe and gentle and all consuming. Every bit of her wanted it.

She kissed back, nipping at his bottom lip, sliding her hands along his chest as she memorized every inch of definition through his shirt. He groaned and tangled his fingers in her hair. That single, primal sound dug into her chest and squeezed. *God, this is incredible.*

He parted his lips, and she darted her tongue into his mouth. Her skin burned with need, and her heart clenched with something achingly familiar she couldn't quite grasp. She shifted her weight against him, sighing at the friction. He rested his free hand at the small of her back and grazed her spine with his fingertips.

She wanted more. To strip off everything between them. To trail her tongue along his skin and taste sweat and desire. Want ached between her legs. She cruised her hands down his chest and tugged the bottom of his shirt.

He nudged her back with a soft *no.*

Disappointment and hurt crashed around her as the cool air rushed in to replace his heat. "What?" She couldn't keep the pang from her question.

He raked his fingers through his hair. "At the risk of sounding cliché… It's not you; it's me. And believe me, you're definitely a temptation."

Bloody fucking hell. He was kidding, wasn't he? He really was too good for something as simple as base lust. She crossed her arms, trying to force anger in to cover her hurt. It didn't block the throb behind her ribs, but it made her feel more in control. She should have known. But the gaping hole inside wouldn't go away. "You felt fine to me."

"Physical and intimate distractions… I kind of try and stay away from them."

Even if he hadn't spent most their time together swapping touches with her, gazing at her, telling her how fucking tempting she was, his explanation didn't make any sense. They shared a kiss, not a marriage proposal. Also, angels didn't actually do things like stay celibate. He obviously held himself to different standards. She just wished she knew what those were. "I get it."

"I don't think you do. Let me explain."

As he spoke and moved, an image flashed into her mind. It was him, but the setting was different. In her thoughts, sand and rolling dunes superimposed themselves over the dojo. Michael still stood in the middle of it all, but instead of workout clothes, he wore robes. The man standing in front of her spoke, and his words overlapped those in her memory. "If we do this, everything changes. It's not as simple as sex."

"What if that's the point?" The words passed Ronnie's lips, but they weren't hers. "We're not supposed to stay stagnant. Imagine what we get in return."

Here-and-now Michael's eyes grew wide. "What?"

The single question was enough to wash away the foreign memory. She blinked and shook her head, and her vision returned to normal. "Nothing. I… Thanks for trying with the fighting and all. I think I'm better off not knowing."

"Met— Ronnie."

The slip in names sent a dagger through her, and she tried not to fumble while she pulled her shoes on.

"Told you this wasn't meant to be your life."

This shouldn't hurt. Ronnie shouldn't care. Sure it was one hell of a kiss, and Michael was kind, but something told her he was good to everyone. So why did her insides feel like an imploded mess? He didn't want anything to do with her. He was only interested in the voice in her head. Even thinking the words made her feel as if she was being forced through a paper shredder.

"Ronnie. Don't leave things like this. Talk to me."

She wanted to believe the pleading was directed at her. That the sincerity in his voice was because he wanted her to stick around, not Metatron.

But Ronnie couldn't buy into that delusion. Was he, even for a moment, spending time with her? Or was today all about reliving things with Metatron? Was yesterday? How had Ronnie not seen that? For as strongly as Metatron reacted to him, of course he felt the same way.

God, she was a fucking idiot. She had a guy who cared about her, and made her feel so much, and instead she was wounded by a lovelorn angel who missed the ghost living in her head.

The entire thing dug a vast hole in her chest. She couldn't look at him. They'd pretend this never happened—as long as she could make the ache inside go away—and then life would go on. "I'll see you around."

Chapter Eighteen

Michael sank to the mats and scrubbed his face in frustration. Why didn't she let him explain? Besides the obvious reason: he made a terrible slip. He didn't have any difficulty noticing Ronnie was her own demon. She radiated a uniqueness. She even picked different weapons from the ones Metatron used—a sword and dagger instead of two blades of the same length.

But in his head, for so long, he associated *Ronnie* with an affectionate nickname for Metatron. It was careless, even so.

That kiss… It still hummed on his skin and flooded his thoughts. He hadn't been celibate over the centuries. Staying in a physical form as much as he did, he wasn't sure he would have survived without getting laid.

He didn't have a better way to phrase his hesitation, though. Telling her this was more emotional. That he didn't want to fall in love. It felt a bit severe given they just met. He didn't mean anything immediate, but people always took things wrong.

Not being able to get her out of his head told him it was the right decision. He just didn't know how long he could stick to his resolve. If that kiss had lasted a few seconds longer, he would have pinned her to the wall, stripped off her shirt and shorts, and explored every inch of her. Another kiss like that, the right smile from her, and he wouldn't push her away next time.

If he couldn't exercise control where Ronnie was concerned, he needed to back off.

Someone knocked on the dojo door, jarring him from his rambling thoughts, and he frowned. Technically, he was in heaven right now, and he doubted Ronnie was back in his condo, so someone with enough power to see the door wanted to talk to him.

Grateful whoever it was used the existing door instead of creating a new one in the middle of his practice mats. He hopped to his feet and crossed the room to open the door, expecting to see Gabriel or Lucifer on the other side.

He stepped back in surprise. His guest was almost as tall as he was and thin with blonde hair reaching halfway down her back. "Abaddon."

She leaned against the doorframe, arms crossed, posture casual. "Do you have time for an old friend?"

"I do." That'd be a nice change of pace. He stepped aside. "Do you want to come in?"

"I was hoping we could walk. I need an excuse to stretch my legs."

It was curious how so many pieces of Michael's past were converging now. In his experience, coincidence only went so far. "Just let me grab my shoes. I have to admit…" He tugged his sneakers and socks on. "…you aren't at the top of my people-I-expect-to-come-knocking list. How long has it been?"

"I lose track." Her tone was casual. She fell into step next to him when he joined her. They were really in heaven.

He hadn't been here in ages. Work didn't call for it. The atmosphere of the place collided and coursed around him like highly-charged air. It was almost foreign, but at the same time, comforting. It was nice to be home. "Two, three hundred years?"

"Something like that. Great Northern War I think."

The visit was starting to feel less casual and friendly and more contrived. He didn't like second-guessing his associates. Did dealing with Lucifer so closely have that impact on him or was there more to it? "What brings you to my neck of the world?" he asked.

As they strolled, flowers and green bloomed, changed, and shifted around them, lining the stone path. Heaven rearranging itself to their mixed ideas of beauty. Michael wanted to appreciate it, but it was ethereal—not tangible—so the vibrant colors, the potent floral scents, were all in his head. Literally.

Abaddon fiddled with a snap on her denim jacket. "Are the rumors true?"

An open-ended question, given how often life turned on its head over the past few days. "You know I'm not one for gossip."

She was loyal to Gabriel, something that bothered Michael since hosts were supposed to serve Him, not other angels. If she wanted information, other sources offered more than Michael did, making him wonder what he knew that she couldn't get elsewhere.

"I heard you sold your soul." She glanced sideways at him, a smile playing on her face.

He raised his brows. "I don't think the devil's buying what I have to offer."

She laughed, and it sounded forced and hollow in the ever-shifting environment. "Rumor is you've gone corporate. Upper management at Ubiquity."

"That's hardly a secret."

"What happened to individual reformation?" she asked.

He missed it terribly. Already. "I'd like to get back to it, but this is a priority right now." He left out mention of Ronnie and wasn't sure why. She didn't seem to be much of a secret either. However, he doubted many people knew she hosted Metatron, or was anything more than a demon getting special treatment.

"I want in."

"To Ubiquity?" Michael stared at her for several seconds. Did he misunderstand? She was old and powerful. A warrior and assassin. Not a paper pusher.

She didn't meet his gaze, but moved to the next button on her jacket and twisted it in circles. "I want to make a difference."

"Why wait until I'm there? Why not go to Gabriel?"

"I'm asking you, as an old friend."

The hosts of heaven may not be as gifted at double-talk and deception as Lucifer's students, but when an angel wanted to keep a secret, they could go to a lot of lengths to pretend it didn't exist. "I'm more of a figurehead than anything. Even if I did have that kind of sway, I can't push you to the front of line. You'd start at the bottom like everyone else. The world's got better uses for your talent."

"I want to help." She was starting to repeat herself. "This is big stuff, right? Getting worse? Maybe there's an opening in security."

"Ubiquity doesn't really do security. If they did, you'd be stuck behind a desk a lot of the time anyway." He tried one more time. "Why do you want the job?"

She jammed her hands in her pockets, and kept her gaze on her sandaled feet. "I was just thinking… If there was some newbie angel or demon out there doing captures, and they didn't know how to fight, they might need an escort."

That was oddly specific.

"I hear rumors," She added before he could decide if he wanted to prod for more, or shut down the conversation. "That, you know, maybe training methods are shifting…? Some recruits are starting work without the proper physical training?"

Michael had never been good at interrogation or dragging the truth from someone. He could tell when humans were lying, and that was where he spent most of his time.

He could peck at Abaddon's story all day, and probably not get anything more than awkward answers. He might uncover her intention after enough slips, but he wasn't in the mood for that. "I'll see what I can do."

"Really?" She grinned—the most genuine expression he'd seen on her since she arrived.

"Sure. I'll let you know." It would be interesting to get her in the door there, if for no other reason than to keep an eye on her and see what she was up to.

Chapter Nineteen

Irdu hated keeping this secret from Ronnie. As she told her story, he had a pretty good idea of what she was dealing with. Her situation might not be identical to his, but it was close.

Unlike the majority of cherubs who landed in human hosts, the one that possessed him so many decades ago wasn't a blank slate. It had served Lucifer. It had its own memories.

And for the first few months Irdu shared a body with it, he'd dealt with a voice.

But when Lucifer found him, made him a demon, the voice didn't just vanish, its memory melded with Irdu's.

Why wasn't Lucifer doing the same for Ronnie? And how did Ronnie end up that way in the first place?

Tia's safety was the only thing keeping him from heading back to Ronnie's place and telling her everything about his past.

This was yet another reason for him to find answers though.

It took him about two seconds of being in Fiji to figure out he had no idea how to find Izzy.

Calling him didn't work, which made sense. If the fallen angel was working with one of the tribes here, it was unlikely he was within range of a cell tower.

Irdu needed to do something. He'd exhausted all his reasonable outlets for research years ago. Anything he did now was digging for needles in the haystack that was the world wide web.

Except Lucifer knew something, and from what Ronnie told him about Gabe's strange questions, the angel did too.

Irdu had dug deep into the Ubiquity servers several times. He'd found the code that gave Gabe's favorite angels the best hits on cherubs. He'd seen how the system was rigged. Demons were never top performers, because a large portion of the programming was outsourced to Gabe's third party, who ensured angels always shone.

But there wasn't any information that was useful for Irdu's issue. Finding a way to keep Tia immortal, while yanking her out from under Lucifer's thumb.

He headed back to his apartment and fired up his computer. Within seconds, he had a VPN and a series of IP address masks and blocks in place. There was no guarantee Lucifer or Gabe would keep this information digital.

But if it had happened to Irdu, and now to Ronnie, it couldn't be isolated.

The first thing he stumbled on was digital fingerprints. Messy ones. Someone had been in here before him, and didn't know how to hide their tracks.

He traced the information back to Michael.

Interesting.

Irdu erased all traces of Michael's presence in the system.

As he dug deeper, he'd find hints. The start of threads that snapped each time he followed them.

His eyes burned and his brain ached, but he couldn't look away.

He didn't realize how long he'd been working, until his phone chimed with his Monday morning alarm. Had he really been up all weekend?

Fuck. He needed some sleep. He'd call in sick, and pick up his search again in a few hours.

*

Ronnie had wanted to call Irdu on Saturday, after things went bad with Michael.

But it felt like running into one guy's arms because another rejected her.

Besides, Irdu was looking for answers. She needed to let him work.

"Or you don't believe him when he says he's sorry about the past."

Ronnie knew he was hiding something from her, but that wasn't it.

"How do you know?"

And that was the rest of Ronnie's weekend—an onslaught of doubt, questions, and incessant chatter in her skull.

Her Monday wasn't going any better. Irdu had texted her to say he was taking the day off, but that he was onto something.

Great, but she missed him.

And Raphael steered clear of her, but the gossip followed her like a swarm of angry hornets. She was nuts. She was fucking around. She was only here because she sucked cock better than anyone else.

It was wonderful. Not.

She found an empty corner in the breakroom and leaned her head against the wall. Only few more hours to work. She could make it. Or maybe she couldn't. For the millionth time that day, she wondered what would happen if she walked out. Tossed her key card at Raphael and found something less mentally strenuous to do.

"Like...rocket scientist? Really, what else are you qualified for?"

"Being a demon."

"You're already a demon."

Ronnie gave up trying to ignore Metatron about halfway through Saturday. She didn't have the strength to keep Metatron caged nonstop. Besides, Ronnie arrived at some conclusions, even without her memory.

Angels and demons weren't made to be hunting down their own kind, cherub form or otherwise. They were supposed to help people realize their potential. All the stuff Michael said he did before he got to Ubiquity.

"Because he's definitely not interested in you. Besides, you're a servant of hell. Your job is to do what Lucifer tells you."

It didn't matter what Ronnie's position was on anything. Metatron disagreed.

"How's it feel?"

Ronnie pushed away from the wall. She should get back to work before someone saw her lounging. Though, Raphael bitching her out was almost better than this eternal, circular conversation.

"Liar."

Staring at a queue of false leads must be better than talking to herself. Er…Metatron.

"Whatever. I wonder… If I fantasize about Michael, can I drive you into a little more of this wallowing? Because I have to say… Wow, it's a blast watching you mope." Sarcasm bled into Metatron's taunt.

Please let that be an empty threat. Ronnie wasn't fond of the images Metatron sent rushing through her thoughts. There was no way this would be any better. Back to work.

Something caught her attention out of the corner of her eye, and she spun toward it. The blinds in Michael's office just closed all at once. He wasn't there this morning. She tried to ignore it. It didn't have anything to do with what happened between them over the weekend. It couldn't have.

"You haven't convinced yourself, and you're sure as hell not convincing me. I mean, it might be true, but you don't believe it."

Ronnie should talk to him. Tell him it was okay, no hard feelings, apologize… *Something.* Habit made her glance around for Raphael, but he'd steered clear of her all day. She turned away from her desk and made a line for the corner office instead. She knocked tentatively.

"Yeah." The voice wasn't quite right.

She stepped into the room and leaned back against the door to close it, grip staying on the handle. Surprise flooded her when she looked up. That was why it hadn't sounded right. Gabe sat behind the desk instead of Michael.

"If I had to get busted, at least it was by you." His smile was too big—too toothy—and something she couldn't identify flickered in his eyes.

"Deception, maybe?"

"Hey." The less thinking Ronnie did, the less reason for Metatron to talk.

"Oh, brilliant logic. You know it doesn't work that way, right?"

"Then tell me how it does work," Ronnie thought.

"Nice try." Metatron's response was snide. *"You don't want me to exist anymore than I want you in this body that should be mine. Any answers I figure out are mine."*

Screw her. "What are you doing here?" Ronnie asked Gabe. "I mean, not that you shouldn't be. Or that I have any say in where you go or what you do. But..." She trailed off before she could babble herself into oblivion.

"Michael asked me to grab something for him."

"Why couldn't he grab it? He's coming back, right?" She didn't mean that last bit to slip out.

Gabe raised an eyebrow. "He's been gone a day. Why wouldn't he return?"

"Way to look paranoid."

"Long day. Don't pay attention to me. I'm sorry for interrupting."

"Wait."

Ronnie paused, eyeing Gabe expectantly.

He crossed the room. He traced a hand down her arm as he pulled her closer, away from the door. The familiar shock of his touch rolled through her, pushing away days' worth of mounting tension and replacing it with indecision. The familiar fog clouded her thoughts, muting the scream of her brain to pull away.

"I'm glad you're here," he said. "I wanted to find you, but I wasn't sure it was a good idea."

His power shoved aside Ronnie's aches and misery. *God, what an amazing feeling.* Unlike with Michael, this was sharp and distinct. It made her pulse race and her gut churn. It didn't promise the safety or intimacy Michael's did in the dojo, and it was definitely lacking the playful, erotic companionship she felt from Irdu. "I'm here now," she said.

"About the other night at the club..." His words were hesitant, but only confidence shone in his expression.

Right. The club. With Ari, not at work today either, and whatever happened between Ari and Gabe. It was funny—everyone was happy to point out to Ronnie that agents didn't get sick, when she'd passed out. And three of the people she knew were taking *sick* days from work.

What did Gabe expect Ronnie to say? She still didn't understand half of what transpired.

"I can't stop thinking about that kiss. Tell me I wasn't the only one who experienced how potent it was."

"Would you even listen if I asked you to please, for anything that's ever mattered, walk away now?"

"You weren't the only one." The confession spilled out. That wasn't what she wanted to say, but she couldn't make herself take it back. Michael obviously wasn't interested in her. That didn't mean Gabe was a reasonable alternative. Something about his power wove around her, though, and obliterated her reason in a way she didn't like.

It was almost an ethereal roofie, and that made Ronnie's skin crawl.

"Can I kill him now?"

Though, he'd gotten rid of Metatron once…

"Bitch."

"Headache-inducing nag."

"I'm so glad." He traced a thumb over the back her hand. "I can't get it out of my head. You're all I'm thinking about."

An irrational giggle rose in her throat, and she clamped her lips shut before it could escape. Her gut clenched, and her head fluttered, and she didn't know if she was flattered or just going to be ill. "I, um, really?"

"Smart. Move over. Let me talk. I'll kill him, we'll go find a real man, and you'll be much better for it."

But the contact with Gabe gave Ronnie enough strength to stop listening, even if she couldn't shut Metatron up.

He tugged her closer. "Hear me out, and then I'll let you get back to work."

There was more? "But what about temptations of the flesh and all that?"

"Of course there's more. He's more of an elaborate liar. Kind of a flaw, if you ask me. But, you rarely do."

Metatron had a point. The best lies were simple ones. But continuing this conversation pissed her off.

"And lets Gabe weave his magic voodoo around you so you act contrary to character. Maybe he'll buy you some pretty new white wings to go with your delusion."

"I—" Gabe paused. "It's not that simple. You do understand that, right? We barely know each other, but this isn't base lust I'm talking about. I enjoy your company. And everything about you."

Apparently Ronnie didn't understand at all. Sure, he was a great noise filter, but his tone made her think he was talking about something more serious. That was awkward. Her brain ticked back to the shared moment with Michael, and the realization he saw more of Metatron than Ronnie when he looked at her.

"Truth hurts, doesn't it?"

Irdu liked Ronnie for Ronnie, though.

"Oh. My. God. Irdu this. Irdu that. Could you be any more pathetic?"

"I know you're having trouble here and what Lucifer is like. I'm concerned about you. And..." Gabe sighed. "I think I'm falling for you. Mostly because after thousands of years, I can't afford to ever be concerned about the individual. But now I find myself always worried that you're not doing okay. That and I can't get that kiss out of my head."

"You're buying this, aren't you? You're not even wondering what's in it for him. What he's up to."

Ronnie wasn't buying into anything, especially some sort of implied confession of maybe-lust after only a few days. That didn't stop her from having to fight the flush his last statement brought. Contrary to Metatron's lack of faith in her, Ronnie wasn't ready to fall into his arms and profess her undying love. Radiating creepy seemed to be his default setting. And a relationship? Like a romantic one? From a guy who hadn't given her the full truth at any point in their short time together, and who seemed to be magically drugging her?

"You're awfully quiet." His grip tightened on her hand.

Right. She needed to talk to him too. Not just Metatron. "I'm immensely flattered."

"But you're not interested." He dropped her hand.

Pain rocked through her skull as the fog vanished, and the edges of her vision blurred. She recognized the warning signs of Metatron trying to push her aside to take control. She struggled to speak through the onslaught. "It's not that at all. I'm just..."

"Incredibly desperate for someone to take you seriously. And hey, he might be a good lay."

He didn't interrupt.

"You caught me off guard." And she'd seen him in his full glory. If she pissed him off, the way Ari did the other night, would she be subjected to that?

"What do you need to hear to let me kill him?"

"Really?" He raised an eyebrow. "The subtle flirting never cued you in?"

"I thought you were an affectionate guy." If affectionate meant stalkerish.

He rested a hand on the back of her neck. The contact quieted the chatter in her head. "I wanted to be more direct. Your loyalties lie in a different place than mine, so I wasn't sure how much you would put up with."

"That could still be fun. If you won't let me have control, I can watch him destroy you far slower than he did me. You'll lose a friend along the way. That'll make you miserable, too."

Ronnie was already losing her mind. If he only slowed the process, there was no reason to trade his affection for Ari's.

He tilted his head closer and kissed Ronnie, lips hungry and demanding.

A wave washed over her, burning and soothing at the same time, making it difficult to think, and filling her with immense power. She reached for it, wanting to wrap herself in it. Like a downpour on a hot day, she could stand in it forever. She grabbed for more wisps and wove them around herself. The web grew, and she languished in it.

The connection snapped, and she opened her eyes, blinking a few times before she focused on Gabe. He had stepped back, face as pale as the walls.

"Oh, that was interesting. I was starting to wonder if I'd ever get to take a cherub again. But this could be much better."

Whatever. But damn, that was a rush. Tingles of his power still danced on her skin. Her resolve to not fall into his pretty words lingered in the back of her mind, faint and whimpering for attention. "Um, wow." Maybe there *was* some chemistry there.

"Or enough power to pretend it can rival what you have but won't use. Look at him. You practically drained his reserves."

As in stole his power? How would Ronnie do something like that? And she did too have her own power, or else she wouldn't be able to do things like phase in an instant. Metatron was trying to distract her.

"No, you do a really good job of that on your own."

"See? The kind of spark that's difficult to ignore." Despite the confidence in his tone, Gabe looked as if he was ready to pass out. The toes of his shoes bounced in an uneven beat—something she'd never seen him do before. "But unless you're okay with rumors, you should probably get back to work."

Like the rumors could get any worse at this point. "Yeah. Okay."

"I'll pick you up after five." He didn't finish the suggestion and vanished before she could tell him no.

"So you'd sell your heart for a little well-placed power display? At least you have your price."

She hadn't thought of it that way.

"Liar. I'm not talking to you anymore today."

"What, like that's supposed to be a threat?"

"It's not that simple. You can't fuck him and work for hell at the same time. And office romances never work out."

Given how the rest of Ronnie's life was going, she'd take a complicated office romance in exchange. Not with him. The one she had with Irdu seemed to be enough to piss off Metatron.

"Trust me. They never work out."

Chapter Twenty

The moment Ronnie stepped from the Ubiquity building, Gabe approached her. "Are you ready to get out of here?"

"Wow. Super stalker creepy."

Ronnie wasn't willing to fall into the relationship he proposed, but she was curious about why he pushed so hard. "Sure."

"I have something I'd like to show you." He took her hand.

"Ooh, his magic spear? His rod of destiny?"

"Shut it, you."

Ronnie was prepared for the rush of power at his touch and let it flow through her when they phased into the ether. They reappeared in the middle of his coffee shop.

"I know you've already seen the main room." Gabe's voice wove into the dim surroundings. "I'm hoping you'll let me give you a more intimate tour of the apartment upstairs later."

"If you like the way he kisses, just imagine how he fu—"

"We'll see." Ronnie talked over Metatron, hoping her attempt at being coy hid the uncertainty slithering through her. Now that she was here, would her curiosity hold out longer than her discomfort?

"There's time." He traced a line along her ear with his lips and circled her waist with his arm.

Without the intense brain fog—or whatever he did to her in the club—her skin crawled away from his touch. She tried to be subtle about stepping back and forced enthusiasm into her voice. "I didn't get to see much of this place last time I was here. Do I get the grand tour?"

"There's not much else to show you. At least here. But…"

She allowed herself to be led toward what she assumed was the back room. The wooden door creaked on its hinges when they pushed through. Something told her the noise was there to add ambiance. No one else was around, and it made her edgy.

He led her down a flight of stairs, the rotted wood protesting with each step. They passed through a second door—stainless steel, which swung open without a sound. The room they entered looked a few yards deep. Rows of weapons, armor, and other trophies decorated the wall, hinting it would extend as needed to hold everything.

She missed Michael. The quiet comfort, the security of being around him, knowing where they stood—even if it wasn't together. What made her think of him now?

"Good question. When you've got someone as amazing as Gabe by your side, who else matters?"

"Mmm… Sarcasm." Ronnie crossed the marble floor, distracted by the items on display. A battered shield with angelic characters caught her attention. "Where did you get all of this?"

"I've been around for a long time. I'm sentimental. Over the years I've either used every one of them or knew the angel who did."

His openness piqued her curiosity. A straight answer? Could it be the first time? "I bet you have some amazing stories to tell."

"You'd get tired of them quickly. I promise. It's like the heavenly version of watching someone's vacation slides."

"Eww."

Ronnie didn't want to mimic Metatron, but she admitted he made the experience sound less than enticing. "It can't be that bad."

"You're too polite. Maybe someday I'll share a couple of tales." He stepped behind her, rested his hands on her hips, and kissed the back of her neck.

His touch sent ice sliding down her spine. She tried to mask her shudder under the motion of spinning to face him. "Like why there are only three of the originals left?"

He wrapped his arms around her waist and placed a line of soft butterfly kisses across her lips. "That's a very boring story."

"Fuck you, it is. Some of us consider it a matter of life and death."

The potency of his touch intoxicated her, and she struggled to convince her body to put distance between them. He pushed up her tank top, brushing her stomach with his fingers. The unpleasant crawl raking her frame, telling her the desire was inspired by an external compulsion, won out over the euphoria of his touch.

He frowned when she broke the kiss, and then the corner of his mouth pulled up in a crooked smile she hadn't seen before. "We can pick up where we left off in a minute. What I wanted to show you is over here." He pointed toward the back of the room.

The light didn't reach that far, leaving everything draped in shadows, but if she squinted, she could see the outline of something that looked like a pedestal.

"What kind of twisted fucking game is he playing?" The familiar wash of emotion that came with Metatron getting worked up made Ronnie stumble.

"Someone's being paranoid."

Gabe nudged her forward. "Imagine an entire group of beings who are immortal. Untouchable. And in their own minds, perfect. And then one day, someone comes along and proves they're as corruptible as any of the creator's works. When Metatron plotted to destroy us, everything changed. This is my reminder of *never again*."

"I didn't do any plotting, but I'm starting to. At least you've got the never again *part right."*

As they drew closer, the temperature spiked. Within seconds, Ronnie flipped from wishing she wore sleeves to tugging at her tank top to keep it from sticking to her skin. Sweat trickled down her neck and ran between her breasts. Pain assaulted her, though she couldn't name a source.

"Her death is the reason I don't wield my spear anymore." Gabe paused a few feet back from the pedestal.

"Oh, how noble of you."

Any questions died on her lips. A spearhead sat in front of them, smooth obsidian amid tattered fabric. The air around it pulsed, each beat mimicked in her head.

The heat and pain inside her cranked from irritating to excruciating, and every inch of her screamed in agony.

"We should go." Metatron's usual snark was gone, replaced with tortured pleading.

Ronnie didn't know this kind of pain was possible.

"Are you all right?" Gabe eyed her with concern.

"Yeah, fine." She massaged her temple and moved nearer to him. Her panic rose when she didn't find the relief his touch normally granted.

He nodded at the weapon. "It unmakes things, separates the light from the tangible, from the shadows. People. Angels. Possibly reality."

They stepped closer, and Metatron howled. Sweat beaded on Ronnie's forehead, and she wiped it away with the back of her hand. Something yanked at her skin. No, that wasn't right. It jerked at something inside, pulling at her skeleton and everything wrapped around it.

"I didn't feel right wielding that kind of power, so I keep both memories here." He brushed a thumb over her cheek, wiping away the sweat. He left her side and crossed the short distance to the spear.

"Great. Your insanity is inducing hot flashes."

Maybe sharing her head with an extra occupant was inducing hot flashes. The heavy atmosphere sucked at her flesh. "I need some air."

Giving her one last glance of concern, he grabbed the stone spearhead off its pedestal. It was sleek and black, like carved onyx. The light bouncing off it didn't reveal any flaws. He held it out in her direction.

Heat seared her skin when he drew closer, and her skull erupted in a cacophony of roars. She recoiled in pain and stepped back to put some distance between her and the spearhead. Razors tore through her body, and she fell to her knees, struggling to breathe through the agony of having her body ripped from her bones.

"Holy fuck, what is that?"

Gabe set the spearhead down and kneeled in front of Ronnie. "Are you all right?"

The pain was still borderline unbearable but was the glory of hell compared with drawing close to the spearhead.

"My God, that hurt."

Ronnie swallowed and then forced her response to sound even. "I don't think I like your spear."

He helped her stand and held her upright as he guided her toward the stairs. "I didn't expect that. I'm sorry."

"He's not. Fucking asshole. Talk about agony."

"Yeah. Of course." The dry air rushed to fill her lungs as she inhaled. She didn't know what else to say. Why did it bring her so much pain? Was it the answer to why Metatron lived in her head?

"Who cares? Let's just agree not to ever do it again."

Chapter Twenty-One

"That sucked."

"Are you sure you're all right?" Gabe brushed a strand of hair from Ronnie's forehead.

"I swear to everything ever, I'll kill him for that."

Ronnie pushed aside Metatron's venom, earning another wave of weakness. She swallowed and forced her voice to remain steady. "I'm better."

"I really am sorry. There's something I want to ask you, and I was hoping the spear would help me convince you. But it's not necessary."

Reason bulldozed her fading pain. She didn't know if she could handle any more of Gabe's surprises. "What does an agony-inducing spear have to do with convincing me of anything?"

"You need to sit down."

"I think that's a good idea." It didn't escape her that he avoided the question. She followed him into the coffee shop, more from the overwhelming desire to retreat from the pain than anything else. Even with distance between her and the haunting museum of weapons, uneasiness churned in her gut. She was the heroine in a horror movie who goes into the dark basement without a flashlight even though people are dying around her left and right.

"You know what they say about curiosity."

"That irritating dead angels use it to be even more irritating."

"That didn't even make any sense. The spear screwed up your head. Want me to drive for a while?"

"Not ever."

Gabe led Ronnie to a stool behind the counter and took a second one himself. He gave her a peck on the cheek, and the kiss nudged aside any residual pain from the spear. She didn't like his assumption that the contact was okay, but she welcomed the relief.

"I have one more surprise for you," he said.

Not having her flesh ripped off in agony was nice. They should quit on a high note. "Maybe another day. I need to lie down." At home. Behind her wards. Where he and his spear couldn't get to her.

"Maybe he's going to bow down and let me sever his head from his body. We can stick around for that."

Metatron's venom surged, and Ronnie swallowed it back.

He grasped both of her hands in his, expression turning somber. "I know this is atypical among our kind, but... Well..."

"Oh geez, really? Melodramatic much?"

Ronnie wanted to leave, but something in his grip compelled her to stay and hear him out.

"I was wondering if you'd come work for me."

"A new job. It's exactly what you wanted. Rah."

Ronnie stumbled over her response, not prepared for the question. "Huh?"

"Oh, brilliant. Good answer."

"I want you to work for me. I know you're struggling at Ubiquity, and I have a handle on something you might enjoy a little more."

"Which is...lattes? Sure, you're trained for that."

Ronnie shook her head, trying to ignore that Metatron's questions mirrored her own. She swallowed back the bile. She should say yes, right?

"You don't know anything about the job. You have no idea why he feels you're qualified over anyone else. Sure. Why the hell not? I mean, if I want you to, you won't, so..."

Gabe watched her, smile frozen in place.

"It's a big change." That wasn't what Ronnie should be saying. She needed to tell him no and hightail it out of there. "I mean, Ubiquity is the only job I know." Not that she was doing it anymore, considering the number of cherubs she walked away from instead of capturing them. Could she even just decide to go work for someone in heaven? She was pretty sure her orders needed come from Lucifer. "What does the job entail?"

"That's the trick. It's not as public as what you're doing now. So it's not the kind of thing I can fill you in on, unless you say yes."

"Wow, what a great offer."

"You can't give me any more details at all?" She'd seen things like *top secret* jobs on TV, but heaven and hell weren't really like that. Or were they? Technically, they didn't make what they did public, but in her experience, agents didn't have assignments they couldn't talk about.

"All I can say is, if anyone at Ubiquity knew about it, they'd drop their position in an instant to snatch up the one I'm offering."

That was the least reassuring thing she'd heard all day, and she'd almost had her flesh ripped off by a spearhead a few minutes ago.

He rested a hand on her arm. "Don't say no right now. At least sleep on it."

Ronnie smiled, feeling fake. "All right. I won't say no right away."

* * * *

"I have to get back to work." Izzy gave her a quick hug and a knowing smile. "I want details tomorrow, though."

Heat flooded her cheeks, as she watched his robes swish around him one more time before he vanished. She might have tried to argue valiantly, at least for show, but he'd coax the details out of her anyway.

The afternoon sun didn't reach this back corner of the temple, and there was no reason for the priests to light the room. She could have done it, but the shade was pleasant. She paced the packed dirt, her woolen wrap swirling around her legs. She wanted so badly to expose her shoulders. To let her wings show. It was the one thing she didn't like about being here. Now Greece…that was a country. Cherries, wine, and togas.

Maybe she'd find an excuse to go there next.

Giddiness distracted her. A gentle tug in her belly reminded her he'd be here any minute. Even though she saw him only a few days ago, she missed him. She didn't know if she could do what they discussed—walk away from heaven and being an angel, surrender it all for the experience of mortality. They'd become a flash in the grand landscape of eternity, but there would be so much to learn and experience as humans. With him, anything felt possible.

"Ronnie." Michael's voice brought a smile to her face, as did the nickname. He never called anyone else by anything other than their full name. And she loved the sound of affection rolling off his tongue.

She whirled midpace. He stood near the edge of the room, mostly in shadows. Something wasn't right. She frowned and tried to make out the details on his face. Was it his eyes? She wasn't sure.

He crossed the room in a few short strides, placed both hands on her cheeks, and pressed his lips to hers. The hungry kiss spilled through her, filling her with intense desire and fogging her thoughts, so her hesitation waned. This was him. It had to be. Nervous anticipation was making her imagine things.

She tilted her head back as he skimmed his mouth along her jaw and throat. His words vibrated against her skin. "Everything I asked you about. Everything I promised."

Her heart clenched with affection.

"I lied."

What? Something pierced her abdomen and tore through her like a million fiery daggers. She looked at him in disbelief. Shock, betrayal, and unimaginable agony filled her. Her attention dropped to the sword.

No, it was a spear. How was she thinking clearly enough to realize that? The edges of her vision blurred. As she dropped to her knees, he extracted the weapon. She looked up, finding eyes that weren't Michael's. Gabriel's sneer taunted her.

Fucker killed me. Why? She might have sobbed, but consciousness was slipping away.

"Ronnie." Michael's voice cut through the haze. He shoved the imitation him aside. Gabriel. Right. It was difficult for her to hang onto her thoughts.

Michael cradled her head in his lap, muttering and brushing her hair from her forehead. In the background, Gabriel babbled. Everything coming out of his mouth was a lie. She knew it, but she couldn't make her lips move. Couldn't push out the words to tell Michael the truth.

Ronnie's own yell woke her up, and she sat up in bed with a start, sweat sliding down her face and neck. She dropped her head in her hands, willing away the images of the dream. It was too vivid. As if she lived it. This wasn't a metaphor-based dream like the one of the market. Metatron was bathing Ronnie in her past. She didn't question Metatron's version of things. The sick pit in her stomach told her she witnessed the reality. At least Metatron found an effective way of torturing her even when she slept. Nowhere was safe.

"It's pretty safe in here. Want to trade places and see?"

Something needed to change. Lucifer wasn't helping. Gabe exposed her to the most painful thing she'd encountered in her short life, and she wasn't any closer to a solution. And she was pretty sure Michael was seeing her to get to Metatron.

"God, could you be any more wishy-washy? Nobody likes me. Everybody lies to me. *Grow up already."*

Ronnie had to admit Metatron was right. She was floundering like a child instead of facing things head on. Lucifer was the only one with the answers. And one way or another, she'd get them from him. She phased to hell.

The oak door in the middle of white sterility mocked her. The familiar aura tugged at her senses. *Home?* But more like a lingering scent than an immediate presence. And she didn't miss it. Not at all.

"Liar."

She knocked. There was no answer. She could wait. She had all night. Her back to the door, she slid into a sitting position and hugged her knees to her chest. She'd come back tomorrow and the next day and over and over, until he was ready to talk. He knew she was here, and he'd give in eventually.

"You wish."

Okay, so Ronnie might not have her sanity long enough to win a battle of wills with Lucifer, but it was a plan in progress. If he didn't show up in the next couple of hours, she'd reevaluate. All this missing sleep was catching up to her. Maybe she could just rest her eyes for a few minutes. Lucifer would wake her up when he got in.

"Ronnie?" Michael's quiet voice startled her.

She opened her eyes and jerked her head up. How did he sneak up on her? Better question, why was he here?

When she realized how close he was, her breath caught in her throat, and her questions evaporated. He kneeled in front of her, studying her with concern. Reminders of the other morning rushed back to greet her—the kiss, the intimacy, and being pushed away.

Something unreadable played on his face as he offered her a hand and then pulled her to her feet. He tucked a strand of hair behind her ear and brushed her cheek. "I'm sorry about the other day."

In her head, Metatron whimpered. Ronnie's thoughts joined in.

Heat sped along her skin, teasing her nerve endings to life, but she didn't know how much of it was hers. It seemed to be attached to the inky strands that penetrated every inch of her body. She wanted to pull away, but at the same time, wanted to lean closer.

She licked her lips, forcing her voice through her dry throat. "I'm not her. You know that." That wasn't what she meant to say.

"I do. But you've got a lot in common. Intelligence, beauty, and resilience, to name a few things."

"Except one of us is a whiny little brat."

Ronnie felt the same. Michael's comment left a dull ache in her chest, and she backed away when he reached for her. "Don't."

"You're right. I need to earn that."

She crossed her arms and summoned as much resolve as she could. After the way they left things in the dojo, she couldn't do this. Admitting there was any compassion or affection in the way he talked to her was another reminder he saw Metatron where she stood. "Stop comparing me to her. I know you want Metatron here. I'm not her. I'm pretty sure at this point I'm better off that way. Whatever happened between the two of you, whatever ghosts haunt you, I'm not the way to exorcize them."

"I never meant to give you that impression." Stepping closer, he wrapped his fingers around her hand. She didn't want to enjoy it. Didn't want to acknowledge the way he made her pulse race.

"Move aside, let me do this."

"No." Sparks screamed along the dark ribbons all through her, and she pushed Metatron back. "It sure seemed like it."

"You can't take this from me. It's not yours.

"But it is. It's my life."

Michael slid his hand to her neck and stroked her cheek with his thumb. "If you spent more time being yourself, instead of worrying about what you were before, it might make it easier to get to know you."

"Don't waste your time. She won't be here long."

Ronnie struggled against Metatron's efforts to take control. "But I can't walk away from my history, whatever it was."

"I'm not suggesting you do." He leaned closer and rested his forehead against hers.

Despite her resolve to push him away, and his insistence they avoid a physical relationship, the simple gesture fanned the conflict roaring inside her.

His voice was low but firm. "But you also have to live for now, and so do I. So I'll make you a deal. I'll stop picturing her where you stand, if you stop assuming that's what I'm doing."

"No."

Ronnie's sadness mingled with melancholy. Such a simple suggestion. She knew it wouldn't go down that way, but she liked the idea enough to give it a try. "Yeah, all right."

More sparks flooded the inky threads within her, catching her off guard, and she stumbled in her own mind. She tried to blink, but her eyes didn't close. She was aware of her hands resting at the base of Michael's neck, but she wasn't the one who put them there.

"Don't listen to her." It was Ronnie's voice, but Metatron spoke. "I'm exactly who you remember."

Michael's eyes grew wide, but he didn't step back.

Metatron stood on Ronnie's toes and pressed her lips to his.

Ronnie stopped struggling to regain control of her body. The rush filled every inch of her until she thought she might burst. Similar to Gabe's, but more…real. Her heart hammered. It was like nothing she'd ever experienced.

"Suck it, bitch. This is my life. Move over."

Metatron's taunt drew Ronnie from the awe. The entire situation was surreal. Metatron's love for Michael pulsed through her, but Ronnie's emotions were still there. It was like living an intense movie.

Michael traced his hands up her arms, until his palms rested on her cheeks, holding her close.

A moan tore from her chest, but she wasn't sure who it belonged to. It was as much Ronnie's as it was Metatron's. Was this really what it was like to be in love? Could Ronnie really have this if she surrendered?

"No. I could. But you can watch."

Lust, desire, being wanted—all raced through her. She wanted to feel more. Wanted him, not the Metatron-diluted version of him. She pressed closer. *God,* it was so amazing. The incredible lust—

"Love"

—he had for Ronnie.

"Me."

He smelled of pine and fresh air, and his hard frame didn't yield when Metatron pressed Ronnie's body against him. He trailed a finger down the side of her face, and she parted her lips at the tender gesture. His coaxing tongue pushed aside any thoughts except experiencing the moment.

He twisted his fingers in her hair. She traced lines along his chest, barely aware they were still in the middle of a hallway in hell.

He moved his other hand to her waist and slid his palm under her shirt without shoving the top out of the way. She wanted to feel more of his skin against hers. Would he balk if she wanted to take this back to her place? To remove themselves from prying eyes and take their time exploring each other?

"Please?"

The begging rocked in Ronnie's skull, jarring her out of the moment. How did she forget Metatron? Was any of this even Ronnie's?

"Of course it is."

Ronnie wrested back control of her body—unlike previous attempts, the transition was smooth, sliding into a comfy pair of jeans smooth—and broke away with a gasp, confusion assaulting her. She couldn't look him in the eye. "Me or her?"

"Uriel?" The concern in his voice couldn't completely mask hints of disappointment. She was pretty sure she wasn't imagining it.

He used the right name. Ronnie shook her head and stepped out of his reach. She was such an idiot to let her guard down with Metatron sharing her skull. Now she'd found a more subtle way of taking over.

"Holy hell. You're fucking paranoid. Was the kiss really that bad?"

It was incredible. And not all for Ronnie. So much for him resisting temptations of the flesh. "I can't. I'm just— I just can't."

*

"Tell me." Michael wrapped his fingers loosely around Ronnie's wrist. Another shock of want spilled over him. He might be a servant of will, but when it came to internal resolve, his was apparently shot.

He was surprised she stayed. When she wasn't fighting herself, she was powerful. His grip wasn't enough to keep her here.

She flopped back against the wall next to him, never breaking free of his grasp, and tilted her head toward the ceiling. "I don't even know where to start."

Prompting her to explain was easier than trying to put his own thoughts into words. But it wasn't fair of him. "I'm sorry."

She laughed and shook her head. "For as many let downs as I've had recently, I think you and Irdu are the only people saying that. What are you sorry for? Don't doubt for a second I've got a list, but I'm curious what you think you should be apologizing for."

Who was Irdu?

Not important right now.

Ronnie's attitude. Unapologetic and direct, even amid her confusion, was another reason Michael adored her company. Watching her in the diner the other morning with her appreciation for life. The way she approached everything with a refusal to back down. It drew him in. "For kissing you when it wasn't all you."

"So you did know." She shook her head. "Wait. You said not all me. That wasn't any of me."

His concern grew. "I don't—are you sure?" Her aura was there, spiking and dancing with its neighbor. Her unique taste still lingered on his lips.

Never pulling away from the wall, she worked her wrist free and glided her fingertips along the back of his hand before sliding her fingers between his to lace them together. At least she still trusted him. He wasn't sure he'd earned that, but he appreciated it.

She inhaled in a shaky-sounding breath. "When we... When we kiss, it's incredible. The problem is, I don't know if it's me feeling it. That's why I stopped. I don't know if these are my emotions."

"Did you enjoy it?" It wasn't fair of him to ask, but he despised the thought he'd just taken advantage of her.

"Yes." The single word, a drawn-out hiss.

"I won't try and pretend I know what that's like. I don't know if this helps, but I see you here."

"But you see her too."

"I'm not kissing *her*." The explanation sounded weak even before he said it, but he needed to try. "The power flowing through you? The energy that belongs to you when you're not hiding from it, it's more than just a feeling, or a pretty glow around you. It radiates from you in every way. Cool heat when I touch you, spring rain when we kiss. That's *you*. She's scorching chaos mixed with pepper."

"Even if those aren't just a bunch of poetic words—and they're pretty endearing—what if that's a mistake? You compared my situation to someone hosting a cherub. What if I'm not even a demon? What if I'm just a vessel for an angel who wants another chance?" She finished with a noisy exhale.

He rolled his head to the side to see her better and traced his gaze over her. Not her body, but the light flickering around her. "You're a demon, I promise you."

She stepped in front him, never letting go of his hand. "How do you know?"

"I know. I can see it. Whatever else is going on, I know that, as distinctly as I know any agent when I see one. It's part of who I am." A part of himself he only called on when he absolutely had to. Being back at Ubiquity, working within their mess of an infrastructure, he remembered it wasn't such a bad thing to own what He created him for.

She smiled. "Because you're the great and mighty Michael?"

"Something like that." He didn't know any other way to make her understand. Everyone around them was keeping secrets, spinning tales, and he wasn't interested in it.

"Even if you're so certain, I don't know if what's going on in my head—or heart—is mine." She searched his face. "If it's really her, she loved you so very much it almost knocks me over, and I don't know if anything I experience when I'm with you is my own. She *feels* everything with an intensity I think most people would kill for a taste of. Love. Vengeance. I lose myself in her emotions."

He knew that kind of desire. It was the exact thing he wanted to avoid a second time around. So far he was doing a poor job.

She didn't need that burden though. He squeezed her fingers. "I don't think that's true. The things you feel and think and see. The passion you have for the world around you? That's all you. You radiate intensity, and I see it in your aura. *Your* light flares when you talk about something you love. When I say I want to be here with you, I know who I'm talking about."

Which was why he needed to be more careful around her.

"So how do we get her separate from me?"

That was far more important than a crush he shouldn't have and needed to move past. "We'll figure it out."

She pursed her lips. "I've heard that before. No offense. But at least this time I actually think you mean it."

"No." He corrected her. "Not I'll figure it out, or maybe it'll happen eventually on its own. *We'll* figure it out. *We'll* dig and scrape until it all starts to make sense."

"I still don't think it'll do any good, but thank you."

"Get to work. We'll meet up after." He pressed his lips to her forehead. He wanted more, but even this pushed the boundaries of what he should allow himself. The simple contact spread through him, carried on the wave of cool she radiated, and seeped into every inch of his being.

They had to make this right. She deserved that.

Chapter Twenty-Two

Michael should be looking for more information about how to help Ronnie. He told himself he was.

But that didn't explain what he was doing in the Human Resources system, looking up this *Irdu*. A name said in passing, by the demon he should not be lusting over.

The system said Irdu was an incubus, and he'd been with Ubiquity from the start. A week after Ronnie started working here, he was reassigned from a management spot in Reaping to Development.

Someone knocked on Michael's office door. "Come in."

Irdu stepped into the room, and kicked the door shut behind him.

That was unexpected. And bold. And the timing too perfect for it to be a coincidence.

"It's Michael, right?" Irdu dropped into an empty seat, crossed one ankle over the other knee, and leaned back.

"Yes."

"You were poking around in my files, so I thought I'd come down here and let you ask whatever is you want to know to my face."

Michael raised an eyebrow. "How did you...?"

"Know? I wrote the HR system. And it's possible I slipped in a bit of code that tells me when someone is peeking at my file. Besides that, you leave fingerprints everywhere. You need to learn what an IP mask is."

Michael had a lot more important things to worry about. "I look at a lot of records. It's part of my job." That didn't come out as plausible at all.

"Right..."

"What can I do for you?" Michael didn't know what to make of Irdu's attitude. He wasn't angry, but he also wasn't friendly, and he was most certainly confrontational.

"About that." Irdu sighed. "Ronnie is one of two centers of my universe. I don't know how it happened, but there it is. She thinks you can help her. I'd like to see that happen."

What had Michael stepped into? The middle of a relationship of some sort. At least from this guy's perspective. "I'd like to see that happen too."

"Fantastic." Irdu clapped once. "First step, stop fucking with her heart. I don't care if you sleep with her, but don't yank her chain on this. You're mourning a ghost from the past. Everyone knows that. Everyone has known for centuries, or I wouldn't know it. Ronnie's not your ghost. She's her own, incredible demon."

And she apparently had someone very loyal and defensive looking out for her. The knowledge twisted inside Michael in a strange cocktail of relief and jealousy. "I realize that. Believe me. I know."

"Okay, then…" Irdu's bravado slipped. "Glad we're on the same page."

Did he expect Michael to argue? So far the conversation was odd, but not unreasonable. "Is that all?"

"No. I have information you probably don't, and I suspect you have some of the same. I think things will start going more smoothly if we share."

"All right." Michael didn't take issue with sharing what he knew. It should be public knowledge anyway. He gave Irdu a detailed rundown of what he'd spent the last couple of decades doing. Finding possessed individuals. Assessing them one-by-one. Helping them either adapt, or reaping their cherubs so they could go back to their lives.

Irdu nodded through bits of it, but never looked surprised. "That's cool. I'm glad you do that. Thank you." he said when Michael finished.

"You're welcome." Weird. But all right. "What did you want to tell me?"

"The system is rigged." Irdu launched into an explanation of his own, about how Gabe's people got all the good jobs, and that some of them were probably keeping cherubs.

Michael should have guessed. It seemed so obvious to hear it. But it was a deceptive kind of thought process that he wouldn't delve into on his own. "I see. Thank you."

"What next?" Irdu asked.

"I'll talk to Lucifer and Gabriel."

"Okay. I was hoping for something a little more realistic. Did I mention, you can't say you heard this from me?"

"I'm not much of a liar, but I'll work to keep your name out of the conversation."

"So that's it?" Irdu almost looked disappointed. "Just more *I'll look into it?*"

Michael shrugged. "I don't know what you want from me beyond that. I'm trying. This isn't a brush-off. I can confront them with what you've told me. And how do I know Lucifer didn't send you in here?"

He hated thinking that way, but he needed to.

"You don't. Lucky for me, I don't give a fuck if you trust me. I only care that Ronnie does." Irdu stood. "Thanks for hearing me out."

After Irdu left, Michael paced his office, irritation and fury crawling under his skin.

Too bad he didn't know what to do with the data Irdu gave him. It shouldn't be his concern, and on the surface it didn't seem related. Angels and demons had rules to follow. Orders that, if they disobeyed, cost them immortality. It happened for a variety of reasons: greed, lust, ego, or just the desire to live a different life that wasn't eons old. Technically, the Ubiquity situation didn't break the rules.

But he couldn't ignore the crumbling structure. What should be a joint venture between heaven and hell was turning into the same underhanded backstabbing it was created to eliminate.

While Michael's job wasn't justice, he did know His will, and that wasn't the kind of growth He wanted for his children.

Michael snarled at the empty room. What bothered him the most was that Gabriel and Lucifer knew these details. He wanted to believe not. Something like this would detract from any other projects they worked on. But they both knew what was going on with Ronnie.

She was a problem all her own. Unpredictable, unreadable, and two separate entities.

He turned for another circuit around the room and halted. Lucifer sat in the chair across from his desk. Michael let the irritation and sarcasm flavor in his tone. "To what do I owe the honor?"

Lucifer lounged, one ankle over the opposite knee. "Do yourself a favor and walk away now." There was no threat or malice in his words.

So he was onto something. Michael's phone chimed, and he ignored it. "You'll have to be more specific."

"It's a pretty open-ended suggestion. Go back to helping the underdog or find a church in the middle of nowhere. Find yourself."

"Did you put her up to this?"

"The little scene outside my office? No. I don't know what she was trying to do. You, on the other hand, I have a pretty good idea. I should have said this the day you showed up in mud-caked shoes, and I hope it's not too late now. Walk away. Don't stick your nose in this."

So this really was about Ronnie. Michael dropped into his chair and leaned forward, arms resting on his desk. "Who is she?"

"She's not Metatron."

Not quite a direct answer, but more of one than he expected. "They've got a lot in common. Did you know she hears a voice who calls herself that?"

Lucifer's long exhale stretched on for several seconds before he replied. "Uriel's a cherub who used to work for me directly. She was good, she was loyal, and I liked her. So I named her."

"Did you just admit to having a sentimental motivation for something?"

Lucifer snorted. "Don't try and read between the lines, it doesn't suit you. She earned the job, so I made her a demon."

"Sounds status quo." Michael's phone chimed again. Irritating thing.

Lucifer raised his brows. "Except she doesn't remember who she is. I need a drink. Are you thirsty? Let's go somewhere else."

"I'm fine." There was more information here than Michael expected to find in weeks of digging. Except he still couldn't make the pieces fit. "So she's telling the truth about her memory." Part of him hoped she wasn't. Finding out she lied would make it easier to keep his interest professional. "How does a demon get amnesia?"

"I wish I knew. I'd fix her in a heartbeat. And I can't even admit it to her. I don't know why, but I can't find it in me to tell her I can't make this better." Lucifer raked his fingers through his hair. "I don't know what to do."

Michael kept his shock to himself. It was true—whoever this was, Lucifer actually seemed to care about her.

Or he cared that she was carrying Metatron.

Lucifer shook his head, expression returning to impassive. "But I need to tell her the truth. That I don't know how to help her."

Not a tangent Michael expected to linger on. "So what are you doing here?"

"I told you. It's friendly advice. And something made me think you needed to hear it before she did."

"You don't tell me anything out of the goodness of your heart."

"And I'm not this time either. I'm not here for you, I'm here because I don't like Gabriel."

Michael struggled to draw a connection and failed. It was the obvious statement of history, after what Gabriel did to Metatron. "And?"

"And nothing. I tell you to leave, my odds are better if for some reason this comes down to taking sides." Lucifer stood. "This is a bad place for you to be."

The shift in subject was so rapid it almost gave Michael whiplash. "What are you up to?" He felt like a broken record, but each new poke seemed to chip Lucifer's armor further.

"Stay out of this. It's up to me to make this right for Met— Ronnie."

"What did you mean to say?" Michael knew exactly where the slip came from.

Lucifer stared back, expression impassive. "I have to figure out what to do about Uriel. I can't have a demon running around with a voice in her head."

Michael watched him vanish from the room, replaying snippets of the conversation in his head. Damn it. He slammed his fist into his desk. For a minute, he almost believed everything Lucifer told him. Had there been any truth in the conversation at all?

Michael's phone chimed again. "What?" he yelled at the empty room. He clenched his jaw and took a few deep breaths. Temper under control, he grabbed the device and pulled up the series of text messages. More of his foul mood evaporated when he saw they were from Izrafel.

Back in town.

You wanted to talk?

Stop by anytime.

He pocketed the phone, sent Ronnie a quick email, and made his way to the elevator.

Moments later, Michael stood in front of the apartment above the church. The door swung open the moment he knocked.

Izrafel grinned and stepped aside. "This must be important."

"Most likely. More so now than it was a week or two ago." No reason to be rude, though. "How was Fiji?"

Izrafel laughed and flopped into an easy chair, gesturing to the sofa across from him. Overflowing bookcases covered the surrounding walls and more books—both ancient and new—littered the coffee table between them. A laptop sat open on the orange carpet, and two tablets were plugged into the wall next to it. "Incredible. Did you know they have a tribe there who believes as long as they leave every second coconut on the ground, they incur His favor? I've been trying to trace back the origins of that since I returned to civilization."

"How do they know they're leaving behind every second and not every first and third?"

"Faith."

Michael smiled at that. The banter was familiar and friendly, but they both knew the meeting held a deeper purpose. "Did you get my email?"

Izrafel nudged an open book across the table with his sock-covered foot. "You've met her, then. Angels coming back from the dead, possession, and falling but not losing power. Do you have any idea how many variations there are on that theme across the world and centuries?"

"I have a little idea. But I was hoping your knowledge might make it easier to find the common elements and extract the reality."

"Oddly enough, this is a difficult one to pin down." Izrafel leaned over and pointed to highlighted paragraphs in the book. It was fairly new—pages still white, and cover, a glossy, full-color paper. "This sums it up most succinctly, but it's still vague." He grabbed another book from a tumbling stack, cradling the yellowed pages. "But this one backs up the claims." He reached for a third and added it to the stack. "And this one—"

"Can you summarize for me?" Michael knew this could go on for days if he let it. Sometimes he did. Today it didn't feel as if there was time.

"Not a single documented case, or anything resembling one, of an angel who once was reappearing as someone else."

Concern rolled into agitated illness in Michael's midsection. That was what he was afraid of. "She's got Metatron."

Izrafel shuffled the books around, not meeting his gaze. "You're sure?"

"Without a doubt."

"Shit." Izrafel jumped to his feet and strolled to one side of the room before whirling and storming back to the other. He muttered unintelligibly under his breath as he paced.

He finally stopped and looked at Michael again. "Can you bring her here? Soon?"

Michael had never seen the former angel so serious. Not in thousands of years. Any trace of levity was gone from his voice, and his posture was tight and coiled. How bad was this? Michael stood. "Yes."

Chapter Twenty-Three

Ronnie drummed her finger on the right mouse button as she sifted through the queue. *Dud, dud, dud.* What a surprise. Most of these didn't even remotely look like they might be cherubs. Or maybe she wasn't interested in finding them anymore. What gave her the right to take their lives from them?

The air shifted around her, and she flinched at the familiarity of it. Her eyes were drawn toward Michael's office just in time to see the blinds flip shut. Lucifer.

"You know talking to him doesn't really work for us these days."

Ronnie gritted her teeth, hating to agree. But why was he talking to Michael? What happened to her and Michael doing this together?

"The whole of life doesn't revolve around you. They had jobs before you, and they'll continue to after. I should know."

Ronnie slouched in her seat and forced her attention back to her work. Stupid, reasonable voice.

Besides, she trusted Michael—at least as far as his not colluding with Lucifer to make her life worse.

"Nice qualifier."

She had other things to worry about anyway. For instance, Ari still wasn't at work. It was Tuesday, so she'd only been gone for two days. But the weekend felt like an eternity ago. Then there was that whole *angels don't get sick* thing. If she was out on assignment, she would have shown up to retrieve the information, and she wasn't on vacation, so where was she?

"She tried to steal my soul. Why do you care?"

She tried to help Ronnie. Now who was being egocentric and overreacting?

"Fuck you, too."

Some of Ronnie's tension evaporated when Lucifer's power vanished from the office. The relief nudged a sadness inside she couldn't quite place. It was true, Lucifer was good to her, but heavy disappointment filled her because they were barely on speaking terms. Why should it matter?

"None of your business."

Great. More feelings that weren't Ronnie's.

A few minutes later, her email chimed with two messages. The first was from Michael. *Have to look into something. Meet me later this evening?* She was pleased he seemed serious about what he said this morning, but at the same time, she was concerned about how much of her reaction to him was her own. His confidence there ran far deeper than hers.

The second was a meeting request from Irdu, for five minutes from now.

She couldn't help a smile at that. And who cared if Raphael didn't think she should be meeting with development.

She took her time strolling up the few flights of stairs to Irdu's office, trying to time things right so she'd arrive just at her scheduled appointment.

Ronnie knocked, and waited for the typical, *come in.* Might as well pretend she was being professional until they were behind closed doors. Everyone might know that everyone else was screwing around, but most of them didn't flaunt it.

Fortunately, once she was in his office, all that could change. The building had some exceptional soundproofing of the magical variety.

When he opened the door himself, she was surprised, but not disappointed.

Irdu's smile lit a spark of warmth inside, and wrapped her in comfort and anticipation.

When he locked the door behind her, knotted his fingers in her hair, and crushed his mouth to hers, intense need joined the glowing spark.

She pressed into him—the way he devoured her mouth, her body molding to his—until she was breathless, and even then it wasn't enough.

He broke away with a groan, and pressed his forehead to hers. "I missed you."

"Me too." She wanted to wind the strands of their auras around her and fall into the feeling.

Irdu grasped her fingertips, and tugged her to his side of his desk. He shoved aside his keyboard and a stack of paper, gripped her hips, and lifted her to sit on the polished wood. He didn't let go of her as he slid between her legs.

This was nice. Better than nice. A wonderful salve covering and erasing the stress of the last several days.

Irdu brushed his lips over hers again. "I talked to Michael this morning."

"How'd that go?" Not exactly the sexiest bit of conversational foreplay. Were things about to fall apart again? If so, she needed to memorize every second of what happened now.

He bit her neck, then layered a row of nibbles up to her jaw. "I told him I didn't care if he fucked you, but if he kept using you to mourn a ghost, I didn't care who he was, I'd find a way to destroy him."

If it was possible to be mortified and touched at the same time, Ronnie was. "Was that the entire point of the conversation?"

"You're not impressed?" Irdu worked his fingers down the front of her blouse, undoing the buttons one at a time. "I thought chicks were into that caveman shit." The corners of his mouth tugged up and amusement danced in his amber eyes.

He was having fun with this. A good sign.

"Some *women* are, yes. But I'm not sure what you did qualifies." She dragged her fingertips up his back, enjoying the texture of fabric and muscle under her touch, and liking the way he pressed closer into her.

He kissed along the top of her breast, just above her bra. "No? Should I bring a club next time?"

Ronnie laughed. This felt good on so many levels. His touch was rough, but one she wanted.

The banter made her thoughts soar. Being here with him healed her heart. All the reasons she'd been draw to him in the first place.

There was this underlying hint of possession, or maybe it wasn't so hidden. Not in a *nobody fucks you* kind of way, but more in a *nobody fucks with you* kind of way. This was the first time she'd seen him be so literal about it, and she adored it.

"Why did you really talk to Michael?" Ronnie wrapped her legs around Irdu's waist and pulled him closer. He was half-hard, and his shaft teased her.

His throaty groan said he was fond of the sensation too. "He was pawing through my HR file, so I thought I'd introduce myself in person. Offer any assistance in his quest to help you. Point out that I might be better suited for digital research than he was."

Irdu trailed his fingers over her nipples, teasing through lace. Liquid emerald and gold energy flowed from his touch, making her squirm against him with need.

"You're willing to double team just for me?" Her playful question trigged a whole new avalanche of fantasy. One that had her pressed between playful, aggressive Irdu, and proper, attentive Michael. She was playing more with that imagery when she had the chance. Just the hint of it throbbed between her thighs.

"Phrasing."

"I know what I said, and I'm not taking it back."

He pushed a breast free from the cup of the bra. "In that case, yes. I'm definitely up for that. Not today, though. Today you're all mine." He lowered his mouth to her nipple to suck and lick and nibble.

She pressed into his mouth with a moan. "I'm great with that." She stroked him through his slacks, smirking in satisfaction when he bucked against her hand.

He undid her jeans, and she kicked off her sandals. She lifted her ass off the desk enough to let him shove her pants to the ground. When she lowered herself again, the polished oak was warm and smooth against her skin.

She unzipped his pants, and wrapped her hand around his shaft. His growl sent shivers through her.

When he slid inside her that delicious sensation of being stretched out almost too much flowed through her. So incredible.

Ronnie wrapped her legs around him again, drawing him in as close as possible.

He sucked on her neck, hard enough to sting. He'd leave a mark if he wanted. If she wanted. It was tempting. To display his brand on her skin.

Irdu pounded hard and fast, building to a frantic pace. His bites grew sharper against her skin. Each new shock ticked her senses more, building and pushing her toward the height of pleasure.

She dug her nails into his back when she climaxed. He didn't ease up. The edge of one orgasm had barely faded before the next one flooded her body.

Something she'd never complain about was that extra hint of magic he used to make her come.

She was drowning in ecstasy, her thoughts vapor and her pulse roaring.

He dug his fingers into her hips, letting out a long moan when he spilled inside her.

Their auras mingled and wove together, blanketing her in a cloud.

She leaned her head against his chest. This was so good. So perfect.

Silence spread through the room, adding to the lovely floaty feeling in her head.

"I probably should have opened with *how are you*," he murmured against the side of her neck. His voice blended with the feeling in the room rather than disrupting it.

"I'm really, really good right now."

His chuckle rumbled through her. "Dig a little beyond right now."

"Do I have to?" Her pout was half for show. Why couldn't life always be this simple? No voices. No missing memories. No secretive bosses. Just a sexy incubus boyfriend, and afternoons filled with sex and ice cream.

Now she wanted ice cream. And to eat it off Irdu. That was always fun. "Same as I have been. Happy to see you. Worried about Ari. Wanting answers."

"What's wrong with Ari?"

And now the real world was sinking in. It was going to happen eventually. At least she very much enjoyed the mini-vacation. "She hasn't been to work, and she's not out on assignment. She's just… gone."

"Hmm… So I have a brilliant thought."

"Does it involve sex on your desk, and ice cream? Because I should probably get back to work soon, but that would be hard to say no to."

He laughed, and kissed her. "My brilliant ideas almost always involve sex. Before. After. During. It all depends on the timing. It can also involve ice cream."

"I love it so far." She snuggled into him.

"Izzy is back in town. Go check on Ari after work, and then we'll go see him about that irritation of yours. We'll do sex and ice cream after."

"That is brilliant." Ronnie kissed him again. She was reluctant to break away, but with this pleasant buzz, even Raph yelling at her couldn't wreck her mood.

Chapter Twenty-Four

Ronnie was anxious to check on Ari as soon as she was off the clock. Which, as the minutes continued to drag away in slow ticks of the clock, took forever. The moment the display clicked from 4:59 p.m. to 5:00 p.m., she logged off and grabbed her purse before transporting herself to Ari's front landing.

Ronnie knocked. And waited. Was she not home? Maybe she *was* on assignment, and Ronnie didn't know it. She should have called. As she was turning away, the door creaked.

Ari poked her head out. Her normally almost spring-loaded curls hung limply around her face, dark shadows circled her eyes, and her aura was barely visible. A tiny smile forced some color into her cheeks when her gaze met Ronnie's, and she opened the door wider. Her voice was quiet. "Hey, what are you doing here?"

"Worrying about you." Ronnie stepped into small apartment. The studio looked a lot like hers: minimal furniture, tiny not-quite kitchen. But the closet was stuffed to spilling over with a rainbow of clothing, and she knew from past experience, at least half the contents of the fridge was butterscotch pudding.

Ari snorted. "After Friday? You should be leaving me to rot. Did you see how furious Gabriel was?"

"Which I don't get. You were just doing what I asked you to."

More of the shadows faded from around Ari's eyes. "You're too sweet to be from hell."

Ronnie didn't know what to say to that. She did know what should lighten the mood, though. "We should go to dinner. Someplace nice. Blow any extra cash we have for the week."

"Maybe we could just walk."

That didn't sound right. "Or we could go for coffee, if you're worried about the money."

"I don't have ti—"

The shrillness in her voice caught Ronnie off guard.

Ari clenched her jaw. It took her a few seconds before her expression softened. "I don't want good coffee to go to waste. I'll explain, I promise. Let's just walk."

"I'd like to go on record as saying I don't like this. I'd like to, but I know you won't listen, so, meh."

Ronnie attached the thought to her own misgivings. But she couldn't find a source for the uneasiness sliding through her. Besides, she missed Ari. "A walk sounds good."

Ari slipped on the pair of flip-flops by the door, and seconds later, they meandered down the sidewalk. Curiosity and concern grew under Ronnie's skin when the silence stretched on.

"I don't have a lot of time left. As in, I could be sent back to heaven at any minute."

When Ari finally spoke, Ronnie jumped and stumbled on an invisible crack in the sidewalk as she processed the words. Despite the warmth of the afternoon sun, a sliver of cold trailed through Ronnie. "Why?"

"Did Gabe offer you a job?"

"Ooh, random. Her tangents and mood swings are almost crazier than those of someone who hears a voice in their head."

Whatever. Ronnie was curious about the direction of the conversation. "He did, but he was a little vague on the details, and I'm not sure I'm cut out to be a barista."

Ari's barked laugh echoed off the nearby buildings. "Really? You're too naïve for your own good."

That was the second time she said something like that, and it didn't sound like a compliment. "So…fill me in?"

"He's not just running a coffee shop." Ari kicked a pebble and sent it scurrying down the sidewalk half a block. "And that job was supposed to be mine. But he won't return my calls, he's never in when I stop by, and now, today, I find out I don't work for Ubiquity anymore either. It's back to ethereal form for me. And all because—" She snapped her mouth shut. "Never mind."

"What happened?" They turned down another street and into a small park. The sun was bright, the temperature was perfect, and there wasn't a cloud in the sky. Yet, the entire place was empty. So strange.

Ari dropped onto a nearby bench. "I'm jumping all over the place. I'm sorry. I'll back up a little. Ubiquity doesn't do all of their own software development. They outsource a lot of their programming."

Ronnie stayed on the sidewalk in front of Ari, shifting her weight from one foot to the other. "Like, overseas? How's that work?"

"No. Like to a different building down the street. That's what Gabriel does. He heads up these contract developers. In addition, he's got a very small group of us—sorry, them, I'm not one after all—who seek out the challenges. There are the cherubs the regular Ubiquity staff goes after—the newbies who don't know how to hide themselves, who give in to every temptation out there. And then there are those like the guy in Israel."

How did Ari know about him? This encounter sent nervous energy coursing all the way into Ronnie's fingernails. She was talking to her best friend, her confidant. So where did this doubt come from?

And Ari was implying this other team of Gabriel's had better algorithms than Ubiquity did. Why weren't those universal? "I'm still missing something."

Her laugh made Ronnie's blood run cold. "You're still missing so much, I'm surprised it doesn't make you dizzy. The top performers at Ubiquity? We get the good leads. The hard to spot ones. Think of it like auditioning or proving yourself for a promotion. If we can handle them, we get to move on. Or they do."

Something triggered in the back of Ronnie's thoughts, and she grasped it. "You said hard to spot ones. Like… the one in Gabe's coffee shop? Why don't you capture all of them?"

"Why didn't you take the one in Israel?"

"How do you know about that?" Ronnie knew she didn't tell Ari about him.

"Gabe asked me to pass him to you. To see what you would do. Your unwitting trial run became another nail in my coffin. Why did you leave him behind?"

"Look at her aura. It was nearly dead when you showed up, and now it's almost neon. I don't think a random rabbi is the biggest concern we have."

Ronnie hadn't noticed, but now that Metatron pointed it out, it seemed strange. "Because he was already doing more than any angel ever could. Sending him back to heaven or hell wouldn't help anyone."

Ari smirked and stood. "Exactly. You, for instance, you don't deserve what you've got. I don't know where you took it from, or how you don't know, but you shouldn't have it."

Ronnie's uneasiness scaled from wary to full-blown what-the-fuck in under a second.

Ari's aura flared. "They found out I kept a cherub and took it away. That's why they're sending me back. But if I had whatever it is you've got, whatever it is you won't even touch that makes originals flock to you like you're the only demon ever to inhabit a female body, they couldn't take me away from this plane."

"I'll kill you where you stand."

The roar screamed through Ronnie's skull, but instead of feeling like foreign ribbons, this was familiar and safe. "It's not yours."

"It should be." Ari spun in a blur, foot sweeping to the side, kicking Ronnie's legs from beneath her and knocking her to the ground. Ari straddled her, one hand on Ronnie's upper arm, and the other resting on her neck.

Ronnie struggled against the weight on her chest. The edges of her vision flickered and dimmed, sliding into black. Being strangled wouldn't kill her, but it wouldn't be pleasant either. She needed to shift to her ethereal form, so Ari couldn't incapacitate her physical one.

"We need to destroy her."

"Don't you dare." Ari's sneer cut through Ronnie's fading consciousness before she could phase away her flesh.

A new level of pain rocked through Ronnie's body as if every inch of her was being torn in different directions simultaneously. It dragged back the unpleasant memories of the spear in Gabe's basement.

"It's funny you showed up today. I was trying to figure out how to get you to talk to me again without looking suspicious, and you didn't even know enough to realize you should be upset with me. You never realized I meant to take this from you for myself at the club." Ari's taunt swam through the agony. "We're not doing things the easy way this time."

"No. No we're not."

Ronnie agreed one-hundred and ten percent. An itch rolled through her palms, and before the realization fully formed, she knew what it was. She didn't want the swords yet but soon. She closed her eyes and focused inward, driving past the pain to grab hold of the inky ribbons she so frequently tried to get rid of.

This time, Ronnie slid into them instead. Diving into the power the same way she would if she were touching Gabriel. As she opened her eyes to the world, a snarl escaped her throat. She rolled from underneath Ari, knocking her back.

Ari stumbled but landed on her feet, moving into a defensive posture in a flash—hands up, legs spaced for stability. "You won't keep this from me."

She aimed a kick at Ronnie's head. Ronnie ducked and rolled. She didn't know any of this fighting stuff, she wasn't even sure how she was doing it, but she was. It was as if she'd been fighting for centuries.

"It feels good to let loose after so long."

Ronnie didn't know or care who the thought belonged to. This time, she didn't stop the blades from appearing in her hands—a long one in the right and a dagger-length one in her left. Different from Metatron's in the chapel and far more comfortable.

Ari narrowed her eyes. "You can't do that. No one but an original can."

"I'm a special little snowflake." Ronnie advanced slowly, Ari taking a step back for each step she took forward, until Ari's back was to a nearby tree. This was her best friend. The one person Ronnie shared everything with. Now Ari wanted to kill her for something inside her head she didn't even understand. Betrayal and fury throbbed in Ronnie. There really wasn't anyone she could trust.

"Except Michael."

"Maybe."

And Irdu. Always Irdu.

Ronnie raised the tip of her blade to Ari's throat. As far as Ronnie knew, she didn't have the power to kill her, but she could send her back to heaven early.

"You could do to her what her boyfriend did to us."

Gabriel. Ronnie was heading there next. Spoon feeding her power and convincing her it was lust—or more? He was definitely next. Fury poured through her, and she reveled in it. Vengeance tasted better than she thought it would.

Orange glowed in Ari's hands, and before Ronnie could react, a ball of flame slammed into her chest and sent her stumbling back. Ari smirked. "We don't use swords anymore, because projectiles are far more effective."

Ronnie found her footing and adopted a defensive posture. "Or because you don't have the focus to summon a real weapon."

Ari snorted. "You sound like you were trained eons ago. You need to get that fucker out of your head and hand it over to me before you start believing you and it are the same."

"Too late."

Ronnie ignored the taunts and lunged again. Irritation and rage filled her. Lying, sadistic, pretending-to-be-her-friend-to-steal-from-her bitch. Time to fix that.

Ronnie backed Ari into another tree, but apparently she expected it this time. Ari ducked under one blade, drove a shoulder enveloped in ethereal flame into Ronnie's abdomen, and then rolled aside. A dull throb spilled through Ronnie, and she doubled over. Pushing the pain aside, she whirled and faltered.

Michael stood at the edge of the clearing in his full angelic form, sword drawn. He made Gabe's glory look like a cheap magic trick. He both blended with the sunlight and exuded it, and his wings were a stunning charcoal.

Fortunately for Ronnie, she wasn't the only one at a standstill. Ari's eyes were wide, her gaze locked on Michael. He wasn't going to distract Ronnie from the fight.

She snarled "Ariel! Are we doing this?"

"What is *this*?" Michael's tone matched the aura he radiated.

"I'm so sorry." His presence drained the fight from Ari. She stepped back, eyes wide and sunken. "I didn't… I just wanted… I'm sorry."

Ronnie gave a short laugh. "Don't you dare. Don't turn your phony, bullshit, puppy dog eyes on him. You're only sorry you got caught."

He narrowed his eyes. "Judgment isn't your place, Uriel."

Part of Ronnie wanted to shrink under the glare, and bits of her shriveled at the way *that name* rolled off his tongue, but she was intent on her goal. She never took her attention from Ari. How dare he interfere? "You don't know that. What if judgment was my job before this?"

"Don't forget who the enemy is."

"If you do this because of a personal vendetta, you won't be happy with the outcome." His response shook the trees.

"I've lived through worse."

"Uriel."

The name made her mind flinch. Why didn't she like hearing the sound of that? "My name is Ronnie." She struggled to keep the anger and force in her voice, but her blades sparkled and faded from sight. She stepped closer to Ari. If Ronnie couldn't finish her off and send her back to her ethereal home, the fight was still going to end on her terms. Ronnie would send her away because she wanted Ari to go, not because Michael ordered it. "Maybe he deserves a little of your worship after all. He just saved your life. Go."

With the single command, Ronnie made Ari vanish from sight, phasing her back to her apartment, while Ronnie stayed where she was. Neat. It was nice to know she could do that. Ronnie turned on Michael. "Why did you stop me?"

"I told you why."

She laughed, but his response made her ache inside. Had he really picked Ari over her? "I thought we were in this together. Is this going to be like last time? When I thought you were by my side, and you let Gabriel slaughter me instead?"

Wait. That wasn't what happened. And how did Ronnie know that?

"It might as well have been."

Michael reached for her. "No, this isn't like last time, and that wasn't you. We *are* in this together."

Ronnie stepped away. "Then will you stop me, if I pay Gabriel a visit?"

He exhaled loudly, disappointment shining in his eyes. "Yes."

Ronnie frowned and turned away. That he would stand in her way hurt more than any sword to the gut. "Then I should be grateful you can't." And with that, she left.

Chapter Twenty-Five

Ronnie didn't know what raced through her, but it was exhilarating and maddening and euphoric, all at the same time. Snippets of memories danced at the edge of her thoughts but flitted away before she could grasp them. There was too much rage and vengeance for her to focus on anything else for more than a few seconds.

She should have listened to Michael. It was wrong for her to be here.

"He's still got his weaknesses. He doesn't understand this. Do you really think Ari would have let us live? Do you think she cared?"

No. Ronnie knew it in a way that sent daggers of betrayal through her chest. She appeared in front of Gabriel's coffee shop. He'd give her answers, or she'd draw them out with her blades.

"Stop." Michael materialized between Ronnie and the door, wings spread and sword drawn.

"Move." Fire and ice raced across her skin, through her hair, and all around them. Her aura clashed and danced with his.

"No."

She studied his form—so much ancient power, and so much weaker than he used to be. How did she know that? There were tiny fractures in his aura. As he shifted his weight from one foot to the other, whispers of light snuck through his blade.

"Even if you were serious about stopping me, which you're not doing a great job of, you're not strong enough."

Everything angelic about him faded. His blade sparkled into a pile of glitter and vanished, his wings evaporated, and the lightning radiating from his quasi-mortal form ebbed. "Talk to me."

She stepped in, shoulder to his, to shove him aside. He moved with her, resting his hand on her cheek and drawing her gaze to his. "Uriel. Please." His tone dropped in volume, but not strength.

A whimper rose in her chest—hers, but not. *That's not my name.* But it was. She shook her head to get rid of the confusion, and forced indifference through her mind. "Move or I'll cut you down."

He dropped his hands at his sides, palms out. "If that's the only way to do this."

"No. Make him move. We have to finish Gabe once and for all."

The mental plea wasn't enough to make her act. "Let me find Gabriel."

Finger under her chin, he raised her head. "There are other ways to get answers, and we both know one of them."

Answers? For us?

"There's no better way for revenge, though." Even as half her brain considered Michael's words, the other half tore on toward obliterating Gabriel.

"He killed us in cold blood. Took away everything. Stuck us in this shitty life. We will make him bleed for eternity."

The thoughts were so distinct, they might as well have been hers, but the words didn't feel right when she tried to force them out. He hadn't done those things to her. He was an insistent bastard about their relationship, but...

"He needs to pay. And then we'll find Ari. When this is all over, we will have our life back."

We? They weren't— Dizziness rocketed through her skull. She cringed and tried to shake it away. "I don't... I need..." *What was I trying to say?*

"Stop." The command was gentler this time. He glided his fingers along her jaw to the back of her neck and dipped his head to brush his lips over hers.

The barely-there kiss chased away some of her fury, and she scrambled to cling to the anger. But why?

"This isn't fair. Why now?"

He broke away and rested his forehead against hers. "You know why you can't do this, don't you? Why it's not right to hunt down Gabriel and Ariel and exact vengeance on them?"

"No."

The protest was weak, and no part of her believed it. He was right earlier. Vengeance wasn't her place.

"No, it's Gabriel's, and he deserves to get as good as he gives. He took something from us. Let's take something from him in return."

The rage wasn't there though. It evaporated as rapidly as it set in.

Michael still watched her, waiting for an answer.

"I know," Ronnie said.

"So we can talk about this?"

"I don't want to talk." She heard too much talking as it was. In her head, at work… There were always voices. And she didn't even know which were hers.

"Okay." He intertwined his fingers with hers, and the world faded around them. She clung to the emptiness as the seconds dragged on, confusion racing back in as they solidified in front of Izzy's church.

"What are we doing here?" Not that she minded visiting Izzy, what were Michael's reasons?

She was supposed to meet Irdu here. The new name helped push aside more of the haze, but not enough. Why would she spend time with him? He was no one. A middle-management demon.

Ronnie's heart clenched at the dismissal. That wasn't right. He was so much more.

Michael pulled her toward a side door that opened to a flight of stairs. "I told you. Answers."

She let him lead her, still struggling with the rage that had enveloped her and then vanished as quickly as it appeared. They paused at the top of the stairs, in front of a gray door with so much paint chipping away, she saw the metal underneath. All the confusion tumbled to the back of her mind when the door swung open.

"Izzy." She threw her arms around his neck. Relief and joy coursed through her at the familiar face.

He gave her a squeeze. "Angel. I shouldn't have left when you were last here. I've been looking for your other half for centuries, and I just hopped on a plane to Fiji instead."

"She's not my *other half.*" She pulled back, studying him with a scowl.

Izzy looked at Michael. "You haven't had a chance to fill her in. Come on in. You're not the first ones here."

*

Irdu was still reconciling how he felt about Michael. The guy was willing to help. He'd seemed genuinely concerned about Ronnie earlier. And now he was nudging her into Izzy's apartment.

"It's been an interesting couple of hours," Michael said as he perched on the arm of the couch farthest from Irdu.

Izzy shook his head and settled in his favorite chair. "You tell me our mutual friend hosts an original in her head and what came *after* was interesting?"

Ronnie looked between Michael and Irdu. Something wasn't right. Her aura was muddy, and the look in her eyes distant.

She settled on a spot somewhere between the two of them.

Irdu couldn't ignore the disappointment that spiked inside.

"So, everyone knows everyone." Irdu wasn't going to overreact. He did want to find out what happened to Ronnie, and wrap her up and comfort her.

"But I might be the only person who doesn't know why we're here." Ronnie's voice held a sharp edge.

Irdu wondered the same about Michael. But the more the merrier?

Unless he wanted to share his secret. An original angel—one who had admitted he couldn't keep secrets—wasn't the guy Irdu wanted to tell the one thing he wasn't allowed to tell anyone.

Izzy nodded to a stack of books. "We're here to tell you what's happening to you, and discuss a way to fix it." He focused on Ronnie again. "It took some cross-referencing to make sense of it, but the gist is there are angels who fall but still find a way to have access to His power. I understand the big guy over here outed me as having done this myself. So I have a little bit of an idea of what you're going through."

Irdu did a double take with Izzy. Why had he never seen that before? The glow wasn't residual power, it was a distinct power source?

Izzy met his gaze. "I'd rather no one at Ubiquity know. I'm not worried about you, but the more people who know…"

"I understand." All too well. "But Ronnie's not the same." Irdu was certain, because he wasn't the same. "You fell, and took on a cherub without any memories of its own."

Izrafel shuffled the books around. "It's true. Metatron's an original. Since there were only four, no, there's no precedent."

There was a little precedent. Would Irdu sharing his fate help here? He'd assumed that since Lucifer knew about both cases, the ruler of Hell had already done what he could for Ronnie. But what if that wasn't true?

"What about angels or demons coming back from the dead in general?" Ronnie's voice was tiny. Almost scared.

"They don't." Izrafel finally looked up. "They don't die—not as angels. They fall and die mortal, or they stay where they are."

"What about Metatron?"

That was the one difference. The cherub who sought out Irdu did it to get a body without having to be named. It wasn't run through by a pissed off colleague.

Izrafel shook his head. "Metatron didn't die."

Michael frowned. "You were there. You know otherwise."

"You and Gabriel were there, and even you can't tell me what actually happened."

"She faded. Her energy left. She was nothing but an empty shell." Michael sounded as though diving into that past caused him physical pain.

Irdu could only imagine. Seeing Tia or Ronnie die once would kill him. Having to relive that death thousands of years later, if grief let him live that long, even the thought of it gripped his chest and made his entire body tense.

"Yes," Izrafel said. "As far as I can tell, that all happened, but she didn't die. The shell that was still there? A representation of her. It would have vanished if she did. I've never, anywhere, found anything to indicate she's gone for good. Her light left, but she wasn't destroyed."

All those years. The grieving. And Michael had never known she was still out there. No wonder he was fascinated by Ronnie.

But he shouldn't be. He needed to leave the Uriel part of her alone if he didn't care about the demon who was suffering.

"Why haven't you ever told me this before?" Michael asked.

Izrafel's eyes softened with sympathy and pity. "You've never gotten over her. I wasn't going to make it worse. Even if she's not dead, she's not here. Or she wasn't." He turned to Ronnie, gaze traveling her entire form before locking on her eyes again. "What's your name?"

"You know my name." She pursed her lips. It would have been a kissable response if the situation weren't so serious.

"I do. But do you?" Izrafel said.

Her jaw worked up and down for several seconds before she responded. "Ronnie."

"Your given name."

The exchange fascinated and concerned Irdu. Right now her aura wasn't mud. It flared and sparkled like a million colored gems in the afternoon sun. There was no question, both auras shone were shining through.

Irdu never dealt with that either, since half of him had been human.

She opened her mouth, but no sound came out. "Uriel," she finally blurted out.

"Making sure." Izrafel looked relieved.

She sank back into the cushions, drumming her fingers on her leg.

He moved from his seat and kneeled in front of her. "You wanted to say Metatron."

The light went on for Irdu. The reason she showed up with Michael... The tightness in her voice and the words that weren't quite her. She wasn't completely Uriel right now.

"This isn't fun. What do you know that I don't?" Ronnie said.

Izrafel explained in detail about fallen angels, cherubs, and what he called *going rogue.*

Ronnie rolled her eyes. "Old news, really. Since one just tried to off me in the park."

"What?" Irdu's question came out louder than he intended.

She looked at him, somehow managing to pull of cold and sympathetic at the same time. "Ari attacked me when I went to see her. She tried to take part of me."

"She tried to take Metatron. Which is not part of you." Irdu liked this less with each passing moment.

"Yes, but no. Ronnie's special." Izrafel traced a line down the side of her face before standing and making himself comfortable in the chair again. "This wasn't an instance of a random cherub and a willing agent. Someone intentionally stuck Metatron inside your head—you, an individual with your own life and memories—without consulting either one of you first."

Like Lucifer had done for Tia. Except Tia's cherub didn't have a life beforehand. Fucking hell.

Ronnie gave Izzy a weak smile. "No offense, but I've pretty much already guessed most of this."

He didn't flinch. "And the two of you are finally starting to merge."

Irdu understood the changes in her aura correctly. He didn't know how he felt about that. One personality always became dominant when two clashed, even if they merged. Memories would be shared, but someone would lose out. When Ronnie squeezed his hand, his doubt magnified.

He wouldn't lose the Uriel he'd fallen for to some bitch from the past.

Ronnie glanced at Irdu. "Michael told me he helps cherubs merge with hosts, but that he couldn't predict the outcome in my case. That's not an option for me. I like being *me*."

"I like you being you, too." Irdu slid closer to her on the cushions, and kissed the back of her knuckles.

She smiled and leaned into him, rather than scooting away. "Why is she in my head in the first place?"

Michael spoke quietly. "You'd have to ask the person who put her there. I don't suppose you know who it was? Lucifer maybe?"

Good luck getting answers there. Irdu's confession about his origins hovered on the tip of his tongue.

"Why would he do that?" Ronnie asked.

"What's the first thing you remember?" Izrafel asked.

"Sand? Vast patches of people-free land. A temple in the middle of the desert?"

Michael tensed.

Ronnie hadn't lived that life. Those were Metatron's memories. Irdu had no doubt.

Izrafel shook his head. "First thing *you* remember, not Metatron." His voice was soft and coaxing. "You can tell the difference. Focus on what's yours."

"Waking up in Lucifer's office in hell."

"Then you have to ask him why you and Metatron share a body."

Michael growled. "Show of hands… Who here thinks he'll give a straight answer?"

The lack of hands in the air was louder than the most powerful shout.

Irdu swallowed. Should he tell this story? This would put Tia at risk.

Only if Lucifer found out.

At least three people in this room could keep a secret.

Would the fourth keep her safe, if Lucifer made good on his threat?

Ronnie squeezed his hand again. "You still here?"

She was coming back toward herself. That was a relief.

He focused on Michael. "I may have more information. It's not an answer, but it might offer insight. If I tell you this, *you* have to swear to do everything in your power to keep my sister safe."

"Demons don't have sisters," Michael said at the same time Ronnie said, "You have a sister?"

Irdu had already said too much to turn back now. "Tia is my sister. Promise me."

"Tia, the demon who sits next to me at work?" Ronnie sounding perplexed was much better than Ronnie being cold and half-Metatron.

"I promise," Michael said. "Everything in my power to keep her safe."

Irdu took a deep breath, and gathered his words. *Please let this be the right decision.*

Chapter Twenty-Six

Ronnie listened to Irdu's story, about a demonic cherub bonding with his mortal body; about Lucifer finding and helping him deal with the process; about the voice Irdu dealt with, until Lucifer merged the two entities…

Her disbelief warred with hurt. He was the one person who had any idea what she'd gone through, and she held off telling him, because they were arguing over stupid bullshit things like how she felt about original angels.

And even when she did tell him, he didn't share with her. He never once said *I get it. Here's why.*

On top of that, Lucifer knew. He had a solution. And he hadn't fucking used it.

"Ronnie?" Irdu studied her, concern dancing in his amber gaze.

How was she supposed to respond? She couldn't. The words weren't there. Even Metatron was silent. But this wasn't like every other time with Irdu. Metatron wasn't gone, she just lingered quietly in the back of Ronnie's mind.

"I need… I need some air." She stood and walked away, her mind still reeling with the information.

She wandered downstairs, and into the chapel. It was quiet in here. Peaceful. With Izzy back, the feeling was even more potent.

Because he carried the power of an angel, without actually having to be one.

That was so very much the least of her concerns.

She wasn't sure how long she sat in the pew, staring at her feet, when she felt the energy in the room shift.

It was Irdu.

"I'm sorry." His voice was quiet.

She didn't look up, but she could tell from the energy flowing through the room that he remained at a distance. "So I've heard."

"This is different. I promise you."

She didn't want to hear that. "How?"

"I would have told you. I wanted to tell you. And at the same time, I shouldn't have said anything today. This isn't about me. It never was. I'm tired of being under Lucifer's thumb. He can do whatever he wants to me. This is for Tia."

His sister. He was related to the fun, friendly demon who sat next to Ronnie at work. Actually related. Not just a *we were born of the same demon* kind of thing.

"I get it." And she did. She patted the bench next to her. "I'm hurt, but I'm not angry. I understand why you did it. Is she going to be all right?"

"I don't know. I trust Michael when he says he'll do what he can." Irdu crossed the room and sat by her.

"Yeah. He kind of gives off that air, doesn't he?"

Irdu wrapped an arm around her, and she leaned into his shoulder. "We're making progress," he said. "It's slow. But I'm not going to let them pick some ancient bitch over you, and I'm not letting you go insane while we figure out answers."

She believed that, too. As much as she trusted anything Michael said, this meant more. "I know."

*

Ronnie winced at the streams of light striking her closed eyelids. She forced one eye open, trying to figure out when her northern-facing window started facing east. It wasn't daylight after all. Darkness still reigned, and the brightness of the full moon shone through the temple door.

Her surroundings swam into focus. Her head rose and fell at a steady pace, heat seeping into her cheek. Michael's chest. She must have fallen asleep against him. Vague memories of a few hours ago drifted back as she pressed closer. Did they really fall asleep talking in the temple?

A soft groan escaped from him when she tried to stretch without waking him up. His shoulders shifted with each breath. He muttered and wrapped an arm around her when she shifted.

"Don't." His soft command was whispered on the late-night air as he grabbed the back of her tunic and held her in place.

She settled against him, a smile creeping onto her face. "Don't what?"

"Don't move." He didn't open his eyes. "You're warm. I'm comfortable."

Her smile grew, and she lay back down, trailing her fingers along his chest. "As you wish."

He brushed his lips over the top of her head. "Unless you have somewhere more important to be."

"Nope."

Ronnie's eyes flew open, gaze landing on an unfamiliar coffee table. That was right; they stayed up late, talking to Izzy. Her thoughts were clear, the lingering traces of the dream enhancing each one. It occurred to her that for the first time since she started dreaming about the past, she didn't wake in a cold sweat. She was lucid and aware. She had no idea why Metatron chose to share that with her, but she didn't mind the warmth it filled her with.

She leaned into the figure pressed against her back. Irdu's arm draped across her stomach. The gesture was so comfortable. So right

Michael lay on the floor in front of the couch, as if he thought he could keep her safe, even while she slept. With the silence sinking in around them, and the lingering sensations from the dream dancing in her thoughts, she wanted all of this to last beyond tonight.

She'd pushed Michael away because of the adoration he and Metatron shared. But Ronnie didn't question his concern for her. He was trying to help. Somewhere along the way, she started to fall for him.

But she still adored Irdu. She wanted them both. How selfish was that?

Damn it. Something told her that was one of the worst things she could hope for.

A glance at the clock in the kitchen told her it was both too late and too early for anything to be open. It didn't matter. She needed air. Solitude. More than she'd find even if she didn't run into anyone else, but the stillness of the early morning would be a nice start.

She extracted herself from Irdu's arms, an ache echoing inside at leaving safety behind. She could have phased out of the room, but she enjoyed the physical contact too much to rush away from it.

Moments later, she tiptoed from the apartment and down the stairs. She paused on the sidewalk in front Izzy's church, reveling in the simplicity of the night air brushing her skin.

The struggle with Ari in the park seemed forever ago. A damp breeze glided across her bare arms, and she smiled. The clean air and quiet street added to her clarity. She wished the lucidity came with more answers, but at least she could think about the questions now.

"Are we on speaking terms?"

Ronnie walked, not caring about direction. If Metatron could talk to her in their dreams, ignoring her was pointless.

"Took you long enough to figure it out. But, you still could try."

A hint of smoke floated past her, carried on a dry breeze. Sirens wailed in the distance. It wasn't Ronnie's fault no one taught her how to interpret the subconscious messages of the dead angel living in her head. Maybe if Lucifer imbued her with the knowledge of what to do when the voices talked back…

The acrid stench in the air made her grimace. A flash of orange lit up the night sky, flickering in the distance. She hoped whatever was on fire didn't hurt anyone.

The pain of heated razors sliced her skin—the too familiar sensation of being separated from Metatron. It crept up in intensity. Ronnie frowned. As far as she could tell, Ari wasn't anywhere nearby, and Ronnie wasn't trying to get rid of Metatron.

"You're not? Since when?"

Since she was tired of feeling as if she was being flayed alive, which hardly made her unreasonable. Flashes of orange spread over the city skyline. She hoped the fire wasn't spreading. What a terrible way to wake up. Her dreams were nothing compared to that kind of horror. Speaking of her subconscious, if Metatron was so helpful, why was Ronnie still in the dark?

"One assumes it's because you're still not listening."

The pain she associated with trying to suppress Metatron intensified, slicing through her and making her stumble. Stronger than she ever experienced before, the scalding cuts shredding her. Where was that coming from? Outside her—that was certain— but beyond that, she couldn't find the source. She leaned against a nearby post, struggling to catch her breath. Each inhale sent the daggers deeper into her lungs. She coughed.

"Let me help you fight this."

Ronnie may not be trying to evict her, at least not using any previous methods attempted, but Metatron wasn't taking over again. Ronnie wouldn't let her. Ribbons of Metatron's inky power crawled under her skin, and she searched around them, summoning everything she could find of her own strength to block the pain. Ice flowed through Ronnie, and the throbbing ebbed. Where did that come from? It wasn't Metatron, for sure.

"You're delusional."

So much for a truce with the voice in her head. That conversation went downhill fast. Except, as the flow of chill rolled through her, she realized something. She looked inside herself with her second sight to confirm. The icy sensation came from wisps of gray tendrils—Ronnie's. Her own power. How did she not see that before? Had Metatron kept it from her?

Another flash lit up the night, an orange ball rocketing into the sky and hovering. It sent a wash of knives across Ronnie. She gasped, leaning heavier against her support. Why the fuck did that hurt so much?

"Start fighting."

"I can't breathe." Ronnie collapsed to her knees, gasping.

"Let me help."

No. She wouldn't surrender herself, even for relief.

"This pain, whatever it is, could kill you."

Ronnie doubted that. Heat scorched her bare back, and she didn't know if it was the warmth of the fire-filled air or something worse. It hurt like God-only-knows-what, but it wasn't doing any discernible damage. She struggled to find the threads of ice there moments earlier.

"You can't have them."

Holy hell. Really? How did she take that away? Where was it hidden now? Ronnie wheezed, each breath hurting more. Did Metatron want her dead? And what was she doing with Ronnie's power?

"I thought this wasn't going to kill you."

"The pain won't. Having my insides torn from me by an unseen source might." Ronnie smiled as something occurred to her. Sometimes she was so dense.

"Sometimes?"

"Shut up."

With a flash of thought, her form flickered, and she shifted to a quasi-mortal shape. The pain evaporated as her physical body faded. She continued walking, still not interested in being anywhere specific. Fury and hatred tickled the back of her mind when Metatron growled.

Ronnie flew backward before she registered something hot collided with her chest. She slammed into a nearby wall with a grunt and stumbled before finding her balance.

"Don't ignore me." Ari's threat rolled over concrete and shook the walls.

At least now Ronnie knew where the being-torn-asunder sensation came from. She wished she knew how Ari found her. That might be useful information to have.

"Make her let go of me."

Ronnie summoned every memory from earlier and reached for the ethereal swords. Static and white noise flowed through her arms, nothing like the power she felt the last two times. Nothing happened.

Fuck.

Another burst of flame, this one only golf ball-sized, struck Ronnie's shoulder and knocked her back.

Ari stalked forward. "Last cherub I kept was brand new. No memories, just enthusiasm and power. This one is different." A roar filled her words.

She already had another one? Why would anyone do that willingly? Especially twice. "So you can stay now, right? That's what you wanted."

Ari cackled—an honest-to-God-evil cackle. Ronnie might have been amused except the sensation of having her flesh torn from her still consumed most of her focus. Why couldn't she fight back? Did Metatron want to go with Ari?

"Make her stop, please."

The terrified whimper echoed in Ronnie's skull. Was she kidding? Weeks of torment, and she chose now to break? The remainder of Ronnie's bravado vanished when she stepped backward and tripped on a rock. She fell, and a stabbing pain rolled through her spine and legs.

Ari paused a few feet back. "I have all his memories now. Everything from your priest buddy. Angel of music? Really? How lame. I know how much he adored Lucifer and Metatron, why he had Michael help him keep this little ball of light. That he hopes you won't be you when this is over." She smirked. "I don't want to just stay on Earth. I want what you have and won't use."

Oh, shit, she was talking about Izzy. The realization added a heavy layer of dread to Ronnie's growing panic. What did Ari do to him? Ronnie had to get back to him. But she needed to stop Ari from tearing her apart first.

"If this is what his past is like, yours will be a decadence wrapped in glory." Ari kneeled in front of her and cupped Ronnie's cheek. "Just a couple more tugs, and I'll know what Michael kisses like. What Gabriel can actually do with that spear. And I bet *she* was immensely powerful. She was an original. I can't believe I didn't see that before. You have a fucking original living in your skull, and you not only won't use her power, you don't even want it."

Agony tore through Ronnie. If every bone in her body shattered at once, she didn't think it would hurt so much. She couldn't hold back a scream and couldn't find the strength to make Ari stop. Metatron's energy slipped from her veins and the mental voice faded.

Without warning, an icy wave rushed in to take her place. Similar to what Ronnie found moments earlier. It wasn't like Metatron. It was Ronnie. She let it flow through her, and though it didn't stop the pain, it gave her the strength to fight back. She kicked with all the force she could muster, landing a foot in Ari's gut. Ari stumbled back, and Ronnie was on her feet in an instant.

Ari caught her balance, but it gave Ronnie enough time to summon her swords. Something she could throw would have been nice, given her reach, but she'd settle for what her muscle memory knew.

Ari held her arms out to the sides, and the buildings around them erupted in flame. "He was intensely powerful and never used it. He only wanted immortality. What a waste." She looked at Ronnie again, eyes hard and jaw set. "What's your excuse?"

Was? He'd better be alive. *Please don't let him be gone.* Screwing with Ronnie was one thing. Fucking with Izzy? He didn't deserve that. With the ice flowing through her, and Metatron cowering in the back of her skull, she could mute the pain. If Ari hurt Izzy, Ronnie was going to make her suffer. She needed to go on the offensive, and that meant getting closer.

Ari's attention shifted to something behind Ronnie, and instinct reacted before Ronnie's thoughts caught up. She lunged, longer sword already aimed for Ari's neck. This wasn't the fury that consumed her earlier. It was self-preservation, vengeance, and one hundred percent Ronnie's. Ari ducked under the first blade, twisted around the second, and then planted a foot in the back of Ronnie's knee. Ronnie was already turning. She recovered and sliced the edge of blade through Ari's shirt, leaving a red slash across her back.

Ari snarled and whirled.

A new voice roared through the flames. "This ends now."

Ari smirked and slid into a defensive posture. "Oh, goodie. One of your boyfriends is here. Have you told him yet that you're the office whore?" The snarl rolled under the growl of flames. "This ends when I have what I came for. Walk away, has-been." Her gaze never left Ronnie, even as she taunted Michael.

The insult rolled off Ronnie. It was so minor compared to the fear Izzy was dead. Even if Ronnie didn't hear Michael's voice, she'd know it was him. His aura filled the air. She tasted him in the single threat—every one of her senses alive and aware. Clouds rolled in, and thunder rattled the sky. Wet smoke surged as black raindrops fell. Seconds later he stood by Ronnie's side, mouth near her ear. "Walk away."

He must be joking. "Fuck that." Her blades flickered, the left one growing and then shrinking again every few seconds.

"I used to look up to you." Ari's raw voice danced with the dying flame. "But you're nothing. None of you. The greats are just names. And *you*." She narrowed her eyes at Ronnie. "You have this incredible gift, and all you do is whine about it. So I'm going to relieve you of it."

She reached out, and Ronnie stepped back, raising her swords. Rain sliced through the semi-transparent blades. What was happening? "Don't touch me."

"Come on." Ari's expression melted into something grotesquely angelic. "It'll only hurt for a moment and then never again."

Ronnie swung, but whatever gave her the knowledge to fight was gone. She faltered. Ari stepped back long before the blade reached her.

Who was Ronnie kidding? With Metatron cowering, she was a joke. "I'm sorry," she said to no one in particular. Her voice melted into the pouring drops.

"Aww, she wants absolution," Ari mocked. "Death bed repentance doesn't work unless you mean it."

Arrogant assumption. Ronnie clenched her jaw. "I'm sorry all you see when you look at me is her. I'm not her. I'm not sorry that I never will be." She was sick of people expecting it of her. She sucked in a deep breath, and the weapons in her hands solidified. "And I'm tired of everyone overlooking me, in favor of fawning over a memory several thousand years old."

The words carried every frustration she held inside, and she knew this was all her. There was no doubt to whom the feelings belonged. The ground shook with her realization, accompanied by her tremendous roar that rattled the buildings.

"This is still my life." Ronnie lunged forward, all hesitation gone.

Ari dodged, tossing the occasional fireball, but for the most part, she stayed on the defensive. "It's not yours. What life? What you do isn't living, and no one's going to remember you after tonight."

Ronnie's calculated swing caught her in the arm, and vibrant red joined the dark night. Ari recovered quickly, ducking under the sword as she slid behind Ronnie.

The next few seconds moved in slow motion. Ronnie whirled in time to see a softball-size flame form in Ari's hand. Behind Ari, power surged through Michael. The glow of faith enveloped him until he was almost as bright as daylight. He held his palms together and then moved one hand up and one down, and his sword appeared between them.

He lunged, and the blade sliced through Ari's middle. His weapon sparkled and then vanished into nothing, taking her with it as the glow around him faded. And just like that, it was over.

Ari's destruction didn't rid Ronnie of the roaring emotion inside her, but it did snuff the confusion. An eerie, sound-dampening blanket draped the night, muffling the cacophony. Ronnie stuck a finger in her ear. A melody of sirens cut through the haze, accompanied by a concert of terrified screams. *Nope, hearing is fine.* She stared at Michael, not sure what to say. She didn't even know what to think. *Wow, I'm screwed up in the head.*

"Is Izzy okay?" That was a good start.

"He's been better, but he'll be all right." Michael crossed the space between them, rested both hands on her cheeks, and then kissed her deeply. Her confusion quieted, and she sank into the peace. She memorized the soft sensation of his lips against hers. She'd stay wrapped in this forever if she thought it would solve everything.

Too bad that wasn't a real solution. She broke the kiss long enough to mutter, "I'm still not her."

He caught her lower lip between his teeth. "I don't want you to be."

"But what if I'm no one?"

"You're someone. I promise you. It radiates from every inch of your essence." He traced a damp strand of hair off her forehead. The simple touch hurt almost as much as having Metatron ripped from her but in an entirely new way.

That was enough. It would have to be. Ronnie couldn't process any more in that moment. The adrenaline evaporated, and exhaustion rushed in to take its place. "Okay." She slumped against him. "Thank you," she whispered.

He kissed her forehead, and before she passed out, she was aware of his arms encircling her, catching her.

* * * *

Michael lay Ronnie on his couch, and sank onto the floor next to her. It was a simple trick to draw the water from her soaking clothes to dry her, but he didn't know how to wake her up. Physically, he felt more alive than in centuries. So much power coursed through him, but mentally, he felt ancient.

He'd left Irdu with Izzy. The incubus argued up a storm, but in the end, he admitted he couldn't fight. He was a liability against Ariel. He was a shield if he stayed with Izzy.

Michael swore to protect Ronnie, not that he needed someone else to prompt that, and made Irdu promise to keep himself and Izzy alive as well.

Ronnie's apartment was another casualty, proof Arial looked for Ronnie at more than just Izrafel's place. Michael didn't look forward to breaking that news to her. If he hated the idea of hurting her with something so trivial, he was screwed when it came to more.

When he saw Ariel fighting Ronnie, a fear he never expected to feel again surged back. Terror that someone he cared about was about to lose their life. The objectivity he hoped for by trying to keep his distance while staying in her life remained elusive. He was still falling for her.

When he and Metatron were in love, they could have stayed angels and still been together. No rules prevented it. Living as a mortal was a different experience than temporarily assuming a mortal form, and it was one they wanted to share. An ideal he abandoned when she vanished.

For the last several decades he'd been dangerously close to making the same decision. Spending more time in his physical body. Shunning the politics of the heavens.

However, experiencing the world through Ronnie's eyes reminded him he wasn't living. Simply existing.

Outside, sirens and rain still sang in painful symphony. He blocked it all out, sinking into the darkness of the living room.

His phone rang, startling him. A glance at the caller ID told him it was Lucifer. "Yeah?"

"Is she safe?"

Michael glanced at Ronnie, pleased to see her still curled up in a peaceful ball. How did such a simple sight warm him to the core? "What makes you think I know?"

"Because it's been less than twenty-four hours since I asked you to walk away from her, one of heaven's former best and brightest tried to burn the city to the ground, and you've finally owned up to who you are. Welcome back, by the way."

He meant the power Michael drew on to destroy Ariel. Izzy was wrong. An angel could be killed. The new knowledge had filled Michael as he witnessed the struggle. He stripped her of the cherub she stole from Izrafel, shattered her own essence, and forced her to fall before slaying her.

Michael didn't have a comeback, and wasn't in the mood for Lucifer's all-over-the-board conversation. "Izrafel confirmed who Uriel is."

"He'd know. But then again, you already knew too."

"Why did you do it?"

*

Something chimed in the back of Ronnie's thoughts, and she struggled to push aside the haze of exhaustion and claw her way toward it.

Somewhere in the background, she heard Lucifer's voice. It was muted, and Ronnie realized it came from Michael's phone. "What makes you think it was me? What good would it possibly do me to drive one of my own insane and then drop her in the middle of a situation as volatile as Ubiquity?"

That was what Ronnie wanted to know. That she heard him at a distance, through a phone, must be why it sounded as if his voice held regret. There was no way Lucifer did something without a backup plan. *Wait, how do I know that?*

"I know that."

"Oh, good. You're done whimpering and cowering."

"I knew you'd miss me."

"I was hoping you'd tell me," Michael said.

"I won't. Is Ronnie safe?" Lucifer asked.

He called to check on her. The thought warmed her. He might be lying and keeping the key to her sanity a secret, but at least he still cared.

"If you won't tell me what's going on, will you tell her?" Michael's voice was a combination of threat and hope.

"No." The line went dead.

Ronnie shifted on the couch, unable to keep quiet anymore. "Did you really think that would work?"

He tilted his head back to rest it on the cushions. "I didn't. But I can't help trying anyway."

That made her smile. She really was falling for him. And they didn't even have to jump into anything. Irdu had given his okay. And the three of them, or however things worked out, had the rest of eternity to figure this out. She rearranged herself to rest her head on Michael's shoulder. "I probably would have done the same thing."

"And you might have done a better job."

"I doubt it. He's the reason I'm like this to begin with." She hooked a hand around Michael's arm. "Thank you for coming for me, for sticking up for me, for everything."

"I didn't save as much as I should have."

Ronnie didn't want to know, but she needed to. Given who Ari took her cherub from…her gut sank as she remembered. *Please let him be all right.* "Irdu? Izzy?" Michael hadn't really answered her question earlier.

"The church is gone. All of your apartments are gone. Ariel tore large chunks of the neighborhood up looking for you." He rested his cheek against hers. "Izrafel will be okay. He says every inch of his body was dissected by a laser—or might as well have been—when she separated him from his cherub, but he survived. He might not like mortality, but beyond that, he's just got a couple broken bones. And Irdu is fine. He's keeping an eye on things at the hospital."

She exhaled in relief. Best news she'd heard all day, at least given the circumstances. Not the lost apartment thing, but she didn't own much, and could find a new place. Irdu and Izzy—her real friends and the demon she loved were okay; that was what mattered.

Chapter Twenty-Seven

They sat there, Ronnie on the couch and Michael on the floor, time ticking away, not saying anything.

She finally broke the silence. "We need our rest." She would have rather kept him there, but she couldn't ask him to sit up with her all night.

"Do you want a real bed to sleep in?" He stood and offered his hand. "As opposed to the couch?"

He didn't mean…? No, he couldn't. Maybe his bed? Anticipation fluttered in her chest, rising above the horrors of the night. "I wouldn't complain."

"You can stay in the guest room."

She couldn't ignore her disappointment, but she also wasn't about to turn down the offer. She followed him to one of the doors. He gestured to the room. "You stay here as long as you need. Not just tonight, but until you find a new place. The room is yours indefinitely. If you want to wash some of the dust off, there are clean towels in the bathroom, and you can snag something to wear from the drawers or closet."

She couldn't to talk herself out of wanting him. She forced the question out before she could take it back. Shyness when it came to sex was new to her, but with Michael, so much was different. "Will you help me?"

"With…?"

She stepped closer, thumbs hooked in her belt loops, pulling down the waistband of her jeans a little. She needed something to go right. She needed him. An ache of longing grew in her chest, and she tried to hide it with flirty words. "Washing the dust off."

She watched him through her eyelashes, gauging his reaction. He hadn't said yes, but he also hadn't said no, turned her away, or left. With any luck, she wasn't about to humiliate herself. She pushed her luck a little more. "If you're worried about Irdu, he and I have an agreement. I know angels aren't celibate, and those kisses you and I have shared…they steal some plausibility from the *temptations of the flesh* line."

"He told me about your agreement. Sort of." Michael rested a hand on the small of her back. His voice was heavy, sliding down her spine and seeping into her. "Right now, I don't want anything else. I'd love to help." He stripped her top off.

"Good." Relief and lust flowed through her. She ran her fingers down his chest, undoing each button she encountered along the way. "Because I was thinking…" She nudged his shirt off his shoulders and let it fall to the floor. "We're a series of false starts. Entirely too many of them. Even if tonight is just tonight, I'm tired of stalling out. I need you close."

"You've got me. Here, now, just us."

She unbuckled his belt, and his slacks dropped to the ground. He led her to the master bedroom and then through to the adjoining bath. She paused in the door and took it all in—tile, glass, a huge shower. It was as big as the guest bedroom. "So this is where you keep the opulence."

He pulled her into him and reached around to unbutton her jeans. Shoving them to the floor with her panties, he kissed her shoulder. "There are things that immortality has taught me not to take for granted. Indoor plumbing is one of them."

That made a good amount of sense, and she might have been more impressed with the logic, if she wasn't drowning in every touch and caress as his hands roamed her body.

He nudged her toward the walk-in shower, shedding the rest of his clothing as they walked. He opened the glass door and closed it when they were both inside. The bathroom may have been decedent, but his naked form was opulent sin. Chiseled body, the little trail of hair leading the eye down past his stomach to his impressive assets... Talk about a positive self-image. He turned on the water and tested it—she assumed for temperature—before switching it over to the nozzles dotting the other three walls.

She sighed and leaned back against him as the water cascaded over and around her. His hard length pressed into her ass, tempting her. "This is nice."

He squirted a dollop of body wash into his hand from the dispenser on the wall. The sharp scent of soap filled her head. He settled his palm on her stomach.

She gasped, her back going rigid, and then giggled. "It's cold."

"Not for long." He ran his lips up her neck and sent pleasant chills down her spine. He slid his hands over her torso and then lathered along her hips and waist. Each new touch spoke to something both familiar and new. Metatron knew Michael's caress but not like this. Ronnie only had internet images, her imagination, and play with the vibrator for comparison, and they were in a different league. He traced along the bottom of her breasts, eliciting a moan.

That whole *temptations of the flesh* thing was bullshit. She had no doubt. Every brush, stroke, and graze was deliberate. She didn't care about his past. This was now and with her.

When there was nothing else left for him to lather, he glided his hands over her breasts. The feather-light slide made her senses plead for more. She ground against him, and he slipped his fingers over her nipples, pinching and rolling them between his fingers in time to her moans.

He moved one hand to her stomach and then lower. A throb spread between her legs. Intense and vivid. Sharper than anything she felt playing with herself. With soapy fingers, he found the strip between her legs. She whimpered at the spike of pleasure when he dipped between her folds. She thrust her hips to get closer to his touch, but he pulled back, teasing.

Her head felt as it if were floating away, and her every sense heightened. When he finally rubbed her aching button, his fingers gliding around it without friction, she let out a soft cry.

He stroked harder, and breathy inhales punctuated her whimpers. She was close, but she wanted more than this. Wanted him. He glided along her slit and then dipped two fingers inside her, pumping in time to her thrusting. The smooth penetration stretched her and catapulted her to the edge of climax, holding her there until her thoughts fuzzed and stars danced in her vision. So incredible.

He pulled out and found her swollen nub with ease. She squirmed and pressed closer. Her breathing was barely more than short gasps. She bucked her hips against his hand when she peaked, her screams echoing off the tile.

When his touch became too much, she grabbed his wrist and guided him from the overly sensitive area. Her legs threatened to give out. It was a new kind of weakness; one she could see herself becoming addicted to.

He laid a series of soft kisses along her neck, erection digging into her lower back. She still wanted more. She turned to face him, leaning one shoulder against a wall, and traced a finger down his chest. "What's next?"

He hesitated, and wounded disappointment dug inside her. Would he to tell her that was it? Her heart threatened to burst from her chest when he wrapped his hand around her wrist and pinned it to the wall. He tangled the fingers of his other hand in her hair. Yanking her head back, he kissed her. The slow build was gone, and flames raced over her skin at his intensity. Not a shared angelic power, something more primal. More human. He ground his lips into hers.

She slid against him, memorizing every inch of his bare flesh while their tongues explored each other. A wave of hunger replaced her exhaustion, starting in her belly and traveling lower, begging to be filled with something more. He broke the kiss with a grunt, and need ached below her waist. He released her wrist and hair to grip her hips. His fingers dug in hard enough to feel in her bones. He lifted her and pressed her back against the wall. She bit the inside of her cheek in anticipation and wrapped her legs around his waist. Another cry tore from her throat when he thrust inside her. It was frantic and fast and exactly what she wanted. He bit her shoulder, and she fell into the exquisite combination of pleasure and pain.

She rocked hard against him as the frantic pace built. She didn't know which of them finished first. It blurred together, grunts and screams and pleasure, until her throat was raw, her breath was gone, and she didn't know if the dampness on her forehead was water or perspiration.

He lowered her to her feet, and she wobbled. He reached out a hand to steady her. With his other palm braced on the wall behind her, it looked as though he sought the same kind of stability. He rested his head against hers, heavy breathing matching hers. The gesture weighed on her, significant and reassuring, despite its simplicity. She buried her face in his chest and inhaled, memorizing everything. The weakness in her limbs, the hum on her skin, and the scents of body wash and sex.

"That was incredible." He slid his hand along her back, his voice vibrating against her cheek.

She nodded in agreement, not sure she trusted herself to speak. After a minute or two, they broke apart to rinse the soap away, turn off the water, and then step from the shower. He brushed the droplets from her skin with a fluffy towel, each touch gentle. She didn't interrupt the attention or speak. She wanted the moment as it was.

When they were dry, she urged him toward the bed. "You're not going to make me sleep alone, are you?" She winced at the trace of hurt and panic in her question. That was supposed to be seductive.

"I'm not." He lay down and tugged her next to him, guiding her head to rest on his shoulder.

*

Michael heard the trace of hurt when Ronnie asked if she had to sleep alone. He couldn't have told her no even if she didn't look wounded by the possibility of rejection.

He lay there, listening to her breathing until it became steady, and she drifted off. He suspected sleep would elude him tonight. This was why he didn't want to let her get close. Now, he didn't want to let her go. He wasn't sure if he'd been created to fall hard and fast, though two times over the course of his lifetime hardly seemed like a habit.

But the impulse with Ronnie was almost overwhelming. To keep her safe. To take her away from all this. To stop playing the stupid games Lucifer and Gabriel did, and go experience a mortal life. Maybe Ronnie would stay by his side. It was likely they wouldn't last, given she adored someone else. But her joy for living made him want to see more the way she did.

When he saw her fighting Ariel, a dangerous question teased him. If it came down to it, would he let the rest of the world burn to save Ronnie? He would have for Metatron. Not directly, but his falling would leave the world to fend for itself. It was the kind of selfish decision he would have pounced on back then, but couldn't allow himself to now. He couldn't give himself to someone completely—not the way love deserved—and guarantee he could still do his job.

At least Ronnie had someone to be with, even without Michael.

He lay there until light crept through the windows, burning the night into his memories. Saving it for the wonder it was. Knowing it couldn't happen again. He untangled himself from the sleeping demon curled up against his side and then pulled some clothes on before making his way toward the kitchen.

He padded to the fridge, grabbed the juice, and then slammed back what was left. He tossed the empty carton in the trash, rehearsing what he had to say to her, or trying to find a script at least. Everything inside was raw, and he couldn't numb any of it.

The kitchen door squeaked, and he swiveled toward it.

Ronnie stared back, cheeks bright pink. She had found one of his clean shirts, and it hung halfway down her thighs, taunting his imagination. As the seconds ticked away, neither spoke.

Ronnie finally cleared her throat. "Can we talk?"

He nodded. Never good words, but one of them needed to say them.

She gave him a tiny smile and slid onto a stool on the other side of the breakfast bar.

Michael watched her, not having any idea what to say or how to say it.

"I'm— It's just… I want to ask you something, but only if you promise to be completely honest with me. Give me a straight answer. I'll know if you don't."

Honest. He could do that. It would hurt, but it was the right way to go about things. "Only if I get the same in return." He stepped to the bar and slid his hand across the granite to cover her fingers.

She smiled. "Sounds reasonable."

He traced tiny circles over her skin, marveling at how delicate her fingers were. It was time to ease off the intimate contact, but it wasn't as if it would hurt less stopping now or five minutes from now. "I promise. Straight answer."

"Do-you-still-love-her?" Ronnie's question tumbled out so quickly the words ran together. "I mean, you promised to be honest, and I need to know. If Metatron was here instead of me, would you give her another try?"

Michael opened his mouth to say no.

She cut him off. "You can't answer so quickly. I know how she feels about you. I don't care if the answer is yes or no. I mean I do, but regardless, I'm not going to believe you unless you've put some thought into it."

It was a reasonable request, and something he'd already put so much thought into. Still, her question tugged at things he tried for centuries to hide from himself. Thoughts and emotions spun in his mind, mingling with memories, feeling old and distant. "I wouldn't give her another try. She's in my past."

Ronnie's aura flared and fractured for a moment, but the gold and red won out, her shoulders relaxed. "What did you want to tell me?"

He didn't want to do this, especially with the tentative calm between them. But even as the bright morning poured through the windows, chasing away last night's shadows, he knew it was the right decision. It had better be, as much as it ached. "I know we said this last night, but it's important we both agree, and I'm sorry I have to do this."

"Okay?"

He forced iced through his veins, but it didn't numb the sting of what he had to say. "I can't walk the line between serving Him, and loving someone else. Some agents can. I'm not one of them."

She clenched her jaw, and her nostrils flared. "I never asked you for eternity, or even next week. I'm just trying to figure out where we stand."

"And I'm telling you. There's a chasm between us, and it has to stay that way." He forced an edge into his words despite the tear it left inside him to say them.

She nodded, eyes hard. "You were willing to surrender immortality for her, but you're going to strip away the one night we had together. And you insist she's in the past?"

"That's not what I'm saying." *Damn it,* he hated being so bad with words.

"Then explain it to me. Make me understand. I so desperately want to. I don't think you have any idea how nice it would be if something, anything, made sense."

He summoned his decision from the sleepless night of pondering. "This isn't about her, or you, or me, or any one of us individually. Angels keeping cherubs to make themselves untouchable? Not falling when they should? That dead angels can be stuffed back inside someone else and given new life? It's bigger than anything since Lucifer walked away from heaven to do things his own way. I don't want to reach a point where protecting you means putting the interests of the rest of the world aside. Some angels can balance duty and love. I can't."

"I don't need you looking out for me." She turned away. "I just wanted an untarnished memory I knew was my own and to know where we stood. Thank you for that at least." The kitchen door swung shut behind her as she pushed out of the room.

He knew this was the right thing to do, but that didn't make the ache in his chest fade.

*

Irdu sat with Izzy all night, watching over his friend, and watching the news.

Not that they were going to tell him if Ronnie was all right. The media was spinning this as a freak series of lightning storms.

What kind of leverage did Ubiquity—or heaven—have to convince them of that?

Irdu was terrified thinking of it.

He'd called Ronnie several times, but didn't get an answer. Maybe he should have made a note of Michael's phone number.

Light crept through the windows. The only thing that kept Irdu from going out of his head with worry was a series of questions—could he do for Tia what Ari did to Izzy? Not the nearly killing him part, but taking a different cherub, and replacing the one Lucifer had given her.

Would she survive?

Would it keep her safe from Lucifer in the future?

"Step away from him for a minute." Lucifer's voice came from the doorway, startling him. "We need to talk."

Irdu gave Izzy one more glance, and joined Lucifer in the hallway.

"Ronnie is all right," Lucifer said.

Irdu sank into his relief. "Thank you."

"Don't thank me. Michael saved her."

Whatever. As long as she was all right. "Okay. Thank him."

"Speaking of…" Lucifer draped an arm over his shoulders, and led him farther down the hallway. "We have a deal. You and I. I don't require your silence because I'm an evil bastard."

Ice spilled through Irdu's veins. How did Lucifer know? He laughed to hide the nervousness.

"I'm serious. I do this for your safety. For yours, and Tia's, and Ronnie's."

"That sounds like a threat." Not that Irdu's entire existence was anything else.

Lucifer pointed back to Izzy's room. "That's what happened to him when someone found out. What happens to you—who can't defend yourself— and your sister, if someone discovers who you are?"

"I had to tell Ronnie." Irdu didn't like the tension cranking through him. "She needed to know—"

"Because you love her?"

"Yes." Irdu didn't have a problem admitting that. He thought he would, but the admission flowed out easily. "But she needed to know anyway. It could help her. Why haven't you helped her?"

"If I could, I would. I'm going to tell you something you need to keep to yourself, even though apparently you're not capable of such a thing." Lucifer's reply was filled with regret and fury. "I love her more than you could ever know. I've spent millennia on this. You will *not* fuck it up for me."

Irdu clenched his jaw. "You don't love Uriel. You love a memory. Just like Michael does. You're infatuated with the voice in an innocent demon's head. One that's driving her insane. It's not that you can't help her. You won't."

Lucifer's chuckle was dry and humorless. "You have no fucking idea. But I promise you, I have it under control."

Irdu heard something he'd never expected from Lucifer. A hint of doubt. And he suspected if things went bad, Ronnie would be the one to pay the price.

He had to find a way to stop that from happening.

Chapter Twenty-Eight

Michael checked the attitude at the gates to hell when he went to visit Lucifer. He didn't grovel to anyone, but he needed a favor. He knocked on the heavy oak door, feeling enough of Lucifer in the air to know he'd get a response.

The door swung open, and Lucifer sat at the desk. He nodded to the chair across from him. "You're spending a lot of time here lately. Thinking of switching sides?"

Michael raised his brows at the bad joke. "We both know I wouldn't last a day playing by hell's rules."

"It's true. Thousands of years old and never learned how to lie. I don't get that."

"I don't suppose you would." Speaking of, Michael needed to cut to the chase. The sooner he did this, the better. "I need a favor."

"Just like that? No foreplay? You're not even going to buy me dinner? Tell me you at least showed Ronnie a better time last night."

The memories slammed back into Michael like a freight train, assaulting him with both physical and emotional sensations. He struggled to keep his face impassive. "That's between her and me."

"Yeah, yeah. A gentleman doesn't kiss and tell. And I don't want details. Your response tells me all I need. You couldn't keep your hands to yourself." Anger crept into Lucifer's voice. "I had one request. A simple, simple thing I asked for, and that was for you walk away from her. And you've got the nerve to come in here and ask for a favor when you couldn't even give me that?"

The rage might have made someone else back down. Michael recognized the shift in the air, the glow in Lucifer's eyes, the rumble in his voice. Michael wasn't fazed. "This is bigger than a single demon."

"*So's she.*" Lucifer's response rattled the walls. "And some little Gabriel prodigy almost took her out last night. I'm grateful you were there, but I have to wonder, if you had backed off when I asked, would this have happened before she figured things out on her own?"

"We don't deal in hypotheticals," Michael said. "So we won't talk about how this is close to driving Ronnie into isolation and insanity, and how maybe if someone helped her sooner…"

He shook his head. Lucifer was distracting him, and he wouldn't let that happen. "That *meltdown* last night is why I'm here. Gabriel has more of those. Angels with cherubs working outside the confines of Ubiquity. Ariel won't be the last, and we need to step in at Ubiquity."

"This from a guy who's been all about going it solo for decades."

"You said it yourself last night. I'm back. Things are changing. I'm one of them."

Lucifer stared at him for a long minute. "I still don't understand this *we* statement of yours. You're working there."

"I'm not enough. You put this structure in place, and you can navigate it. Things are out of control. Gabriel's development team rigged the system. All the top performers are spoon-fed the best leads, and they're all heaven's. It's time we went hands-on."

"*Fuck*." Lucifer slammed his fist into the desk. "All right. I can't have this…" He snapped his jaw shut. "I'll step in."

"Perfect. Then one more thing."

"You've used up your favors for the next decade." Lucifer spoke through clenched teeth.

"You'll like this one. Abaddon wants a job at Ubiquity."

"I fucking hate that. What in eternity makes you think that's good news? And why the hell would she do that?"

"She wants to *make a difference*." Michael let the sarcasm leak into his words. He held up a hand when Lucifer opened his mouth. "I know she's lying, but not why. If we let her in, we can keep an eye on her."

Lucifer shrugged. "You and I both know this *we* thing is bullshit. She's only going to answer to you or Gabe. Besides, if you want me to sift out the mess at Ubiquity, I can't babysit. Bring her in yourself if you want, but I'm not touching it."

"But you want the answers."

"I do. But that woman scares me a little. You get answers. Share them with me."

"Why would I do that?" Michael asked.

"You owe me. Offices open in what? An hour? I'll be there."

* * * *

Ronnie shouldn't have to go back to work. Wasn't there some kind of bereavement leave for losing one's apartment? Or for their supposed-best friend's trying to kill them? But she was there because the alternative spoke to her every negative emotion—past and present. She could have stayed in Michael's condo, pretending. He'd be at Ubiquity, but that didn't make it any less awkward sticking around at his place. She could have gone house hunting, but nothing was in her price range.

She'd hoped to find Irdu here, but knew better. He'd called Michael's phone last night, to let her know he was staying with Izzy. The fallen angel was in intensive care, but Irdu promised to let her know as soon as he had a room number and a place she could come visit.

Neither of them was comfortable talking with a third person watching. She was grateful Izzy wasn't alone, but she missed having backup in the office.

At least if she had to be somewhere, here should growl and snap at people. She could take her frustration out on Raphael.

She stepped off the elevator, and an almost tangible sense of chaos and panic rushed past her. No one was working. Angels and demons alike were rolled out of their cubes, heads bent together, whispering.

She caught snatches of words, and some heads turned in her direction as she passed. "Ariel…" several of them whispered.

"…devastation…"

"…corruption…"

"…politics…"

"…Lucifer…."

The last word sent her stumbling over an invisible spot in the carpet, but she caught herself before she fell. She managed to make her way to her cubicle without another incident.

"He's here."

Ronnie noticed. *"Thanks for the update, Miss Obvious."* She was only in her seat for a few seconds when she heard the creak of plastic chair wheels.

She turned to find Tiamat behind her. She was a demon with pixie-cut dark hair, gorgeous violet eyes, and skin that would have made a porcelain doll envious. And now that Ronnie knew the truth, she saw the facial similarities to Irdu.

"I heard you know," Tia said.

Ronnie wasn't supposed to say anything. With Lucifer here, it was even more dangerous. She nodded.

Tia smiled. "After work, we should go get ice cream." She looked so friendly and sincere.

So had Ari, and that betrayal still ached through every inch of Ronnie. "I'm probably going to the hospital."

"Right. Makes sense. Have you heard?" Tia asked.

Ronnie heard a lot of things. Normally she got her office gossip from Ari. The name welled inside, stuffing her with ambivalence. She tried to force the feeling away with her response. "Nope."

"It's Lucifer." She leaned closer, voice low—which was ridiculous since *everyone* was talking about whatever this was, but Ronnie wasn't going to point it out.

This wasn't the first time he was in the office since Ronnie started here. "And?"

Tia's grin reminded Ronnie of the Cheshire Cat. "You heard what happened last night, right? With the fires and the destruction and stuff?"

Ronnie's gut sank. She needed to put everything from last night as far behind her as possible. Catching up with Izzy and Irdu was about the only thing she wanted as a reminder. *Go figure.* All this time she fought for her memories, and now she didn't want the ones she had. "I heard a little bit."

"Apparently, it was Ariel. She went on some kind of insane rampage because she lost her job. Can you believe they fired her? If she wasn't safe, none of us are."

No mention of the cherubs Ari stole and kept. Had Irdu not filled her in? Maybe he hadn't had a chance. As long as Ronnie's colleagues maintained their ignorance about the option, no one else was in danger of losing their jobs. "What's that got to do with Lucifer?"

"He's stepping in. Says this isn't the organization he helped build, and he wants to keep a closer eye on things."

Lucifer was enforcing order and going hands-on? Uneasiness slid under Ronnie's skin. That didn't sound like him. "Isn't that why Michael was here?"

"I don't know." Tia shrugged. "But he's an angel, right?" Her voice dropped lower. "You know what Raphael's like. I bet Michael's just as bad."

Ronnie ground her teeth together to fight back the surge of desire mingled with loss over what she did and didn't have with Michael. Thank God Metatron was quiet this morning. "I doubt it."

"Whatever. So Lucifer is holding one-on-ones with everyone. He's already laid several people off today."

Maybe no one was safe after all. Would he fire Ronnie? No. Her luck wasn't that good this week. "Bummer." She turned away. She didn't want to be rude, but she wondered if she made it onto his schedule. Would she actually have a chance to talk to him today? "I should get to work if they're laying off agents."

Tia made a sound that was half squeal, half *eep*, and Ronnie heard the casters roll away behind her.

"I don't care which VIPs are in the office, you still have to log into the queue." Raphael's threat greeted Ronnie from behind.

That was what she needed. She held up her right hand, middle finger extended, while she used her left to log in. "Yes, sir."

He growled, and she braced herself for more, but there was nothing. She wouldn't look. Wouldn't give him the satisfaction.

"Just do your fucking job."

She stopped herself from saying *language* and dove into her work. It was more to keep her mind occupied than because of Raphael's threat. The leads that came across her desk were so completely not cherubs, it wasn't funny. At least that meant she wouldn't have to ignore any of them.

Michael's office door stayed closed all morning, and she was grateful. So did the one to the office Lucifer appropriated, and as the hours ticked by, it infuriated her more and more. Lucifer was right there, closer than in ages. And Ronnie was going to make him tell her... *Yeah, who am I kidding?* She couldn't make him tell her anything. She doubted she could get in to see him.

"Are we still going on about this?"

"Oh hey, I missed you. Not."

Ronnie's email chimed. Her gut twisted in on itself when she saw the message from Gabe.

Can we talk? I'd rather not set foot in that building right now. I'm across the street, if you'd like lunch.

"He can kiss your hurt feelings better." Metatron's snide comment broke into Ronnie's reading.

"Shut up." Why didn't he want to be here? Did he really have to avoid Lucifer?

"Or maybe he's not avoiding anyone. He just likes fucking with your head."

At this point, it wouldn't surprise Ronnie. Everyone else was.

"Whine, whine, whine. Do you ever stop?"

Metatron was one to talk. Ronnie glanced at the clock. It was close enough to noon. She could get away with heading out for lunch. She didn't want to see Gabe, but curiosity compelled her. There was a reason he kept pursuing her, and if it gave her any hints about how to split Metatron from her, she'd grit her teeth through his creepy come-ons.

She sent him back a quick reply that she'd be there soon and set her queue to *Away*. Grabbing her purse, she made her way to the lobby.

She took her time strolling the block to the strip mall. Gabe's message wasn't specific, but there was only one place to eat there. An office building full of angels and demons with borderline sensory addictions was plenty to keep the bakery in business.

Ronnie stepped inside. The incredible aroma of fresh bread and caramelized sugar rushed over her, and her stomach growled. She didn't know when she last ate, but it would have to wait a little longer.

Gabe was at the far end of the room. He raised his head from its resting spot on his palms and stood when he saw her. His familiar smile didn't reassure her the way he probably wanted it to.

"If Michael doesn't want you..."

Yeah, she and Metatron already had that conversation. Ronnie wasn't in the mood to do anything with Mr. Creepy-Crawly. She wasn't in the mood for much at all unless it came wrapped in answers.

When Ronnie drew close, Gabe grabbed her fingers and kissed the back of her hand. A familiar rush flowed through her, and she relaxed despite herself as the gesture sapped her anxiety.

"But not all of it."

"Shut up." She slid onto the seat across from him in the booth, trying to be polite about pulling her hand away.

"I'm glad you came." His smile appeared genuine. "I hear there are changes going on over there."

"I bet that's the understatement of a lifetime. But only like a human lifetime, not like Lucifer's."

How much did Gabe know? And how much would he let on, even if he knew it all? "I guess. There was a fire or something downtown last night."

"So I heard. Kind of hard to miss. Something like a rampaging fallen angel makes people talk."

Ronnie didn't like how casually he took the whole thing. Ari might have gone off the deep end, but she'd liked him. Hell, Ronnie might have even said Ari was crushing on him. And he brushed the entire thing off like a minor bit of inconvenience. White-hot fury singed her nerves, and she struggled to contain it while she searched for a way to keep the conversation rational enough to prod Gabe for answers.

"I know you need to get back to work." He reached for her hand again. "But I need to talk to you, and it can't wait."

"Okay…" Maybe Ronnie didn't need to coax anything out of him after all.

"I know you're hesitating about my offer." He traced the back of her knuckles with his thumb.

The power soothed her, chasing away her exhaustion and replacing it with a new layer of hesitation. His non-specific job offer, the vague bullshit wrapped in nothing? "I'm sorry about that—"

"It's okay. I think I know why."

"Because you're desperate, clingy, and insecure? Because you're such an amazing angel of vengeance that you've managed to convince yourself everyone is beneath you? Because you're not as stupid as you want me to believe?"

Ronnie pushed Metatron's taunts aside. "You do?"

"I haven't been completely honest with you about my motives."

"You think?"

Sigh. Possibly the most straightforward thing he'd ever said to her. Then again, a lot of people were dishonest with her, so maybe she was learning to appreciate the lies.

"And I think you deserve to know the truth."

"Too bad she won't get it from you."

Ronnie was kind of glad he couldn't hear Metatron, though it would make the conversation more interesting. "You've got my attention."

He gave her a confident, full grin that made her feel like she was on the menu, but there was nothing tantalizing about it. "I'm sorry. It's taken me a while to figure out whether you knew and were just hiding it, or if no one told you."

"Oh, this ought to be good."

Ronnie couldn't argue with that. Not reasonably anyway.

"That's never stopped you before."

"Still in the dark here." Ronnie didn't want to rush him, but her stomach growled, and she wanted to go back to stalking Lucifer's office.

"I'm getting there. I don't know why Lucifer or Michael or whoever hasn't told you all this, but the voice you hear isn't just calling herself Metatron, she actually *is* Metatron."

Yay. Old information.

"Ditto."

This was so not helpful.

"Except it means he knew."

True. But she figured he would. Ari knew. Even with Ronnie's limited knowledge, she reached the conclusion days ago. "Why didn't you tell me this sooner?"

"I didn't know how much you knew. You use her name—the one only Michael called her. I needed to find out if you were setting me up."

"Setting you up for what? Why would I do that?"

"I know why Lucifer put Metatron in your head."

"In theory, or he actually knows? He fucking killed me. He told Lucifer and Michael—the men I loved—that I was a megalomaniacal fiend hell-bent on destruction. What kind of bullshit has he come up with now?"

"Or rather, I'm pretty sure." Gabe kept talking, oblivious to the second conversation he evoked. "I don't have confirmation. It's not like he's going to tell me, but it makes a lot of sense."

Gabe believed what he said. Ronnie knew it for certain, though she couldn't explain how.

"That doesn't mean he's not trying to deceive you."

"What makes sense?" Ronnie sat back in her seat, more interested in the conversation now than in getting back to work.

Gabe reached for her then pulled back. "When Metatron betrayed us, she didn't completely vanish."

"For the last fucking time, I didn't betray anyone."

"You think?" The snide comment slipped out before Ronnie could stop it.

He raised an eyebrow. "I'm not sure how he accomplished it, but Lucifer managed to save a part of her. I'm assuming similarly to the way we keep cherubs alive before they have a purpose, but she wasn't a shapeless, thoughtless ball of light. She was already a personality."

Ronnie waited... *"What, no come back?"*

"What? I've got more personality than he does."

Ronnie almost laughed. The tension and this drawn out fucking conversation were getting to her. "What does that have to do with me?"

"Think about it. You witnessed Metatron's potential yesterday. That's an intense power, and we all know it. If she's still Metatron, she's everything an original is. That's why Ari wanted her."

So he knew Ronnie was involved last night.

"Surprised?"

Not really. But he also didn't know Ronnie relied on her own strength when Metatron cowered in the corner. "And that's why Lucifer gave her to me?"

"Kind of." He glanced away, studying the scratches in the table, tracing lines over them. "He wanted someone he could control. You didn't meld with her correctly. So he's focused on ripping her out of you and trying again."

The notion shredded Ronnie from the inside out, and she couldn't put words to the pain it left in its wake. Sure, it hurt like hell when Ari tried to remove Metatron, but if Lucifer could do it, the voice would be gone, on to her own life, and Ronnie would get hers back. Everybody won.

"I don't know why no one else is telling you this. It's in your aura. It's fractured and splintered. If Lucifer pulled the two of you apart, it would probably destroy you."

The words slammed into Ronnie and tightened like a fist around her chest. That wasn't true. "He'd kill me just to have a powerful ally in someone else?" Lucifer wouldn't. *Would he?* He was keeping something from her, but not her inevitable destruction, right?

"I don't know." Gabe shrugged. "Odds are high he knows exactly what's going on in your head. And he changed a lot when he lost her. There's no guarantee Lucifer is rational anymore."

"This isn't right. Lucifer is cruel and brushing us off, but he still cares. He hasn't lost it. Not because of me."

The wounded pouting hurt. Ronnie wished it didn't hit her so hard when Metatron sulked, especially when Ronnie was already drowning in her own reaction to the information.

Gabe stood abruptly, offering her his hand. "Anyway. I had to tell you. It's not fair you be kept in the dark."

Ronnie was too preoccupied to snatch away more of his essence. "Thanks."

"I don't want that to happen to you." He kissed her on the cheek. "I like you. I like who you are, how you think, and your independence. I can help you find a solution, if you come work for me."

He was gone before Ronnie could respond. Something nagged at the back of her mind, pushing aside the hurt his revelation caused. What was it?

"You know."

Yeah. Ronnie did. That was a lot of power, if he was telling the truth. People were willing to kill Ronnie for it, and Gabe would let her tuck it away for eternity, in order to have her by his side?

"How romantic."

Despite Metatron's sarcasm, Ronnie desperately wanted to believe it. At least it would mean someone wanted her around, instead of Metatron.

"Moron."

Ronnie wanted to believe it, but couldn't. The man tried to kill one of his own, lied to his peers about his reasons—which she still didn't know— and eons later, still kept up the illusion. Why would he tell Ronnie the truth about anything related to Metatron?

Chapter Twenty-Nine

Ronnie was sick of all of it: Michael being all reasonable and dedicated to his work, Gabriel lying to her, angels trying to steal portions of her head. She knew who had answers, exactly where he was, and was tired of waiting. She marched from the elevator down the hall and then pushed into Lucifer's office without knocking.

He wasn't there. *Damn it.* He was around. She felt it. She muttered, "I swear to all you hold dear, if you don't get your ass in here in the next ten seconds, I *will* obliterate this place."

"Interesting threat. You know you should never point the gun at someone if you aren't going to pull the trigger."

"Just the corner office or the entire building?" Lucifer's voice floated from behind her.

She whirled, trying not to show how startled she was that he'd snuck up on her.

"Last angel to blow up entire buildings met their fate at the tip of Michael's blade. But you were there, weren't you?"

Ronnie forced casual apathy into her words. "You're here now. I guess we won't have to see how accurately I can recreate last night."

He brushed past her and then took a seat behind the desk before propping up his feet. "How's work going? I was worried you might not be talking to me."

"Her boyfriends hurt her feelings. She wants someone to kiss her boo-boo all better."

Ronnie growled in her head. "I need to know something. I suspect you're the only person who has the whole story. You're going to tell me."

"You're going to make demands? Really?"

She didn't have another option.

He didn't look impressed. "If I didn't tell you before, odds aren't in your favor now."

"I'll tell you something."

Ronnie didn't want more cryptic answers from a psychotic voice. She wanted someone to come clean. "Please?"

He licked his lips and placed his hands behind his head. "If you want to know why the vending machine doesn't have a better selection, you need to take it up with the office manager."

"Or rather, I'll remind you."

"Of what?"

"He loved me. He adores you. He'd move worlds for you."

Ronnie struggled to keep her expression blank as images of what Metatron meant flitted through Ronnie's mind on a current of comfort she didn't want to feel. Flickers of compassion mingled with instinct and memories Ronnie couldn't grasp.

But if using his affection for a long-dead image of her was an option, why hadn't he broken before now? Would playing the wounded former lover actually push his buttons? Ronnie couldn't imagine, but she was out of alternatives. Ronnie moved to the edge of his desk, scooted her butt up on an empty spot, and then crossed her ankles.

He studied her, a flicker of surprise registering before he shoved back and sat straight. "Tell me what you want, Uriel."

She stuck out her lower lip and tried to summon her best wounded look. "Tell me about my predecessor."

He didn't meet her gaze. "I'm not sure what you mean. You're the only Uriel there's ever been."

She made her chin quiver. Those lessons he gave her in body language were paying. "Just tell me why you decided it was fair to burden me with this."

"Don't ask for answers neither of us is ready to deal with."

"But I'm not—"

"Aren't you?" He kicked his chair back and stood in front of her.

She didn't want to back down. He was the key. He also terrified her with his calm, making it easy to keep the waver in her voice. "Why do I have the essence of Metatron inside me, and how come everyone knew it before I did?"

The name hung between them, heavy in the air.

"Everyone who?"

"Michael. Gabriel. The fucking voice living in my head."

"Ariel, Izrafel…"

"If you're hearing voices, you should probably see someone about it."

Ronnie didn't appreciate the insult, but figured that was why he did it. "I am. I'm seeing you."

"Gabriel is lying." He pressed his forehead to hers.

Heat spilled through her at the nearness, despite the terror that rose inside.

Lucifer's tone was smooth and emotionless. "That's what he does. You think *I'm* the Prince of Lies? Work with him for a couple thousand years. Michael is a lovesick puppy who sees shadows wherever he looks."

"He's not."

Ronnie hopped from the desk, tired of the games both inside her head and out. She moved away from Lucifer and began to pace. "I'm sick of this."

Icy power slipped through her. It was the same familiar help she had last night when Metatron cowered in the back of her skull, hiding from Ari. Ronnie's own strength. "Tell me why you created me. Why you stuck a dead angel in my head instead of just giving her a life of her own again, and why you're willing to destroy me so maybe you can have someone to control instead."

"Whoa." Lucifer slammed his palms against the desk. "Who said you were getting destroyed?"

"Told you Gabe was lying."

Or Lucifer was. Or they both were. Ronnie didn't know anymore. She faltered, hating that her self-righteous demands were already shredded. "Someone."

He sighed as he stepped around the desk and stopped in front of Ronnie. He lifted her chin to stare her in the eyes.

His sorrow peering back gnawed at her resolve. What was she missing?

"I don't make mistakes very often." His tone was low and sad. "And like any good professional, I'd rather fix them than admit them."

Ronnie was a mistake? Today was skyrocketing to the top of her bad-news-that-devours-the-soul list. Maybe she was being melodramatic, but damn that sent tears rushing to her eyes.

"The one thing any ugly baby dreads hearing."

"Or maybe Metatron was the mistake."

"Fuck you."

"I meant to bring Metatron back." Lucifer raked shaky fingers through his hair. "I looked for centuries for a way to do it, and then I met Irdu. A demonic cherub possessed a human. So I tried to recreate the experiment with his sister. And holy fuck, it worked. I rolled the dice, in the hopes Metatron's essence plus yours would make a complete individual, and we could have her back."

"Ha! In your face."

"So..." Metatron's sparks pulsed in Ronnie. Which one of them spoke? Or maybe it was both of them. "You really don't want me here."

"I didn't create you to destroy you." His low, rumbling words echoed off the walls. He stepped closer, nose less than an inch from hers, fury and hurt bright in his unnerving gaze. "I was devastated when Gabriel killed Metatron. And that bullshit about her wanting to rise above everything and annihilate it? That was his deception. I suspect it's his own plan. She never should have died for his arrogance."

"She, her, Metatron." Ronnie hated the hurt growing inside, but couldn't stop it from leaking into her reply. "If this is all about her, why do I have to suffer?"

"Because you won't move aside."

"Why did you do this to me? And then to make me think it was my fault on top of all that? You knew it was her talking to me the first time I brought it up. How did you even get this bit of her to trap in me? Have you been holding onto it all this time? Did you snatch it from the ether?"

Lucifer shook his head. "Not that this is relevant, but what you know so far—the cherubs, the fallen, the rogues. Gabriel. It's nothing compared to the big picture. I've already told you more than you should know."

"What?"

Good question. Confusion tumbled over nonsense, as Ronnie tried to figure out what he was talking about. "What?"

"Another conversation." His composure evaporated further, and his shoulders slumped. "You wouldn't be here if I didn't care. It's true. I meant to bring Metatron back. However, when I realized I made a mistake, that you were both sharing that head and body, I didn't know what to do. I talked to everyone I thought might have answers. I even went to Gabe because I knew he played a hand in what was going on here with the top performers."

Ronnie couldn't process the new information on top of everything else. She still ached from the news she wasn't supposed to exist. "I'm missing something."

"I sent you here because I hoped it would jar something inside. I asked Irdu to keep an eye on you. I pulled strings to stick you with Ari, because I thought she might be able to help you from her firsthand experience. I was desperate. I hoped Metatron would become a single, whole being again once she had all the pieces."

"So…" Ronnie stepped back, hating the tears stinging her eyelids. "You really would rather she were here. She's everything I'm not, right?"

"What have I been telling you this entire time?"

Ronnie's chest throbbed, and her stomach flipped. "I'm just an inconvenience."

"No." Lucifer's single word was forceful. "It's why I stopped pushing you. I tried to bring her back, but you're completely different. I couldn't do to you what I did to Irdu, because I couldn't erase one of you, I should have known you were unique. Even as a cherub, you broke rules. Irdu was the second to do that. You were the first. Those who pop into existence here on Earth? It's not random chance, it's because they have free will." He snapped his jaw shut, as if he said more than he meant to.

"That doesn't matter now." He continued. "I don't know how to separate the two of you, I'm sorry. I don't know why you didn't merge, or why you can't remember who you were before. You should have become her. But I won't be the one to try and fix that, because I adore you both, and I won't choose."

Ronnie started to protest, letting Metatron's screams throb in her skull. But she saw something in Lucifer she never had before. Resignation. She had her answers, but they wouldn't give her a solution.

She stepped away with a frown. "I understand. You know I'll do whatever it takes to figure this out, right?"

"I don't blame you, and I won't stop you. But I won't help. I can't choose between the two of you."

Her throat tightened, and her eyes burned. She turned away, blinking back the tears. It would be nice if this didn't hurt so much, but regardless of the disagreements and fights over the past few months, he was still her mentor. She swallowed and struggled to find her voice. "So, whatever happens from here on out, thanks for the good stuff, and I still hate you for the bad."

"Fair enough."

Ronnie pushed into the hallway, trying not to dwell on how much changed between them. She was a mistake. An abomination. Gabriel didn't want her. He wanted the angel inside. She didn't know why, but none of them was interested in Ronnie minus Metatron.

Metatron was the power and glory. She was an original. Ronnie was a cherub from hell in the wrong place at the right time. Michael didn't even know her. And Lucifer wouldn't help her because she housed a memory.

Irdu wanted Ronnie for Ronnie, but compared to the most powerful of all beings…

Maybe Ronnie should just give Metatron what she wanted.

She turned the corner and smacked into Raphael with a sickening *thud*. A string of profanities rose to her lips, along with the urge to take her frustration out on the new target.

"Get it done now, while you still can. You won't be here much longer."

"Watch yourself, demon."

Everything inside snapped at once, and rage roared over her wounds. She sneered. *"Fuck you.* I don't know what your problem is with me, but I'm sick of it. You don't treat anyone else this way. You always have something obnoxious to say to me. Are you really so hard up that your only joy is being the office equivalent of an internet troll? Is life on Earth really that rough for you?"

He gritted his teeth. "You *know* what my problem is with you. I've never made a secret of it. You were wedged into a job you didn't earn. You drove out a cherub who should have received their name months ago. As of last night, you've cost me a better angel than you'll ever meet again. And you're fucking the boss."

Apparently everyone knew Ronnie was there last night. Big surprise. She was already so raw emotionally, he couldn't make it worse. She drew on everything she held back when talking to Lucifer. "Fucked. Past tense. And I don't know why you care. I do my job. I don't get in your way—"

"You flaunt what you've got. Your gifts, your connections." He stepped closer, standing toe to toe with her. "Some of us are here to make a difference. To do what we were created for. You're flitting along like it doesn't fucking matter. You and every one of Gabriel's star pupils who run through the revolving door. Here to get experience and then move on to other things. While those of us who actually work are stuck here, almost impotent, helping those assholes gather numbers instead of going out and trying to make people's lives better."

"I—" Ronnie's angry retort stuck in her throat. She wanted to fling more insults, and he was a viable target. Except he made sense. He was as fed up and frustrated as she was, but for different reasons. She didn't want to feel sympathy for him, but she couldn't help it.

"Growing a heart won't make you a real girl, Dorothy."

Nice. Mixed metaphors. She looked Raphael in the eye. "I'm sorry."

"Yeah. Me too." He handed her a folded piece of paper. "From Irdu."

Ronnie took it, but didn't know if she dared open it.

A door creaked behind them, and Lucifer said, "Raphael?"

"Wish me luck." Raphael gave me a weak smile.

Ronnie did, and she meant it. She stared at Lucifer's door for several seconds after it closed. This place was a wreck. She shook the thought away and forced her attention to the note.

Her gut sank, and the tears she swallowed in Lucifer's office rushed back when she read it. Relief flooded her.

It simply said: *Izrafel. Room 213.*

Chapter Thirty

Ronnie walked away from work without hesitation to visit Izzy and Irdu. They could fire her if they wanted. She didn't know if she was going back to Ubiquity anyway.

After the last twenty-four hours, it turned out she'd read pretty much everyone she knew wrong. But she still trusted and adored Izzy. He tried to help and didn't use her feelings for him against her. It was her fault he was going through this. Ari might not have known he existed if it weren't for his connection to Ronnie. The least she could do was make sure he recovered. Offer to help, if at all possible. It was too bad she didn't know how to heal—most agents didn't—but she could be there for him.

The hospital wasn't what she expected. Except for the occasional person in an open-backed gown, it was just another building. A map on the second floor told her which direction to go for his room, and seconds later she stood in front of the door. She gave a tentative knock and entered when she heard a grunting response.

Izzy's bed sat near the window, and he looked so pale. His arm was in a cast. Guilt surged strongest in the jumble of emotions in her head. No one else was in the room.

"Just a few broken bones?"

Metatron had a point. Why was he still here if that was all that was wrong?

His smile stretched his face, and he nodded to the chair by the bed. "Hey."

"How are you?" She dropped into the seat, worry growing.

"Eh. I feel like I've had my soul ripped out."

"I'm so sorry. It's my fault."

"Yeah. If you'd let me have control when I got here, this wouldn't have happened."

"Whoa, no." He rested his good hand on top of hers. "It's not."

Metatron was right. Lucifer meant to bring her back. Ronnie only caused trouble. Now Ari was gone, and Izzy lay in a hospital bed, and Ronnie was still a wreck. Maybe Metatron could have done this better. "Thanks, but I know otherwise. I just came to check on you and say thanks for helping me figure things out."

"I don't know what you've figured out, but it sounds final, whatever it is."

Ronnie hadn't meant it to, but when he pointed it out, she realized the conversation with Lucifer stuck a new idea in her head. It was one she didn't like, but it might be the only solution. "What was it like, sharing your thoughts with someone else? Did you ever argue?"

"It didn't work like that. I was it. It was me. We blended. But it didn't hold much when it reached me. Really only a *hey, wow,* and *neato.*"

That would be nice. Too bad that option didn't pan out for her. "I've been thinking, maybe I should just let you have Metatron back. I think that's for the best at this point."

He squeezed her hand. "Where did this come from? Are you all right?"

Concern gnawed at her, and she almost felt Metatron's smugness in her skull, waiting for Ronnie to finish. "Why would you ask me that? That assumes I was all right before. Is it just polite conversation? Do you really even care as long as you get her back?" She shouldn't take this out on him. He was lying in bed broken and battered, and Ronnie was pouting like a child.

He tightened his jaw. "Don't. I understand confusion. I walked away from heaven, and now I'm a preacher. But self-pity? That's bullshit."

The words stung, so she held back the rest of her thoughts. If he didn't want to hear it, she could keep the conversation generic. Depression surged inside. No, really she couldn't. "I'm tired. This takes too much effort, and no one wants me here anyway. Why am I trying?"

"Good question. Why are you trying?" The sudden ice in his tone jarred her.

"I could just leave right now. You don't know me. You knew her. Then you could have your friend back. You could check out guys together. You'd both be happier."

"Damn straight."

"I don't know that." His irritation detracted from the reassurance in his words.

Ronnie didn't want to be a brat about this, but it was too much. She couldn't hide her sarcasm. "You've convinced me."

The edge in his voice increased. "That's your choice. It's true, she and I shared a past. First of all, you can't hold that against me, and second, you and I are friends too. Even before I knew she was there. Remember that? All those days ago? I know what you're going through, at least a little, remember?"

He did, as much as anyone could, and she was shoving him away because of insecurity.

"Or because you finally got smart."

And that might have something to do with it too. A girl could only take so much.

Exhaustion raced in to replace the irritation in his voice. "We got to know each other when you first showed up, and I look forward to your visits. I enjoyed your company last night. I miss Metatron, but unlike those big badasses who have been around longer than the rest of us and still cling to her memory, I realize it's been thousands of years. She's in the past. Other than that, I'm really not liking this *oh, woe is me* side of you. Why do you care what I think, anyway? What anyone thinks but you? So what if you remind a few people of someone they used to know? Are you your own person or not?"

"No," Ronnie barked the word. "I'm not. That's the problem. She's living in my head. I don't even have that to myself, and no one will tell me

how to get rid of her. How to get my life back. Turns out it's because no one wants me to do it."

"I'll ask again, why do you care? It's your life, right? You want it? I mean, unless you're tired of it. If you don't want what you've got, why should anyone else care more than you do?"

Ronnie stomped to her feet, fury and hurt erasing every other emotion. "I never said I didn't want this life."

"You said everything but." He searched her face. "So how does wallowing get you what you want?"

Wow, he's an asshole. Except, she felt better than she had in days. "You're a fucker for making sense. You know that, right?"

He shrugged and dropped back onto his pillow, face pinched. "You wouldn't be the first person to tell me that."

She'd drained him. And it was obvious Michael lied to her about how serious this was. She shouldn't be surprised at this point. Apparently he was better at keeping the truth from her than she thought. And she came in here and made things worse.

Even if she couldn't heal him, and didn't know anyone who could, Gabe taught her one thing. Izzy would know what to do with what she was about give him. She took his good hand in hers, and let the tiniest hint of power flow into his palm.

His entire frame relaxed, and the tension vanished from his expression. "Neat trick."

"I'm sorry I can't do more."

"Stop being sorry." His voice was still tired, but the pain was gone. "Do something about it." He made it sound so simple.

"Like what?"

"If you don't like having her there, get rid of her."

"No. My life." The roar echoed in Ronnie's skull.

She flopped back into the chair. "That's not helpful. Don't you think maybe I might have done that already, if I knew how? Speaking of, what did you people see in her? She's whiny, childish, and immature."

"Oh, like you can talk. You've spent your entire remembered existence moping."

He shrugged. "I was the same way three thousand years ago. Or two decades ago. Or yesterday. Besides, you only know the *her* shoved inside your head. Would you be a good sport in that situation?"

"Obviously not. You'd crumble in an instant. I've survived for millennia."

Great. Now Ronnie felt guilty about wanting to get rid of Metatron. Not fair. "That makes a new problem. Getting rid of her sounds so callous now that I know who she is and what she meant to everyone. Who am I to say she deserves to be shoved aside more than I do?"

Izzy squeezed her fingers. "If that's the choice you have to make, you'll have to make it. I'm sorry I can't help there. In an ideal world, you'd find a new vessel for her to exist in, and you could both stick around."

Something tickled her thoughts. "A new vessel..."

"Without their own name, gifted by heaven or hell, cherubs can't exist on this plane without a host. So they find inanimate objects if they can't find anything else. They don't have to stay there, right? Some even find dead humans. Not like an in-the-morgue kind of thing, but like passed-away-seconds-ago-and-has-already-moved-on kind of thing."

That was morbid.

"You're not *sticking me in a fucking dead person."*

Better a corpse than Ronnie. She didn't mean that, but she liked the spite in the thought.

"I'd say find an inanimate object, something to draw her into, but everything I've read says that could destroy you."

Exactly what Gabe told her. Ronnie sat straight up. Unless something existed that unmade things. Split them into their original parts. "You're brilliant." Could it really be that easy? She would have wondered why Gabe didn't tell her, but at this point, she figured at least fifty percent of what came out of his mouth was bullshit.

"What? What are you thinking? You're not going to stick me in a doll or something. You can't. I won't let you."

But Ronnie learned something every time Metatron locked her memories away and from the way Metatron hid Ronnie's power. She wrapped the thought up in a secure ball, chained and tucked it into a part of her mind labeled *for my eyes only.* If

Metatron could keep Ronnie out of her thoughts, it worked both ways. At least long enough to make Ronnie's plan happen.

Gabriel's spear. If she could use it to draw Metatron out—to unmake what Lucifer did—maybe she could find Metatron a new home. Then people could have their bitchy-dead-angel-friend, and Ronnie could still have her life. "Would you think less of me if I told Gabe I would work for him?"

Izzy shook his head. "As long as you weren't actually working for him. You got that from Lucifer, right? The double talk."

Maybe Ronnie could make this happen. She prayed she could. She pressed her lips to his cheek, letting a little more power flow into him. Not enough to recharge him or anything—she didn't think a purely human form could do that—but enough to maybe help him heal faster. "Thank you."

As she stepped from the room, she was startled to find Irdu waiting in the hallway.

"What the fuck was that?" His arms were crossed, and he wore a scowl.

She winced. "How much did you hear?"

"Most of it. You can't go work for Gabe. Who the fuck cares what everyone else wants? You're you. *I* want you to stay you for selfish reasons. I need you to be safe. I love you." He cradled her cheeks in his palms, and pressed his lips to hers.

It was one of those tender kisses of his that usually came after intense sex. The soft brush of lips that threatened to shatter her heart today.

"I love you, too," she murmured against his lips when he pulled away.

"And none of that matters." He held her gaze. "Not in the grand scheme of what *you* want. If you want to be you, fuck the originals, and ancient angels. Be you."

The passion in his touch, in his words, in the gold and green aura that flowed from him and wrapped around them, all warmed her from the inside-out. "I promise you I have a plan. And even if it doesn't go quite right, and even if these assholes make the world crumble tomorrow, I know you're here for me."

"Not quite the assurance I wanted. If I let you go, you have to promise you'll come back to me."

"I swear it." Except she didn't know if she could keep that promise. She wanted to, so badly, but there were too many variables.

* * * *

On the street outside Gabe's coffee shop, Ronnie paused in front of a window next door to check her reflection then ran her fingers through her hair. Her smile looked forced, even in the wobbly dark glass. A million questions and doubts raced through her mind, none of them receiving a retort. Metatron was still sulking because Ronnie figured out how to keep things from her. The sensation was odd and more disconcerting than Ronnie expected.

Was she doing the right thing? The conversations with Lucifer and Izzy and Irdu echoed in her head. Yeah. She was the only one who could do this. She didn't have a choice.

Gabe rested his hands at her hips, startling her. "Hey, sexy."

She whirled to face him, half her resolution evaporating in an instant. "Hey. I've been thinking about what you said earlier today." The words tumbled past her lips.

He stepped forward to cradle his hand at the base of her neck and wrap his fingers in her hair. He kissed her, mouth soft but hungry. She let out an involuntary groan, swept away by the rush of power. Even though she knew what he was doing, she couldn't stop it. She didn't want it to stop. Her composure faded before he pulled away.

He put some distance between them, and a wolfish smile danced on his face. "You're torturing me unnecessarily. I only want what's best for you. For us. I need you by my side."

"This is a big change for me." She pouted. An intentional—if awkward—deception. "And you lied about what I was." Why was she arguing? She needed to convince him she wanted this as much as he said he did. His presence unnerved her. His power swept over and around her, making her doubt her resolve. Would he see through her? Subject her to a fate worse than Metatron's?

"I was scared." He sounded genuine, but slime flowed in his aura.

"I know." She exaggerated her sigh. "But it still hurt."

"Give me another chance? I need you."

He was buying this. She was in. She let a smile flicker onto her face. "Maybe."

He stepped in again, pressing his lips to hers.

Yeah, this was what she needed to do. A whisper of a memory threatened her determination. Hints of death, betrayal, and lies. She pulled back with a small frown.

He tightened his grip on the back of her neck. Concern passed over his face, and then all emotion vanished. "What's wrong?"

Ronnie shook her head, trying to clear away the sick feeling doubt brought with it. "Nothing. I'm just…" She didn't know what she was.

He didn't let go. "I understand. I shouldn't have expected it to be easy. It's my fault."

She needed to get to that fucking spear, and given where it was, there was no way it was happening unless he trusted her. She struggled for words. Metatron's nagging was still gone, so Ronnie didn't understand her hesitation. "I just… Maybe I need to take *us* more slowly, you know?" Now she was playing his game of deception full force, and terrified she was a noob compared to his lifetimes of experience.

He looked wounded, but something about it wasn't sincere. He brought a foot to rest between hers. "We've shared a lot. You know me."

Yeah, she did. Even without a voice whispering in her ear, she saw flashes of their encounters. His assumptions. The information he kept from her. His indifference for Ari's fate. More.

She tried to be subtle about taking a step back. Could she keep her distance and still win his trust? "Why is it so important I make a decision now? We have eternity."

"I'm worried about losing you. I've seen you with Michael. What if someone else wins you over?" His form flickered, tendrils of ethereal strength flowing in.

"If it's my choice, it's my choice with anyone." Something flitted through her, and she recognized two sources of power. But Metatron kept what she had locked away from Ronnie, didn't she?

"It's not like you've had a use for it."

Metatron was back. Sulking time was over.

"Miss me?"

"No."

"Liar."

Gabe twisted his fingers in Ronnie's hair, tugging enough to tilt her head back. He traced her ear with his lips. "Where did this lack of trust come from?"

Whatever hold he had over her in the past was long gone. The need for charade wasn't. She forced herself to smile. "Maybe we need to step back a little."

"This is a dangerous game."

"It's the most effective approach I can think of."

"Not arguing, just trying to keep this shell intact for when I have my shot at it."

Gabe's grip tightened, pulling on her scalp. He grazed her earlobe with his teeth, and his voice was a soft growl. "That's not up for discussion. We're doing this my way."

"No we're not."

Ronnie didn't share Metatron's confidence, and the threat made her hesitate. What was she thinking? She wasn't powerful enough to take on a fucking original. Gabriel. Vengeance. Ronnie was just a minor demon desk jockey. "I think coming here was a mistake." She tried to break away and failed.

"I think you should hear me out." His breath was hot against her skin. Holding her head at an awkward angle, he slid his free hand under her shirt, and crawled his fingers up her back.

The tantalizing sensation of his touch was gone, leaving only revulsion in its place. She made a more concerted effort to break free, no longer worried about convincing him she cared. Panic swept through her when she failed. She wasn't strong enough to take him on, could she talk her way out of here? "You haven't said anything new yet."

"Don't let him scare you."

Easier said than done. Ronnie tried to draw power from within. To use the same tactic she did with Ari. But she failed. Michael stepped in and saved her in the end, and Gabe was far more powerful and experienced than Ari. Ronnie couldn't do this.

"We can."

He twisted his foot, forcing her to widen her stance and making her balance precarious. He pinned her to the front door of the coffee shop. "This isn't a negotiation, regardless of what you think. I'm done playing these games."

"Do it now."

The only thing Ronnie wanted to do was get the fuck out of here. She grasped what she was looking for, and hoped Metatron would back her up. "Leave. Me. Alone." She shoved from within, summoning everything she could, and focused on sending him to one place and her to another.

Cool air rushed in to soothe her flushed cheeks when she appeared in Michael's guest room. Ronnie didn't want to be here, but given that she pissed off someone powerful, she didn't think anywhere else was safe.

Besides, she couldn't stand any longer. Gasping with relief at being away from the threat, she dropped to her knees. She felt weak and relieved and terrified and powerful. But most of all, acid churned in her gut and threatened to evict any remainder of her breakfast.

"I need to lie down."

Ronnie didn't have the strength or will to argue. She flopped onto the bed. Rolling on her side, she pulled her knees to her chest and tried to process what happened. She didn't know what she should be thinking, but she wanted to pick a specific emotion to make things simpler. Forcibly removing Gabe and sending him somewhere he might not want to be left her drained. Where had she sent him, anyway? Away from her, that was all that mattered.

"Are we wallowing again? Do you ever get sick of that?"

Ronnie had just banished an original from her presence.

What was she supposed to do if not dwell on it? Would he come after her? She *was* safe in

Michael's condo, right? Even if she wanted to do something else, she was too exhausted. Not only that, but she rejected and pissed off her one chance at maybe, possibly, splitting Metatron from her without destroying one of them. *Fuck.*

Chapter Thirty-One

Red numbers glared at Ronnie from the clock on the nightstand. Just after three a.m. Perfect. Not. She was pretty sure being wide awake at this time of night was a bad idea twenty-four hours ago. Whatever drained her when she sent Gabriel away—the overload of information, the physical expulsion—she'd recovered. Her brain moved a million miles an hour with no answers, and she wasn't going back to sleep any time soon.

She'd considered going back to the hospital. She ached to see Irdu. But if Gabriel found her, those around her wouldn't be safe.

At least, given the late hour, she could probably avoid Michael. Not that avoidance would be an option for much longer, unless she found another place to stay.

"Or, you know, if you'd just stop being stubborn and let me out."

Ronnie was glad she kept Metatron at bay one more day, but was so not in the mood for her. Ronnie padded from the guest bedroom and made her way to the balcony. Fortunately, it was easy to move without a sound on the plush carpet. She slid the door open and stepped into the night. The smoke was gone from the air, and while the stars weren't as bright as the streetlights below, they still held her attention.

She stretched and tried to work some of the tension from her neck. Her discomfort wasn't physical, but she needed to do something. She reached up to rub the invisible knots instead.

"Let me." Michael's voice startled her. He covered her hand with his. Contentment whispered through her, carried on uncertainty. She couldn't delve into this, but it was comforting. She leaned back into him, relief flooding her when he didn't pull away. He kneaded his fingers into her neck and shoulders.

Metatron didn't know it yet, but she wouldn't be a part of Ronnie much longer. When Ronnie found a suitable vessel, she was pretty sure Michael would change his stance on *I only see you when I look at you.* "We shouldn't go down this road." Ronnie hated saying the words.

"Do you want me to stop?"

"No." She was grateful he couldn't see her sad smile. "This whole existence thing is a drain sometimes. How have you lasted so long?" His attentions chased away her tension and silenced Metatron's irritation. She wanted to wrap herself in the security, but couldn't convince herself this was more than a single moment.

"You just do." Michael stopped kneading, and slid his hands down her arms until he intertwined his fingers with hers. "I talked to Lucifer."

*

Michael wanted to say *I don't know* when Ronnie asked how he'd lasted so long. Instead he plucked out the one name he knew would be a mood killer. He needed that right now. Anything to maintain a neutral conversation. To stick to his resolution to keep Ronnie at a distance. Not that he was doing a great job of that right now.

"That makes two of us." Her voice was flat.

He couldn't help his chuckle. "Did he have anything interesting to say?"

"Not really."

Michael wasn't surprised. There was more to this than a couple of angels stealing cherubs and Ronnie holding a power older than the earth. Those were big enough on their own, but Lucifer knew more. Michael rested his forehead on the top of her head. "He came to visit the morning after I ran into you in hell."

"You mean Monday? Two days ago?"

Was it really only a couple of days? He swore he aged lifetimes since then, and that was saying a lot for someone who didn't age. "Sounds about right."

"Did he have anything interesting to say?" She mimicked his question.

"That you weren't Metatron. To walk away from you." His laugh was bitter. Michael knew it was a lie, even then, but it hid so much more. Except it was true. Ronnie wasn't Metatron. "You never really knew how she died, did you?"

Ronnie didn't answer.

He squeezed her hands. "I was supposed to meet her that night. I was early, but not early enough. When I got there, she was already dying."

She shuddered. "And Gabriel was already there."

"Yes." The single word carried more grief and guilt than he thought possible. "His story was that she was plotting to destroy us all, and he had to act before it happened." The air conditioner kicked on in the background, blending into his quiet story. "You have no idea how hard that was to believe, but we didn't deal with things like office politics and double-talk back then. Why would he lie?"

Regardless of how far in the past it was, the moment still haunted him.

"He didn't mean for you to find him there," she said.

He tightened his grip on her hands at the information. She did know.

"He meant to frame you. If it looked like you did it, she'd be gone, you and Lucifer would take each other down, and he'd be the only one left."

No. Gabriel wouldn't... Michael tried to reconcile the information. It wasn't right. But he knew better. Gabriel would. He'd never made it a secret he thought he could do this better as an individual than group. Always hated sharing the glory of being an *original*.

Michael kissed the top of her head. "I guess I have always known that." He let go of her hands and turned her to face him. "I'm sorry you got caught in the middle of it. I've said this before, but if you believe one thing, out of this whole mess, I hope it's this. You and Metatron aren't the same person. She was stunning and brilliant and one of us."

Pain flashed across her face.

He didn't say the words to hurt her, but she had to know. He kissed her on the cheek, struggling to ignore the comfort that seeped into him and hoping to convey apology. "But you... You're just as beautiful, just as intelligent, and completely your own person. You see the world in a way I forgot was possible. You're not one of us because you're the most unique thing I've ever seen. She never had that kind of reverent awe for life. I don't know if I would have stayed if she was here instead of you. I'm glad I stuck around long enough to get to know you. I'm sorry it can't be longer."

That wasn't how he meant to finish, but as he spoke, he knew it was the only solution. He phased from the balcony. He should tell her goodbye, but it was too much. Distance would help. She'd grow and become more, with Irdu by her side, and he'd do what he was made for—help people achieve their potential.

He reappeared in the hospital, outside Izrafel's room, and was startled to find Lucifer already there. "I didn't know you two were friends."

Lucifer gave him a dry smile. "I know everyone."

"How is he?"

"Not good."

Michael wished there was more he could do. That wasn't his place, though. "One more favor?"

"You want to open a tab?" Lucifer's tone was flat, almost exhausted.

"Something like that. But this time I've got an offering in return." He pulled his keyring from his pocket and held it up.

"Aww. You got me a hybrid car. You shouldn't have." Even Lucifer's sarcasm was flat. Had this really worn them all down so much?

Michael tossed the keys at him. "I'm leaving. Out of *her* life, though I realize it's not soon enough for you."

"And dumping the Ubiquity clusterfuck on me?"

"It's your project. But no. More like I'm taking a demotion. Remote work."

Lucifer sighed. "That's what you were doing before."

"Except now, I'm looking for more like Ariel. Give the keys to Ronnie, *please*. Tell her the place is hers until she can get established." He turned to leave. He'd rather use the front door right now. He was about to spend a lot of time in the ether, and wanted to appreciate Earth a little longer.

"Michael." Lucifer's voice stopped him, but he didn't turn. "Good luck."

* * * *

Michael was gone, leaving an empty void in the room to keep Ronnie company. His words echoed around her. If he meant the kindness to reassure her, it didn't work. Since he left anyway, it made the hole in her heart more obvious. Her chest throbbed, and she blinked back unexpected tears. Where was this coming from? She knew—pretty much from the first time they really talked—there would never be anything between them.

At least he didn't walk away from Ronnie because of Metatron. Ronnie sniffled and rubbed the back of her wrist across her eyes. She still wasn't sure she understood his reasons. Immortal beings without the restrictions of heaven and hell— what Ari became—were dangerous. Falling in love? Or at least experiencing a heavy dose of lust? Apparently it hurt a lot when it ended, but it wasn't in the same league.

Despite trying to tell herself she was better off without that in her life, she still wanted him to stay. She couldn't ignore the selfish bits of her that already ached from his leaving. She'd see him around, right? He was cutting her off, but there was still work to do. Would seeing him every day make things easier on her or harder to accept?

She stood there, trying to make sense of her thoughts, until the sun peeked over the horizon. Was there even a point in going to work? Her entire world was stripped away.

"So... My turn now?"

No. Fuck that. And why wasn't Metatron torn up about this? Ronnie tried to swallow her grief and failed.

"Because he left you, not me. Part of you knows that."

Taunting was the last thing Ronnie needed. If she couldn't have her past, she'd build her future instead. The resolution didn't reassure her the way she wanted, but if she could dive into it, maybe she could ignore how much losing Michael hurt, at least for a little while.

Ronnie didn't need Metatron knowing what she was up to before she finished. Ronnie rolled the idea over in her head. If she could figure out how to get that spear, she could shove Metatron into it. Not permanently, but long enough to get her away from Ronnie and find her a new place to stay.

She desperately needed something to take her mind off the finality in Michael's tone.

She wandered into the guest bedroom and found Michael's phone on the nightstand. Probably too early to call Gabe. Then again, the bastard all but assaulted her, and for all she knew, waited for a chance to finish what they started. Did she really care about waking him up?

Yeah, she did. If her plan was going to work, she needed to make him think she was sorry long enough for him to trust her. *Fuck.*

The phone buzzed in her hand. She jumped and then laughed at herself for being startled. It was a text from Lucifer. Short enough for her to see the whole thing in the preview window. *It's Izzy.*

"No."

Metatron's reaction echoed Ronnie's. She phased to the hospital room. Lucifer stood outside the door, back against the wall, arms crossed. He frowned when he saw her.

Ronnie wanted to ask a million questions. What was he doing there? How did he know to come? Why did he let her know? Only one thing rushed to her lips. "What's wrong?"

He wouldn't look her in the eye. "They don't know."

"You do." Ronnie wasn't going to listen to his bullshit. A new kind of fear coursed through her. Not like when she faced off with Ari or Gabe, but for the man in the other room.

"He's having a hard time adjusting. He's so weak, and he has to heal on top of getting used to mortality. He might not make it through the day."

Ronnie's heart sank, and she bit back a sob.

He nodded at the door. "No one's going to stop you, if you want to see him."

She wouldn't have waited even if he told her no. She slipped into the room. Izzy lay in bed, head sunken into the pillow. His chest rose and fell slowly, and a steady beep filled the room.

She crossed over to him without a sound, in slow motion, not seeing the world for what it was. If only she recognized who Ari was—a power hungry bitch willing to betray the world for her own desires—or what Ronnie held in time, she might have kept Ari away from Izzy. Or maybe Ronnie could have just kept her mouth shut and not provoked Ari, and the angel would still have her cherub and wouldn't have touched him. This was Ronnie's fault.

She stroked the back of his hand, grief and powerlessness filling her thoughts. He was so gaunt and fragile. And he didn't deserve to be here. In a way, she blamed Ari, but Gabriel drew her into it. Promised her something he shouldn't have. Showed her an existence none of them were meant to live.

Rage rushed in to replace sorrow, and fury filled every inch of her. Fucking originals. They weren't any different from any other agent of heaven or hell. Lucifer did this for so long, he didn't know when the truth was an asset. Michael operated independently, terrified of his own feelings or getting close to someone the way he had Metatron. Gabriel was a bitter, lying asshole. And Metatron wasn't any better, except she was locked away with her own thoughts for millennia.

Ronnie was tired of playing by their rules. She wanted Metatron out of her head, and she wanted her own life.

Chapter Thirty-Two

Ronnie exited Izzy's room. Irdu waited next to Lucifer.

Irdu grabbed her wrist, pulled her close, and wrapped an arm around her waist. The comfort in his touch, the implication in the gesture, it all soothed the fractured cracks inside and gave her strength.

She was terrified of what she was about to do, but knowing he waited. He supported her. He knew her. It all helped.

Irdu kissed her hard and fast. "Come back to me," he murmured against her lips.

She nodded, unable to tell the lie a second time, and broke away.

She brushed past Lucifer and his request for her to wait, and walked down to the front desk of the hospital.

They were happy to let her use the phone. Or terrified of telling her no. She didn't care which it was.

She called Gabe. She was going to see him now, throw herself at his feet, beg forgiveness for the day before, and play the phony bullshit game as well as he or Lucifer ever did. She wanted that fucking spear.

"Fine, ignore me. Keep me in the dark. The longer you hold onto me, the more likely it is I'll push you aside."

Ronnie listened to the phone ring and ignored Metatron's babbling.

"Ronnie." The strain in Gabe's voice was apparent across the phone lines.

"Hey." She forced all the cheer and submission she could into her voice, glad he couldn't see her sneer. "Are you busy?"

"Are you begging? You're really pathetic."

"I'm done begging. I'm taking."

"What do you want?" His question was clipped.

"You. Dead. Not picky about the details."

"To talk things through." Ronnie kept her voice contrite, ignoring the screaming in the back of her head.

"My schedule is full."

She expected that. She'd extended the olive branch and the next step would happen under his terms. "I understand. Do you know when you'll have time?"

"Time for what?" His sigh echoed out of the mouthpiece.

If she could get him to invite her into his vault—possibly with the reminder that the spear had her at a disadvantage last time—she could grab what she wanted. "I want to see you."

"Gag."

Silence greeted her. She checked her phone to make sure she was still connected. "Hello?"

"I'm still here." He sounded irritated. "I'm still not sure what you want."

"I was going to drop by your coffee shop. Maybe in about an hour?"

"I have places to be this morning. I'll be there at four. Make sure you're not late."

"I hate you."

The feeling was mutual.

* * * *

Ronnie arrived at the coffee shop ten minutes early. Gabe's implied threat lingered in her head. Not that she was worried about what he'd do to her—if she put any thought into that at all, she'd chicken out—but she didn't want him leaving before she got what she came for.

He sat at the far end of the room, facing the door, but focused on a laptop. He didn't look up as she approached.

She lingered less than a foot from the table, waiting and watching.

He took his time turning to her, expression shifting to flat when he finally met her gaze. "Care to join me? Or do you need more time to think about it?"

She hoped she seemed appropriately wounded by the passive-aggressive comment as she dropped into the chair across from him. With any luck, they could move past the antagonism quickly. "Thanks for making time for me."

He frowned, gaze drifting to the table. "I couldn't say no. I missed you."

"Gag."

The words didn't move Ronnie—Metatron's or Gabe's. But she'd play along a little longer. She rested her hands on the table, fingers intertwined. "Me too."

He reached across the scarred tabletop and turned one of her hands over, tracing a line down her wrist. "Why here?"

"It's where we first met. Made sense for a new beginning, if we're both willing to work on it."

"Gag."

That was already old. Could Ronnie recreate the making-Metatron-sulk-so-much-she-shut-up trick she pulled yesterday?

"Bitch. Want some sugar with your denial? Oh, that's right. You drink that shit straight now."

Gabe pulled his hands away and dropped them into his lap. "Tell me what I have to do to win you over."

Ronnie paused, waiting for a snide comment from within. Not hearing one, she mentally shrugged. "You told me I had time to think about things. You implied you wanted me to. And then you pushed. You made assumptions. Do you want me by your side or not?"

"Never mind how happy you were to use him for little power-ups before you found out he was an asshole."

And there it was. At least with Metatron, she expected the biting words. The constant was almost a relief.

He sighed. "I already told you this. I was scared. I couldn't afford to take any chances. I've had to walk the line between self-preservation and love since I met you. The person you work for doesn't have the same goals I do. It was unfortunate that something upset that balance. But it's over now. If you didn't understand at least a little, you wouldn't have called me."

She was already willing to go along with whatever he said. But she couldn't make it look too easy. Not after that whole forcibly phasing him thing she did. "It's true. I guess I just want to make sure it doesn't happen again."

"Of course. I think we both know better now. Never again."

She brushed aside the rage that asked how he could make such a promise.

He stood and offered her his hand. "Can we go somewhere more private?"

She hesitated, but only for a moment. A familiar tingle filled her at his touch. It didn't penetrate every inch of her being the way she was used to, and she resisted the temptation to draw on it against his will. She waited for the inevitable lecture from within.

"Why? So you can shoot me down again? Screw that."

Ronnie leaned into Gabe's touch. His power crackled around her, and her surroundings vanished.

"I'm tired of this game." His breath warmed her ear. They were in his vault under the coffee shop. The underlying threat in his voice made her stomach lurch.

"Same." She kept her tone submissive as she struggled to figure out her next steps. Getting here was easier than she expected, him being on guard threw a wrench in things.

He tightened his grip around her waist, and held her against him, her back pressed to his front. He grazed her neck with his teeth. "Why are you really here?"

His power sliced across her skin, but Metatron kept Ronnie from using any of it. Not that Ronnie wanted to. She'd do this on her own. The weight of being surrounded by his essence kept her from pulling away, and she realized how much Gabe held back in the past. She tried to swallow her fear. She'd tell him the truth. Or one version of it.

"Why? Obliterate him."

Ronnie wasn't Metatron. She was just another demon. She couldn't do that. Instead, she used the excuse she hoped would speak to his ego. "I need you."

"Really?" Anger tinged his sarcasm. "You're pushing me out one day and wanting me back the next?"

The seesaw behavior made her insides quake. She expected a methodical deception, not borderline psychosis. Ronnie didn't know if she was prepared for something so intense, but she let the words flow, hoping instinct would preserve her. "I'm a demon. Without a purpose, I'm nothing. Hell doesn't have that for me, and I need something. I'm so terrified of being removed from it all."

"Holy hell, you're high."

Ronnie wasn't. She was tired of the mood swings. But as long as he bought her story long enough for her to figure a new way to get to—

"Let's kill him."

—that fucking spear. She kept the thought locked away from Metatron.

"You're lying." Gabe's accusation hissed across her senses. He slammed her into a wall. "What do you want from me?"

Her skull cracked against concrete, the pain reverberating through her neck and spine. Her instinct was to shift forms to get rid of the pain, but an unseen presence stopped her. The inability to become quasi-mortal made her realize he had all the control in this space. Being here kept her from doing anything with her power he didn't want. She reached up, fingering the tender spot on her head, relieved when she didn't feel anything wet or sticky. The fear in her voice was real. "I'm telling the truth."

"Let me out."

"No." At least Ronnie still controlled what was in her head. Not that she wanted to devote any attention to the mental tantrum. Her joints ached from the crushing pressure around her.

Gabe was in front of her in an instant, forehead pressed to hers. "The naïve demon routine isn't charming anymore. I'm tired of your games."

"Oh hey, we agree on something. Who knew? Let. Me. Out."

Black ribbons spilled beneath Ronnie's skin, vying for control. She whimpered involuntarily at the dual assault. "I'm not playing." Tears leaked from her eyes.

"Kill him or I will."

"What else could I want?" she asked and then winced, expecting another rush of pain in response.

He let go of her and took a step back. A wicked smile filled his face. "I don't know. Maybe vengeance. We both know what you hold in your head, and we both know what happened to her centuries ago."

"Wow. Smartest thing he's ever said. Kill him."

His invisible, crushing control didn't let up, but at least he didn't hurt her again. "No, I swear to you." Ronnie poured all her sincerity into her reassurance. "I want to serve with you, even if it means subjecting myself to the pain of that spear. I'm here for you."

"Wait, what? We're not going near that thing again." Metatron's death-lust fueled ranting wavered, peppered with fear.

Shit. Ronnie shouldn't have mentioned the spear.

"Really?" He grabbed her upper arm and yanked her to him. He dug his fingers into her skin, making her cringe. A haunting chuckle shook his frame. "You'd do that to prove your loyalty? From your reaction last time, I could have sworn that thing was going to kill you." He forced her to walk toward where the spearhead rested.

"We're not going near that thing. You should rot and die."

Ronnie didn't know who Metatron was talking to–Ronnie or Gabe. Both, probably.

The dark threads roiling inside Ronnie singed her bones, burning and screaming for freedom. *No.* It was Ronnie's body. Metatron couldn't have it.

"Then fight back."

Ronnie couldn't fight both of them. She was struggling to survive Gabe. The room swam at the edge of her vision.

"Keep walking." Gabe's command sliced at her consciousness, tearing away more of her control.

"Kill him."

"I'm stronger than this." The thought whispered in a cloud of ice, distinct in a collage of confusion, and Ronnie grasped what was hers.

Gabe sounded distant, even though he was right next to her. He hauled her toward the back of the room, grip never loosening, and growled in her ear, "You do this for me, and then we can talk."

"Fuck you."

Ronnie would do what he wanted. He was right.

"Because you don't have a choice?"

Something like that, but not quite. The ice of Ronnie's power slid through her. Through the haze of pain, she swore she could visualize it weaving together with the foreign elements inside her—the pieces that were Metatron—and wrapping itself around Metatron until she evaporated.

"Wait, what are you doing? Oh, that's new." Awe and realization spread through Metatron's words.

Evaporated wasn't the right word. Ronnie was making them a part of her. *Wait.* Making them part of her? Was this the integration everyone talked about? As the ice raced through her, it swallowed the traces of Metatron, the gray wisps of Ronnie's power chasing away the pain. Was Ronnie absorbing her or becoming one with her? *Fuck,* did this still mean one of them would be lost when it was done?

Ronnie had enough presence of mind not to let her realization show externally. She was terrified of what Gabe would do to her. But the discovery made her pause.

"Don't tell me making me vanish into your consciousness was your master plan?"

It wasn't, but it might be better. Inky ribbons raced through Ronnie, surging to get to her power before she could get to Metatron. Ronnie pushed back, temporarily bringing the struggle between them to a standstill. What if this wasn't a merger? If Ronnie continued and lost, would Metatron be in control after all?

Metatron thought so. She fought back, her dark energy rushing into every inch of who Ronnie was, magnifying the pain of Gabe's power. Agony tore through Ronnie, and she stumbled. Her knees hit the concrete with a dull thud, and she cried out.

"Stand up." Gabe wrenched her to her feet. "We have a spear to use." His fingers dug into her arm.

Ronnie would have smiled through the pain if she could. He was ultimately still in control. In his realm, where his power was strongest, he was the ruling entity.

"Haven't you learned anything? He's nothing compared to me. I'll shove you aside, and I'll kill him."

Metatron's taunt was weak

"Liar. I'm in control here. You're just a copy. Now that I know what to do with your energy, this shell is mine."

Ronnie struggled to keep herself from Metatron. To cling to her own power. But Ronnie was fighting a losing battle. Stopping Gabe from crushing her took too much focus. She couldn't do that and claim Metatron's essence at the same time. Absorbing Metatron was a bad and fleeting idea. She needed to go. The spear waited for Ronnie, offering that solution. Once Metatron was gone, Ronnie only needed to focus on Gabe.

"You're a pathetic vessel. A useless little girl, who doesn't know what she's got. Lucifer meant for me to live again. You'll ruin everything because you're a selfish child."

Maybe Metatron was right.

"Of course I am. I've had millennia to learn. You haven't learned anything."

Another shock of threads spilled through Ronnie, and she screamed involuntarily at the spikes biting into her muscles. They amplified the pressure Gabe applied until she swore her bones were being crushed.

"Shut up." Gabe's bark echoed off the walls and antiques, reverberating in her skull. "You're so much more trouble than you're worth."

They were both wrong. Ronnie knew it. Or at least she believed it enough to convince herself she knew it. Ronnie was powerful, but she wasn't an original. She needed Metatron to defeat Gabe, not some half-assed, mutated conglomeration. Ronnie needed to be one with Metatron.

She clamped her jaw shut and focused inward, finding the icy strands of her power. Some of them were still a combination of Metatron and Ronnie. Ronnie dove back into the corners Metatron had retaken, forcing her out.

"Stop."

Ronnie struggled, unable to penetrate the core of ink that hovered over the sigil on her back. *Uriel.* The mark where Metatron's name would have been. The designator that made Ronnie a demon and not just a cherub.

"Let's go." Gabe yanked her arm.

It was too bad the jarring didn't remove Metatron's surging quest for dominance.

His grip loosened, but his power held her as he pushed her toward the pedestal. He bound her legs moving them one foot in front of the other.

"I'll kill him!"

Metatron screamed in Ronnie's skull and forced herself into Ronnie's veins. Agony tore through her. She was going to burst. She dropped to the ground with a whimper. *No.* Metatron couldn't win. But Ronnie couldn't fight her without cluing in Gabe. Everything ached as Metatron struggled to take control of Ronnie's body.

"My body. Move aside, bitch."

Ronnie gasped, studying the patterns in the marble floor, watching them swim. For a moment she saw through someone else's eyes. Like the morning she woke up to Metatron controlling her. Ronnie's screams sounded distant, fading as Metatron took more control.

"No."

That was Ronnie. *Shit.* She was the voice in her own head.

"Yes." The whisper rushed past her lips. That was Metatron.

Chapter Thirty-Three

"I won't tell you again." Gabe's growl was distant, like it filtered through speakers. "Stand. Up."

He forced her up, trying to force her joints in ways they didn't want to go. It wouldn't have been so bad if she weren't fighting Metatron at the same time. "Why are you so focused on keeping him in the dark? Stop fighting me so we can kill him." Metatron's words came from Ronnie's lips.

Shit. Ronnie didn't want Gabe to know about the internal struggle. Ronnie poured her strength into reclaiming her body. She shoved Metatron aside in her head, ice licking the edges of the ribbons and absorbing them, but not penetrating the dark box Ronnie pictured her living in.

"Kill who?" Gabe glared at her.

Ronnie ground her teeth hating to sacrifice focus to even a simple reply. "Someone else. A not-here guy."

Metatron tried to thrust Ronnie aside again as Gabe half-floated, half-dragged her across the room. Ronnie was grateful for the first time that night for his overt display of power. She grabbed individual strands of the energy he radiated, untangled the intangible bonds, and used them to further the ice flow under her skin.

"Stop." Metatron might as well have shouted, but terror bled through her command.

Ronnie probed the edges of the dense ball Metatron hid her core inside, tucked between her shoulder blades.

"Stop." The command came from outside, and Ronnie's connection to Gabe snapped, cutting her off from his power. He flung her toward the podium with a roar. "You've lost the right to touch that."

Heat enveloped her, the spear's pull grabbing her essence and tearing it from her. It didn't matter. She took enough power from him to finish what she started. Ronnie didn't want to destroy Metatron. Too many people wanted the original back. She didn't see another option, and this was survival. It wasn't the kind of standoff where they both walked away if one surrendered.

Gabe kept talking. "I wish you'd gone along with this. I would have loved to have flaunted you on my arm. Better than destroying Metatron again—she would have been locked away, Lucifer would have been furious, and Michael… That might have driven him over the edge. But you were never more than a trophy. Destroying them—literally or otherwise—is the ultimate goal. I don't have a problem decimating you, if it kills her again."

"I'll demolish you first." Metatron's threat slipped past Ronnie's lips. "See you crushed, leave you alive, and walk away from your broken existence."

"Shut up," Ronnie growled at herself.

She was done trying to hide what she was up to. She pushed at Metatron, focusing on wearing down the black core of her power with the ice of Ronnie's, absorbing all of it. Ronnie wouldn't let someone else take the life that belonged to her.

"That power is mine, not yours." Metatron still had control.

"Have I broken you already?" Gabe's taunt was distant, carried on more pain than Ronnie thought possible.

Through the haze of her internal struggle, she saw him grab the spear. *Fuck.*

"No." Metatron's roar bounced off the concrete walls.

He grasped the weapon, lips curling into a wicked smile, as he hefted it.

Metatron tried to pull away, but with Ronnie absorbing more and more inside, and Gabe's energy holding her body in place, there was nowhere to go. Agony ripped through her, as the weapon drew closer, sucking out her guts, tearing her to ethereal shreds. She couldn't move.

Ronnie withdrew further into her head, both to avoid the pain and to finish absorbing Metatron. But she couldn't grasp the threads. Metatron had blocked her off from her own power again. Ronnie's icy strength was faint, growing cloudier each moment as Metatron took more and more control.

"Now I take what belongs to me."

Why wasn't Metatron talking out loud anymore?

"You'll die instead of me."

No.

"I'll destroy you."

Why wasn't Ronnie surprised?

Gabe stabbed her from behind.

A new pain tore through her. She screamed until her throat was raw, and even then couldn't stop. The walls rattled.

He plunged the spear deeper into her back, between her shoulder blades. He twisted and pushed harder, hitting what she was sure was a lung. A gurgle marred her roar.

Metatron was being stripped from her, unwound from the corners of her mind, being shredded away from aspects of Ronnie she didn't realize the angel was buried in. Wisps and strands rushed into the obsidian sticking out of Ronnie's back.

Holy fuck, that hurt. Metatron dug her claws in, wrapping herself around Ronnie. The edges of where Metatron started blurred with Ronnie, until the two of them were no longer distinguishable.

Revelation sank in amid the agony. Ronnie didn't know if it was a pain-induced idea, or if there was actually any logic to it, but if it didn't work, it wouldn't matter in a few seconds anyway. Suddenly, everything Izzy and Ari said to her about claiming a cherub made sense. Ronnie didn't have to pick which of them survived. Metatron still ran from the spear's pull, and Ronnie used the distraction to dive into what Metatron locked away. To plunge headfirst into *her*.

Metatron gained control of Ronnie's arm, and reached for the spear.

"Sorry, love." Gabe's admonishment was distant. His power pinned her arms to her side, and he gave the weapon another shove.

Ronnie arched her back and whimpered, no longer having the voice to scream. Focus. Needed to focus. Finish this. In her mind, she saw Metatron's core. It was attached to Ronnie's, woven and braided through each other. Ronnie thrust everything toward it. It didn't matter how much the spear hurt, or that Gabe crushed her. If she couldn't finish this internally, she might as well let him do what he wanted.

Metatron recognized Ronnie's target, but not the ultimate goal. Sharp, black rage enveloped her thoughts, trying to shove Ronnie back, but it was too late. Ronnie saw the individual strands of both of them. She plucked at one, unraveling the threads. Metatron's internal protests faded as Ronnie absorbed more of her, and the harmony of the two opposing powers mingled and coursed through her veins.

Ronnie followed the fading trails back to the spear, blending with the remainder of Metatron as she went. She formed a shell around the onyx wedged between her shoulder blades. She let out one last scream as she stripped the rest of herself from the spear. Metatron gave a final protest, and something inside snapped. A rush of memories that hadn't been Ronnie's, but were now, screamed inside her skull. Images of Michael, Lucifer, Izzy. Things she never lived, but did.

Metatron's hatred. Her rage, hurt, disappointment, and sense of betrayal at what she was subjected to—forced into without her consent—because one angel wanted her dead and another couldn't let her go. Her emotions were Ronnie's now. Not clouded by an extraneous voice. She still whispered, but they were a part of the same whole.

Ronnie's memories were there, too. A little cherub helping Lucifer tirelessly for decades. Offered a chance to become more. To be something special.

Ronnie let the glory of both of them rise to the surface and rush over her, wrapping her in golden light, as wings spread from her back. There was no one or the other. A simple shove, and Gabe's hold on her shattered. Power crackled and faded around them. The last of the pain vanished, and Ronnie straightened up with a smile.

Gabe growled and lunged. She knew how to avoid him. Metatron's knowledge of how to fight filled her head. With a whisper of a command, his spear tore itself from her back and vanished. Now that she knew how an original summoned their weapon, it was simple enough to see the source of Gabe's and make it disappear. He could summon it again, but she wasn't planning on giving him a chance. She shifted to quasi-mortal enough to eliminate the gaping hole in her back.

Gabe stopped a few feet away, wary. His smile looked forced. "Welcome back, love. I'm glad you figured it out before it was too late."

"Clever." A torrent of hatred snaked through her, and she entertained the idea of killing him. Getting used to those moments when her memories and feelings contradicted themselves would be interesting. Vengeance wasn't her place.

Concern bled into his voice. "I was so worried you might not survive. I didn't want to do that to you, but I didn't know any other way to separate the two of you."

"I'm sure you only ever had my welfare in mind."

She would give Gabe what he wanted. Or at least, what he thought he wanted. She'd leave him to rule his lonely little corner of heaven and keep him from going anywhere else for a while. She couldn't help one more power play. That part of Metatron demanded she do more than just slap him on the back of the hand and then let him roam free again. She stepped toward him, hands clasped behind her back.

"Uriel?" He backed way.

She smiled, stopping less than an inch from him, coiled and ready to spring out of reach if he lunged. She stood on tiptoe, looking him in the eye, and chewing on her bottom lip. "For a while there, I almost thought you cared about what happened to me."

"I did. I do." His insistence came too quickly.

"I bet." She pressed her lips to his, consciously drawing on his power and funneling it through her body. She didn't need it, and it wouldn't kill him, but she wanted him to be without it for a while. She took more than he ever fed her before. The kiss lasted less than a second, but it was enough. She drained him for the moment.

He broke away with a snarl, face pinched, and hands shaking.

The energy filling her was foreign, almost uncomfortable. Did she really take that much? Good, maybe that would keep him from fucking with her for a little while. He'd be back. His agenda was pretty straightforward, and all three of the other originals were back, preventing him from being the one and only.

"You manipulated the system." She liked knowing every word was her own. "You tried to destroy a balance that exists for a reason. We won't let it happen again. Michael and I know the truth about what you did to me. Lucifer will as well. When you recover—and I know you will, I'm not stupid—things won't be the same."

Everything had changed. There was too much knowledge on the table now. And as much as it still ached deep inside that Michael left, she understood his reasons better than she wanted to. She didn't agree, but Metatron gave her insight she didn't have before.

Back then, in Metatron's original incarnation, he and she would have surrendered eternity for each other. Given it all up to experience mortality. Doing that now determined more fates than their own. If Gabriel was willing to throw Earth into chaos for control, all four of them needed to exist as immortals to maintain balance. Besides, Ronnie liked her immortality too much to surrender it.

Gabe opened his mouth.

She wasn't interested in hearing anything he had to say. She vanished from his basement, leaving him alone and at least temporarily unable to cause trouble.

Chapter Thirty-Four

Gabe's coffee shop didn't have the same haunting darkness Ronnie remembered. She gave Claire a weak smile as she walked out the front door. For the first time in months, Ronnie's destination was unknown on purpose, and not because she was confused. The power singing inside her was fantastic. Different from Gabriel, or Irdu, or the inky ribbons. She and Metatron were one and the same now. Something told Ronnie she was wicked powerful, but she wasn't in the mood to try it out.

The silence in her head was incredible. Cars slogged by, pockets of people shouted and laughed on their way to late dinners or movies, and cicadas blended with the city's music. And it all happened outside her skull. She walked without direction and delved into the memories. So many vivid colors, thoughts, and emotions from both of them.

She wasn't sure how long she wandered, but the sidewalks gave way to parking lots and rows of lights, dotting the landscape like upside-down stars.

The hospital where Izzy was staying.

Ronnie's gut clenched, and a phantom pain echoed inside. Images of his unconscious form flashed through her head. She didn't want to see him like that again.

But she did want to see him. She grabbed an elevator up to his floor. She paused in front of his room then forced herself to knock.

"S'open." His cheerful voice chased away her hesitation.

He sat on the bed, color returned to his skin, and circles fading from under his eyes. Irdu was in the chair next to him. Ronnie all but flew across the room, and wrapped her arms around Izzy. "I'm so glad you're okay. You are okay, right?"

"I've been better, but I've definitely been worse." Izzy nudged her back with his good arm. "What about you? Done moping?"

"What happened?" Irdu's voice didn't hold the same levity.

Izzy scooted over, and she sat on the edge of the bed next to him, so she could see both of them. "You two first. What happened to *he might not make it?*"

"Lucifer's a drama queen," Izzy said. "Apparently, princess charming came and woke me up with a kiss."

Heat and realization flooded her. The tiny bursts of power she sent through him actually did something. "Lucky bastard."

He shook his head. "Not really. No offense, Ronnie. You're cute as a button. But send a prince next time?"

"Prince of sexiness, right there." Ronnie nodded at Irdu, who winked.

Izzy laughed. "Like he's going to give me a second glance with you around. Why is he studying you like a bug under a microscope?"

She met Irdu's gaze again. "I chose."

"I see it in your aura. You figured out how to keep both of you." Irdu grinned.

"Yes."

Irdu reached out to squeeze her fingers. "I was worried I'd never see you again. I'm so glad you're back."

A tiny smirk played on Izzy's face, but he didn't say anything.

"Welcome back," Lucifer said from the doorway.

She looked up to see him studying them. He almost looked relaxed.

"You're an asshole, by the way," she said to Lucifer. "Saddling me with that when you didn't know what you were doing."

"It worked out. I knew it would."

Ronnie snorted. "Whatever. You had your doubts."

Lucifer's expression softened. "I'm glad I was wrong. What now?"

"If I had a choice? Ubiquity would be on the bottom of the list." With all the events of past few days, Ronnie couldn't get behind what they were doing there.

"Technically, you do have a choice."

"Because I'm half Uriel and half Metatron, making me both demon and angel, so I don't work for either side?"

"Sounds like an overdone TV plot. Because you're Metatron. Originals only answer to Him."

She liked the sound of not answering to her peers. "So I can spend the rest of eternity on a beach."

Lucifer scowled.

She raised her hands. "Joking. That sounds so dull. Or, you know, it might after a couple of years of nothing but relaxing sun and laziness."

"Things are changing at Ubiquity. It's why I'm there. It's your choice, but if you're interested in helping to define the company's direction..."

"I'll think about it." Not just because it sounded like a bad mission statement, *defining angelic direction*, but because it would take more than little tweaks to fix the system, and she'd have to speak up if she thought something bigger needed to happen.

"I wanted to give you this when you were here earlier. I'm glad I waited." Lucifer tossed something across the room. "This is for you."

She snagged the keyring out of the air. The sinking feeling returned to her gut, but she wasn't sure why. "What are they?"

"Keys."

"Smart ass." She would have smacked him, but she wasn't sure she wanted to know the real answer.

"Michael's. His condo. His car. He asked me to give them to you. Said it was all yours, until you got established. He's not using any of it right now."

She was right. She didn't want to hear anymore. She accepted his leaving and understood his reasons, thanks to Metatron's perspective. She didn't agree. She was happy with her immortality and didn't understand why he felt he had to surrender his in order to live. It wasn't her decision to make, though. Hearing he was really gone made something crumble inside.

Irdu squeezed her hand, and she returned the gesture. She had the perfect guy right here.

She bit the inside of her cheek, but the emotion and longing surged regardless, made stronger by the memories of two pasts, both falling for Michael.

A heavy silence sank into the room.

"Can I ask another favor, princess charming?" Izzy's cheer was forced, but it was a nice way to crack the emptiness.

"Sure. Anything at all."

He nudged her to her feet. "I don't need anything that extravagant. But I'm dying for some ice cream."

She laughed at the simplicity of the request. It didn't take away the ambivalence over the keys she dropped into her purse, but it helped her feel better. "Absolutely. I'll be right back."

She phased out of the room and returned minutes later with four pints of ice cream and spoons. They made themselves comfortable and dug in. She could get used to this. As long as she learned to ignore the hollow ache in her chest that shouldn't be there. It was best this way.

They all chatted for a couple of hours, until Lucifer had to leave, and Izzy started to doze off.

Irdu grasped Ronnie's hand. "Do you want to go for a walk?" he asked.

"Yes. Definitely." The simplicity of it all sounded amazing.

When they reached the street, a cool breeze blended with the heat coming off the asphalt. Car and streetlights blinked brightly in the night.

Hand-in-hand they strolled down the sidewalk, until they reached the main road. She didn't know how he decided which way to go. It didn't matter.

"It's weird, isn't it?" Irdu's question was soft. "The silence?"

She hadn't noticed it in Izzy's hospital room, because everyone was talking. Now, it was sinking in again, how quiet it was in her head. "I thought it would be all relief and *everything is right again*. I kind of don't know what to do with my brain."

"You'll get used to it. I'm here to listen, or to talk if you'd prefer, as it happens."

Right. Because she not only had a sexy boyfriend, he was possibly the only individual in the world who had a solid idea of what she'd gone through. "Thank you." She squeezed his hand.

"And you have all your memories back? Yours and hers?"

Ronnie nodded. "It's kind of disconcerting. And it doesn't feel right to put it that way. It's more like mine and mine. We're both me?" As far as she could tell, that was why the Metatron part of her was quiet for so long around Irdu. It woke up when Michael came back, and it didn't have anything to do with Irdu.

Until the two halves started to merge.

"Which means you remember loving Michael. And Lucifer." His tone was hard to decipher.

She cringed. "I also remember loving you, and that's a fresh memory. Besides, they're both really fucked up. Have you met them?"

"Yeah, I have." He glanced at her with a smile. "I still won't make you choose. I'll be hurt if one of them does, and you think that's all right."

"You're willing to share?"

He shrugged. "You're a lot of fun. Possibly my favorite ever plaything. But you're not a toy. I'm as okay with you going where your heart pulls you as I've always been."

"Except those couple of days when you were a giant prick."

Irdu grabbed his crotch and winked. "It's always giant, love."

"You're horrible." Ronnie was laughing though.

"I want you in my life. I wouldn't complain about being part of other hook-ups when those happen. I just won't give you up without a fight."

Ronnie's smile grew. "You'd better not."

This was going to take a lot of getting used to. That she was two people melded into one. That she had lived two separate lives.

But this, what she had with Irdu, was wide open for exploration, and she was looking forward to that in the best possible way.

THE END